DON'T TRUST ME

JOSS STIRLING

KILLER
READS

A division of HarperCollins*Publishers*
www.harpercollins.co.uk

KillerReads an imprint of
HarperCollins*Publishers* Ltd
1 London Bridge Street
London SE1 9GF

www.harpercollins.co.uk

A Paperback Original 2018

1

First published in Great Britain in ebook format by
HarperCollins*Publishers* 2018

A catalogue record for this book is
available from the British Library

ISBN: 9780008278656

This novel is entirely a work of fiction.
The names, characters and incidents portrayed in it are
the work of the author's imagination. Any resemblance to
actual persons, living or dead, events or localities is
entirely coincidental.

Set in Birka by Palimpsest Book Production Limited,
Falkirk, Stirlingshire

Printed and bound by CPI Group (UK) Ltd, Croydon, CR0 4YY

For Kate Bradley
Kate, you win the prize for Most Enthusiastic Editor. It's been a pleasure working with you and the team at Harper Fiction. I hope you like your book!

'human kind
Cannot bear very much reality.'
(T. S. Eliot, 'Burnt Norton', *The Four Quartets*)

'She is brave and strong and broken all at once. As she speaks it is as if her existence is no longer real to her in itself, more like a living epitaph to a life that was.'
(Anna Funder, *Stasiland*)

Prologue

The door closed on the man lying broken at the foot of the stairs. Life hadn't yet left him – a twitch of a finger, a shallow lift of the ribs, betraying that there was hope if help got there in time.

But it wouldn't, would it?

Walking with unhurried steps down the suburban street despite a racing heart, the killer felt that congratulations were in order. Thinking fast on your feet was a trait to be regarded with a certain pride. It had come into its own just a short time ago when it became clear something had to be done. His madness had to be stopped.

The act was self-defence really, when you thought about it.

Oh yes, there were plenty of excuses to be made.

A wild glee bubbled up which had to be hidden from other people out and about enjoying a London summer's evening. An innocent face was such an asset. Glimpsing the families lingering in shadowy gardens, citronella candles lit to deter the mosquitoes, memories of childhood games stirred. Candlestick in the conservatory by Mrs Peacock? No, no, that was a stab in the dark. Rope in the library, Professor Plum? Really, was that the best you could do? Lead pipe in the kitchen, Colonel Mustard? Warmer. The police would be left guessing like inept players when they found him – that's if they even suspected a crime had taken place. Underestimated by everyone, the killer knew how not to leave too many traces. The scene was staged correctly. Justice done. Time to fade into the background, just one among the many passers-by. Just look at them. Any one of them, under the right conditions, might also take a cast-iron pan to the back of someone's head and end a life.

Chapter 1

'I'm leaving.'

We have barely just walked through the door when Michael makes his declaration. I'm still standing in my holiday T-shirt and shorts, cradling the duty-free bought at the end of our week in Minorca. Our bedroom is scattered with a week's worth of dirty clothes and he is already repacking his suitcase.

'What? *Leaving* leaving, or just leaving?' I ask, mesmerised as he transfers ironed shirts from the wardrobe to his carry-on. It's like he's become a whole different person after the holiday wear got dumped. Back to business. Item one: deal with errant girlfriend.

He pauses, hand arrested in choosing the right tie. 'I'll stay overnight at Gatwick. I don't want to disturb you by having a taxi fetch me at five.'

And I'm not disturbed now with this sudden departure? 'Oh, so just leaving. I see. I thought, after... you know... it might be *hasta la vista, baby*.' I give a hiccup of laughter and

3

unscrew the top of the lime-green liqueur I bought on impulse at the airport. I take a swig.

'Jessica! I warned you that stuff was vile.'

'Yeah, well. It tasted great on the beach.'

'And now it tastes like bleach.'

He's right but I'm not backing down. 'Cheers. My funeral and all that.'

He shakes his head. He's already finished stowing his conference gear. The Grand Prix pit teams could take lessons from him on efficient changeovers. 'You know how to reach me.'

I really don't, not anymore. 'So we're not going to talk about it?'

'What good would that do? Don't do anything stupid while I'm away.' He walks past me without a goodbye kiss. I hear the front door slam.

I check the level in the bottle. Perhaps it will taste better with ice and lemon?

It doesn't. I'm still lying awake at two in the morning, tossing and turning, getting up to go to the loo a million times. I check the time.

02:36.

The house clicks and settles in that odd way it does when it thinks no one is listening, like it's really some living, breathing beast just pretending to be bricks and mortar. A horrible feeling comes over me of there being something wrong, someone out there, with me alone in the house. It's happened before, usually when I'm in a car after dark on my own, waiting. Be honest, you've thought that too, haven't you? Put your mind to it and it could happen right now where you are. In my nightmare, a man in a Scream-face mask is going to tap on the window. I can see him lurching from the bushes to stare, blank-faced, black circle of a mouth, hands pressed to his cheeks in terror, eyes fixed on me. I know it's foolish but once the image is there, he's there in the dark, the Scream guy, real as anything. And now he's outside my back door as I lie upstairs in bed in a cold sweat.

Stop it, Jessica. You know how this works. It's the late-night drinking that has summoned your personal horror. Yet my body hums with tension, telling me this time it's different. This time he's real. Paralysed, I lie wide awake, listening. There are footsteps in the side alley, I am sure of it, but no way am I going to look. I'm afraid I'll see him – or not see him, which would be almost as bad, as I'll know my brain is tricking me again. I take my phone under the blankets with me, thumb close to the emergency-call option on the home screen, but whoever it is doesn't make another move.

It was probably just a normal intruder raiding the shed, I tell myself, and then laugh grimly at my idea of a small mercy.

Eventually, as it grows light and thoughts of the masked intruder recede, I drift off and sleep through my first alarm. On the second round, I leap up out of the twisted sheets and rush from the house, still buttoning my jacket. On the street, I bump into our neighbour, Lizzy, walking her spaniel. The dog lets off a staccato bark of hysterical joy at seeing me.

'Had a good holiday?' asks Lizzy, tugging on Flossie's lead.

I have no time for the truth. When do I ever? 'Great. Thanks for feeding the cat. I got you a present but I'm afraid I drank it. Believe me – I saved you from the hangover from hell.'

She laughs, as I hoped. 'I don't expect anything, you know that. I like Colette. It's no trouble.'

'Thanks. You're a star. Must dash!' Giving a cheery wave, I run for the station. Why have I let myself get in such a flap? I scold myself in my mind using Lizzy's-voice-of-sense, for letting an overactive imagination cause such paralysis last night. The Scream guy never seems real at eight in the morning. Maybe things will improve today? I'll have a good few hours at work and a decent conversation with Michael later to clear the air. Yes, that's what I'll do.

Then the train from Clapham is on time. Usually that would be cause for a marching band and trumpet fanfare, except I'm not. On time, I mean. I stumble up the station steps to see the 8:04 slide away to Vauxhall. My phone goes flying, screen hitting the concrete with that crack. I pick it up. Sure enough, the screen has gone all modern art – my life through shattered glass, still just about functioning.

Injured mobile in hand, I wonder if maybe I should take it as a sign? I should stop here, turn around and go home – repack the suitcase and max out the credit card on the first standby ticket to anywhere that isn't this life of mine. Would Michael count that impulse as 'stupid'?

The moment passes. Instead, I squeeze myself onto the next service, like a good little rat in the rat race. Suffering the indignities of the short-in-stature at rush hour, I travel with my face pressed against the back of a German student in a Bayern top. That's no hardship. He smells good, all kind of musk and bath soap with a hint of alpine yodelling, and looks, well, far too young for me. Funny that that constitutes my most sensual experience of the month. Maybe of my year.

Change on to the Underground, another change and finally I make it to Dean Street, Soho, having hoofed it down Oxford Street as if someone gave a damn about what time I clocked in.

And then the key won't turn in the lock.

Chapter 2

'Brilliant, just bloody brilliant.' I ease the key out, wipe it on my skirt and try again. Jiggle. Plead. Swear under my breath. 'You will not defeat me, you stupid bit of useless metal.'

I'm coming apart at this last hitch. My head is pounding, hands trembling, tears close. Don't do this to me, world.

I then notice that the Yale lock looks new – a shiny brass face, unscratched, innocent. Right. OK. Reason this through. I've been on holiday for a week so it's possible my boss has had cause to change the locks in my absence – a mugging, a drunken oh-shit-key-went-down-the-drain incident, or maybe he's finally listened to my doubts about the cleaner? I indulge in a grunt of vindication. I've been complaining that she barely wipes the surfaces and seems to think a squirt of air freshener into the scummy bathroom will convince me she's doing the job. But if he has given her the boot, and changed the locks to pre-empt revenge attacks, why didn't he at least text me to let me know?

I thump on the door. 'Jacob, are you in there? It's me, Jessica?' I shout my name with a rising inflexion. Remember me? You know, the research assistant who's been working alongside you for three months.

No response.

Defeated, I sit down on the top step and review my options. This comes as a particularly fat fly buzzing on top of the pile of crap that is my morning so far. This is the way the world ends, not with a bang but a whimper.

OK, some would say I'm being overdramatic. So what do I do now?

I try ringing Jacob but the number is unobtainable. No surprise there, as he usually keeps it switched off, claiming he doesn't like the idea that his position can be triangulated from every phone mast. I'd once made a lame joke about drone strikes but he just looked at me in that way of his. Some men, actually most men, seem to find me the equivalent of the tissue left in a pocket during the wash. My jokes and ill-thought-through comments are fluff to be brushed away with a show of mild irritation. I then try ringing the office phone, just in case. It's only a few metres from me on the other side of blue door and if he is in he'll have to pick it up. I should be able to hear it ringing, but there's only silence. I lift my mobile to my ear and hear the distressed beep of another unobtainable line.

OK, think this through. I don't wait for a solution to come to me; I always act. This is my place of work, right? Starting to doubt myself – and that's very easy to do as doubt is my factory setting – I go back down the stairs and stare at the number 5a on the front door.

Yes, it is the right one, with the busted entrance that yields to a firm push. Our narrow door is sandwiched between the empty shop that was briefly a nail bar and the ex-tapas restaurant that rapidly went bankrupt in the way of overambitious eateries. Both premises are gathering post and circulars on the doormats like letters from an obsessed lover who really just won't give up. They're gone. Get over it.

I go back upstairs and carry on an extra flight. I know there is a flat up here as I have heard the sound of feet and occasionally bursts of loud music as I did my internet searches in the office below. I'd never seen the inhabitants so my mind has naturally run riot. We keep very different hours and I've sometimes speculated as to whether it is home to one of the prostitutes for which the area is famed. Don't take any notice of me though. Little do I know about the contemporary sex industry, not having met a sex worker recently – at least, I'm not aware that I have. I probably have. I mean, do Michael's students count? Some are said to be sleeping their way through college to avoid taking on crippling debt. Well done, government, prostituting the best and brightest.

I realise immediately that I've got my picture all wrong when I see the messenger bike blocking the stairwell – unless this is a form of sexual delivery about which I am ignorant. That is entirely possible as my recent experience has been vanilla all the way – and what came before that I really don't want to remember. I shuffle past, reminded of my less-than-sylphlike proportions as my hip takes a jab from a brake and my butt squashes against the wall. I knock on the door.

After a few seconds, I hear someone approaching. The door opens and a lanky guy wearing an entirely too-small towel, is staring down at me.

'So?'

What kind of greeting is that? 'Um, hi, I work downstairs but I can't get into my office. I don't suppose you know if there was a locksmith here during the week?' Stupid question. Why would he know that? What am I even doing here? I try a friendly smile even though my head is still throbbing. I probably look demented.

He rattles off a reply in a foreign language, Polish I think. I can get the '*nie mowie po angielsku*' (I don't speak English) thanks to a Polish barista who had once taught me a few words and given me a free coffee for my attempts. It dawns on me that the man hadn't said 'so?' at all, but '*co?*' – Polish for 'what', which sounds almost the same.

'No English?' I find myself saying, as if this is in any way relevant to my situation. In post-Brexit Britain I go for an over-friendly, I'm-not-one-of-the-haters, commiserating tone.

'Leetle,' he says. As little as his distracting towel.

'Sorry, never mind.' I back away before the towel gives up its perilous grip on his hips.

'You have problem?' he asks.

Not as long as you keep a hold, mate, I want to quip, but bite my tongue. This month's goal, agreed with Charles, my therapist, is not to blurt out inappropriate comments or jokes. I failed spectacularly last week but am trying the new-leaf approach. Anyway, here is someone actually showing an interest in helping. I feel so grateful to find a human who cares that I begin a pantomime of my predicament, complete with props: key, lock, downstairs, shake of head.

'OK. Moment.' He goes back into his flat and closes the door.

Hanging on to the promise in that 'Moment', I wait for him to emerge, which he duly does a minute later, wearing lycra that looks like it's been slapped on with a roller brush. Soho's answer to Chris Froome, he hefts the bike out of my way and follows me downstairs. I hold up my keys, and point to the lock. Then magically, he produces a brand-new Yale key on a ring with a fob in the shape of a little bicycle-wheel.

Thank God, some sanity is being restored to my morning. Jacob must have had the locks changed and had the idea of leaving the spare with the guy upstairs. He could've told me. My headache begins to ease.

My Polish white knight opens the door and stands back.

'Thanks.' I hold out my hand for the key, but he shakes his head.

'I keep. For boss.'

I don't really hear this explanation because the room I enter is just not right. Ten days ago, my messy desk with laptop sat in front of the sash window, a grey filing cabinet in the corner, a pinboard of all the cases we were working on next to that. Jacob's desk had taken up the majority of the room across from me, a chair for clients and a coffee table pushed against the wall. The decor had been gunmetal grey with water-stain accents. The door opposite the entry had led into a depressing little kitchen and bathroom in the cheap extension, which I guess had been put on in the 1930s when it was decided indoor plumbing was here to stay.

Now I feel like I am walking into the same room but in a parallel universe. The place is bigger. Someone has knocked through to the kitchen, laid a wooden floor and painted the walls white, refitted the kitchen. All in the space of ten days. A treatment table, still wrapped in plastic, has replaced Jacob's desk, and all the paraphernalia for an aromatherapy-cum-massage is neatly laid out on a pale-wood counter that takes up one wall. A feng shui kind of arrangement of ominous forked twig and stones – I mean, where are they planning to shove that? – stands on a low table where my desk had been. It smells new – new paint, new people, new business. There wasn't even a nail mark in the wall to show where the pinboard once hung.

I resist the temptation to slap my cheek to check I'm not dreaming. 'What happened to all the stuff that was in here?' I ask, pointless though it is.

My Polish helper just smiles that bemused 'seen enough, lady?' smile.

'Where is Jacob Wrath? Who's renting this place?' Finally I think of a relevant question with which the key holder might be able to help. 'Do you have a number for the landlord? Landlord? Yes?' Meeting incomprehension, I type the word into Google translate and let him squint through the spider-webbed screen.

He nods and pulls a phone out from God knows where in his close-fitting outfit. Also in dumb show, he selects a contact and turns the screen to me. I jot down the number with a biro on a receipt dug out of the bottom of my shoulder bag.

'Thanks.'

My guide stands back. He's not going to leave me here, clearly, in case I steal a box of patchouli essential oil. I walk back down the stairs and on to the street. A few moments later, my new friend is outside with the bike slung over his shoulder. He dumps the bike on the road, gives me a wave, and mounts in one smooth move.

'*Jen-Coo-Yan*. Thanks!' I call after him in my one remembered coffee-powered phrase.

And then it starts to rain. Of course it does. But not glamorously, not like that scene at the end of *Four Weddings and a Funeral*, where the girl stands looking damp but still adorable. This is thunderous downpour where no one escapes with any shred of dignity. Deciding to take my phone call to a drier spot, I scurry to the coffee shop I like on Soho Square.

Buying an Americano to cut down the wait produced by the arcane art of working an espresso machine, I slide into a table near the back. Chasing a couple of paracetamol with a shot of black coffee, I tap in the number I got from the Two-wheeled Pole.

The phone is answered with an aggressive 'Yes? What the fuck is it?'

God, I wish I was the least bit assertive but that was missed out of the baby shower of cradle blessings thrown by my good fairies. Instead I got impulsiveness, disorganisation and an inability to swear in public. I can swear perfectly well in private – fuck it – see what I mean? But whereas other people seem to regard the f-word as an ordinary intensifier, I can't use it. Not at all. Not even when it is literally what I'm doing. Especially not then.

'Um, hello, is that the landlord of 5a Dean Street?'

'What's it to you? You're not that fucking woman from Number 7? Don't waste my time telling me Marek is playing his music too loud. Fucking racist bitch. Take it up with him.'

I guess Marek is the bicycle messenger. 'It's nothing to do with him or his music. I'm not from Number 7. I work in the office below his flat – or at least I did. I was wondering if you know what's happened to the previous tenant, Jacob Wrath?'

There's silence at his end. I can hear birdsong and the crunch of gravel. Is he on a golf course? I immediately imagine an Essex gangster type, thick gold jewellery and a blonde younger wife. My mind loves these leaps.

'You know that fucker Wrath?'

This doesn't sound good. 'Um, yes. I mean, I work for him. Do you have a forwarding address for correspondence?'

'Ha! Stay right where you are... What did you say your name was?'

'I didn't.' Suddenly, it doesn't seem a very good idea to admit who I am, so I say the first thing that comes to mind. 'Holly Golightly.' It must be the whole adrift-on-the-streets-of-a-big-city-in-the-rain thing that's getting to me if I've gone from *Four Weddings* to channelling *Breakfast at Tiffany's*.

'I'm sending my man round to talk to you. Where are you? Coffee shop?'

He can hear the hiss of the milk being steamed into submission and the Italian being bandied about behind the counter. I calculate what could happen. To lie or not to lie? He needs time to send someone over. 'Yes, I'm in Carlo's, Soho Square. Do you know it?'

'No, but my man will find you.'

'Why? What do you want?'

'I've got something for you.'

That doesn't ring true. He didn't know I existed until he took the call. 'Right then. I'll wait for him here. I'm in the seat by the window.' I mentally picture Audrey Hepburn sitting there over a solitary coffee to make it more real for us both.

'You fucking be there, all right?'

'Of course.' Sending a mental two-fingers, I end the call and then power off the mobile. I have to hope that no unsuspecting girl on her own takes a seat by the window but so far I'm good: there are two Asian boys with laptops who look like they've settled in for the morning.

This is getting ridiculous. I've just talked to a man who sounds like the cliché of the mobster boss. I don't do that. My life doesn't include that kind of conversation. Gathering my things, I leave the cafe, having already plotted my next move into the garden square. I stand in the shelter of the half-timbered hut in the centre, a child-sized Tudor fortress, and keep watch on Carlo's. A damp ten minutes pass and then a man arrives on a motorbike. He gets off, locks his helmet in the seat compartment, revealing he is the spitting image of Idris Elba, and heads into the cafe. Is that him, the landlord's man? Two women follow him in with their pushchairs, children under plastic wrap. Then an older man with a briefcase.

I should've got a description, but I never got the knack of thinking things through.

Motorcycle man comes back out with a sandwich in a to-go box and roars off. OK, not Idris. Through the window, I see the mothers edge out the Asian students with an interesting piece of psychological warfare. They let their two-year-olds occupy the low window seat normally devoted to flyers for local businesses and West End shows. The kids, two boys, lounge on their bellies and wave their heels in the air as they bash toy cars into each other. The Asian students exchange a look, close their laptops and scram. The mothers settle in the still-warm chairs like a couple of self-satisfied generals. The man with the briefcase comes out but with no sign he's bought anything.

Him? He doesn't look dangerous but he looks legal. I don't want to take charge of any papers or writs that the landlord might be trying to serve. I've worked out by now that Jacob must owe him money – just as, come to think of it, he owes me my pay.

The older man, paunchy, grey receding hair, navy suit, makes a call. I would bet that if I had my phone switched on, it would be ringing right now. Then more bad news: he is joined by two serious-looking blokes who have just got out of an SUV, the muscle to the brains. The knee cappers. Spine crackers. My fertile brain comes up with lots of words for them but no hint of how to handle them.

Self-preservation instinct kicks in. I really shouldn't still be here.

Something tips him off. Mr Lawyer raises his eyes and

meets mine across the square. He knows. I break into a run and risk taking the shortest route to Tottenham Court Station. Good idea? Bad idea? How do I know? All I can be sure of is that they'll be in pursuit. If I get into the Underground their car won't help. I reach Oxford Street and feel too exposed on the pavement. I dive into the first shop with open doors, a saucy lingerie store where a woman blends in and three guys stand out like priests in a bordello. I weave expertly through the aisles of satin and lace panties and barely-there bras and take the far exit that brings me out closest to the entrance to the station. Once at the bottom of the stairs, I fly through the barriers with a wave of my Oyster card and vanish down the escalator to the Central Line.

With heart pounding, I get on the first service going anywhere. I'm not even sure if I'm going east or west. I'll work out the route home later. I duck down as I think I catch sight of one of the big guys arriving on the platform just as the doors close. The woman opposite gives me a funny look, but this is London and the trains are full of weird people you really don't want to challenge. She turns her gaze back to her paperback.

That's right, sister. Nothing to see here.

The train goes into a tunnel and I sit up.

Well, hell. It appears that my boss and my job have gone. Time I was too.

Chapter 3

I reach home with only a cracked phone to show for my attempt to fulfil my part of the gainful employment deal. On the doorstep of our Victorian semi-detached house, stone worn into a dip by the passage of so many feet, so many bags of shopping, I have a moment of doubt as I slide my key into the lock, but there are no surprises. It turns. Wouldn't that be the cherry on top of the crap if Michael had taken it into his head to edit me out of his life today too? If he'd given the order for the locks to be changed while I was at work and he was *guten tag*-ing the *frauleins*? I'm like that paragraph in one of his articles, the one around which the copy editor has put a square bracket. *Do you really need this part?*

Stet. For now. I have my uses.

I go inside, disarm the alarm, and walk through to the kitchen conservatory at the back to dump my shoulder bag on the table. Something prompts me to check so I go past the tiny utility room and peer nervously out of the glass in the back door but I'm not sure what I'm expecting to see. An abandoned Scream-face mask? Footprints in the flowerbeds? I still can't shake that feeling of not being alone, the flight from Soho not having helped my rational processes.

I check the door to the basement is securely bolted – it features in another of my nightmares where I imagine the undead breaking through the London clay beneath, climbing up the wooden stairs and invading the house. It's actually not that scary with the light on as it's full of Michael's snow sports gear and boxes of his wife's things that he has never wanted to throw out. He goes down there from time to time just to bury his face in her ski-suit – he thinks I don't know. It's kind of sad really, this wanting to catch the scent of someone who's gone forever. He won't do that with anything of mine if I go.

I return to the kitchen. Here I'm surrounded by the hobbies I have adopted and failed to finish during my recovery: the bulky quilt project stuffed in a bag like a dead Elmer the elephant, the jewellery maker's starter kit, and the half-finished oil painting of the Serengeti – I'd had big plans for that. Beginning to feel a little desperate and a whole lot suspicious, I boot up the old desktop and check my last two months' statements. I had one payment in June, a cheque that I'd cashed myself, but the promised standing order has still not arrived. I can see Jacob now, fingers hovering over his laptop keyboard, handsome 'trust me' dark eyes meeting mine as he asks me what day of the month I'd like to receive my pay. He's a good-looking man, an outdoors type with tanned skin and work-roughened hands. He habitually wears a string of wooden beads around his throat like a dog's collar that he said he carved himself, and I believe him. In that game of 'Which person would you take with you to a desert island?', he'd be a good choice as he'd whittle, build and farm his way to survival.

'I'd like to be paid on the first,' I said, just so thankful that someone would pay me after all that had happened. When my salary hadn't come through in July, I'd raised it with him and Jacob had laughed it off as a mistake, saying he'd missed the deadline to set something up for the previous month but I should get twice the amount come 1st August. I hadn't wanted to push or suggest another cheque. I knew that his finances were tight and my position was tenuous. If he'd asked more questions he would've found out about the Eastfields disaster and then I'd be out the door. The single payment had persuaded me to trust him.

I log off from my account, all too aware my balance is in desperate straits. That is two months' part-time work for which I haven't been paid and I don't need a crystal ball to tell me that I'm unlikely to see the money. I'm thirty and on skid row. Again. Why can't I negotiate my adult life better than this? If I told you what had happened to me recently it would appear to be one crisis after another. I sometimes feel that some cosmic soap scriptwriter has got hold of me and keeps orchestrating season finales. I just want a quiet run of modest happiness with no thrills or spills.

I need to talk to someone about this. I need to vent. But who is there? My half-sister has forbidden me from troubling my mother. She's delicate, vulnerable, says Miriam, it's time you relied on yourself. That always brings to mind Mum as a dandelion clock, a perfect sphere, tremulous, seemingly fixed until a puff of wind starts to unravel it. She only ever seemed competent when with me, never with her capable older child, which is probably why Miriam doesn't understand our relationship. But big sister is right about one thing: I sense Mum is retiring from a world which she finds too much for her, pottering around the edges of Miriam's life on the farm, looking after grandchildren, getting involved in her village community where what happens on *Strictly* is about the most distressing topic of conversation. Her whole aim is to try to keep from being underfoot. Her existence is cast as a form of apology, her epitaph 'I'm sorry I took up so much room'. No, Mum isn't the right person to help me with this.

Depressingly, I find myself reverting to habit and sending Michael a text. *Can we talk?* I don't want to do this by messaging. A minute passes in which I put on the kettle. I can see he's read it, and he knows I know he's read it, so I get a response.

Is it important?

It's important to me.

I mean can it wait until tomorrow? I'm about to go into a presentation.

What would be the point of a conversation, I wonder, dragging him away from his oh-so-vital conference on something or another? Please hold, your call is important to us. Michael doesn't even pretend to give me the pseudo-sincerity of the automated switchboard. I try one last time. *My boss has gone. So has the office.*

The elusive Jacob Wrath. Or is that illusive?

Damn you, Michael, with your clever word play. Couldn't you for once try to care? We had been friends before, even if we're not now. I close the message thread. His comment reminds me that the couple of times I arranged for a social meet-up after work for the three of us, me, Michael and my employer – 'come on, guys, it'll be fun' – Jacob cried off, claiming new lead, head cold, threatened train strike. It was all the more galling as I had called in a lot of home-life favours to get Michael to agree to traipse up to Soho (his characterisation of a simple tube journey). He began to make barbed jokes that Jacob didn't exist, that he was a figment of my imagination. Now I think that Michael just didn't want to discuss me with my boss, or look responsible for my day-to-day welfare, and Jacob was just avoiding making himself real to anyone but me. So much easier to slip away when you've few connections to sever.

How far has Jacob taken it? Paranoia is getting a hold. I search for our website, the one I'd helped create and administer. Wrath Investigations, Specialists in Missing Persons Cases. (Yes, I am aware of the irony that the expert has gone AWOL himself.) Instead of the picture I'd posted of a lost girl in profile against the background of a London station, I get a broken link. I do a more general search and find only one relevant record: my cheery announcement on a business networking site that I'd started work as a profiler at Wrath, the implication being that it was far better than teaching Psychology A level. I'd meant it as a 'look, see: I'm bouncing back' to old colleagues but now I'm ashamed. It seems like I'm trying far too hard. I delete my profile. I don't want the landlord to find me that way now I've not stayed to meet his man.

My phone starts doing an Irish jig on the table. I check the number. I'd noticed three missed calls in my log from the same phone since I turned it back on, which suggests the landlord isn't going to let this go. I decline the call but wait for the person to leave a message.

'Miss Golightly, if that's your name, this is Max Tudor of the law firm Tudor Associates.' The lawyer is more of a film buff than his employer and has recognised the borrowed name. 'I believe we almost met today. My client, Harry Khan, wishes urgently to speak to you. Mr Wrath owes him three months' rent. The only payment he ever received was the first instalment plus deposit, which has naturally been forfeited. We are eager to find a Miss Jessica Bridges, whose name and signature appears as co-guarantor on the lease.'

What? I know I didn't sign anything resembling a lease while working for Jacob. I may be many things but utterly braindead is not one of them.

'As Mr Wrath has decided to make himself unreachable, we wish to pursue our claim with her. You might like to tell her that as her name and address are listed, she will not be able to avoid us. I strongly recommend you ask her, Miss Golightly, to get in touch.' The sarcasm with which he says my fake name makes it clear he believes he's talking to Jessica Bridges. Which he is.

I turn off my phone again. My three-month employer has shifted quickly in my mind from hapless to fraudulent. Have I really been set up? For real? And why?

I sink on to a kitchen chair and beat the table top with a fist, hissing swear words. The very worst thing is that no one will believe me if I tell them. I've tried that before and it has never gone well. Despite what Michael thinks, it's not the 'Cry

Wolf' situation; there's always been a wolf in my mess-ups, but I've always managed to escape – just. This time it looks like the wolf knows where I live and is coming to eat me.

The landline starts ringing, making me start. I rub my aching fist. No one ever calls us that way, not unless they are trying to sell us something. I bite a hangnail, looking at the handset as if it will make the decision for me. It's probably the man again, having traced me via my address on whatever agreement Jacob has forged. Jacob knew where I lived because I'd filled out a form with all my details when applying for the job, as any normal person would do. I'm not speaking to the lawyer; I'm learning Jacob's lesson and not making myself real. I have to go out before the landlord sends more people round to bang on the front door. Fortunately, the house is in Michael's name, so the lawyer can't burst in with bailiffs. As far as the law is concerned I don't own anything worth seizing. When Mr Khan works that out, he'll back off, surely?

I grab my bag, stuffing in keys and phone. Entering the utility room, I step over the drift of laundry waiting to go into the washing machine and pluck down a change of clothes from the dryer. They've been hanging there for over a week and need an iron but I'm not an ironing kind of person. That's Michael's phrasing about me. 'You're not a tidy sort of person'; 'you're not a focused kind of person'; 'you're not a careful kind of person'. No shit, Sherlock.

That reminds me to fetch my tablets. I go up to the bathroom on the half landing and pack my wash bag, including my disposable contact lenses and little box of Ritalin capsules. In my hurry, had I remembered to take one this morning? I think not. I quickly pop one from the blister pack and wash it down with a gulp snatched from under the running tap. It's supposed to help my concentration but, to be honest, I've not noticed much improvement since I started the course, not unless I take a couple and I'm not supposed to exceed Charles' prescribed dose. Tempting though. I find myself staring blankly at the green glass bottles arranged on the windowsill for a drifty moment. What am I doing? Oh yes, packing. Getting the hell out of Dodge, as they say in American novels.

Pocketing the pills, I enter the bedroom and step over Michael's holiday clothes. How have we become the couple where he expects me to pick up after him? It's the not-having-a-proper-job thing that's done it to us. Or maybe he was always heading that way but I'd just not woken up to my expected role? Next he'll be leaving me housekeeping money on the table like my dad used to do for Mum and expecting dinner on the table.

Speaking of money.

I go through Michael's bedside drawer, looking for his wallet. He has a travel one – currently with him in Berlin – and the one he carries at home, stuffed with loyalty cards. I find it and borrow forty pounds. As I put it back, I can't help but notice the framed photo of his wife, dead now just over five years, smiling up at me in her perfect pose of windswept black hair and sultry smile, forever young. He says he doesn't keep it on display out of consideration for me, despite the fact that I've no problem sharing my life with her picture. I never met Emma, she's dead; so why should I feel bad? It would be healthier to have her out in the open. Instead, I've had to put up with the knowledge that she's snuggled down next to us at night. He usually lies on his side, turned towards her, presenting his back to me.

The lovely Emma. I've begun to call her that in my mind, sometimes chatting to her when I'm on my own. Was Michael such a bully to you too? Were you 'an ironing sort of person'? You don't look it. I bet you made him do his own shirts. He might've even done yours. Did he nag you about forgetting to put the sharp knives away at night? He has this hang-up about preventing someone breaking in and using them on us. It's all that reading about psychopaths. Michael has such dark expectations that even a kitchen is first and foremost a potential crime scene.

I rarely delve beyond the photo as Michael has snapped at me several times for prying but I decide to have a proper root through the bedside shrine. You know how it works, while the cat's away…

A little blue box with a wedding ring. I've opened that up before. You clearly had something I don't, Emma, if you brought him to the point where he got down on one knee. Only way I'd get him there would be if I set a trip wire for him to fall over and that wouldn't end in a proposal.

There's a bundle of cards tied with a ribbon. Variations on 'Happy Anniversary, darling' followed by a row of big kisses. Her writing is a surprise – large loopy words in turquoise ink. A risk taker on the pen front. I conclude that she felt confident about covering more space than most of us do. Some photos. Emma at work. A couple of nice studio ones in the little album from their wedding in the US. I approve of her dress. She looks so glamorous. Very very sexy. No wonder I don't measure up.

Right at the bottom there's a new addition to the shrine: a Moleskine notebook. I wonder where that's come from? I have a soft spot for that brand myself, a hangover from the teenage diary days, and I usually have several on the go at the same time, one for work, one for my random thoughts. I flick open the cover and find that it is filled with Emma's, rather than Michael's, handwriting. Unlike my notebooks, hers is meticulously kept – dates, neat little anecdotes, not my jottings, highlighting and underlinings. I read a couple of sentences. 'Michael took me to Venice for a surprise weekend to make up for the bad news. I love that man more and more each day.'

Romantic Venice? I should be so lucky.

Before I have time to quash my own impulse, I've pulled out my phone and begun capturing any page that takes my fancy, just snapping, not taking time to read. I can't remove something so personal to Michael, even for a day, but I have to know more about this woman – this wife – who haunts our relationship. If I understand her, then maybe I'd get a better handle on what she was to him and I'd know where I've been going wrong?

At least that's what I tell myself. Maybe I'm just plain nosy and what I'm doing is way out of line? It's a bit like grave-robbing, isn't it? My jury is out and decided to go for a long lunch break while I carry on taking photos.

I make myself stop at twenty images. More would be obsessive, wouldn't it? I bite my lip, seeing another entry that appeals.

OK, now that really is the last. No more. Step away from the diary, Jessica.

The last page, handwriting no longer so exuberant, some of the words illegible, I see that she mentions getting a cat to cheer Michael up. It was a nice thought, to give him something to live for afterwards. My mind takes another swallow dive off the top board. The cat. I've forgotten the cat. Lizzy had fed her while we were away, but Michael will not be pleased if I abandon his beloved Colette to fish her dinner out of food recycle bins. Pocketing my phone after a last photo, I hurriedly put the Emma shrine back exactly as I think I found it. I then make sure I walk on Michael's dirty boxers on my way out of the bedroom.

I fill up the kibble bowl and change the water. Radar ears alert for the rattle of food, the cat flap slaps and Colette winds round my ankles, a black-and-white silk scarf of a creature. I stroke her. I am a cat kind of person, one of my few remaining plus points as far as Michael is concerned. I wonder if that's the only reason he's not evicted me. Who could he get to feed Colette at such short notice? He can't keep asking Lizzy. She has her own life to lead and we can't expect her always to pick up the loose threads of ours. The old lady next door, Mrs Jessop, is grounded with a bad hip, waiting for the op. The rest of the street are nodding acquaintances only.

'I'll be back, Colly. Don't eat it all at once. And don't answer the door to strangers.' I grab my bag and head out, leaving her in regal charge of the house. She does it so much better than me.

Chapter 4

There's really only one place I want to go. The undertaker's. It's not as desperate as it sounds. My best friend works there, responsible for fulfilling the weirdest contract in the world. Payne and Bullock, a family concern, is paid to deal with the dead who fly into Heathrow. There are more of them than you might think. Some are already dead and are being repatriated – one sangria too many and lights out in the Costa Brava. Others join the exclusive mile-high-die club, less popular than its sexual equivalent. If it's a busy long haul over the Atlantic, they are strapped in as discretely as possible and covered by a blanket. Mr So-and-so is not feeling well. Please respect his privacy. Why have you put the blanket over his face then? Madam, can I offer you any duty-free? A stiff drink next to the stiff?

My mind runs through what it would be like to be the passenger in the seat next to the body. I suspect I'd be tempted to behave badly and would want to touch it. I've never felt what death is like and this would be the perfect opportunity. I would only do it if no one was watching, of course. We are all interested in death; some of us are just more ready to admit to it.

Don't Trust Me

That's what kicked off my friendship with Drew Payne. We met at a local bar when Lizzy and I were out on a girls' night with colleagues from her school – her attempt to cheer me up and my first venture into public after my breakdown. At the start, it felt like an awkward evening with her staffroom friends all trying so hard not to talk about the fact that I'd recently been given the push from my teaching position at Eastfields. I suspect Lizzy had banned the topic but it was the equivalent of the instruction 'don't think of a blue elephant' – these nice primary-school teachers, unsullied by the experience of tutoring hormonal teenagers, couldn't help but feel the holes in the conversation were forming the big-elephant shape of my disgrace.

'Let me get the next round,' I announced, in part so I could flee the niceness. Lizzy followed me to the bar as I attempted to order. As usual, I failed to attract the attention of the server.

'I'm sorry. I can feel I'm making the whole evening a disaster,' I said. 'Do you want me to go so you and your friends can enjoy yourselves?'

Pretty, confident, blessed with a swatch of honey-blonde hair that I had seen make straight guys weak at the knees, Lizzy merely rolled her eyes and took the crumpled twenty from my fingers. She elbowed her way past the shirt-sleeved businessmen blocking the counter.

'You really don't want me to leave?'

'Don't be silly, Jessica. Just give it time – and a few more drinks. They'll all loosen up after that.'

'Hey, it's Lizzy, isn't it?' The man next to her at the bar, who had been nursing a pint, turned on hearing her voice.

Lizzy frowned, ready to deter all boarders, but then her expression cleared. 'I know you, don't I? Let me guess: guerrilla gardening club?'

'Guerrilla what?' I laughed.

The guy grinned. 'There's a group of us in West London. We descend in the dead of night on public spaces like verges and roundabouts and plant stuff – bulbs, vegetables, even trees.' He thumped his chest. 'Reclaim the streets for nature, yo!'

'Lizzy, I did not know that about you!' I accused my friend. 'You rebel.' I'd known she was into the Green Party but hadn't realised she'd taken things further.

'I like to keep my secrets secret. It's Drew, isn't it?'

'Yeah. Can I buy you a drink?'

'We're getting drinks in for our whole table, but thanks.' Lizzy saw her chance. 'Hey, can I order, please?'

Her attention now on the bartender, I was left to make conversation with the guerrilla gardener. I gave him a quick study. Medium height, edgy looks, he might look a bit too alternative for most of the women in this posh bar. I couldn't see him coming here as his first choice.

'So, um, what brings you here? A couple of neglected hanging baskets that need filling on the sly?'

He laughed. 'No. I was abandoned by a disappointed date.'

'Oh, I'm sorry.'

'Don't be. It happens a lot. Once they reach the "what do you do?" part of the conversation, my profession puts a lot of people off.'

Lizzy picked up the first three drinks. 'Can you bring the rest over when they're ready, Jessica?'

I didn't want to leave the conversation with Drew at this intriguing juncture. 'Of course. No problem.'

'Nice to see you again, Drew. Catch up another time, hey? I'd better get back to my friends,' said Lizzy.

His eyes followed her, another in the disappointed Lizzy fan club.

'She doesn't date much,' I told him.

'Oh.' He turned his attention back to me. 'How do you know her?'

'Not gardening club. Same street. Known her a few years now. We live really close, in and out of each other's houses, you know the kind of thing: watering plants when we go away, feeding each other's pets.' Hauling the broken fragments of a friend to the bar to cheer her up. 'But you can't leave me guessing. What profession is it that sends your dates running for the hills? Paid assassin? No? Uh-oh, not a...' I whispered as if it was a shameful secret, '... a tax collector?'

'Undertaker.' He wiped condensation off his Corona and lime. 'Someone's got to do it.'

He wasn't my idea of an undertaker, too young and wild for that with a range of piercings. I suspected tattoos up his sleeve. To find him doing something so unexpected ticked my boxes. 'You don't need to apologise. What are you called? Dead Guys R Us?'

He snorted at my stupid joke, which was lovely.

'No, Payne and Bullock, almost as bad. I'll suggest yours to Dad as the new company motto.'

'Frankly, Drew, your date was an idiot. You're doing a necessary job. Interesting. All walks of life and so on.' The bartender put the last of the drinks in front of me. 'Not walking obviously – at least I hope not. I mean, corpses rising off the slab: cool in a horror flick, not cool in real life.' Enough, Jessica. Don't say any more. I glanced over my shoulder but Lizzy's friends were happily chatting now I wasn't there. 'Um, so how did your family get into it?'

His eyes sparkle. 'There were all these dead bodies, see? And no one to bury them.'

I was wondering now if I'd got him wrong about his gaze following Lizzy. Was his vibe a bit on the gay side? He certainly seemed at ease with me. 'Ah, one of civilisation's oldest problems.'

My table waited a long while for their drinks. I only returned once I'd persuaded Drew to come with me. I'd assured him that the girls' night rule only existed to be broken. And if later Lizzy happened to mention to Michael how well I'd got on with her guerrilla gardening friend, then that would be all to the good. I was hoping that Michael would be a tiny bit jealous as I feared we'd already entered the 'I couldn't care less what you do as long as you stop dragging me down' phase in our relationship.

So it's to Drew's house I am fleeing now. Watching for pursuit by Khan's men on the mean streets of Clapham, I take the train to Feltham.

Chapter 5

Michael took me to Venice for a surprise weekend to make up for the bad news. I love that man more and more each day. I don't know what I've done to deserve him in my life just when I need him most. The doctor was expecting more progress. She thinks we should try a different treatment but I shudder at the prospect of yet more chemo. But there's no choice really. It's either that or give up now. The months ahead look grim, but I've got to keep believing I can beat this.

Yet sometimes you can get one over on life, lick up a dollop of happiness before it slides from the cone. That was our little weekend break. I don't know how Michael managed it during carnival – I'm imagining he offered all sorts of interesting and illegal sexual favours to the travel agent – but he booked us into a quiet hotel near the La Fenice opera house, which is the Italian for 'phoenix'. The theatre, I was pleased to see, has risen again after burning to the ground some years back. Did they foresee its future when they named it, I wonder? I'm not a high-culture fan but I can appreciate history as long as you

35

don't make me sit through a performance. Me, I'm more likely to go to a Lady Gaga gig than *Madam Butterfly*.

The hotel is on its own little canal which is not wide enough for much boat traffic. The water there is a strange slate blue, unexpectedly teeming with black fish right up to the front doorsteps. I wonder if people cast lines from their windows? I forgot to ask the hotelier. The walls have a weathered look, like stippled old-lady skin. I imagine that if anyone does repaint they are immediately instructed by the city authorities to mess up the finish so nothing stands out too strongly. The place is so crowded you get important buildings stuck down what in any other city would be back alleys. I loved the limp flags hanging from the official buildings, washed-out colours and little or no wind to make them flap. You get the sense that the whole of Venice is like that, just hanging and hoping nothing blows her away. The cruise ships have a good go, ugly white blocks dwarfing the city as they churn along the lagoon, the backwash doing plenty of damage. It's like Manhattan trying to invade a medieval city – or one of those alien invasion films where a huge flying saucer drops out of space, reminding Earthlings how insignificant we are.

Have you noticed how Hollywood sci-fi does superpower invasions with heroes who always end up in a punch-up despite having laser blasters, whereas the UK does *Doctor Who* and *A Hitchhiker's Guide to the Galaxy*? Odd bloke in a telephone box and another hitching a lift in a dressing gown. I listened to *Hitchhiker's* on perpetual loop as a teenager, my way of combating exam stress. Something about the bemused outrage of Arthur Dent before the absurdity of the universe just hit the spot for me. Still does. The alien constructor fleet destroys the Earth to make way for a bypass. That sums up the British sense of humour and I think is closer to the shit-storm that is the universe than Hollywood's grandiose ideas that anyone could be bothered to invade us. Stuff just happens – a meteorite arrives and kickstarts life, then another takes out the dinosaurs, and maybe yet another will bring down the curtain on this human experiment we're running not very successfully. It would help if I could take comfort from this big-picture perspective but it's hard when it's your life, your cancerous meteorite.

Enough.

But back to the cruise ships. If I were in charge of the city, my first directive would be to keep them well away – make the tourists transfer by smaller vessels. It's not as if Venice is short of visitors. They are killing the thing they love.

That's the human condition, I suppose.

Thanks to the perfect choice of hotel, we didn't have to go very far to find the carnival in full swing. We hired some costumes – not as elaborate as many on display – and joined in with the street party. It was a relief to have a couple of days off from that conspicuous group – the cancer treatment patient with a hairless head. I was gloriously anonymous in a gold dress, cloak, wig and mask; Michael wore an outfit in red and black which made him look like Zorro. He was very careful of me, mindful at all times of the doctor's words, like I was a delicate confection of spun sugar that would fracture on the slightest brush against anyone. I wanted to tell him that I'm tougher than I look – I've had to be, considering my recent experience – but I think he was getting a kick out of being protective. It reminded me of the incident last year. I shouldn't bring that up again with him, though. We're both keen to forget how close we sailed to complete disaster. The might-have-beens still keep me awake at night.

I found it liberating to walk a city with my mask in place. We all dissemble, even with the ones we love most, smiling when we feel like crying. I'm so used to wearing a mask that lies just below the skin, that to have it out there for all to see was the most real, most truthful I've been for a long time.

Chapter 6

Jessica

It's hard to read Emma's diary on my cracked screen. I'll have to download it to a computer if I want to finish the rest. I like the sound of her, though, with her asides on sci-fi and opera. We could've found plenty to talk about.

The train pulls into Feltham where Drew's family have their business. The undertaker's is on the corner of Manor Lane and the High Street, near the bright lights of Tesco and the shadier dealings of a government intelligence collection centre. Feltham has that unfortunate mix of no-longer-modern and not-that-old that screams airport suburbia. Planes are a constant companion roaring overhead as if the Viking God Thor has driven a thunderstorm to the long-stay car park and forgotten to collect it. Drew's shopfront has pale-grey vertical blinds, half closed to give the clients some privacy, and a curly black script announcing the firm's name which must be hell to read for someone with dyslexia. It's a font favoured by the front covers of romantic novels, Regency tearooms and dealers in the dead – go figure that one out. I know from Drew that the funeral director's is not a place many of the bereaved actually visit, with most transactions done on the phone. That means that when I arrive I'm not too worried that I'll be interrupting a sensitive meeting, but it's a possibility. I breeze in, ready to breeze back out immediately if I've called at an inopportune moment. I'm relieved to find Drew manning reception with his lunch and he's alone.

He puts down his Tesco sushi, wipes his fingers on a napkin and gives me a welcoming hug. 'Hi, Jessica, nice surprise! What are you doing here?'

'Come to see you, of course. No DB to report. I've not done away with Michael, not yet, so I'm not asking you to bury him.' Of course I have made that joke before with him: a good friend will help you move, a true friend will help you move a dead body. I've told him that under this criterion he is the perfect true friend.

'So what do you have to report?' He pushes a chair out for me and shoves the black sushi tray to halfway between us without asking.

I reel off the morning's events while folding strips of dead-skin ginger over rice pinwheels. Am I the only person in Britain who finds those shavings of ginger root to be like something that's been pickled for decades in an anatomist's laboratory? I'm craving chocolate, my go-to comfort food, but Drew is unlikely to have any to hand as he is ruthless about healthy eating.

Drew fetches some water from the cooler and sets it down in front of me while I finish my story. He's dressed in a white shirt and black tie and trousers, suit jacket hanging on the back of his chair, which means he's probably already done a funeral today. On duty, he takes out his piercings but he normally has one in his eyebrow and several in his earlobes. With his slicked-back black hair and trim beard styled like an Elizabethan privateer, he carries a hint of feral even in a suit. What I love most about Drew is his optimism. He's philosophical about death, and cheerful about the prospect of an afterlife. Bodies are just husks, he says. When you've handled enough of them, you realise that. Either the soul has buggered off to be somewhere different or dying takes the batteries out of a person. If option one, then great; if two, then we won't know, so why worry? I once told Drew that he was restating Pascal's Wager but he gave me a funny look and teased me for having a near-useless university education. I didn't like to say that this was something I'd picked up from *QI* on Dave, not my psychology degree, because I enjoy him claiming I'm more intelligent than he is. It counters all those 'dumb blonde' moments I seem to get with Michael.

'So what would you do if you were me?' I ask at the end of my account.

'I'd pack a bag and go visit a friend.' He grins. 'Especially if that friend has a fold-out bed they can offer.'

'Thanks. Huge relief.'

'So what are you going to do next?'

'I don't know. I really don't.'

'I think you need to find this Jacob wanker. It's his mess. You need to make sure it's dumped on his doorstep.'

'How do I do that?'

'Jess, have you or have you not just been working for a missing persons agency?'

I wonder for a fleeting second if he means to doubt my version of events but then I realise what he is implying. 'Yes, I have.'

'Have you or have you not learnt a few things along the way about how to find someone?'

'I was just doing the psychological profiles to predict where the runaways might end up.'

He raises a brow.

'But yes, I learnt a few things along the way.'

'Then profile your boss as far as you can and see if you can trace him. This landlord guy will be after him too. It'll be a race to see who gets there first. Consider it a professional challenge.'

The phone rings. I'm so nervous, I jump. Drew lays a hand on my shoulder and answers it.

'Yes, this is Payne and Bullock. I see. No, I'm afraid we don't do pet funerals. No, never. Really, we don't. I'm sorry for your loss.' He puts the phone down. 'Jeez, a Saint Bernard for burial as it's too big for the back garden, but why is it my problem?'

My faith in the absurdity of humanity restored, I rest my head briefly on his chest and then help myself to another piece of sushi.

Chapter 7

Emma, 28th April 2011

I freewheeled down Box Hill once when I was a teenager. I had the whole of the Surrey Hills stretched out before me and I was planning to ride to the coast. Best-laid plans... About halfway down I hit a pothole, sailed over the handlebars and ended up in the ditch. My friends laughed when they realised I wasn't badly hurt. I was unbelievably lucky. Of course, I wasn't wearing a helmet, though I've given that talk to my fair share of students since I moved into training. Like they do, I thought I was immortal. Thank God for bushes. Branches broke rather than my neck.

Why am I back at Box Hill? That's the closest I've ever come to what it felt like sitting in that office to hear the specialist's verdict today on how the treatment was going – a sickening ride through the air with the prospect of a not-so-soft landing, when I thought I'd get to the coast. I'd seen my life as an eighty, or even ninety-mile ride; I'm in fact getting only twenty-nine, thirty if I hang on for a few more pain-filled months. It's the shock of rearranging it all in my head that has really floored me. I can't get a handle on it – I find it almost impossible to believe. This voice, this me, that's been chatting away in my mind, will fall silent. I won't exist.

I don't 'get' death. Don't even want to write the word. I'm still flailing in that tumble through the air, as my mind has not quite caught up with what's happened since the pothole.

We are so bad at dealing with death as a society. I've been sick now for a while so I've got to see how most people cope. Many of my friends at work, and Michael's colleagues too, go for all that clichéd angry stuff, telling me 'don't go gentle into that good night'; they like to quote Dylan Thomas when something so unfair happens, as if it helps, as if rage is a good choice. I don't like poetry and this advice is not helping. To me that's the fake bravery of the generals sending the squaddies over the top, safe in the bunker themselves. I'd settle right now for 'don't go so fucking scared and confused into your grave' and some answers on how not to do that. This is not how I want it to happen. I want some comfort.

But you don't get what you want. I'm hearing my poor mother now – also dead too young from this same serial killer. I've got some shitty genetic markers. *If life hands you lemons, make lemonade.* She was big on the homespun wisdom. I now appreciate that she made a better exit than I am managing, finding a kind of calm in the storm that I can't – just can't – reach.

Hearing the verdict in that sunny office, Michael gave a sob then gathered himself. He held my hand, stroking my wrist, trying to comfort, but what could he do? This is a journey I make alone. I floated in a not-really-there daze as

Dr Jackson gave me the options of pain meds, support groups and leaflets, like she was a travel agent and I was a client going on some bloody holiday.

How do you get a grip on what is a death sentence? Don't tell me we're all living under one; mine's come early, too early. I'm not done with life yet, only just started. I have all this regret and nowhere to direct it. I am so—

I am angry after all. Raging against my own dark.

That was last week. I sound like a harpy. I'd rip out the page but Michael told me not to. Warts and all, he says. I love you, warts and all. I don't have warts, thank God, but what about bald and sick? That too – more than ever, he says.

I've been too pissed off to write anything since. I worry someone will read these notes after I'm gone, so I don't want to show my worst side here. Let that go with me. I want the courageous one to be remembered. Laugh in the face of a foe I can't beat. Metastasised Me. I can't control the timing of my exit but I can influence my legacy.

You know what I did today? Of course you don't, because you're an imaginary audience in the future. I persuaded Michael to get a cat – a kitten, really. This house has felt so bleak recently that I wanted us all to have something to make us laugh. When Michael agreed – he'd do anything for me, my poor love – Biff swung into action and got one from the rescue home. Predictably, Katy loved it at once even though it sank its claws in – tiny, not really hurtful spikes, so it was OK. I found I could still feel light-hearted when I watched the two of them playing. Michael is yet to be convinced that introducing a cat into our lives is a good idea but I'm leaving him with such a burden, he needs something to lift him out of his depression. Something to live for. Colette can be it.

Chapter 8

Jessica

Emma is haunting me and I'm trying to read more of the diary on the shattered screen even though I really should wait until I download the photos. I think I would've got on with her – apart from the bit about not liking poetry. How could she not? She comes across as sane and righteously angry about her diagnosis. The most perplexing thing from my point of view is that the Michael she describes shows tenderness towards her that I can only envy. I hadn't realised how Colette came into the house. In my share of cat responsibilities, I've fallen into the life Emma ordained for Michael without being aware that it's been her pulling the strings.

A warning flashes up and I have to put the phone on charge. I am parked for the afternoon in Drew's flat above the under-taker's. His parents lived there before they made enough money to move to a house near Windsor so it's always been a family home rather than a temporary lodging. The wallpaper in the guest bedroom is small flowers on a blue background, an old Laura Ashley print, suggesting a last makeover in the Eighties

47

when Drew's older sister was little. Blu Tack marks show where posters once hung. He has replaced them with a photograph of a sunrise over the sea and a quote by his favourite nineteenth-century poet, Walt Whitman: 'To me the sun is a continual miracle, / The fishes that swim – the rocks – the motion of the waves – the ships with men in them, / What stranger miracles are there?' I mull over the phrase 'stranger miracles' for a moment, like sucking on a boiled sweet. My thoughts turn more prosaic. I'm standing in a minor miracle: the luxury of a spare room in London. Able to afford to live without a flatmate, Drew has set up the room as a study with a fold-out sofa. I unpack my bag and join him in the living room. He gives me the password to the wi-fi and leaves me to my searches, explaining he has to be at the crematorium at three.

First, I prowl the flat. Drew knows I do this so I don't feel guilty. It's part of my restlessness – I can't settle until I've opened all doors, and peeked into every cupboard. I don't know what I'm looking for, I just have to do it, like a dog circling before settling down on her bed. I pause in front of his drinks collection, heavy on beer, light on spirits and wine. No, I've got to be a good girl. I open the fridge and kitchen cabinets. He needs milk and some more indulgent cereals, as he's bought the most bargain muesli. I see a trip to Tesco in my future. His visible music collection stops mid-2000s, a dusty rack of CDs. Metallica and Killing Joke feature strongly. There's a man-sized TV screen. I flick it on to find it tuned to a sports channel – it goes off immediately. His pot plant, a ficus, is a little dry so I water it. A few leaves drift off on my touch. I hide them in the bin. I really should stop interfering.

Neurotic, that's what Michael calls my behaviour. I prefer nosy. Sounds more normal.

Right, get down to work. I return to my bedroom and type in the most obvious search – Jacob's name. It doesn't throw up anything or anyone remotely like him. A film noir about murder, a wine seller in South Africa, a verse in Genesis. That raises the likelihood of it being a pseudonym. So what else do I know about him? I'm not the police, so I can't demand his phone or bank records. I have to go on the information he's let slip over the last three months. I make a list, realising I can't trust any of the surface statements he's made. I mustn't think I know him. I have to dig deeper.

1. About thirty-five years old, from his cultural reference points.
2. Not talkative, brooding, but not unkind. He brought me lozenges one day when I lost my voice. Made his own tea and coffee without expecting me, as the office junior, to wait on him.
3. I would've said he was good at what he did, methodical in the presentation of his research. From a psychological point of view that clashes with the idea that he had chaotic finances.
4. Dark-brown hair thinning at the temples and on top. Work-roughened hands which he explained as due to his hobby (gardening), so does he have a garden or allotment? Frameless glasses. Five nine? Smart casual clothes.

5. Grew up or has lived in or around Swindon, as he was familiar with local landmarks I mentioned – the White Horse, the Wyvern Theatre.

And now it gets trickier.

6. He was prepared to employ someone with a dubious dismissal-cum-resignation on her CV. That suggests a certain level of desperation or underhandedness (I should've asked more questions).
7. He has not hesitated to run away and leave me with his mess.
8. Unlike all the other lies, he really is an investigator. He had already compiled case files on the missing girls before I joined his one-man firm.

These girls are real. I've been investigating them for three months so I'm sure about that – all tragic, kick-you-in-the-gut cases of young lives cut short by sudden disappearance. I'd assumed he'd been employed by the parents or friends when the police searches had turned up nothing. Now I have to rethink.

I jot down in my notebook the names and dates of the girls while I can still remember them. Ramona James. Lillian Bailey. Clare Maxsted. Latifah Masood. I need to get my hands on the files and notebooks as there's so much more in there. I've done ample research on them already, I don't want to lose that. In the case of Lillian Bailey, I'd thought I was close to a breakthrough before I went on holiday. Just coming out of social services care, the eighteen-year-old had gone missing from Harrogate. I'd dug deep in her social media profile, not updated since she disappeared, and found a reference to a friend in Southwest London. From the profile I generated about her, I feel I'd got to know her. She was the kind of girl who took to strangers and would've been blind to the dangers of meeting them in a place where she was vulnerable, over-estimating how streetwise she was. She might well have been lured down to London. That's the darker explanation. The other, more likely scenario I'd come up with was that she seized on a chance to make a new start away from her old friends. She'd fallen out with her boyfriend of six months and spent a lot of time saying how she hated Harrogate and wanted to break free. She was an adult on paper so didn't have to tell anyone. I handed the possible address over to Jacob to follow up but I've no idea if he did or not.

So what was Jacob's motive in setting up the business in the first place? There doesn't seem an angle on it where he benefits, or am I just not imaginative enough? Is the interest in missing girls genuine? If so, then he might be carrying on the same work somewhere without the overheads of an office. He obviously got his business plan catastrophically wrong.

I tap the notepad with the end of my pen. It's a habit that drives Michael mad.

Then why add fraud to financial incompetence? Is this a pattern that Jacob repeats: hire someone so desperate for a job that they don't ask questions, then run off and leave them carrying the can? Are there others like me out there? I can't see the point but maybe I'm just not good at penetrating into the darker sides of human nature? I should be, what with the whole profiling thing, but I'd not liked the criminology part of my course, sticking instead with social and developmental psychology, the wider focus. Investigating my own motives for taking that path, I think I'd wanted to understand where my own dysfunctional family life came from, where it fitted, but it's never a good idea to do a university degree to get personal enlightenment. I understand the runaway girls, though. I can ace that part of my professional life if I'm given the opportunity. I thought Jacob was that chance but that now seems just wishful thinking on top of something much more malign.

Searches on Jacobs in the Swindon area are leading nowhere – too many and it might not even be his real name. I'm stupid even to try. I have to concentrate on the concrete clues I have. There was an office with case files, physical evidence of his existence in fingerprints and coffee mugs. The cleaner – Rita – where had she come from and how had he recruited her? And why go to the extra expense, if he wasn't planning to stick around? The girls. Why these particular cases?

I need to find the documents. I have to discover if Jacob moved everything out or if our stuff was just binned after the landlord took back control of the office. Only a week has passed. Jacob must've know he was in trouble before I left for my holiday because surely the landlord would have sent the usual warnings and final demand before taking the drastic step of repossessing the premises? Had Jacob been waiting for me to fly off to Minorca before hightailing it away from Soho, knowing Mr Khan was going to throw him out? Let's assume that was the case – he left quickly and maybe didn't take much. Counting back, if the super-fast makeover started last Monday, I might still be able to find something. What day was rubbish collection? It's possible the stuff I need is sitting in the wheelie bin in the yard behind the office. Looks like I'm going back to Dean Street.

Drew is not keen on my plan of rooting around in the bins behind the office. He's changed out of his suit into black trousers and a T-shirt, accessorised with a tea towel tucked into his waistband as he gets started on the stir-fry.

'Isn't that trespassing? What if you're caught?'

'The bins should be out front by now for collection. Who's going to care about a few bins on the public highway? Anyway, I can just say I'm looking for my personal stuff, dumped by mistake in my absence when the office was cleared. That's sort of true – I had made my own notes. Do you always wear black?'

He looks down at himself as if he hasn't even noticed. 'No... well, maybe, yes?'

I smile. 'You do.' I bite into an apple. 'It's your camouflage. You feel comfortable being the brooding guy in the bar, belonging to the tribe of slightly Goth slash late punk. What do you feel about wearing, say, a blue flowered shirt?'

He shudders histrionically. 'Are you trying to mess with my head, Jess?'

'It's the anthropological psychologist in me. I can't help seeing people in terms of their social groups.'

'What are you then?'

'God knows – pale, stale and female?'

Drew chuckles, thinking I'm joking, but I do feel like that last slice of bread in the cellophane that's too thick for the toaster. The one that lurks until it grows mould then gets put in the food bin. Being around Michael last week has done that to me.

I nibble around the core until only a size-zero catwalk model of a piece remains. 'Another question is what's happened to the computer equipment? It wasn't top of the range but I doubt that's in the bins.'

He slides some red peppers into the wok. 'Look on eBay.'

'I'd prefer not to fish in that ocean of possibilities. The memory will be wiped by now if it's being sold on.'

'Those police dramas always claim you can't remove all traces.'

'Possibly, but I'm hardly a computer geek. Like most of the population, I can use the things, not understand them.' It crosses my mind that Jacob Wrath has done a Wrexit on me, leaving me to tidy up in the way unreliable men expect of responsibly-minded female politicians.

My phone buzzes. I've blocked the calls from Khan's lawyer and decided not to worry too much about triangulation – I mean, there's no obvious link between me and an undertaker's, so why come knocking on the door? With any luck, if they trace me here, they'll assume I'm dead. I glance down to see who's ringing. It's Michael. So *now* he wants to talk to me.

'Aren't you going to answer that?' asks Drew.

I really want to punish Michael for failing me last week and last night but I don't have the self-control that would take. I pick it up.

'Hello?'

'Jessica, it's me. Lizzy's rung – she couldn't get hold of you. Our alarm is going off. Where are you?' Each sentence is served like tennis balls from a too-fast opponent. I manage to get my racquet to the last one.

'At Drew's.' Had I been right about someone watching the house? There was the noise last night, and now Khan's men had to be added to the mix.

'Then you'd better get back home and sort it out. You must've left the door to the kitchen open again. You know Colette sets off the alarm if she goes out of her designated zone.'

I can't return serves at 147 miles per hour. I decide to have the conversation I would like to be having with him, the equivalent of gentle Sunday afternoon lawn tennis – long rallies where each plays so the other can reach the ball. We might've had that conversation five years ago. 'Please, don't worry about me. Fortunately I was out so I'm not having to face the burglars alone. Yes, yes, I'm fine – apart from finding out my job was bogus and my boss is a crook. How's your conference?'

Michael sighs. 'OK, I see what mood you're in.'

'I'm glad it's going well with lots of admiring Frau doctors, police experts and grad students to polish your ego. I look forward to seeing you tomorrow so you can ask about my day.'

'Jesus, Jessica, this is petty, even from you. You need to act like an adult for once.'

'That's so kind of you. Yes, Drew's fine. He says "hi", by the way.'

Drew grimaces, holding the chopping knife over a carrot like a Tudor executioner. I imagine it as Michael's... well, not his head.

'I'll ask Lizzy to go in and switch it off.'

Concern for our blameless neighbour sweeps me. 'Michael, tell Lizzy not to go alone. It might be an actual break-in – not the cat. Things are happening that you don't know.'

'I never know with you. Always it has to be a drama, never a simple mistake of forgetting to shut the bloody door.'

God, he's turning into an irate Michael Caine. If I'm beginning to find his rants amusing, does that mean I'm getting over his rejection? Consciously decoupling, isn't that the phrase? 'It's probably my fault, usually is, but I can't get there for at least an hour. Tell her to be careful, OK? I'll go over as soon as we've finished dinner.'

'I don't know if I can trust you.'

'No, you don't, do you?' I end the call.

Drew raises his brows.

'Michael. The alarm's going off at our house – his house.'

'How bad has it got – you and him?' He sweeps the carrot matchsticks into the pan.

'Are you going to add any meat to that?'

'I'll add grilled halloumi at the end. I've gone vegetarian. Trust me: it'll be great.'

My spirits sink – no chocolate and now no meat. 'Our basic problem is that he doesn't like me anymore. The things I do – well, you know me...?'

Drew nods.

'I can't help them sometimes. It's part of my condition. He

used to find them amusing but now he's embarrassed. He'd prefer me just to go but I haven't got the money to rent somewhere, so...' I catch a glimpse of Drew's expression. 'I'm not asking to stay here more than a night, don't worry.'

'I wasn't worried about that.'

'You should be. I'd drive you crazy if you had to live with me. I drive everyone crazy after a time. Michael's up for a sainthood, having survived five years.'

'Jess, really, it's not a problem how long you stay. I'm worried that you are in an unhealthy relationship which is destroying your belief in your own self-worth.' Drew is into self-help books. There's a whole shelf of them in his living room.

I laugh. As far as self-worth goes, I've always been an atheist.

'Why are you with him again?'

'I don't know really. It made sense at the beginning. We met at his college. He was supportive when I did teacher training.' I curled a carrot peeling around my ring finger. 'He found it unthreatening. He was just beginning to really take off in his career as the media's go-to psychologist on socially deviant behaviour, and my job was always going to be second fiddle. He liked that. What he didn't like was the development where I needed more from him than he was prepared to give. He only wanted a witty and amusing girlfriend, not a partner, and certainly not a partner with problems.'

Drew is silent while he tosses the vegetables. I can imagine what he's thinking. She sees it so clearly, so why is she so feeble as to stay? I don't want to admit it to him but, apart from new friend Drew, I don't really have anyone of my own. My relationship with Michael cut me off from my old friendship groups as I moved in his circle rather than keeping mine. The colleagues I made at Eastfields – well, they went with the job. I am disgusted by myself. I've lost all confidence in my ability to make decisions, and that's with good reason, as the ones I've made tend to be impulsive and end up as disasters. Michael had got accomplished at sweeping in to rectify them for me. He was the one who persuaded me to resign from Eastfields before I was dismissed – that was sound advice in retrospect, though it felt like I was surrendering. He sorted out the counselling when I had my breakdown. I'm not convinced I'd survive on my own.

'I've always thought he was a bit of a prick,' announces Drew, plating up the stir-fry and adding the grilled cheese on top.

'Funny, he thinks the same about you.' I laugh. 'Though he would give it a posh term.'

'I'm pleased he classes me as one of his social deviants. Might get that put on a T-shirt.'

'A black T-shirt?'

'Obviously.'

Chapter 9

August 8

To: chaslam@wellmindassociates.org
From: dr.michael.harrison@expeditedmail.co.uk
Subject: Jessica again

Dear Charles,
I apologise for interrupting your long weekend in Edinburgh but Jessica's behaviour is causing me deep concern. After a relatively quiet few months during which she occupied herself with a range of new hobbies, she appears to have gone wildly off track. The new crisis centres on her claim to have a job as a 'psychological profiler'. I did wonder, as I told you at the time when she announced she had got this position, whether this was a shot at me and my career? I thought then that she was disguising some office temp job, but I increasingly have begun to suspect that she is inventing the whole thing. This has been worrying me, so I followed her to her place of work the week before we went away and discovered she spent most of her time in a local café,

drinking coffee and scribbling in one of her many note-books. The writing in these is still as you will remember: obsessional, full of lists, underlinings and highlightings, writing from various points of view as if she is that person. It's very hard to decipher but I can see that I don't come out very well in any of her entries.

I tested her on a number of occasions as to the nature of her work but her attempts to introduce me to her employer all conveniently failed. You warned me that her fantasies are real to her and there will always be a good excuse for her inability to make them concrete. Just in case, I searched for evidence of her boss's existence and found no trace of the man and just the barest front door of a website that Jessica admitted while we were on holiday that she had constructed herself. That caused a particularly spectacular row between us. Now she claims to have lost said job, and mislaid her employer, marking the start of a second paranoid phase to the job fantasy.

We've seen this pattern before over the Eastfields debacle. She barely escaped prosecution then and I'm not clear where this current fantasy is leading her. To give me peace of mind, I would be eternally grateful if you would persuade Jessica to come in for another inpatient stay at your clinic. I know we've discussed this before but it's far more than adult ADHD with her; there is something profoundly out of kilter in her psyche and I think she needs rest and a controlled environment if there's any hope of her recovering. At least this time there doesn't appear to be a sexual element to her fantasy, not like when she turned on me and that poor student at Eastfields – you can see that I'm reduced to being grateful for small mercies.

I would also be most appreciative if you would reconsider her medication. As before, I'm happy to pay for this and any other costs of treatment. I will suggest she contacts you when I return from my Berlin conference. I'm due in Washington in two weeks and I really don't feel safe leaving her on her own again. Her only friend appears to be drawn from the shadier fringes of society, picked up at a bar, no less. Her talent for charming people on first acquaintance hasn't faded and she's extremely engaging to begin with, knowing how to deploy her good looks and vulnerable air. She claims her new friend is an undertaker, which again shows how rampant her imagination has become. I've met him and he is far more likely to be living on benefits with a pitbull named Spike, but you can't stop Jessica once she gets inventing.

On a happier note, I send greetings from Miles and Tariq. We are all sorry you were unable to make the symposium this year and just about forgive you for putting your daughter's wedding first.

Many thanks in advance.

Michael

Chapter 10

Jessica

I am expecting to have to face dealing with the alarm and bins on my own but Drew insists on driving me over there. He has a moped with lots of shiny accessories, so we set off like Gregory Peck and Audrey Hepburn in *Roman Holiday*, except this is West London and it's raining, but I have a good imagination.

We reach my home to find the light on the alarm flashing, indicating that it has indeed been tripped. Leaving Drew on the scooter, I knock on Lizzy's door. She opens it, penning in her excitable spaniel, Flossie, behind bars of denim. As usual she's looking very together, tawny hair neatly styled, make-up perfect even though she's having a day in. I wouldn't have bothered if I were her.

I give her a hug, made awkward by the fact that she was trying to stop Flossie escaping. We laugh as we bump heads. 'Michael rang me. So, so sorry about the alarm, Lizzy. What am I like?'

'No problem, Jessica. First time it's happened in weeks.'

'So, no break-in?'

'Not unless you count your live-in cat burglar.'

I think I'm relieved, but part of me wanted to discover it wasn't my fault. 'Well, OK, sorry once again.' I turn to go.

'Don't worry, Jessica. We all have our moments.' She looks past me and raises a brow. 'Hi, Drew.'

'Hello, Jessica,' he calls. 'Sweet-peas are looking good.'

'Thanks. Grew them from seed. Do you want to come in? I can make coffee.'

'Another time. We've got plans. Jess is just going to do a quick walk-through.'

'Right, I'd better put Flossie in the garden before she keels over with the excitement of visitors.' She closes the door and I hear her shooing Flossie out the back.

'Won't be long,' I tell Drew, secretly pleased that he has turned down the chance to be with Lizzy to stick with my agenda for the night.

I let myself in the front door. The entry to the kitchen is now firmly closed. Had I really forgotten to shut it? I thought I'd stopped doing that. When I'm inside, I like to be able to see through from the front to the back of the house, it helps me not to feel trapped, but I'd trained myself to leave in a certain order: keys, phone, kitchen door, alarm, front door. I can see myself doing that this morning but evidently it's a false memory.

I go into the kitchen. Colette isn't there. There's a second alarm pad in case we want to go out the side entrance. No sign of any break-in at the back. It must've been me. I don't linger, thinking of those bins waiting for the dustmen. I don't want to stay here anymore. The place no longer feels like home.

'Everything OK?' asks Drew as I join him outside.

'Think so.'

'Did you close the kitchen door this time?'

'Yes, I closed the kitchen door.' I resist the temptation to check. I did. I can see myself staring at it a few seconds ago. Shut. The problem is, I also can see myself closing it when I left at midday. My brain has become accomplished at filling in gaps with plausible images, an inventive liar. If it does it over something so trivial, is it doing it at other times when I don't realise? And if my mind is rewriting my reality, what does that make me? I'm like the actress who finds her role replaced by a CGI character, her actions just discernible as the foundation for the pixels.

'Jess, don't beat yourself up. No one's been hurt; problem dealt with. Let's go.'

'Yes, you're right. Perspective.'

He pats the back seat and I get back on. Revving the little sewing machine of an engine, we scoot off through the evening traffic.

It's getting dark by the time we reach Dean Street. 5a and the surrounding buildings are in a much quieter stretch than the parts further north towards Oxford Street and south towards China Town with their pubs, clubs, theatres and restaurants. I'm relieved that I have Drew with me. These streets make me cringe, especially after dark. *Come on, Jessica. Don't go there. Concentrate on why you are here.* Many of the premises have already put out their bins for collection the next morning, making the road look like it's in the middle of an invasion by square green Daleks, victims reduced to slumped heaps of black plastic beside them, innards of non-recyclables leaking out where a dog or urban fox has attacked. The pile outside 5a is encouragingly big, a massacre of bags.

'What are we looking for?' asks Drew, wrinkling his nose as he crouches down beside me.

'Anything – everything.'

'Great. Glad you were able to narrow that down for me.'

I tug open the top of the first bag. Yuck. Marek appears to live on takeaways. The next includes some empty paint cans – 'White with a hint of apricot' – I totally missed that hint. I take them out and find only paint-stained plastic beneath.

'What about this?' Drew lifts up a corkboard leaning against the wheelie bin in the hope of being free-cycled.

Thank God. 'Yes, that's ours.' I undo the ties to another sack and hit the jackpot. 'Drew, my notebooks.' I fish them out. They're a little swollen with damp. Under them are two mugs, one chipped, the other with such a faded design that no charity shop would take them. I recognise them as they were my contribution to our kitchen. I dig in my shoulder bag for the foldaway carrier Mum gave me last birthday – a disappointing gift to open but, hey, isn't it proving useful? I load up my treasure.

Drew, meanwhile, has been searching the last bags and the wheelie bin itself. 'Nothing obvious. Do you want to check in case you recognise anything?'

He's right. No computers or office equipment, just the things belonging to me. Unless Jacob drank out of my mugs that last day and only swilled them out rather than washing them, I wouldn't even have a physical trace of him.

'It's like he never existed,' I say.

'I guess he must be a pro at that. But why leave your note-books?'

I flick through them. These are the ones I designated for my missing persons research so I'd kept them at the office. My handwriting is atrocious and I have a methodology of high-lighting and footnoting that only I seem to be able to understand.

'He didn't need these. I typed up my findings in the computer records. This is just the background stuff.'

Drew knuckles my forehead lightly. 'You are so analogue, Jess, actually writing things down.'

'But it's a good thing I do, as I can reconstruct most of what I found out from here.'

Two police officers turn into the street and approach us at a leisurely pace. Drew begins furtively resealing the bin bags.

'Everything all right?' asks one, a twenty-something blonde with her hair tied back in a no-nonsense ponytail.

I show her my mug collection. 'Yes, just looking for my things. Got chucked out by my old landlord.'

'Good luck with that.' As I predicted, the officers aren't that interested in people stealing from bins. 'Try not to make a mess.' They walk on.

Drew sits back on his heels. 'You weren't the least bit worried, were you? Why am I the one to feel instantly panicked when confronted by anyone in uniform?'

'Guilty conscience?' I've been moved on for far worse than ferreting through stuff that no one wants. This is nothing.

We stack the sacks more or less how we found them.

Drew sniffs his fingers then grimaces. 'I need to wash my hands before I touch the scooter.'

Carlo's will be closed but there's a pub on Bateman Street, a short walk from here. 'I know a place – and I'll even buy you a drink for being such a star.'

'I would ruffle your hair and say "what are friends for?" but that, at the moment, would just be gross.'

'Thank you for restraining yourself.'

We sit across from each other in a quiet corner of the Dog and Duck. It's cramped inside, combining eatery and bar with all the polished wood and colourful tiles such a small space can embrace. I find it strangely reassuring. Drew sips on his half while I indulge in a Bloody Mary, needing the kick of fiery Worcester sauce to drive off the taste of rubbish. It feels the right kind of retro drink to have in such an antiquated place.

'So what are you going to do now?' asks Drew. He flicks through one of my notebooks. 'You've done so much work on these girls. You're not going to give up, are you?'

'I don't know. I don't understand right now. What was Jacob doing investigating them in the first place?'

Drew scans the other people in the bar, fairly quiet on this Monday night, a couple of office workers, some tourists in optimistic shorts, a gaggle of student types looking effortlessly young. That's what I notice but I wonder what he sees when he looks at people? Coffin sizes? God, that's macabre. He's not like that. His job makes him celebrate life; I'm the one with the Gothic imagination.

'Jess, if he was asked to do that by family or friends, then they might have another way of contacting him. He'll want to be paid.'

'Don't we all?' I wonder how it would go, trying to contact some of the nearest and dearest to the missing. I cringe at the thought.

'I suppose there's another possibility.'

'What's that?'

'He's insane, obsessed by these cases for no particular reason, living out some kind of fantasy where he's the intrepid detective and you're his Dr Watson.'

I don't like to leap so quickly to the accusation that Jacob was living in a world of his own invention; that has come my way too before and I know how difficult it is to wriggle out from under such an allegation. 'Surely I should've sensed if he were delusional? He appeared perfectly rational to me.'

Drew just smiles. 'You, my friend, are easy to fool because you are so nice. Me, I'm a little nastier, and I suspect everyone.'

'You're not nasty.'

'Oh, I am. But you don't see it. I have motives within motives.' He reaches out and takes my hand where it is loosely looped around the base of my glass. 'It's not anyone I'll go through bins for.'

I let my hand stay in his. Right now, I just need the comfort that someone finds me the least bit necessary to them.

'It's too soon, isn't it?' Drew brushes my fingers with his.

'Too soon for what?'

'You and me.'

Major gaydar malfunction. 'Drew, are you saying... oh my God, you are, aren't you?'

He gives me a funny look. 'Not exactly the reaction I was hoping for. Polite refusal, yes; incredulity, no.'

'I thought you were like my gay best friend.'

He moves back. 'You thought I was homosexual?'

'Or maybe bipossible. Oh shit, I've made a hash of this, haven't I?' I'm blushing worse than when I was thirteen and asked the out-of-my-league boy to a party.

Drew gives a grimace. 'Or maybe the hash is mine?'

'No, no, it's my fault. I just assumed... kind of built a picture of you based on...' I tail off. What had I based it on? The fact that he made me feel at ease. That is all, really. I've made a fantasy role for him and moulded him into it in my ridiculous mind.

'I thought you knew me better than that.'

'I'm sorry.'

'God, this is embarrassing. Bit of a dent to the old ego.' He sips his drink.

'No, no, it's not you, it's me.'

He laughs at my joke, which is also the truth. 'Jess, you are something else.'

I shrug. 'I'm so sorry for being dense. And I want you to take a long hard look at me. I'm this.' I gesture to my own hopelessness.

'That's fine by me. You need to get away from that dickhead Michael. He's destroying you, you know that, don't you?'

I didn't really. There were times when I thought he'd been saving me. 'I can't blame him, Drew. He's tried his best. People do, and I still mess things up.' I gaze out at the street. A girl in a brief black skirt and off-the-shoulder blouse is coaxing a guy into an alley with the practised moves of a pro. He looks furtive but follows. I shudder. There is so much that Drew does not know.

He squeezes my hand and lets go. 'I get it. This is a process. You need to make the break, then we'll talk.'

'Now that I know you're not gay.'

He manages to laugh. 'Yeah, that'll help my case. Speak to him when he gets back. Not because of me but because you really need to do this for you.'

Drew's right. This train has been coming down the tracks for a very long time now. If I had any objectivity about my own relationships, I would've told myself, lying on my own therapy couch, that something that started with such an unequal balance of power, made more exciting by being a rule-breaking secret, would fail when it became respectable and had to face real problems. Michael accuses me of spinning fantasies but he has as well over our relationship, using me to flatter some version he has of himself. I need to free him so he can either grow up or, more likely, enter another round with a younger model. He is going to be nothing but disappointed with me from here on. None of us, the women in his life, live up to his dead wife, so he is destined to repeat unless he works out how to move on.

But that's now his problem, not mine.

'OK, I'll talk to him when he gets back.'

Chapter 11

Emma, 13th January 2011

It's been a rough week. This treatment cycle is no picnic and there are times when I just want to opt out, pretend none of it is necessary. I can see myself doing it, ripping out the IV, flushing the pills, striding out into the sunset. I would if I had the energy but I've had a continually streaming nose and felt like death since the weekend. Funny, as the treatment is the thing that's supposed to stave that off, not bring it prematurely into my body. I sit on the sofa in the kitchen, too tired to do much else but watch Michael at work. I'm so grateful to our friends helping out to give us this time. Biff has gone with Katy to the shops getting food and some supplies for the house. They'll enjoy that time together and it gives me a break.

I wish they'd stop asking me what I want to eat, though. I don't bloody well want to eat anything.

I asked Michael how his book is going. He went off on a little lecture about the limitations of Eysenck's personality types as applied to the personalities of serious offenders in the judicial system. I won't tell him that it's not what he says but how he says it that I'm listening to as I murmur 'really?' and 'that's interesting' at appropriate moments. He has hopes the book is going to take his work to a larger audience than he's managed so far on the conference circuit. The police might appreciate him but I know he craves a bigger stage. I'm pushing him to come up with a catchy title. Anything with Eysenck in it will remain on the academic shelves. *Type M for Murder* is my best so far, with a wordplay on Michael's use of the concept of personality type. I'm sure I can come up with something better if I lay on the sofa much longer; some good has got to come of enforced inactivity.

Michael certainly has the face for popularising psychology; the camera will love him with his square jaw, astute gaze and wavy auburn hair – no geeky egghead here, no sir. He may not be the most academically successful psychologist ever, but he certainly is in contention for the most handsome. It's like Hollywood has already cast him in his own biopic. I tease him that he wants to be a celebrity and he gets flustered, so I know I'm on the right track there. I can read people; I suppose that's one of my talents.

Being this sick gives me plenty of time to think about my own career – one of the drawbacks, really. Have I done the right thing with my life? If I do get out of this and recover enough to return to work, would I go back to the same job? No, I think I'm done there. I can't imagine walking into the classroom to preach what I didn't practise. I can't tell the students that I got away with skirting the rules just barely and some of the things I did seem crazy in retrospect. God,

I was so driven – I saw myself as a crusader, saving young lives from radicalisation, ends justifying the means and so on. I can't claim that I wasn't warned. You get sucked in, thinking it's your responsibility to save the day. It's not a job where you can shelve your concerns as you approach home and put some distance between yourself and what weighs on you. Even doctors have that luxury. No, like a soldier in a combat zone, you have to live it twenty-four seven.

And what does weigh on me? I don't think I've been fair to some people I met. They might've had better intentions than I gave them credit for and still I reported them. But I have a priority now that goes above and beyond any person I brushed up against in the job. Biff says I made the right choice leaving. Michael is a great guy, a safe pair of hands. He'll make up for any shortcomings that I introduced into the situation. On my own I'm pretty crappy; with him I make half of a good team.

That's got to count for something. I hope Katy will think so when I explain.

Chapter 12

Jessica

Drew tells me he has to go out to deal with a DB from Florida so I decide I'd better go to work too. I minimise the photo of the page in Emma's diary that I've been reading on the laptop and resolve to spend the day reconstructing my cases. I hadn't realised she'd moved into teaching. Had she been tasked to keep a watchful eye out for student extremists? That's what I took from the last paragraph. I don't think I could do that. It must've been so awkward. I'm enjoying reading her words, though, puzzling through the hints of people around her, the regrets. I can get back to her later. I have to focus on the now if I'm going to get out of this fix Jacob left me in.

I'd reached some conclusions about the missing girls individually but seeing them like this, I begin to make some new connections. They've all vanished in a two-year period with indications that they were headed to London, or at least away from their home town where things had become unbearable. Lillian and Clare had both come out of the care system so had the smallest support network but Ramona and Latifah have families who are presumably still anxious to know what has happened to their daughters. I remember I had suspected that Latifah's exit had partly been motivated by the desire to avoid an arranged marriage – there had been talk of a cousin coming to meet her last summer. She was an all-A-stars A-Level candidate but missed out on taking her place at Royal Holloway. I'd felt particularly close to her when I saw that she had been down to do Criminology and Psychology. The irony is that Latifah would've been one of Michael's students now if she had taken her place last autumn. I make a mental note to check she hasn't reapplied this year. I don't suspect foul play with her; I think she's just biding her time. I suppose I have to consider that there's a vague possibility, a notion prompted by Emma's diary, that she might've been radicalised and gone to Syria, but there is no sign of that on her social media or in anything her friends say about her. It would be lazy to leap to such a conclusion just because the press sees every story about a Muslim runaway in terms of terrorism. No, I think Latifah has her head screwed on. She's OK.

I am more worried right now about the other three. They seem more vulnerable. From some of the things Ramona let slip, her father looks like he might've been abusive. I can well imagine her running away, but with little or no qualifications and no money, she is unlikely to have landed on her feet. Same goes for Lillian and Clare. They all seem to have vanished into the crowds of the city.

> *A crowd flowed over London Bridge, so many,*
> *I had not thought death had undone so many.*

T. S. Eliot is haunting me at the moment. Little fragments pop up in my mind every time I hear an echo of one of his words. I can't make a hot drink without his Prufrock telling me that he's measured out his life in coffee spoons. I wonder how many other people suffer from this same cultural commentary as they go about their ordinary business? I suppose there could be worse poets to carry around with you.

Where was I? I tap the pen on the notes I made on Ramona. Margate, February 2014 was the last sighting. I remember visiting the seaside town around then with Michael. It's an odd place: great beach, tatty seafront, boarded-up shops in a failed high street and then this world-class art gallery on the quayside.

> *On Margate sands,*
> *I can connect*
> *Nothing with nothing.*

Thanks, T. S. How true. We were attending an event at the Tate Contemporary and I'd enjoyed the landscapes by Turner that Michael had abhorred. He's got this thing about anything impressionistic. He accuses late Turner, Monet, Manet and their followers of chocolate-box painting, softening reality, avoiding sharp edges. He is not interested in the theories of light that they were exploring or their message about art being in the fleeting perception of the artist. His own taste runs more to the blocks and shouting colours of the De Stijl movement and Pop Art. Our house – his house – is decorated with reproductions and the occasional canvas by a contemporary artist who meets his exacting standards. Perhaps my rebellion when I furnish my next home will be to make it a homage to Monet's water lilies, what Michael calls the apogee of Impressionist wallowing.

Apogee? Who even uses that word in everyday life?

'I like Impressionism.' I say it out loud to the humming silence of Drew's flat. Take that, Michael. You have a partner – soon to be ex-partner – with conventional tastes.

I look back at my notes on Ramona. Something else has shaken loose in my mind. I hadn't noticed or put much store by it before but the one area at school in which she excelled was art. I had found articles online in the local press about her winning a competition when she was fifteen. One of the few photos I have of her is from that time. Dark-haired and daunted, she stands beside a big canvas of the sea and beach at Margate. She had given the holiday scene a disturbingly stormy sky and the faces of the people were pained and haunted, a view of Margate as the Expressionist Emil Nolde might have depicted it. Where would a girl running away from her family, but drawn to art, go in London? If she has avoided the downward spiral of the desperate into prostitution and drugs, what would be her goals, her aspirations? Art college maybe? Or finding jobs as a model? I know from my time as a student that you could earn some useful money as a life model. I've never been overly self-conscious – it goes with my impulsiveness – so stripping off to be sketched by a bunch of art students had not been a problem. I found watching them draw me as interesting as I hope they found me as a subject.

I close the notebook on Ramona and get up to make a sandwich for lunch. I've never told Michael I did that for money. Somehow I don't think he'd understand as he is uptight about nudity, always donning a robe to walk from bathroom to bedroom whereas I'm happy to flit around naked. Odd, really, as he's the one with the great body.

I make a round of sandwiches for Drew and head downstairs to find him. Mrs Payne is on reception. A curvaceous woman with dyed red hair and a fondness for floaty scarves, she reminds me of a fairground fortune-teller. Not that she has the least interest in the occult; she is one of the most resolutely grounded people I know.

'All right, dear?' she asks on seeing me.

I wonder what she thinks I'm doing here. How has Drew explained my presence? 'Yes, thanks. I've got some lunch for Drew.'

'He's out the back with Ron.'

'Can I go out there and give it to him?'

'Of course you can!' She pats my hand. I can see where Drew gets his natural warmth. 'You can't offend anyone there. They're all tucked up in our refrigerator so you won't see a thing. I hope the families hurry up and arrange funerals. In the summer we always get pressed for space, oldies keeling over in the heat, families on holiday so funerals delayed, and storage filling up faster than we can move them.'

This insight into the logistics of juggling bodies is fascinating to someone with my kind of mind, so I head to the behind-the-scenes department of the funeral business. I've not been in here before but I find a purpose-built area with a concrete floor, complete with cold-storage compartments in a special fridge like I've seen in police dramas. Who wakes up one morning and thinks, 'I know, I'll go into the business of making corpse refrigerators'? I'd like to meet them, whoever they are.

Drew and his father, Ron, have just finished closing a coffin for the afternoon's funeral. They have a special mechanised loading platform with the casket on rollers to minimise the lifting. Care of backs is a chief health-and-safety concern for funeral directors, it would seem. I wonder if there is an inspection regime? A government department for the regulation of the dead? There's one for abattoirs.

Cease and desist, Jessica, this is not the same thing at all! I wish I could tune out my stupid internal monologue sometimes.

'Hi. I've made you some lunch, Drew.' I hold up the plastic bag of cheese, pickle and salad sandwiches. Is it odd to have food here? I'm not sure of the protocol.

Drew checks his watch. 'Is there time, Dad?'

'Of course there is. Take a break. We'll leave at two.' Ron winks at me, a small jovial man with a sun-tanned complexion, the result of a couple of weeks in the Bahamas last month.

Drew takes off his overalls and washes his hands. It's very warm outside in the little courtyard compared to the air-conditioned shed. We sit side by side on a bench, the only free space as the rest is given over to the shiny black hearse already backed up to load from the double doors.

'How've you got on this morning?' Drew asks, making a start on his lunch.

'Good, thanks. If I'm going to ask one of the families whether they have a contact for Jacob, I think Latifah's might be my best bet, or Ramona's mother.'

'But you don't sound keen.'

'It'll be a difficult conversation and they have no reason to help me.'

'Except you've tried to help them by investigating what's happened to their daughters.'

'I'm not sure I would've given them the contact details if I'd got that far. Both girls may have had good reason to run away. I tend to be on their side.' I close my eyes and tilt my chin so the sun warms my face. A plane rumbles overhead. 'I ran away once.'

'Really?' I can feel him shift to look at me but I don't open my eyes. 'Seriously, or when you were little and only got as far as the end of the road?'

'No, the real deal. I was gone for four months – missed the beginning of the school year. I slept rough – not something I'd recommend.'

'I want to ask why, but you don't have to tell me.'

'I don't mind telling you.' But I'm not going to tell him the whole story; no one will ever hear that. I've buried it deep and am not going to dig it up again. I choose the simple version. 'Imagine your dad and now imagine his absolute opposite – that's what I grew up with. My father was an evil bastard, impossible to live with. In our house, we were in terror of him and his moods. He would fume then explode. Nothing my mother and I did was ever right.' A knot of anger forms in my chest like a fur ball I've never been able to cough up. I swallow, trying to force it down as I can't get it out. 'Any show of emotion on our part was forbidden, as nothing could divert from his stage-centre performance. We weren't allowed to be angry or challenge him over anything. His word was law. It was his house, his garden, his wife, and I was his daughter.' When I think of him, all I remember now is a pair of screwed-up muddy-grey eyes and a flushed face. He's become a cartoon of himself in my memory. It lessens him, and that helps me no end.

'Jess, he sounds an appalling man. What happened to him? Tell me he died of testicular cancer.'

Life isn't fair like that. Nice men get horrible diseases; ones like my father hang on like cockroaches after a nuclear winter. 'Don't know, don't care. He was actually Mum's second husband. She had a daughter already, my older sister Miriam.'

'Didn't I meet her once? Formidable woman.'

'Yes, that's Miriam. She should be in charge of the free world, not just a farm. Anyway, her dad was a good bloke called John but he died of a heart attack in his forties. Miriam left home as soon as she could after the second marriage as she didn't like my father, so she never saw the bastard at his worst. After I ran away, Miriam finally realised how bad things had got and helped Mum leave.'

'That was brave of her.'

'Yeah, we got lucky. Miriam had just married Bill – he's a

farmer, great guy – and could offer Mum a home well away from my father. By the time they found me, Dad was history. I was sixteen so my opinion was taken into account in the divorce settlement and I wasn't forced to see him again.'

'Rough, though.'

'It could've been much worse. You know those news stories where some guy flips and kills his ex and her kids? Well, I thought that would be us. I was convinced for a long while that he'd come round and murder us all in revenge one day, but he never bothered. Maybe Bill's farm dogs and rifle scared him off. He's probably still sitting in his house, moaning about how his wife, his daughter, abandoned him.'

Drew scrunched up the empty bag and stuffed it in his pocket. 'I have to say it, Jess, but don't you see a similarity between your domineering father and Michael?'

'Are you saying I'm repeating family history? No, Michael's not that bad.' He isn't, is he? 'He recognises I have a life separate from his – he positively encourages it. He often says he doesn't want us to live in each other's pockets. My father would never have done that.' My phone pings. A text from Michael. *Come home immediately.* 'Speak of the devil. The eagle has landed. I've got to go back. Thanks for looking after me.'

Drew leans over and tucks a strand of hair behind my ear. He smells of cheese and pickle with an undertone of varnish. 'You know you're welcome back anytime. I like having you around.'

'I like being around you.' It's true. He makes me feel wanted. I rest my forehead on his shoulder. 'Thank you.'

* * *

I arrive back in Clapham to find a police car parked outside our house. Christ, not another tripped alarm? It's really not my fault this time. I definitely closed the kitchen door and set it correctly. Drew will be able to back me up on the latter, as he would have heard the buzz as I locked the front door.

I use my key to enter and call out a wary 'Hello?'

'In here, Jessica,' replies Michael from the conservatory half of the kitchen which is out of sight of the hallway. I go in and find he is serving tea to the officers, two of them sitting at the scrubbed pine table. They look up expectantly as I enter.

'What's going on? Did we have a break-in?' I drop my bag on the fourth chair.

'Where've you been?' asks Michael. He's still in what I think of as his conference uniform: lichen-green linen suit, jacket, and shirt. He cuts a patrician figure with his thick auburn hair and large frame. In the States, he would've done well as a newscaster or TV evangelist. Here, we seem to like our newsreaders to have an ordinary vibe and our clergy less polished. A new shoulder bag is hanging from the back of one of the chairs advertising the name and date of the symposium. He has at least five of these freebies, the boringly grown-up version of the T-shirt with the band tour dates.

'At Drew's.' I feel I need to explain a little more for the benefit of the silent police officers. 'He's a friend from Feltham. With Michael away, I didn't want to stay here on my own last night.' I decide not to add that debt collectors might be after me for rent I did not owe them or that I suffer from sleeplessness caused by fears of intruders: that would lead to too long a story.

'And you staying away has nothing to do with the state of the bedroom, I suppose?' Michael's hand slices through the air, a typical gesture of annoyance which means 'cut the crap'. 'Don't give me your usual excuses; I want the truth. I'm not playing nice this time. You've gone way too far. I'm pressing charges.'

'What?' That's a kick in the stomach. The police are here for me. 'What am I supposed to have done?'

'As if you don't know!'

'I don't!'

One of the policemen stands. 'Perhaps Miss Bridges would like to accompany me upstairs so she can see what this is about.'

I trail after the constable. It's odd to see his heavy shoes on our carpet. Michael is usually so insistent that we change out of outdoor shoes before going into the carpeted areas. The policeman leads me to our bedroom at the front and opens the door.

'Oh my God.' The room has been trashed – not just turned over by thieves but systematically ruined. The covers are ripped off the bed and the mattress has been slashed on Michael's side. White stuffing leaks out and you can see the springs. Our carving knife has been left in the material, stabbed where his heart would be if he were in bed. His clothes are out of the wardrobe and drawers, some shirts torn in two. There's a strong smell of aftershave in the air from the smashed bottle that had stood on his side of the dressing table. His stack of bedside reading – mainly psychology related – have been tugged from their covers and turned into clumps of confetti.

But my side is untouched. Clothes hang limply. Lotion bottles still lined up on the glass top. An iPad and a stout Kingsolver sit waiting for me. My glass of water hasn't even been spilled.

'This wasn't me.' I don't dare cross the threshold.

'Perhaps you'd better come back downstairs with me, Miss, and we can discuss this in the kitchen.'

'It wasn't me. Have you swept for fingerprints?' I follow him. 'Was the alarm tripped again? Our neighbour would've noticed. You must ask her.'

Michael is standing with his back to the oven, arms folded. 'Well?'

'You can't think I'd do that, Michael.' He obviously does. 'It wasn't me, I swear it.'

The policeman who took me upstairs gets out a notebook. The other one, I notice, is stroking Colette surreptitiously under the table.

'You came back here last night after Miss Huntingdon reported the alarm had gone off, correct?'

'Yes. At about nine.'

'You came inside and saw no evidence of a break-in?'

'No, it all seemed normal.' Then I realise. 'I didn't go upstairs, though. I was in a hurry because I had to get to my old office to fetch some things before they got thrown away.'

'Were you with anyone?'

'Yes, with Drew. Andrew Payne, the friend from Feltham.

He's employed in his family funeral business. We came after he'd finished work for the day.'

Michael gives a sceptical snort. For some reason, he's never believed Drew has a job and refuses to accept any proof I offer. I've given up trying and I know Drew, on the rare times they've met, believes it a point of honour to present his worst side to Michael, as he is so ready to think badly of him.

'Did he come in with you?'

'No, he stayed on his moped outside. That's another reason why I didn't go upstairs. I didn't want to keep him waiting.'

'So when were you last in the front bedroom?'

'Yesterday morning, about midday, when I grabbed a few things to stay away overnight.'

'And how did you leave the room?'

I'm tempted to blurt out 'by the door' but this isn't the moment for inappropriate quips. 'Mainly tidy.'

'Mainly?'

'Michael had left some laundry on the floor. I wasn't in the mood to pick it up.' I shoot Michael a glance but his expression is granite.

The policeman leans forward. 'What mood were you in?'

'I was in a hurry. I didn't have time for moods.'

'Why a hurry?'

'Because I didn't want to stay here alone and wanted to go to Drew's. Look, officer, I know it looks bad up there but I didn't do that. Someone else got into the house. There must be signs of how they did it?'

'There's not been a break-in,' snaps Michael. 'Believe me, that's the first thing I checked.'

'And can you tell us what you took from the bedroom when you left yesterday?' continues the constable.

'Not much. Change of clothes. Wash bag. Night stuff. Oh, and I borrowed some money from Michael's wallet as I didn't have any cash. I'll pay you back, Michael.'

'I don't care about the fucking money, Jessica. I just want to know why you did it. Why take Emma's picture, the diary and wedding ring?'

This is the second time I'm blindsided. 'What?'

'You know exactly what I'm talking about. Her picture, a diary and the little blue box with her wedding ring are the only things I've noticed that are missing. I didn't think to count the cash, but I suppose I should add that to the list.'

'But I didn't... I mean, why would I do that?' I hadn't taken anything else and forgotten, had I? I remember looking at the picture, the rings and the notebook but I'm sure I put them back. I took photos rather than remove the diary. Oh God, that's going to look really suspicious if they ask to see what's in my phone's photo app.

The policeman clears his throat. 'Miss, Dr Harrison said before you arrived that you have a history of mental illness, that you're on medication.'

'Hardly. I suffer from ADHD which is, as I expect you are aware, a mild condition that about five per cent of the population have and can be controlled with treatment. It's not a personality disorder of the magnitude to do that.' I jerk my chin towards the stairs.

'He said you had spent time in a clinic to straighten yourself out after an episode of delusions about a pupil at your last school where you were employed.'

God, it is all circling back to haunt me. 'I had a breakdown due to stress. I'm better now.'

The policeman lowers his voice, getting all pally with me. 'Look, Miss, if you do have those items on you, things will go much more easily if you produce them now. Otherwise Dr Harrison has said he wants to press charges.'

'But I didn't do it – I don't have them. How can I produce something I don't have? Look, here's everything I have on me.' I take my bag and tip it upside down. Two mugs fall out, one smashes, followed by my notebooks, and then miscellaneous rubbish that accumulates in the bottom of my handbag. I throw out my arms. 'You can search me. See, I really don't have them.'

Michael has the gall to look inside the bag I've emptied. 'You've probably stashed them at your friend's – or thrown them away.' His voice breaks a little on that last suggestion. 'I know things have been bad between us, Jessica, but I never thought you'd be so cruel as to stoop to taking that picture. You know how much it means to me.'

'Yes, I do – clearly it means far more to you than I do, because you're not even trying to imagine that I might be innocent.'

He throws my bag down. 'Who else could've got in here?'

'I don't bloody well know. Isn't it their job to find that out?'

I gesture to the two policemen who are watching our little meltdown. 'Whoever it is certainly has a grudge against you, if the state of our bedroom is anything to go by. You need to ask yourself who hates you that much?'

Michael turns away, dismissing me. 'See, officer, she's admitting it indirectly. Her doctor will tell you that much of Jessica's paranoia is directed against me. She makes things up, like this ridiculous job she was supposed to have had. As for her case notes, you'll never be able to work out what's real and what's fantasy from her words. No, I've had enough of it. After what you said to me on holiday, Jessica, this is the final straw. I want you out of here tonight. I want to press charges.'

The policemen exchange looks. 'But really, sir, there is no evidence,' says my constable. 'I can see how you might conclude she is responsible, but there's nothing we can hold her on. If we found the missing things on her, that would be different.'

'She stabbed the bloody mattress with a carving knife! That's not the action of a sane woman! Then I want her sectioned. I'm ringing her doctor.'

'Sir, calm down, please,' says the cat-loving officer.

I sit down, feeling so weary. Drew's right. Michael is like my father after all. It's his feelings, his life that matters here, not mine. 'He's not my doctor, Michael. He's my psychiatrist, my therapist, but he's really more your friend, isn't he? I'm not going back to see Charles. He's not impartial. He listens to you rather than me. I only got out from under his thumb because I started to say the things I know you wanted me to, but I'm done with that.'

'See what I'm dealing with?' says Michael, appealing to the officers in that awful man-to-man thing he does. 'She's even projecting her paranoid fantasies onto the expert who's done so much to stabilise her.'

The constable closes his notebook. 'We'll send a team round to dust for prints. Please don't move anything in that room until they've given you the all clear. We'll also take your prints for elimination purposes.'

'Take my prints!' Michael looks ready for another round of explosions.

'They won't be kept – it's just a formality.'

'But they'll be in some database somewhere. It's an infringement of my civil rights.'

The policeman's mood has swung from sympathy to annoyance. 'We can't do our job without collecting evidence. Are you saying you don't want this investigated?'

Michael struggles for a few moments, choking on his words.

'We'll go away as soon as you say you've changed your mind about pressing charges.' Both officers are now on their feet. From their point of view, I can see this is a minor crime, probably domestic in origin, nothing of great value stolen.

'Yes, dammit, I'll drop the charges. I'll settle for getting her out of my house.'

'And, Miss, will you be all right if we leave you now?' the officer asks.

I nod. 'He may huff and puff, but he won't blow the house down. I was thinking of leaving anyway. You can see how welcoming he's become recently.'

'Very well. We'll show ourselves out.'

The sound of the door closing behind them punctuates the silence between Michael and I.

'How did we come to this, Michael?'

'I want you out in fifteen minutes. And you'd better return Emma's things or you'll be sorry you ever crossed me.'

'Believe me, I already am. I didn't do that to our room.'

'You just say that you didn't but who else could it be, tell me that? I'm afraid you're so lost in your own fantasies that you don't even know if you did it or not. You need help, Jessica. I've tried and I've tried but I can't save you if you don't want saving. You're on your own from here.'

Chapter 13

Emma, 5th January 2010

It's odd how you can be thinking your life was heading in one direction when suddenly – bang – you come into a room and everything changes. What has caused this epiphany? OK, confession time: I met the most gorgeous, wonderful guy today. God, I sound as if I'm about sixteen, not twenty-six. I'm going to be so embarrassed when I read this back. Please forgive me, future self – you will if you remember what it was like to see him today. Coming out of a rough patch as regarding men, I have to be wary. He could be too good to be true, has to be. Surely, I'm too cynical to think he is a) intelligent; b) single; c) solvent; and d) did I mention gorgeous?

I quickly google him before I get too carried away. Hmm. He sounds pretty much the real deal and no mention of a wife, not even an ex. He's in his early forties so, if this profile is to be believed, somehow he has reached his fifth decade without a litter of failed relationships or children he doesn't see except at the weekend. Not bad, Michael. You don't mind if I call you Michael?

Wow, I'm flirting with him and he's not even here. That guy must be like catnip. I'm taking a break to splash my face with cold water.

OK, I'm back and I promise I will behave. Let me give you the full story. It was quite by chance that I signed up for the conference on youth psychology. I was only prompted to do so by my line manager who thought it would help me adapt to the responsibilities for which I had volunteered in my new part-time position at the college. Dr Harrison, Michael, was there as the guest speaker. I do not lie when I say that all the straight females in the room, and probably all the gay guys, perked up when he strode in to give the seminar. Battered brown leather jacket, anyone? That just does it for me somehow. Joe in the seat next to me arched a brow but I just grinned.

'No chance,' I mouthed. Move over, boys, this is one man who is not going to be playing with his own team.

I spent the entire seminar trying to think up an intelligent question. I was aware Dr Harrison's gaze fell on me a few times, probably because I was looking pensive. I hope he didn't think I was tuning out. I came up with something decent in the end and waited until a few others had broken the ice with their queries.

'Would you say, Dr Harrison, that there is a predictable age at which psychopathic and sociopathic tendencies can be diagnosed in the young?'

That sounds OK, doesn't it? And my voice didn't squeak or do anything embarrassing as I asked it.

He complimented me on my question and went on to give

a long answer about the difference between the two conditions. It was actually very interesting so I jotted it down. Just for future reference, both are obviously an antisocial personality disorder and can exhibit quite similar behaviours. To fulfil the definition of a disorder, they will show at least three of the following: regular law breaking, lying, impulsiveness, aggression, disregard for the safety of others, irresponsibility, such as not meeting financial obligations, and not appearing to feel remorse. But where they differ, that's also fascinating. The current theory is that psychopaths are born that way and are without a conscience. There's possibly a brain malfunction in the limbic system, so in the future you may be able to diagnose the condition with a brain scan – that was the answer to my initial question. Sociopaths often have a conscience, weak though its voice may be, and are more often created by their upbringing. Basically they are messed up by their parents – or lack of parents. Neither are necessarily harmful to society, there's a whole range from mild to severe in both conditions, and there will be many on these scales living perfectly decent lives among us. Possibly even in this room.

That got an uneasy laugh.

It's what they choose to do next that causes the problem. Harold Shipman, for example.

I suppose that's reassuring. The courts can't hold someone responsible if the person is prey to their brain chemistry. In Dr Harrison's description of the mentality, there are still checks to behaviour available to the person with the disorder. The mental vehicle is not completely out of their control. Some prison psychiatrists are having success in treating offenders by helping them recognise where their thought processes differ from the mainstream experience. In a sense, helping them construct the idea of a conscience they don't naturally have.

When he finished his answer he made a point of coming back to me and saying he'd be happy to discuss this further if I had any follow-up questions. As I was walking out of the lecture hall, he gave me his card so I don't think I'm being over-confident when I say that I believe the attraction went both ways.

He might be a good person for me to go out with as a way of re-entering the dating arena after a long drought. Life is a struggle at the moment, and I would appreciate someone to help me get over the bumps, someone with whom to have just simple adult fun. Biff, and Katy too in her own way, try their hardest but they can't be the man in my life. Both sense I've been down in the dumps since November. But, hey, new year, possibly new man. I'd say things are looking up.

Chapter 14

August 9

To: chaslam@wellmindassociates.org
From: dr.michael.harrison@expeditedmail.co.uk
Subject: Developments regarding Jessica

Dear Charles,

Sorry to contact you so soon after my last email but there has been a development regarding Jessica's behaviour which demands your immediate intervention. She has escalated from her usual fantasies to destroying my belongings and my half of the bed. She has also removed Emma's picture, one of her diaries and her wedding rings – a theft calculated to injure me where I am most vulnerable. This is the last straw and I have told her to move out. Indeed, I'm not sure I'm safe with her now, as she took a carving knife to the mattress. If I had been here, would it have been me? She is upstairs packing her belongings but whether or not she actually leaves is anyone's guess. She made a joke to the policemen who interviewed her in my presence, comparing me to the big bad wolf, so I have no hope of her treating this as seriously as I do. I certainly can't stay under this roof with her here.

However, I would not be a responsible friend to Jessica if I did not try for a final time to get her appropriate care. I truly believe she might be a danger to herself and those around her. I understand that it is difficult to get adults sectioned but as her responsible clinician, surely you can get her detained under the Mental Health Act and see that she gets the treatment she requires? The accusation that she sexually groomed a child at Eastfields will help, as will today's violent outburst. She denies everything and I sometimes wonder if she doesn't believe it – that she is having periods that she blanks from her memory. You're the expert on her state of mind, so you'll probably be familiar with other patients with similar conditions and will know the appropriate action to take. I know from my work that family permission is often sought before sectioning is undertaken. If you wish to speak to Jessica's closest relatives, she has both a father and mother still living. The mother is somewhat detached from reality – I sense she has some of the same mental issues that afflict Jessica – so you might be better off contacting her father who still lives in her old family home. I've not met him but understand from Jessica that she hasn't seen him for years and has no wish to heal the breach. Knowing Jessica, he's probably a decent guy who just had the temerity to call her bluff on her fantasies. You might not want to go down that path but he could be useful if family permission is necessary. I attach his details.

The best outcome would, of course, be that Jessica surrenders herself voluntarily to your care. Now I've calmed down a little from my initial dismay over her actions, I will suggest it to her, but I don't anticipate that she will welcome this from me. If you could see your way to talking to her tomorrow, she might respond better as she knows you have your patient's best interests at heart.

Regards

Michael

Chapter 15

Jessica

It is difficult to imagine the man who swept Emma off her feet could be the same person as the one downstairs. I can hear Michael typing furiously on his laptop on the kitchen table. I bet his message is all uptight and so... so Dr Harrison, I presume, God's gift to the universe. He has got out one of his prized ten-year-old single malts from his whisky collection so I know he is serious about pampering himself to get over the shock. Folding my clothes into the second-best suitcase, I wonder who he is writing to? Probably his friend, Charles, who also doubles as my psychiatrist. That was not the best idea I ever had, now I come to think about it, but I had been desperate at the time when I agreed to start seeing him as a patient. Michael and Charles went to Cambridge together – Emmanuel College in the early Nineties – and seem to be on the same wavelength: both fond of women but with no genuine respect for us. I learned that after three weeks of inpatient treatment at Charles' clinic. Once you get the key to his behaviour, it is then easy enough to say the right things to get yourself discharged, like seeing the answer to a riddle that has eluded you. I wasn't going to get out any other way, so I became the patient he wanted and showed the recovery he predicted. Some of it was genuine.

Stopped halfway between wardrobe and case, I catch myself staring down at the ruins of the bed. It would've been a good revenge if I'd caught Michael cheating on me, but I haven't and I really don't have that kind of energy. At lunchtime, I had been planning a civilised conversation and a mutual parting of the ways, not Armageddon. Does Michael know me so little that he seriously thinks I'm capable of this? Shouldn't we be putting our heads together to work out who really is behind it? He might be in real danger.

That's not Michael's way. Once he found out I had a condition with a label, he immediately assumed I was completely crazy. He's like a doctor seeing a mild cold giving a diagnosis of bubonic plague. He doesn't get it. I suppose he spends his life studying those on the extreme and forgets the rest of the range. Mental illness is complex. Most of us suffer from it in some degree at some point in our lives. My condition is very small fry compared to some issues with which others have to deal.

I move to the chest of drawers and start transferring my T-shirts and underwear. I'll need a second case if I'm making this in one trip. There's a crunch under my shoe and I pick up a photo frame containing a picture of Michael, Charles and me and one of Charles' short-lived girlfriends, taken when skiing last year. I don't mean she died or anything; just that he dumped her after a couple of months. What was her name?

Katherine? I don't think she's the same as the Katy in Emma's diary as she didn't stay around very long. As a divorcee, Charles shows no signs of settling down again and risking his assets by hooking up with anyone so they have a claim on him. At least I can be slightly grateful to Charles for working out that I was suffering from undiagnosed ADHD. Most people these days associate that with unruly children, the kind who are bouncing off the classroom walls after two minutes of sitting still, but girls are more likely to go undiagnosed as our reactions are less disruptive. Not being able to pay attention is usually the first sign there's a problem. When I was little, my restlessness was put down to naughtiness and my lack of focus was labelled daydreaming. My blunt comments were called – variously – refreshing or loud-mouthed, depending on whom I'd upset. It's like I'm missing a filter between brain and mouth – things just emerge which I wish I'd kept as private thoughts. Mostly, that's not a problem because I can laugh it off, but sometimes it lands me in serious trouble, as it did at Eastfields.

I'm not blaming my condition for that debacle – I am responsible for my actions – but I do claim it as a mitigating circumstance for how I handled the false accusation. I am truly my own worst enemy.

The front doorbell rings. It's probably just Lizzy checking up on us. She will have seen the police car.

I hear voices – male – Michael's growing louder with each exchange.

'Jessica!' he bellows.

Oh God, Kubla Khan's men. I'd totally forgotten, in all the

drama of the last few hours, that I am also hiding from my ex-boss's ex-landlord's debt collectors. I don't reply. I curl up on the armchair by the window, waiting this out.

'Jessica!'

Not here, not listening. 'Weave a circle round him thrice, And close your eyes with holy dread.'

An argument ensues on the step. I hear fragments.

'No, I bloody well am not letting you into my house. Nothing here is hers so you're wasting your time.'

The men are being insistent.

'I'm not fetching her for you. I'm not a bloody butler. It's between you and her, nothing to do with me. Now get off my land or I'll call the police.' The door slams. Feet stamp up the stairs.

'What the hell is going on, Jessica?' Michael throws a sheaf of documents at me. I don't touch them. If I haven't actually picked them up then they can't be said to have been served on me. 'Those men say you owe them rent for an office in Soho.'

'Thank you for not letting them in.' I hug my knees to my chest. 'Will you listen to an explanation or will you just shout at me?'

'I can't believe you, renting something like that without the means to pay for it! What were you thinking? You've taken playing at having a job way too far!'

He has picked the shouty option.

'I don't owe anyone anything.'

He picks up the documents, rolls them up. 'That's not what these say!' He pokes them in my chest. 'Go on, read them.'

I try to fend them off. 'Stop it!' He starts hitting me over the head with them as I flail at him with my arms, trying to get free. 'Michael, stop it!'

'I've had more than I can take of this!'

And then somehow the pokes with the rolled-up papers convert to a slap with his free hand. As I reel from the chair, he grabs me by the back of my shirt and hauls me up. He forces the papers into my face, grinding them against my mouth and nose like a twisted version of the custard-pie joke.

'You will... take... responsibility... for this, Jessica!'

I claw the papers away and catch sight of him. He's panting, face flushed, frightening.

'You fucking hit me!' Now I can say it. He's finally done something that breaks my last taboo.

He looks surprised by the accusation. 'I didn't.' He lets go of my shirt and steps away.

I rub my cheek where I can still feel the sting. My eyes are watering. 'You fucking did and you know it.'

'It was a heat-of-the-moment thing – you got in the way. Christ, you deserved it.'

I clench my fists. 'Never say that again. No one deserves to be hit. You say I have problems? Michael, you just hit a woman – you know what that makes you? An abuser. There's no defence.'

He's still breathing heavily. 'Just the once – and don't you go making more of this than an accident. Try to blacken my character and no one will believe you.'

I'm cold inside now. Any impulse I had to explain the rent matter has vanished. I don't want to do anything except leave.

'It's not about me going to other people, Michael. I can't see the point in that. You and I both know what you are.' I go back to packing my things, pretending a calm I don't feel. Inside I'm like a volcanic island still undergoing an eruption, shivering, shaking with shock. 'When you look in a mirror, think of that. There's one person in this world who has seen you without your mask.' My sense of injury gives me strength. 'Go away so I can finish this.'

With a string of expletives, Michael storms out. I immediately ring for a taxi and text Drew to say I'm coming back tonight. I could, of course, stay with Lizzy, but that would be too close. I want nothing more than to escape the threat of Michael's presence and can't bear the idea of bumping into him on the street. The rest of my things I chuck into all available bags, including Michael's favourite suitcase, the one I'd been intending to leave him. He no longer deserves any such attention.

The taxi hoots as it pulls up. I drag the cases downstairs. I don't regret the scuff marks I leave on the oxblood paintwork.

I find Michael huddled at the kitchen table. 'I expect I've left lots of other stuff scattered about the place. I'd appreciate it if you would put it all in a spare corner and I'll arrange for Lizzy to collect it.'

Michael grunts as he scowls at his laptop.

'Right then. I'll leave my set of keys on the hall table. Oh, and one thing more, it really wasn't me who did that to the bedroom. You have an enemy, Michael, and it isn't who you think it is.'

I'm quite pleased with my exit. For once I've managed

dignified. Michael being so clearly in the wrong has helped me be in the right.

'Any more luggage, love?' asks the taxi driver once I've passed him all my bags.

I glance back at the pretty Victorian semi that has been my home for five years. 'No, that's it. There's nothing else I want here.'

Chapter 16

Emma, 23rd July 2010

It's Katy's birthday today. Biff arranged the party so we could keep it a secret from her – not that a two-year-old is that good at sniffing out plans when you want to keep them hidden. She lacks guile. Michael found it all a bit of a strain, poor love. He didn't quite realise when we got married how much he would be involved in this side of things. He didn't mix well with the parents of the other young children Biff had invited and I suppose it did sound like one of the circles of hell with all the howling going on as they fought over the wrapping paper – the kids, not the parents. Michael is not used to toddlers. I see him as a man who would be good with older ones when they can hold a conversation with him. He'd find them interesting then. He spent the whole time watching the chaos with something like horror on his face.

It's cute how Katy knows he's not yet a potential playmate. When neither Biff nor I are around, she will approach him, but it's always with a sober plan in her little head. He's OK for reading a book, or putting on the TV, but not for the hours of 'let's pretend' that she likes. Mind you, to hear him read *The Gruffalo* with such disbelief in his voice makes me wonder why she persists. Perhaps she's cleverer than we think and is secretly laughing at him as she tortures him with her requests. That's Biff's theory.

She's got Biff and me, though, to entertain her, and we each step in when the other is feeling tired and, God, I feel so tired all the time these days after college. When we found out that Katy was on the way, Biff and I made an agreement to do this together and we've both stuck to our word. Biff has a great corner in her kitchen with a play stove and cupboard. Katy feeds us both meals of plastic food, chattering away in that birdlike language of hers that makes a kind of sense if you listen to the intonation.

Biff and I have talked about pre-schools. She, naturally, knows them well and recommends to all her friends the Montessori nursery a short walk away. I'm not sure I like the sound of it – all a bit too Yummy Mummy. We'll have to go and visit soon to get a feel for the place. In what is still a man's world, I want Katy to grow up kick-ass like her mum; I'm not sure that's part of the Montessori curriculum. Biff will probably get her way though. She tends to call the shots on childcare arrangements.

Chapter 17

Jessica

Drew is so good about finding me back at his with my suitcases. He even pays the taxi, which is a mercy as I'm down to my last – Michael's last – twenty.

'You've left him?' He picks up a suitcase to carry it over the threshold.

'I thought that was self-explanatory.' I gesture to the bags. 'Sorry to clutter up the place.'

He brushes this off with a shake of his head. 'As if I care. You've been crying. And, hey, what's that on your face?'

In the mirror at the top of the stairs, put there to reflect more light into a dingy corner, I see myself rising up to meet me at the turn before the door. There's a red blotch high on my cheek like the pressure mark you get from sleeping funny. I don't think it'll bruise. I hope it won't – that would just be pathetic.

'It got a bit physical at the end.'

'Jesus. You should've called the police.'

Dumping my load in the hall, I laugh without humour,

wrapping my arms around my middle. I'm feeling like my sides are splitting, and not in a good way. Life has never been more unfunny. 'He did that before I arrived. Someone had trashed our bedroom and he thought it was me. He was hoping to get me arrested.'

Drew pulls me to his chest. Just comfort. 'God, Jess, I should've gone with you.'

'I didn't do it, you know.'

'I wouldn't blame you if you did.'

I push away. 'I'm not lying. Someone got in the house, probably during the afternoon, you know, yesterday between my two visits?'

'Superglue on the loo seat – that would've been a good revenge.'

'Drew!'

'I know, I know, Jess. I'm just imagining.' He transfers my bags to the spare room. 'He hit you. He deserves much worse than a messy bedroom.'

Something clicks. 'You... You didn't do it, did you?'

'What? Me?' Drew laughs then realises I'm serious. 'Bugger me, no, though I wish I'd thought of it. I'd have pissed on his books on deviant behaviour. So it wasn't you, and it wasn't me. What about Michael, trying to give himself an excuse for booting you out after five years? You probably have a claim on him. You've rights, haven't you? You've contributed to the household?'

'You think he'd do that?'

'He's the one who found it. He's the one making the accusations.'

'There was no break-in.'

'See? We have ourselves another suspect, m'lord. Whoever did it, vindictive ex or intruder, I'm pleased you're out of there.'

'So am I.'

'And I'm seriously considering going round there and decking him.'

'Drew, you're not exactly Hercules and Michael is six foot one and goes down the gym.'

'He's also nearly twenty years older than me. I bet he has a glass jaw. Those kinds of guys look impressive but can't take a punch.'

'Don't joke about this. I don't want one of my few remaining friends in jail. I mean, where would I stay then?' I poke him in the ribs.

'But I would make the perfect criminal. Think how easily I could dispose of his body. I could double him up in a coffin and no one would know. Mrs Bird – we're doing her funeral tomorrow – she was a little thing at the end. We could fit him in and still manage to lift the coffin.'

His revenge fantasies are having the effect of cheering me up – that's the kind of friendship we have.

'I'd settle for taking his conference suits and bags and burning them on a bonfire – as well as his books and articles. And I don't want any harm to come to the cat.' Emma's cat. 'I'll take her with us.'

'That's a good thought. I do the grisly deed, you burn his stuff, and we live happily ever after with Cauliflower.'

'Colette.'

'No, we'd have to rename her to put the police off the scent.'

'Ah, cunning.'

He sits me down in his lounge and goes into the kitchen to prepare us something to eat.

'Risotto?' he calls.

'Ri-yes-oh. You know, Drew, it feels after the events of the last two days that my life has fallen out from under me. No job, no home, no relationship.'

He comes back with a tall glass of white wine. 'Drink this. Think about safety nets, not falling. Everything will look much better in the morning. You're a bright woman. You'll come up with a plan. Out with the old, in with the new.' He gently brushes my cheek where the mark sits. 'All that's over now.'

Drew's right. The next morning my strategy has crystallised. Though I did not want to go down this path, I decide to contact one of the girls' families. Ramona's mother is no longer with the father as far as I can tell, so she poses the least risk. I get her number by the simple method of telling the truth as to why I want it to one of Ramona's old friends. This isn't so hard, as I've already contacted her earlier in my research. She's happy to hand over a number if it will help find her mate.

'Mrs James? Hi, er, my name's Jessica Bridges. No, no, I'm not trying to sell you anything. It's about your daughter.'

The poor woman goes from desperate to fend me off to eager to hear everything I know.

'No, I haven't found her but I have been looking. That's why I'm ringing. I work for a small investigative agency specialising in missing persons cases – Wrath Investigations. Have you heard of us?'

The hope in her voice is heart-breaking. 'No, I haven't. Did the police ask you to look for Ramona?'

'So I don't suppose you've heard of my boss, Jacob Wrath, either?'

'Should I have done?' She sounds genuinely bemused. 'I'm sorry, I'm not very with it at the moment. Things haven't been the same since... and I feel ill from worrying, in pieces really. You can't understand what it's like. My only child. The stuff the doctor gives me – it knocks me out.'

'I'm sure it's not your fault, Mrs James. You haven't forgotten him. Mr Wrath probably didn't contact you. The police didn't ask us to look for her, as far as I know.'

'But you'll carry on? I need someone to take this seriously. The police say she's over eighteen now, has every right not to call, but she's my daughter. She'd get in touch if she could, she really would. You believe me, don't you?'

'Yes, I believe you. And I'll keep looking, I promise.' Why am I saying this? I can't just kill off the tiny glimmer of hope I've offered her – I don't have that in me. 'If it's any consolation, Mrs James, there's nothing I've seen that suggests, you know, foul play. Lots of girls run away each year. Often it's just a question of being patient and keeping the door open for them when they are ready to return.'

'Thank you, thank you. But where has she gone then? I can't help being worried sick about her.'

'I'll try and find out, I promise.'

'I'll pay – I really will – pay what I can.'

I almost refuse but I don't have an income. I have to be practical. 'Let's talk about that if I have anything concrete to offer. But I'm not doing this for money.'

'I know you aren't – I can hear it in your voice. You care, don't you?'

She's being far too kind to me. 'Yes, I do care about Ramona. And if I find her I'll let her know you've not given up looking. I'm right in thinking you live alone now?'

There's a choked sob at the other end. So she found out, or guessed, what her husband had been up to. 'Yes.'

'Then I'll let her know that too.'

I end the call as gently as possible. She may not have been a strong enough mother when needed but at least she is still there for her daughter; Ramona has someone in her corner, which is more than many do.

I carry my results to Drew, having a sudden image of myself as Colette bringing in a dead mouse. I have to shake this habit of wanting to please the men in my life.

'Jacob wasn't employed by the families, or at least not Ramona's, so I'm guessing the others will say the same thing.'

Drew looks up from the ironing board. He's getting his afternoon shirt for Mrs Bird looking all spit-spot. His tattoos – I was right about them – flex as he works. A jester and some kind of lightning bolt on his bicep. *Dashing away with the smoothing iron, dashing away with the smoothing iron, he stole my heart away.* Where do I know that song from? Primary school or my mum, I think.

Keep focused, Jessica. Stop leapfrogging your thoughts. Take your tablet. Take a couple.

'So what does that tell you?' Drew asks.

'That he picked them himself – he had a reason, even if a crazy one. They weren't the result of families reaching out to him.'

'Learning she is, my young apprentice.' Drew slips into the shirt and quickly fastens the buttons. 'And your next move?'

'I'm feeling kinda crazy myself, being the only one, other than the irate landlord, who ever dealt with Jacob.'

'Were you the only one? Didn't he sign for packages? Interview anyone?'

'He always sent me out when he was expecting a client. He said they'd not speak freely if I were there.'

'Did you ever see any of these clients?'

'No. No, I didn't. Probably didn't exist either, did they?'

Drew shrugs and flips the long end of his black tie over the short. 'Can't say. What's he living on if he's not being paid?'

I snap my fingers. 'But there's Rita.'

'Rita?'

'Cleaner of Doom. I swear to you that she exists – I met her many times. Came in once a week to do the bathroom. I say "do" advisedly. We often fell out over her cleaning technique of spraying the area with air freshener and calling it quits.' I sit on the arm of the sofa and hug a cushion to my stomach. 'But I don't get why she came at all? If Jacob was planning on doing the midnight flit, why have another employee?'

'Are you sure she's his employee? Some landlords have a cleaning service come in to keep an eye on their properties.'

'So she was Khan's spy?'

'Maybe. So how are you going to track down Rita?'

'Lovely Rita, meter maid.'

'Educating Rita.'

'Rita Skeeter – it's one of those names that just begs an internal rhyme. Easy. Wednesday is her morning. If she hasn't changed her schedule, I can stake out the place and catch her as she leaves.'

'A stake-out. That sounds very grand.'

'OK, I'm getting up early and going to lurk in a doorway. Happy now?'

Drew grins and puts on his jacket. 'See you later, Detective Bridges. I've just got to put the bird in the oven.'

'Ouch. Very bad taste.'

'Nah, she would've laughed herself silly over it. Viewed life as the end, full stop.' He brushes his hair, straightens his tie. I've noticed that he spends more time in front of the mirror than I do. 'Knew she was on the way, no family, very unsentimental about the arrangements, according to Dad. We're going to make it special for her – us and the carers from her home – as she didn't know many people, having outlived most of her friends.'

I feel a sudden sympathy for the lonely old lady, thumbing her nose at the world that didn't do well by her, from the sound of it. 'Would you like me to come with you?'

'Would you?' Drew looks delighted by the offer.

'Of course. I'll just get changed.'

'Five minutes, Jess. Then we have to go to be on time for our slot.'

'I go, I go, swifter than a something from a whatsit bow.'

'An arrow from a Tartar's bow. And I know you know it, as you say it often enough. Don't dumb down for me, you Shakespeare hack.'

'Educating Andrew.' Smiling at the ease with which we riff off each other, I dive into my bags and pull out my most suitable clothes for a funeral: black skirt, grey flowered shirt. I'm ready in four minutes.

I'm not sad at Mrs Bird's ceremony. It's sobering to see how you can come to the end of a long life with so few anchors holding you to the ground, but there is something of the exhilaration of the opening of the Pixar film *Up* as we let her go weightless into whatever comes next. The crematorium officiator does a good job making it personal, having bothered to speak beforehand to the staff who knew her best. But Mrs Bird's past is something of a mystery; she's managed to erase it in a way that few modern people can, with our digital trails. She leaves to 'The Lark Ascending', which has to be the most sublime bit of music ever, and the point at which I well up for this unknown lady and, I suppose, for all of us.

They all go into the dark.

Another fragment of Eliot bobs up in my mind. I've made it worse by rereading him before I go to bed, refreshing the pages in my memory where the words I first met years back have begun to fade. Emma wrote that she didn't like poetry but she might've found him a help as she faced her own dark slide. He might have fitted her personality more than Dylan Thomas. Who was at her funeral? From the last entry I read,

I can't quite work out who Biff and Katy are – sometimes it reads like Katy is Emma's child and sometimes she sounds more like Biff's. Michael has never mentioned either so I guess Biff has to be the mum, and a good friend of Emma's from way back. I'm guessing it was an unplanned pregnancy with a father who buggered off, so Emma stepped in to help Biff manage on the 'it takes a village' principle. Biff definitely would've been at the funeral as well as Emma's colleagues and other friends. From the sound of it, Emma didn't have any living relatives, no mention of father or siblings, just an already deceased mother – and Michael, of course.

I look around Mrs Bird's funeral and wonder who would come to mine if I fell under a bus tomorrow. What's nice about this funeral is how I feel embraced by Drew's family and even the care staff. That's a gift from the departed to me, a chance comer at her farewell. I think, from what I've heard, she'd have liked that.

> *Not fare well,*
> *But fare forward, voyagers.*

Drew looks at me and raises a brow. I smile reassuringly, only now aware that I've been muttering. Crumbs, I must look mad to most people. I'm not sure if I'm saying it to the dead people I've been thinking about or to myself. I now have a bigger focus than my own problems. I do want to do something for the girls I feel I've come to know.

Chapter 18

Emma, 14th October 2010

This week has been almost a complete disaster, if it wasn't for a final sweet conclusion this afternoon. Michael is on sabbatical so we took Katy away to Center Parcs in Norfolk to give Biff a break from childcare responsibilities. I'm a bit worried about Biff, to be honest: she's getting completely wrapped up in Katy and her life and is forgetting to make one for herself. I'm hoping this time apart will prompt Biff to get out a little, look for a man, for Christ's sake. She's been living like a hermit. Worry for Biff is no excuse, though. I don't know what possessed me to make the booking. Michael at a Center Parcs? That is akin to inviting a nun to an orgy and as predictably as bad an idea. He just didn't get the hedonistic pleasures to be had and looked faintly horrified by the antics of the families having loud fun in the pool and bowling alley.

'It's all so artificial,' he would bewail every now and then. 'If you want waves, go to a beach.'

I had to bite my tongue not to explain about parental fears

118

of rip tides and pollution. He thinks tidy packages of anything made by someone else are suspect – and that's what Center Parcs is on a grand scale. He turns his nose up at those lists of best books of the year or prizewinners – he has to judge for himself. This man is never going to listen to a playlist anyone else has created on YouTube. Come to think of it, I doubt he'd consume his music that way in any case. It will be a CD, bought from a specialist retailer, played on a high-quality sound system where the digital information hasn't gone through too much compression (I've had the lecture).

To be honest, though, it's my fault. I'm the one dragging him to a place that would be to him yet another of the circles of Dante's hell in a modern version. What did I expect? It's quite funny really.

After two days of existing in a mild state of horror, he relaxed a little when I booked Katy into a nursery this afternoon and we went to the spa. I had a hot stones massage to help with lower-back pain. He went in the sauna and child-free pool. When I came out I found him chatting to an obviously lovely young blonde in a high-cut swimming costume. She reclined next to him like a model posing for a statue of Venus. He was sitting up. I had my suspicions why. I have to admit my stomach is no longer as flat at this end of my twenties as it was at hers, so I couldn't help feel that claw of jealousy. I did the inevitable. Came up behind him and wrapped my arms around his neck.

'Hi, darling, sorry to keep you waiting.'

He introduced me to Jasmina. We gave each other toothy grins: blonde beauty faces off against brunette wife.

'Sorry to pull you away but we'd better hurry along to get the baby,' I dropped in oh-so-casually so she would infer that we are a close-knit family unit, no poaching.

Michael didn't spoil it by telling me to go ahead to collect the sprog while he stayed to chat to his new friend – a point to him. As we walked back to the childcare centre, I couldn't help a little grumble.

'You looked like you'd got very friendly with Jasmina in a short time.'

'What can I say? She started chatting to me first.' He grinned, knowing exactly what was going through my head. 'Nice girl. Graduated with a first in English literature from Oxford but struggling to get a job. I was giving her some pointers.'

'As long as that was all you were giving her.'

He took my hand and swung it in an easy gesture. 'Oh-ho! Is this jealousy I hear?'

'No!'

'So I can't talk to other women now?'

'Not glamorous ones with tits like watermelons, no.'

'I didn't notice. And if I had, I'd say they were more like cantaloupes.'

'Michael!'

'Well, forgive me for being a man, darling. She was rather spectacularly endowed.'

'Probably purchased them from a plastic surgeon.'

'Money well spent then.'

'This is not making me feel better.'

He knew I'd had enough teasing. 'Would telling you that I

found her beauty unsubtle compared to yours? That while I may admire other women in an impersonal way, I have no desire to touch anyone but you? That yours is the only body I want to see beside me in bed? You are my wife – you wear my ring – that says it all.'

I checked my watch. 'You know, we actually have an hour before we have to fetch Katy.'

He picked up the pace. 'Now you're talking. How far to the cabin?'

'I know a shortcut.'

It's not only children who get to play here.

Chapter 19

To: JBridges@expeditedmail.co.uk
From: chaslam@wellmindassociates.org
Subject: Your treatment plan

Dear Jessica,

As you may be aware, Michael has been in touch concerning recent events and his worries that we have not got your treatment plan right. I think it would be beneficial if we brought your next appointment forward so we can discuss this as a matter of urgency. I'd like to hear directly from you how you feel you are doing and whether you are in need of another rest cure at Willowbank. Please phone my PA and she'll book you into the first available slot.

One further word – I know it will be tempting not to face up to acknowledging any deterioration in your mental health but I really do think it would be better to get you back here as soon as possible so that any slippage can be caught before it develops any further.

Best wishes
Charles

August 10

To: chaslam@wellmindassociates.org
From: JBridges@expeditedmail.co.uk
Subject: re: Your treatment plan

Hi Charles,
I'm fine. Consider this email me discharging myself from your care, so you are no longer my therapist. Thanks for your advice to date but, from here on, I'll seek help if I need it from people unconnected with Michael. That's best for all of us.

I hope you enjoyed your daughter's wedding.

Bye.

Jessica

P.S. It's Michael who needs treatment for anger management. Ask him why I say that and see if he denies it.

Chapter 20

Jessica, 11th August

Rita is still working at the office. I watch as she lets herself in at eight to do her quick spit-and-polish of the new business at 5a. No one else is with her so I decide to confront her inside. A firm shove on the door and I'm in. The hallway has a different smell – something slightly floral and musky like potpourri. I knock on the office door.

'Yes? Oh, it's you.' Rita frowns at me. A woman of my own height, she manages somehow to look down at me along the slim line of her nose. Her limp brown hair is kept back by combs. 'Didn't expect to see you back here.'

'Hi, Rita. I was wondering if I could come in for a moment?'

'There's nothing for you here. I bagged up all your old rubbish and threw it out last week – Mr Khan's orders.' She stands there, a formidable guard in her navy jumper and jeans, maroon tabard apron to protect her clothes.

'Yes, I know. I'm not after anything. I just want to ask you a question. This all came as a bit of a shock to me, as I was on holiday.'

She sniffs. 'Yes, I suppose it did. And these new people, they don't complain about me, not like you.'

'And I'm sure it's much easier to keep clean now the land-lord has done a proper job on decorating. You were fighting a losing battle before, I see that now.'

My concession gets me inside. She picks up the kitchen spray from where she left it and carries on scouring the pris-tine sink. It looks like the new tenants do the cleaning each day and barely need her services.

'I hardly recognise the place,' I admit.

'Neither do I. Wouldn't mind a massage. My back plays me up something terrible in the hot weather.'

'Um, Rita, I've been left in something of a pickle.' Did I really just say 'pickle'? 'You see, Mr Wrath hasn't paid me.'

'He didn't pay his rent neither.' She wipes the table holding the twig and stones, dislodging several pebbles. With some-thing close to satisfaction, I imagine all the good vibes running screaming from the room. She straightens, knuckles on hips, cloth dangling. 'Wait a moment, didn't I hear something about Mr Khan wanting to talk to you about the money?'

I see no point in denying it. 'Yes, but I've also found out that Mr Wrath forged my signature. I'm afraid it turns out that Jacob was a complete crook.'

'Was he?' This interests her. 'He was always so pleasant to me.' 'Not like you' is the unspoken conclusion to that sentence.

'But you remember how it was, don't you? I wasn't his equal, not a partner. How could I be responsible for the rent when I worked part-time and he barely paid me?'

She nods at the justice of this, moving on to clean the

windows. I've never seen her be so conscientious before. Maybe my attitude towards her was the problem, not her skills?

'So I really need to find Mr Wrath, but he doesn't seem to exist, at least not under that name. I was wondering if you knew any more than I do?'

She finishes the pane then puts her cleaning gear back in the bucket she carries on her rounds.

'I'm not nosy,' she begins, and my hopes rise.

'No, no one would ever think that.'

'But I did think him an odd sort of person, always keeping his desk clear and leaving you doing most of the work. A queer duck, I told Mr Tudor – that's Mr Khan's man who manages things round here. I had a little look once in Mr Wrath's bag – you remember the satchel thing he carried around with him?'

'Yes.'

'He left it sitting on the desk once when he went to the...' she jerks her head towards the toilet. 'I took a quick peek.'

'And?'

'It struck me as peculiar that he was carrying someone else's post – a bank statement – same bank as me – but it was sealed.'

'Whose post?'

'Mr J. M. West.'

'I don't suppose you got the address as well?'

'I wasn't snooping.'

'I never said you were.' I'm enjoying this conversation; I hadn't expected it from Rita, of all people, but it's like we're dance partners, both knowing exactly what the other means but able to do the moves around each other so nothing looks ugly.

'It was John Ruskin Street near Kennington Common – I remember it because my sister lives round there; we walk down that road to go to the park with her kids. Not that I've seen him there, though.'

'Did you get the number?'

She shrugs. '16 or 36 – something with a six in it.'

'Thanks, Rita. And I'm glad to see you've still got your job.'

'Mr Tudor, he's not a bad man. I'll tell him I saw you.'

'I'd rather you didn't.'

'I know.' She smiles, scoring a final victory for her in our three-month tussle.

Back on the street, I contemplate my choices. Drew would say to wait for him but he's busy all day and I don't want to put this off. I decide to head directly over to John Ruskin Street and at least find out the right number.

After consulting an *A to Z* in a newsagent's – easier than trying to squint at my phone screen – I catch a bus to the Oval cricket ground. As I watch the familiar streets of the West End pass, my mobile rings. My mum.

'Hi, sweetie. How are you?'

'Oh, er, good, I think.'

'Only "I think"?'

'I broke up with Michael.'

There's a pause. 'I can't say I'm surprised. He didn't make you happy, did he?'

Mum might be dandelion fragile but she also has the knack for nailing a situation. 'You're right. He wasn't good for me.'

'So where are you living now?'

'Drew's?'

'That nice young man from Feltham?' Drew had predictably charmed my mother when he met her on one of her rare forays to London.

'Yes.'

'You stick with him, dear, until you're on your own two feet. How's the job going? Can I meet Mr Wrath when I'm next in town? I can call in when I go to the matinee, say hello and then take you to lunch.'

'You're coming up to town?'

'Silly, have you forgotten? My ladies' group has tickets for *The Bodyguard*.'

'When?'

'Next week.'

'Mum, look, things are a bit complicated – on the job front.' I can hear the stress in her voice. 'But you said you were enjoying it – that it was your path back.'

'I know, but I'm in a slippery patch right now. My boss has money troubles. He's had to let me go.'

'Oh, darling, what are you going to live on? First no Michael, and now no job.' I can almost hear the gears in her mind shifting. 'You'll have to come and live with me. Miriam won't mind – really, she won't, not after I explain to her.'

Miriam would hit the roof: a grown-up half-sister sponging off her! Not while I have any respect for myself left. 'I'm fine, really, Mum. I'll get something else.'

'Are you sure?' Mum's panic is subsiding.

'Yes. Drew's been great.' She always responds better when

a man's name is mentioned – she comes from that generation. Even though her second husband was a complete shit, she still has faith. 'He's a really kind person and he's not going to throw me out.' Not like Michael did. 'Let's do that lunch next week.'

'Wednesday, at noon. My treat.'

It really is going to have to be, as I am more or less penniless. 'Thanks. I'll meet you near the theatre – we'll go somewhere close.'

'Bye, darling. Love you.'

'Love you too. Take care.'

The call has distracted me and I almost miss my stop. I'm saved by an elderly lady taking her time with her shopping trolley giving me a chance to reach the doors. I help her lift it down to the pavement, then strike out in the direction of John Ruskin Street. Funny man, Ruskin, a wonderful artist and writer but now mostly remembered for being squeamish about his wife's pubic hair. The relationship was never consummated and she went off to be someone else's artist's model. Millais, if I remember. Ruskin was definitely a man born in the wrong century. It's a mistake, though, to imagine that he'd be happier now or that he was a repressed homosexual. I just think he didn't like the physical side of human life. All kinds of sex are messy, so maybe he really just wanted to be celibate, and not get involved in all those body fluids? He'd have been better off being born at a time when being a monk was a career option.

I'll have to work out soon what my own future looks like as I'm not a Ruskin. I need someone but sex also has the potential to destroy a relationship. It can't be the only tie because that soon works loose. If I really love Drew…

This isn't the moment. I wander the suburban street looking for clues at the houses 'with a six in it'. It's a nice street with a mixture of flats and Victorian semis and a pleasing number of trees shading the parked cars, but it's also very long. I know from my experience of living in London that it is a rare area where people know their neighbours by sight, let alone by name. I could try the electoral roll but my instinct here is that Jacob would've kept his name off the public one, if he bothered to register at all. Nothing else for it: I knock on the door of 16.

By the time I reach 46, I'm losing hope. I've only had one door answered. Most of the houses are multiple occupancy so I'm leaving behind plenty of possibles. No reply. I try 48 and after a wait an elderly man using a walker answers. He's bent over by arthritis so has to look up at me through bushy eyebrows to meet my gaze.

'Oh, I thought you were meals on wheels.' He gives me a questioning look but has been raised not to slam the door in the face of a lady.

'Sorry, no, sir, but that does sound a lovely concept. I wish I were. I'm looking for someone who lives in this street but, stupidly, I've forgotten the number.' I try my best disarming smile.

'Who's that, dear?'

'A Mr West. He might live next door at number 46.'

'Oh no, that's a Spanish family. Nice people.'

'Right. Well, thanks for helping me cross them off my list.' I start to go.

'There's a Mr West at 49. Been there about a year. Not very friendly but we say hello when we meet.'

'Dark hair, slightly receding? About thirty-five?'

'That's him.'

46 was in fact 49. Rita had probably misread it when she glanced at the address upside down. 'Thank you. I don't suppose you've seen him today?'

'No, dear. Not seen him for a few days, actually. Not that I watch the street all the time, but I do often sit in my window to catch the light, you know?'

'Yes, I'd do the same.'

'What day is it now? I think I saw him Monday.' He chuckles. 'But don't put much store by me. All the days merge into one now.'

'You've been so helpful. Thank you.'

A car draws up behind me.

'Ah, there's lunch.'

'I'd better get out of your way then. Thank you.'

The lady delivering the meal gives me a hard look as she passes me on the path.

'It's perfectly all right, Mrs Bishop, she was just asking about a neighbour across the way,' calls the elderly man.

I turn out of the gate and cross the road to 49. The front garden has been stripped of any living thing, leaving maintenance at zero. Little white stones like they use in graveyards crunch underfoot. The curtains are still closed. What exactly am I going to say to him? I take a deep breath and ring on the bell. No response. I press again, and make sure I can hear it sounding inside the house. I then rap on the frosted-glass panel.

'Jacob? Jacob?' Nothing. 'Mr West? It's Jessica Bridges.' I remember that I've been here before but that was Monday outside an empty office. Has he also fled from his home? I crouch down and push open the letterbox to peer inside. A grill covers the slot so the letters don't drop to the floor but, when I move a pizza delivery brochure aside, I can see through the mesh. It takes a little while for my eyes to adjust.

There's someone lying at the bottom of the stairs.

I shove at the door but it's firmly locked. The meals lady has stopped by her car to watch me.

'There's been an accident! Call an ambulance!' I shout. Using a half brick that had been weighing down the lid of the food bin, I smash the panel and reach in to undo locks. The woman is hurrying over, already talking to the emergency services.

'Yes, number 49. Not sure yet. Oh, I think he's fallen down the stairs.'

I crouch beside Jacob Wrath – West – whoever he is. He lies face down; blood from a gash on his head has trickled down his neck but is dry now. I touch his wrist, hoping for a pulse, but he's cold. 'I… I think he's dead.'

Chapter 21

It doesn't take long for the ambulance to arrive. The police draw up at almost the same moment. I can hear them talking as I sit in Jacob's front room with a metallic blanket wrapped around my shoulders, 'to help with the shock', says the kindly paramedic when he realises his services aren't needed elsewhere. The meals lady, as the one who called 999, is giving her version of what we saw first. She's in a hurry, she explains, as she has elderly clients waiting. I take a couple of my pills to help clear my thoughts before they interview me. I'm feeling shaky and sick and the medicated hit shoves me past that.

What a horrible, terrible coincidence. I've been blaming Jacob for leaving me in the lurch when maybe it has all just been because he was dead?

But the old man across the road saw him on Monday, or so he thought. That meant Jacob had not taken steps to prevent me turning up to an empty office.

Jacob's motives and thoughts remain a mystery.

I gaze around the room, trying to get a sense of my former boss. He hasn't bothered to do much by way of personalising, but there is one A4-sized photo on the side table. I pick it up to take a closer look. Jacob is with a woman and baby in a forest clearing. It's a lovely shot of the three of them on a picnic blanket. The woman's face is slightly turned away; she's looking down at her child.

But I know that face even in half profile like this. It's Michael's Emma – that, or she has an identical twin. I guess that it was taken around the time of the photo that Michael used to have in his bedside table.

Oh my God, did Jacob know Emma? My mind leapfrogs a few theories to settle on what is possibly the most obvious: were they having an affair? Is this the link that I've been missing?

Stop jumping to conclusions, Jessica. Could she be a relative? I stare at the photo, willing it to spill its secrets. No, I really don't think so. The pose looks loving – they seem to be a family. The little girl – could that be Katy, the two-year-old from Emma's diary?

I notice now that Jacob has left his messenger bag beside the sofa, tucked in by the wall. Checking the police are still busy outside, I reach down and gather it onto my lap. I flip it open. A laptop, paperwork, black moleskin diary and a framed photo are inside. I can't examine the picture properly now but I am sure it is the same as the photograph that went missing from home.

So Jacob was the one who broke in? And did that to the bed? But why?

Think quickly, Jessica: what to do? I'm only carrying a light handbag. Would anyone notice if I took this bag and pretended it is mine? Maybe not. Probably not. And if someone does, I can say it was what I'd called round to collect as I'm pretty sure it's the office laptop – Jacob's, not mine, but it's relevant to the missing persons cases. Right, finders keepers.

Oh God, is this me being my usual reckless, impulsive self, or is this a stroke of sleuthing genius?

I cuddle the bag on my lap and decide to let fate dictate if I walk out with it. If the policemen query it, I'll hand it over immediately. If not, then it's mine to investigate.

'So, Miss, can I have your name?' asks the sergeant, entering the room. He's wearing a suit rather than uniform and has the polished crown of the prematurely bald. He carries it off well, having an attractive dark-brown tone to his skin.

'Jessica Bridges.'

'I'm Detective Sergeant Lloyd, CID. And your connection to the deceased?'

'I used to work for him.'

'Recently?'

'Yes, I mean I thought I still did until I got back from holiday on Monday and discovered he'd closed the office.'

'And you waited until Thursday to track him down?'

'I wasn't sure where he lived.'

'You didn't know?'

'He was a very private man. In fact he told me his name was Jacob Wrath. It wasn't until today that I learned his real name from the office cleaner.'

'I see.' The policeman looks at me speculatively. 'What was it that you did for him?'

'He ran a small investigative agency looking into missing persons cases. I was his part-time researcher.'

'And what does that entail?'

'Profiling runaways and trying to work out where they might end up.'

The policeman makes a note.

'So what happened to him? Did he fall down the stairs?'

'That's the problem, Miss; no, we don't think he did.'

'What?'

'The early indications are, he took or was administered a sedative, then collapsed at the bottom of the stairs. He could have hit his head then or been struck – the medical examiner will verify.'

'Maybe he was trying to get help – trying to get to the door?' My voice is a desperate squeak. God, I sound guilty even though I've done nothing.

'Maybe. Do you know if he was on any medication?'

I'm still shaken by the 'took or was administered'. Are they implying it could be murder? I can hardly waltz off with Jacob's bag if that's the situation. But now my prints are all over it. Oh God, this is getting terribly muddled.

'Miss?'

'Er, medication? No, not that I've noticed in the office. I've not been to his home before.'

'Yes, so you said. Have you been anywhere else in the house other than the hall and this room?'

Here was a question with a straightforward answer. 'No.'

Another man enters the room and the police officer springs to attention. The newcomer is below average height and has an everyman vibe to him. I wonder if that makes him more formidable? You are more likely to make mistakes in front of someone who appears harmless.

'Detective Inspector Randall,' says the sergeant, 'this is Miss Jessica Bridges, a work colleague of the deceased. She found the body and is responsible for the broken window in the front door. The property was secure until that point, no sign of any earlier break-in.'

'Thank you, Sergeant Lloyd. May I have a word?'

The two go outside to confer. Irrationally, I'm beginning to feel guilty about more than just hugging the bag. Police are arriving in greater numbers and tape is appearing outside, fluttering like grim bunting.

Inspector Randall re-enters to take over the questioning, Lloyd now hovering by the door to intercept messages. 'I'm from Lewisham CID, Miss Bridges. We are called in to investigate any death where there is the possibility that a crime has been committed.'

'Who are all these people?' I ask. I've seen enough TV dramas but somehow this calm invasion doesn't fit the pattern. The only sign that anything is wrong is the flashing blue lights and the traffic jam of emergency vehicles. There are no sirens and nobody seems in a hurry.

'I've called in the Homicide Assessment Team, as there are enough questions as to how Mr West met his end to raise a red flag. First we have to eliminate other possibilities. Do you know any reason why Mr West might end his life by his own hand?'

I find his calm tone reassuring. I get the sense that nothing would surprise Randall. 'No, other than his money troubles. But I really didn't know him well. I know next to nothing about his personal life. I think he might've come from Swindon but that's about it.'

'Do you know anyone who has a reason to harm Mr West?'

'He owes our old landlord rent – that's the money trouble I mentioned. I found out that he even forged my signature on the lease, so I think his affairs must be in dire straits.'

'So you were angry with him?'

Perhaps I shouldn't have said that, but it would come out once they phoned Khan. 'Honestly? I don't know what I was. Disappointed and confused, maybe? I came round today to ask him why he put my name on the lease and if he could straighten it out for me, as I've been left in an awkward situation. I didn't kill him, though, if that's what you're asking. I haven't seen him for almost two weeks. I was on holiday until Sunday night and then he didn't come to work on Monday, as I explained.'

'Can anyone confirm where you were last week?'

'Yes, my boyfriend, um, ex-boyfriend. We just split up. What a great holiday that was.' I grimace. 'Sorry, too much information. My passport details should be at Immigration at Heathrow. I went through that automatic gate check where it scans your passport and your face. I'm guessing that goes to a database somewhere, doesn't it?'

The policeman stands up. 'Thank you, Miss Bridges. Here's my card so you know who you talked to this morning. I'll just take down your contact details and then you can go. We've got to process the scene. Once we've got a better picture of what happened here, we'll be back in touch. I'd be grateful if you would make yourself available for further questioning.'

'Of course.'

'Will it be all right with you if we contact your ex-boyfriend to confirm your movements last week?'

I choke back a laugh. 'Fine. But you should know we've just gone through a stormy break-up and he's not happy with me at the moment. You might like to mention that Mr West really exists – existed – as Michael didn't believe in him.'

The policeman looks at me curiously.

'We have a difficult relationship – that's why we split.' I give him Michael's details.

The inspector taps his notepad. 'Dr Michael Harrison? Is that the same man who's the expert in deviant behaviour?'

'The one and only.'

'I've heard him talk at Hendon Police College.'

'Good for you.' It's depressing to find his fan club everywhere I go. Michael loves scattering his pearls of wisdom in front of the senior officers and boasts about his regular date at Hendon at dinner parties.

'He's very impressive.'

'Yes, he is; just hell to live with.'

I escape with the bag still in my clutches. This is a bad idea, isn't it, removing evidence? I can't seem to help myself. I've left the top of the waterslide and am letting impulse carry me along. After whisking myself north across the Thames, away from police cars and incident tape, I splash down in the National Portrait Gallery café. It's the most harmless, innocent place I can think of round here. I set up at a table with an overpriced pot of tea and go through the contents of the bag. There's not much in it: the laptop, diary and photo, of course, some bills and receipts, and at the bottom a set of keys. They look familiar – a Yale and a deadlock. I can't be certain without my own set but I think they are identical to the ones I had for Michael's house. No wonder there was no sign of a break-in: Jacob had copies of my keys.

I don't understand what's going on. Jacob destroyed Michael's side of the room but carefully removed the photo, glass intact. Emma is the only one in it, taken at her graduation. It has to have meant something to Jacob.

I open the laptop and find it left on standby. The prompt for the password comes up. Jacob was a careful man; he's not likely to have used an easily guessed word. I try some obvious ones but know it's hopeless.

Think, Jessica, think.

My phone pings with a message from the policeman asking for a call back as soon as convenient. Guiltily I close the computer – not that he can see what I'm doing but it just feels better that way. 'Hello? Inspector Randall?'

'Thanks for getting back to me so quickly, Miss Bridges. We've been conducting a search of the house and found a message addressed to you.'

'What? You mean a suicide note?'

'Not exactly. It doesn't read that way. It's more a note to tell you something left among a pile of things on the kitchen table. It could be old, of course, from before your holiday.'

'What does it say?'

'Not much. Just says "Ask Bridges if she knows a Kaitlin

Morris", then a question mark. That's Kaitlin spelt with a K. Does that mean anything to you?'

I rub the bridge of my nose. 'Nothing obvious. We worked together on a number of missing persons cases but that's not one of them. It might be a new one he had in mind.'

'OK, I'll run the name and see what comes up. Thanks. I'll be in touch.' He ends the call and I lift the lid of the computer. Why not? I type in 'kaitlinmorris'. Then 'KaitlinMorris'. Finally, just 'kaitlin'.

Oh my God, it works! The desktop loads and I find myself inside Jacob's secrets. Is this the point where I call Inspector Randall back and explain that I have the office laptop and Emma's diary? I can fudge exactly how they came into my hands.

But then I'd never find out the connection between Jacob and Michael's dead wife, Emma. I know, I know, I should stop, but I can't. Fortunately for my curiosity, no saner people are on hand to prevent me.

Tea is forgotten as I begin to dig.

Chapter 22

Emma, 11th November 2009

I can't stand this situation any longer. I've decided to leave him. He's getting suspicious, asking where I go with Katy on my trips up to town. I can hardly tell him I'm seeing Biff as he doesn't even know that I know her so well, though we've seen each other from time to time across group meetings and exchanged a few rolls of the eyes as the others get more carried away than normal. It would be good timing because Biff has broken off her relationship with Milo, saying that was getting too intense. I know how she feels. He acts as though we're his, all part of some great crusade to achieve the perfect life-style. It's like he's Noah and we're Noah's wife and daughter shut up in the ark with him. God, if I ever see another wood burner again it will be too soon. I'm longing for a fillet steak, nice clothes, killer heels on expensive shoes, pavements instead of fricking bark chippings, disposable nappies and central heating, not necessarily in that order. This little cottage in the woods is no rural idyll but neither is it the centre of the revolution, as he would like me to believe.

'We change the world one step at a time,' he told me last week when I called him on it.

Yeah, but it's not him scraping baby poo off cloth nappies and washing them in the tub by the back door. I feel like I've travelled back in time to the Victorian era. When he gets home from his work for the Forestry Commission, he makes a great show of saying, 'Hey, Ali, let me do that. You can make a start on dinner.' He takes the basket and hangs the washed cloths around the fireguard as if that's the hard part. No, you idiot, that's the easy bit. You missed all the backbreaking, disgusting work while you were out tree-hugging. And does he care that the nappies give Katy a rash and I can never get them dry quick enough at this time of year? No, Mr Save-the-world-but-not-his-own-family is unmoved by any of that.

I've done all I can here and, more to the point, we're never going to see eye to eye on Katy's upbringing. He wants all this back-to-nature stuff with which I've rapidly fallen out of love since Katy: no inoculations, no records, no health visitors, no contamination with the modern world. Forget that. Back to nature meant half of under-fives dying of what are now preventable diseases. My daughter is getting the best that the NHS can offer. I'm not playing Russian roulette with measles and mumps. Plus inoculation only works if a high enough proportion of the population participates; it's a parent's social duty to see their children get their vaccinations. Put that in your pipe and smoke it, mate. It'll do you a great deal more good than the weed you grow.

OK, decision made. I'm out of here. I don't need much. I left most of my stuff in London in the flat. Fortunately, he has no idea about that. I'll just grab Katy's things and then I'll be on the train to civilisation. She's too young to miss him and he has never taken that much interest in her, as he is on fire for the world, not one little citizen of the planet. He'll probably be relieved to see the back of us once he gets used to the idea. We will significantly reduce his carbon footprint by leaving. I'll get a decent childminder and report back to the office. There's a training conference in a few weeks' time that my line manager wants me to attend, so that can be my new start. I'll put in for a post near home, rather than out in the field. Sanity will be restored to my life.

Chapter 23

To: chaslam@wellmindassociates.org
From: dr.michael.harrison@expeditedmail.co.uk
Subject: Need to talk

Dear Charles,

I'm sorry to bombard you with emails this week. I have to admit to feeling particularly low since my altercation with Jessica, and particularly vulnerable, if I'm allowed to admit to such a thing. I was wondering if you could find time this week to meet up for a drink? This would be friend to friend and not a professional call – not couples' therapy – I wouldn't want to drag our friendship through that thorny hedge. I just want to talk to someone who can get my point of view. From the damage she did, Jessica clearly didn't understand me and never has. She was always very breezy when mentioning Emma, saying she was fine to discuss her with me. She did not realise that the problem wasn't her feelings but mine. I can't talk about something so vital to me. It's like amputating

145

my own arm, something you do only in survival situations like that mountaineer. In fact, you'll recognise that this email is maybe the first time I've really mentioned it to you. I've tried to keep it all to myself, but now the pain of it all is just spilling out.

Sorry. I've got to maintain my sanity. I can't let myself break – that would embarrass both of us. It helps me very much, though, that you remember Emma. So few people in my life now do. You remember what I was like after I met her at that conference in my college on youth psychology? I couldn't stop talking about her, how she owned any room she walked into, how her wit enchanted me. Forgive the romantic widower and his nostalgia but I remember thinking at the time that the turn of her cheek, the style of her hair had a kind of pure beauty you find only in Renaissance portraits – a hint of something eternal. That's why I loved that photo of her taken at her graduation years before I knew her: it captured all that in one quick click of the camera. I didn't have a digital copy so it's gone for good, I suspect.

As for what came next, line up the clichés because they describe exactly what I felt in her presence: struck dumb, love at first sight, instant connection, soul mate, a fool for love. I've struggled to find a less hackneyed phrase, something that plays in your context, and all I can come up with is how a dose of amphetamines makes you feel – focused, intent, hooked – like Dorothy entering Oz, going from greyscale to colour. Remember how we ate them like sweets when we were cramming for our finals back in the '90s? Jesus, we were cavalier about our health in those days. Well, drugs were long in my rear-view mirror when I met Emma and she still gave me that same buzz. I knew within twenty-four hours that I wanted to marry her – so traditional of me but I told myself it would be the only way of stopping her going on to someone else – or back to that nutcase she had just dumped in the woods. I couldn't bear the thought of that. I lived in fear that someone else would also notice how amazing she was and give her a better offer than I could manage as a rather old-for-her university don, so within a month I'd hurried her off to Las Vegas and we were married in a chapel there – not by an Elvis imper-sonator, I hasten to add, but by a decent officiator during a tasteful wedding vacation at Caesar's Palace, two stran-gers as witnesses. You would've hated it but it suited us.

Am I looking back at Emma through rose-coloured spectacles? Probably. Undoubtedly. Over the past five years, when Jessica has been especially difficult, I've reminded myself that I'm attracted to that kind of woman: complex, clever, emotionally subtle. Emma and I had less than two years together so who's to say I wouldn't have found the strains emerging in our relation-ship too – I must be ruthlessly honest with myself. But fate would have it that I only had her for those glorious first year followed by the heart-wrenching final months. She's destined to live on, preserved in my memory as a kind of perfection. I am not completely insensitive: I can understand how Jessica found my attitude difficult to live with and that might've sparked her jealous rage. But I can't forgive her for turning on the few mementoes I had of my marriage. It's unspeakably low of her.

Emma left me an emotional legacy that I couldn't cope with at the time. Grief made me a complete mess and I'm forever grateful for your clear-sighted advice that I had to heal before I could do anything else. Today I'm realising that I never really mended because, when I emerged from mourning, I took on Jessica and look where that led.

Regards
Michael

August 11

To: dr.michael.harrison@expeditedmail.co.uk
From: chaslam@wellmindassociates.org
Subject: Re: Need to talk

Dear Michael,
Thank you for your email – that seems a trite opening but I actually mean it when I write that this time. Despite the turmoil of the last few days, I'm relieved to see that your break-up with Jessica has been the catalyst to you opening up to talk about Emma. I've long worried that you've suppressed your loss and that it was making itself felt in other ways. If I'm allowed a cliché of my own, better out than in. I know you weren't thinking of our meeting as a therapy session – God forbid: with whom am I able to talk PGA golf if not you? – but I would

urge that you seek out a grief counsellor. I can give you some names if this feels right for you. I'll say this much now, though: you aren't to feel guilty for not being able to cope at the time of Emma's death. I've never seen a man more gutted by someone's passing. You weren't able to take on anything more than the responsibility of getting yourself back in a fit state to function, and in many ways that is an ongoing situation. You couldn't carry the burden Emma left you and you can't carry Jessica's when you are still weighed down by your own.

I'm afraid I have some bad news on the Jessica front. She's dismissed me as her therapist. My fear is that she won't seek out another qualified psychiatrist and will end up just going to her GP to keep her prescription running. I doubt he will know how to treat someone with Jessica's condition and he'll just keep the pills ticking over. That would be a bad move. I tell you now in confidence that I was intending to develop the cognitive behavioural therapy part of her treatment to modify her impulsive tendencies and ease back on the pills as there were signs she was using them erratically. They do have potential side effects, including hallucinations and paranoia in some patients, so it may be that some of her behaviour is not a sign of further mental disorder but a reaction to her medication. It may have reached an extreme point if she's taking her feelings out on things she associates with you, like the bed and belongings. In rare cases, the patients have periods of selective amnesia. I was going to explore that with her but now I can't. If you can negotiate a peace with her, that might help me make these points without it appearing as me taking your part in your difficulties.

And yes, of course I can make time for you this week. Friday at my club?

Charles

Chapter 24

Jessica

The picture of Jacob, Emma and the child smiles out at me from Jacob's desktop. It is the same as the photo in his house, the one where Emma is turning away as if she wants to avoid the lens. How had I never seen this at the office? Jacob was very familiar with the cat-who-looks-like-Einstein that I had as my wallpaper. Sitting with my tea cooling in the cup, I think back and remember those times sharing the same small office space. Jacob never left his computer open and always had it facing away from me. He was like Emma in that, trying to avoid the direct gaze. He probably got a thrill from the risk.

'What were you up to, Jacob?' I whisper.

It takes me a while to work out where he kept his work files. First, I have to open and dismiss a whole lot of documents in which he seems obsessed with corrupt global business, land grabbers and polluters. I'm interested in something much more local. I then have the idea – something I really should've thought of first – to see what he was working on most recently. Rejigging the files to 'date modified', a folder comes to the top called 'Harrison'. I'm guessing this is nothing to do with the Beatle.

Oh my God, oh my God, oh my God, I cannot believe what I'm reading! I find that he has detailed, point by point, intersections between Michael's life and the girls he asked me to investigate. Can this be real?

I read it through several times but the times and dates do seem to stack up.

With my pulse racing, I look further into the files. Oh Christ, he mentions me too, saying he wondered if I'd make the connection but notes that I didn't, or at least, 'not visibly'.

Of course, I didn't, because there is no connection to make, is there?

Is there?

I'm being dragged into his crazy fantasy. Stop it, Jessica. You started this to find out more about his relationship with Emma, not to be dragged into The Insane World of Jacob.

But there's nothing about Emma in there. Reading on, I discover that Jacob really has gone overboard. He thinks Michael is some kind of serial-killer-cum-sex-offender and the missing girls are in a shallow grave in a forest somewhere. Why would he think that?

I look up to find life carrying on around me, plates served, drinks poured. Wonderful, sane, ordinary life. I can't believe this. This is mental! I wish I could say it's like some psycho's diary, only it's not rambling and incoherent, it's ruthlessly logical.

Oh God, there's more on me in here too, in a sub folder. I click on that.

My jaw drops. Here is my pathetic application for the job, detailing all my personal information, no surprise there. But Jacob has also written what he calls 'an assessment' of me. In this, he admits that he knew about Eastfields and was only employing me to watch what I did. He was coming round to thinking I was complicit in Michael's sexual perversions, either because I 'wilfully turned a blind eye or because I actively aided and abetted'. Eastfields fitted with the second of these two theories. He doesn't spell out the accusations against me but from his insinuations he knows things I thought only I and a select few were party to.

I feel sick and exposed. Ashamed.

Shaking, I try and sort out my confused thoughts. What have I learned? Jacob seems to have had some grand idea about Michael and me, seeing us as embodiments of evil. Me, he thinks morally evil, failing in my duty to protect the weak – meaning the girls who fall into Michael's path; but it's Michael for whom he saves his strongest words. In his last entry, on the very day he was murdered, Jacob writes that Michael, like so many wrongdoers, has 'an egotistical sense that he is justified or allowed to commit heinous acts. He doesn't scrutinise; he indulges himself in a false sense of entitlement.' In sum, Michael's arrogance means he takes what he wants without any consideration of the harm he does, and I've been shutting my eyes to it.

How could Jacob have thought that about me? He knew me better than that, didn't he? So it must be total rubbish about Michael, right? Jacob has to be insane.

But now he's dead. The police haven't ruled out murder.

I'm so confused. I look again at his long final entry. Jacob clearly expects his life to be in danger if Michael hears of his investigation. Did I do that? Did I unwittingly tip Michael off that a private detective was coming his way?

I rerun in my mind my argument with Michael in Minorca. We'd been sitting over breakfast on the terrace, the 'hello, sailor' Mediterranean mocking us that we weren't having as good a time as the brochure promised. Michael's friend, a TV producer, owns a villa that is predictably fabulous – terracotta-tiled floors, biscuit-coloured walls, hand-carved furniture, a frozen explosion of bougainvillaea from pots, streams of purple stars over arbours, and an eternity pool that even I enjoyed swimming in. Michael had been looking particularly hand-some in his sun-tanned god-man way in navy shorts and white shirt. If only it had been the beginning of our relation-ship and not the end, we could've put that pool to good use. I remember thinking that he would've made the advertising photo but I, with my sunburnt shoulders and not-beach-ready body, would've been airbrushed out. How unsuitable we have devolved to look as a pair. He'd turned away from me when I'd angled for sex that morning, which made me feel about as desirable as takeaway leftovers at the back of the fridge.

Never reheat rice, I remember my mum saying. Never try to reheat a relationship, I might now add. It only ends with a horrible feeling in the pit of your could-lose-a-few-inches stomach.

'It would be nice if for once you took me out for dinner,' grumbled Michael, still fretting about the expensive seafood meal we'd consumed in Mahon the night before.

'Did you know that Mahon is the origin of mayonnaise?' I quipped, hoping to change the subject away from my economic failure.

'Can't you stay on topic for two minutes, Jessica? Are you remembering to take those pills Charles gave you?'

'Mother's little helper.'

'What?'

'Rolling Stones, Michael. Their song on housewife addiction. It's really quite famous and even before your time.' I wafted my heated cheeks with the floppy sunhat that hadn't done well in the suitcase.

'You're not a housewife. I don't know what you are, but I know you're not that. Our house is in a continual state of mess. I spend all my time tidying up after you.' He stabbed at his phone, checking emails even though we were on holiday and we'd both pledged to dump the electronics.

'You do not.'

'Mud on the stairs? Who was that? I always take my shoes off in the porch.'

I rubbed my temples, feeling the headache slink out of hiding and steal the best seat in my brain like an early-bird sunbather covering a poolside lounger with his towel. 'OK, OK, I admit it, m'lord, yes I did forget to take my shoes off last week. I'd forgotten my handbag and I was late for work.'

'Late for work? Jesus, Jessica, why don't you just drop the charade! You sit in a café and make yourself look busy. You no more have a proper job than I'm a Buddhist monk.'

'Then prepare to say Om. It's a part-time profiling job, as you well know, and I'm very lucky to have it.'

'Stop this. Just admit that you invented it.'

'How can I have invented it? I have a salary.'

'Really? How much?'

My wage was just above the minimum level and Michael scoffed at even that.

'I just don't believe anyone would take you on, not after what you did.'

Would he never let that go? Hadn't I paid enough already, both career-wise and mentally? 'Jacob has. He didn't even ask about that.'

'Jacob Wrath is a chimera.'

'He is not.'

'Then explain why I've never met him, why no one has ever heard of him when I ask around, why he never answers the so-called office phone when I ring.'

'He's... he's busy.'

'No, he's a phantom of your overheated imagination. Looking for runaways? That's not even a very convincing invention, Jessica. You can do better than that!'

'Michael, if you'd just come with me to work one day, right into the office, I'll prove he exists. And the work – it's real.'

'Oh yes?'

'Look, I developed the website.'

'Anyone can make one of those.'

'And he's got me investigating these four cases of missing girls.' I reeled off the names, not noticing then that Michael went quiet. 'I think I might even have made a breakthrough on one of them.'

He stood up, throwing his napkin on the breakfast table,

a gauntlet challenge. 'You are fucking kidding me. You think you're some kind of FBI profiler now?'

'Don't rubbish my work just because you don't understand it!' I stood up, a shade too late to look strong and sure of myself.

'Of course I understand it. I'm the expert in this area.' Out came the accusatory finger, pointing at me. 'You wouldn't have a clue how to do it. I've had enough. You pack in this whole pretence or we're through.'

'You can't stand anyone else sharing your limelight, can you?' I folded my arms.

'Limelight? Jessica, don't kid yourself. You are in the dark and getting more and more lost.'

'I'm not, you egotistical ape! I'm getting myself together but you just want to push me back down.'

'I've not pushed you anywhere. It's you, trying to cling to my coattails the whole time, living off me, not supporting me in my career but asking me to baby you in yours.'

'I'm not asking to be babied. I occasionally ask for help but that's normal. That's what couples who love each other do.'

He skated over the mention of the 'L' word. 'And where did your vocation in teaching lead? Disaster. You are frankly a liability to any employer – a complete fucking waste of space!'

There were so many untruths in that statement, I didn't know how to begin a rebuttal. 'I suppose you're going to say it's all about me?'

'Isn't it? You're totally obsessed with yourself and can't see the damage you do to others.'

'Right back at you, mate.'

'Shut the fuck up, Jessica!' He strode away and we didn't speak again unless there were others present.

I agonised about his accusations, of course, for the rest of the week, wondering if I had been unreasonable in my demands on him, if I was a liability. I knew already I was hell to live with, that I had gone very wrong at Eastfields, but I thought Michael had realised what he was taking on when we moved in together. He was a psychologist, for God's sake! He should've recognised I was always going to be prone to impulsive mistakes. I didn't get why he was so sure I was inventing my job.

Now, sitting in the National Portrait Gallery café, I have to ask myself if his anger was a smokescreen. What if it hadn't been about me? What if he had been rattled that someone was on to him? Had he blown up at me as a handy target and then spent those brooding last few days planning how to silence Jacob? And what about his alibi? Did I know for a fact that he had gone to Berlin? He'd been very eager to get away on our return, but from other trips I know that he hates staying in airport hotels. Perhaps he hadn't. Perhaps he'd used the time to hunt down and kill Jacob. I'd found my ex-employer after a morning of asking the right questions. Michael was perfectly capable of doing the same.

Horrible pieces of this new puzzle keep slipping into place. Oh my God, had he even planted the evidence on Jacob and trashed the room himself? Maybe Jacob had never had a chance to break in? What time exactly had Jacob died?

My phone jigs again. The waitress has been hovering for a

while now to clear my cup but the beauty of a pot of tea is that you can always squeeze out just a dribble more as a server approaches, forcing them to swerve off in another direction.

'Hello?'

'Miss Bridges, it's Detective Inspector Randall again. I apologise for disturbing you a second time.'

My heart races. Has someone mentioned that I walked out with a bag that I did not have on arrival? 'That's fine. Anything to help.'

'We're concerned that Mr West might have a dependant who should be informed of his death. There are pictures of a child around the house, also an unidentified woman, and it appears the Kaitlin I mentioned to you is the girl's name, so I'm thinking now that it wasn't a case he was going to raise with you.'

'I see.'

'There are no photographs of her after the age of about a year or eighteen months, but his kitchen calendar claims she recently had an eighth birthday. Can you cast any light on this for us?'

I don't know a Kaitlin but I would find out more if I read further in these files. Kaitlin – Katy? It could be. The explosive entry in Emma's diary when she decides to leave Jacob suggests this is the case. That means Kaitlin was likely to be that child in the photo right here on the computer desktop. I decide playing ignorant is the best holding strategy while I sort through this jumble of facts and speculations. 'I'm sorry, Inspector, but I can't help you there. Jacob never talked about his family at work. He was an extremely private man, as I've already mentioned.'

'So why did he write down that message – the one asking if he should talk to you about her?'

'Maybe he thought he could trust me? I've been working for him for three months now. Perhaps there's some tragedy or a failed relationship in the past that makes, made it painful for him to talk about her? Sorry, I'm just guessing here.'

'That's fine – in fact, it's helpful. One more thing.'

Uh-oh.

'We found two glasses of Scotch on the kitchen table, one with a generous serving still in it, the other drained. There's also a bottle of single malt. Are you sure you didn't go into the kitchen at any point?'

'Yes, and I don't drink Scotch.'

'It would be very helpful, then, if you would come to Lewisham police station and be fingerprinted for elimination purposes.' I sense he's waiting for me to hesitate.

'No problem. When?'

'As soon as possible. I'd like to understand what happened in Mr West's house and at the moment it's not telling a consistent story. Can you come by tomorrow morning?' Randall leaves me with the address before ending the call.

My mind is whirling. Michael's refusal to allow his finger-prints to be taken at our house suddenly takes on a new meaning. Had he known that he could be linked to other crimes if he got fed into the police computer? Has he always been wearing a mask – one that Jacob believed he had detected, a fake persona hiding such terrible acts? Have I been living with a monster and not known? I think through the parts of the diary I've read so far. Even when Emma catches him chatting up the young blonde at the swimming pool but calls him on it before he takes it any further. He charms her out of her complaints and distracts her by taking her to bed. Is he a sexual predator when away from his current partner?

And what about the child whom I had wrongly assumed was Biff's? I seek out mentions of Kaitlin in Jacob's files. 'I wish I'd had a chance to warn Ali about Harrison. When she took Kaitlin and went to live with him, I had no idea of her peril.' This is seriously twisted stuff. He is calling Emma 'Ali' and claims she stole their child away. Skimming over the next part, it looks like Jacob was a back-to-nature kind of guy working on a Forestry Commission plantation and living in a little cottage. That ties in with Emma's diary. He and Ali fell out over living a carbon-neutral life. Having a kid and washing cloth nappies can test anyone's principles. That was Emma's take on the issue too.

Was Ali a nickname? I can see her not hacking the lifestyle and going back to the city after maternity leave but not letting Jacob know where she went with the kid after she was safely established in her own home? That sounds low. I know she said Jacob was uninterested in the child, but surely that didn't mean she intended never to let him see Kaitlin again. That's way harsh, unfair to the child and the man who had been the only father she had known for the first year. It's not like the woman I'd met in her diary. So why? I can only think that she must have had a very good reason. Was Jacob abusive?

But she never said that and I feel she would've said something in the diary.

And what kind of 'peril' did Jacob have in mind?

My mind is full of questions. Possibly the two most pressing are – and it is incredible that I even have to think this way – have I been living with a murderer? And the second: where is Kaitlin? Michael has never, ever mentioned her. Isn't that at the very least suspicious? I need to read the rest of Emma's diary and Jacob's files to find out.

I'm so shaky with this download of so much information that I don't think I can navigate public transport back to Feltham. I put in a call to Drew, blurting out words such as 'dead body' and 'police'. Overhearing this, the encroaching waitress swerves away again without so much as a glance at my empty cup.

'Jessica, stay where you are. I'll text you when I'm outside,' says Drew.

'You don't have to drop everything for me.'

'I think I do.'

Waiting for him to make the half-hour journey into town, I finger my box of pills, wondering if I should take another. I've had two already today but they do help me think. I need that boost to my focus.

But they also make me agitated and I know I need to calm down. I shove them to the bottom of my bag and suck on a mint instead. I can silently hear Charles commending me for my restraint. I don't like him much but in my psyche he does act as a brake on my more reckless moments – must be the grey-haired-guy authority he oozes. *One a day, Jessica. These pills aren't addictive in the traditional sense but people get hooked on the way they make them feel.* I really need to make an appointment with my GP to ask for a repeat prescription; I'm getting through my last one twice as fast as I should.

Receiving Drew's message that he's outside, I bundle everything back into the bag and run. He doesn't immediately drive off but makes me sit down on a step by the porticoed entrance of St Martins-in-the-Fields.

'OK, deep breath, Jess, and tell me what it is that's happened. You found a body, did I get that right? And not one of mine.' He gives me a wry look.

I nod and try to organise my thoughts so that I can recount my story in some semblance of order. I think I manage to get across the main points. I hide nothing, including the fact that I walked out with Jacob's laptop without permission.

'Jesus, Jessica, you realise you've put yourself in a really bad position?' he asks at the end.

'I know, but what about that stuff implicating Michael?'

'You're taking that seriously? Jacob also described you as some kind of Myra Hindley figure and you were able to dismiss that out of hand.'

'So... So you think it's all lies? But there's Emma – or Ali – whoever she was. And then Kaitlin or Katy. I've seen the photographs. I know they exist.'

'Anyone can have a picture Photoshopped.'

'But it looked real – a selfie of the three of them in the woods, natural. It would've been incredibly difficult to fake. And why would he have it at home where no one but he would see it?'

'OK, how about this theory: maybe Ali changed her name to get away from a guy who wouldn't let her go? He sounds obsessed with her.'

'And in this scenario, Kaitlin just, what, vanished when her mother died?'

Drew sighs. 'Look, I don't know the details – neither of us were there, were we? But Jacob's theory just seems so complicated. Wouldn't it be better not to jump to conclusions and go for the simplest, most normal explanation?'

'Occam's razor,' I mutter.

'What?'

'Old theory about making the least assumptions. Right, OK, but the facts don't all fit a "normal"-world answer. Jacob is dead. So is Ali, or Emma, for that matter. Four girls are missing. Michael must know the truth but he's never mentioned a Kaitlin, or told me much about Emma's background, even after five years. Don't you find that strange? Why the silence?'

Drew can sense I am getting myself worked up again. He puts a hand on my knee. 'Jessica, just press pause a moment. You know what happens when people leap to conclusions, add one and one and make fifty-two. Your experience at Eastfields must have taught you that.'

I rub the back of my neck. 'Yeah, well, it wasn't so much one and one equalling fifty-two as one and one equalling about four.'

He removes his hand. 'What do you mean?'

'Look, I wasn't blameless, so maybe Michael isn't either? He might not be innocent. I've never claimed I was, have I?'

I probably had but I would never stick to that if someone asked for details. I'm not above bending the truth now and again but I wouldn't tell an out-and-out lie.

Drew looks at me. God, his expression is so... so disapproving, this from my slightly feral, happy-go-lucky friend whom I thought could understand and accept anything.

'Geez, this is difficult. Drew, that boy who accused me...'

'You said his name was Kyle Parkinson, that he said you molested him, but you hadn't.'

'Yes, his name was Kyle. And no, I didn't molest him against his will. You have to understand he was eighteen, a grown-up-looking guy. In fact, he looked more like twenty-two.'

'But he wasn't.'

'No.' I gulp. 'Right, well, it all started as a joke. You know, *C'mere miss and give us a kiss*. To embarrass me in front of the class. It was a kind of flirtation, I suppose. And then one day he caught me in the classroom when I was on my own. He said the same thing again and I thought I'd call him on it to, you know, stop him doing it again? So I said, *All right*, and laid one on him – a silly lip smacker, nothing serious. But then he grabbed me and we had a kind of... a moment. The bell went and he left. God, I felt so stupid. How was I going to face him?'

'OK, I understand that. And that was it?' I can tell from his tone, Drew would really prefer the story to stop there but I feel I owe him honesty.

'Er, no, Kyle sort of stalked me. I'd worked out by now that he really did fancy me. He kept arriving when I was on my own. We got into the habit of having these little fumbling sessions. It got quite… quite heated on a couple of occasions.' I didn't want to admit even to Drew that I got a charge from the illicit nature of the encounters, another of my less-than-worthy sexual fantasies. It's hard to explain to someone whose urges don't work that way that Kyle was the dominant one and took the lead, despite the age difference between us. 'School broke up for Christmas and thankfully I had time to get my head straight. When we came back in January I told him firmly that I wasn't going to do that anymore with him, that I should never have started down this road, that I was sorry. But that just annoyed him. He got angry, called me several very unflattering names. Next thing I know, he's gone to his head of year, who went to the headteacher, and the whole ice bucket of disapproval got dumped on me. He said I'd started it all, groomed him, and no one believed me when I said he'd been the one who'd pursued me.'

'You know that you're to blame, right? That you were the adult.'

'He was an adult too.'

'Jessica! You had sex with a fucking teenager!'

'Yes, sorry. No excuses. I was the teacher, he was the student. And I shouldn't have even put a toe over the line, as I was in a relationship already. Don't you think I know that I'm bad?' I pick at the fraying strap on my handbag. 'I guess I was just feeling like dirt, thanks to Michael's treatment of me; he'd already begun sneering at me and my less-than-toned body. I went to the wrong person for comfort.'

Drew is ominously silent. It takes a lot of courage to carry on with this confession but I have to get it all off my chest or it'll be worse later.

'I resigned before they could boot me out. I deserved that, I suppose, but Lizzy, you know what? She took my side. She's a teacher so she knows what it's like, how unforgiving the classroom is, how easily things get twisted. She said my union would probably help me as Kyle was of age and we'd only had, you know, sex a couple of times? I should've been suspended, she thought, pending an investigation to get a more even appraisal of what had gone on in the stationery cupboard.'

'You're joking? A cupboard?'

I thump my forehead, wishing I could stop blurting things out. I want to confess but I don't need to spill every single humiliating detail. 'I know: it was part of the thrill. I'm sorry, but there it is – I get excited about taking risks and I think Kyle guessed that about me. It excited him too. I really don't think I did any damage to him. We both found it kinda hot. He was just angry that I was able to reject him before he dumped me.'

'You weren't going out with him, Jessica. He was an eighteen-year-old student in your care.'

'Sorry, bad choice of words. But there was definitely hurt pride in there when he shopped me. And as for going to my union, I had a type of collapse or breakdown so didn't try to defend myself. The upshot is, now I can't teach again.'

'You're lucky not to be on the sex-offenders register,' says Drew shortly.

'What?' I'd thought he'd take the truth better than this.

'You always presented yourself as innocent. I thought you'd been wrongly accused but you were actually going at it with a pupil in a school cupboard – Christ, Jessica, don't you see how wrong that was?'

'Of course I do. But I'm... stupid, OK? I give in to impulses when I shouldn't. I know myself, blame myself, if that's what you want to hear. I'm sorry.' I stand up and shout at the pigeons. 'Sorry, world, for breathing!' They flutter off in protest.

'I'm not a hundred per cent sure you are.' Drew gets to his feet and hands me his spare helmet. 'I'll run you back.'

'Is that it? That's all you're going to say?' He is bearing an enormous grudge against me now. I can feel it like a sandwich board swaying between us, not advertising best exchange rates but the drastic decrease in his estimation of me. 'Look, I know I'm a disaster area. I warned you!'

'Don't press me now, Jessica. I need some time to think about this.' He drops the helmet in my hands, forcing me to catch it.

My eyes are brimming but tears aren't going to solve this. I don't deserve pity. I'd offer to go to a hotel but I don't have the money. I'd offer to crash on someone else's sofa but I don't have another friend I can go to. My God, I'm pathetic. 'Do... do you want me to find somewhere else to stay?' I could ring Mum and ask her to foot the bill for a Travelodge. Just the once wouldn't be too bad, would it?

'I said I wouldn't throw you out. I'm not Michael.' Drew gets on the moped and waits for me to mount behind him. It's about as inviting as getting on a bed of nails.

I gingerly put my hands around his waist. 'No, you're not

Michael.' Except that Drew has joined the club of those who are disappointed in me. If even Drew despises me, why am I bothering? Why don't I just give up now? No one would care and quite a few would be relieved.

Except Mum. It makes me feel even more wretched that I've reached thirty and only have a mother who would miss me. That in itself is almost reason enough to top myself.

Chapter 25

12th August

I wake up with a familiar feeling of hating myself. What is wrong with me? Well, I know what's wrong with me, so the question really is: why can't I handle myself better, knowing what my problem is? I remember this feeling from the sorry story of my learning to drive. I eventually passed on my fourth attempt but when I ventured onto the motorway for the first time, I was scared stiff of causing an accident. My life: knowing the theory but feeling a bit out of control of the vehicle.

I don't drive much now – another result of living with Michael, who wouldn't dream of letting me behind the wheel of his car. He has a nice BMW 1 Series in midnight blue parked outside the house. Three-door sports hatchback, he says at dinner parties when guys ask him, three hundred and forty HP. When asked what my partner drives, I just say it's blue. I do know the specs – he's got the souped-up version – but, God, can you imagine a more boring conversation? In any case, with his academic friends, it's usually the blind leading the blind. I expect most of them don't look under the bonnet of their own cars, so why pretend interest in a vehicle when someone brags? Michael is fond of it, though, because he thinks it reflects well on him. He's prepared for it to get keyed while parked on the street, but not to have me put a ding in it trying to park it at the supermarket. That's a direct quote, by the way.

Damn him.

I get out of bed, anger surging. I don't want to be the timid driver who doesn't know how to overtake a lorry or judge the speed of approaching vehicles. I don't want to pull over onto the hard shoulder to breathe through a panic attack.

OK, new day, new start. I have to get my head straight. I have to salvage my life. When in doubt, make a list.

1. I've disappointed Drew and I don't want to do that. His good opinion is worth earning. I can't change the past but I can change my future.
2. He thinks I was wrong to take the laptop. Well, I agree. I even knew it at the time. If there is any fact behind Jacob's accusations, then I'm also obstructing a murder enquiry. I've got to face up to that. I'll take it with me when I go to the police for fingerprinting. I won't excuse myself, well, not much, just enough to try and avoid arrest.
3. I need to be open-minded about Michael. Things look bad for him but that doesn't mean it all adds up.

Usually when I make a list I include items I can already cross off, but unfortunately nothing comes to mind. That's dispiriting. I've a tough few days ahead. Maybe I can do Point Two before the end of the day. I mentally shake hands with myself not to rabbit out on that deal.

Drew has already gone to work when I emerge from the spare room. If he had breakfast he has removed all traces, not even a plate on the drainer. I don't feel hungry but make myself drink a glass of orange juice. I'm not anticipating a pleasant time at the police station. I wash up the tumbler and put it back in the cupboard.

'OK, Bridges,' I tell myself. 'Time to girl up.'

'Can I help you?' The receptionist at Lewisham police station doesn't smile as I report to the front desk. She is surrounded by posters advertising different police initiatives against burglary, vandalism, drugs and knife crime. The graphics all share a Banksy vibe, which is ironic if you think about it.

Did you know you can use a mixture of orange juice and milk in a high-pressure hose to remove graffiti? Seems like a very motherly solution to a predominantly urban youth problem – almost cute.

God, my brain is out to lunch again. Focus.

'Hi. Sorry. I'm Jessica Bridges. Inspector Randall asked me to call in for fingerprinting.'

She makes a couple of clicks of her mouse. 'Yes, CID. Your name is on the list. Would you take a seat, please?'

'Um,' and here comes the difficult bit, 'is he in today?'

She gives me a pained smile as if to say he'd hardly be off on holiday at the start of a serious crime enquiry. 'Yes.'

'I need to speak to him. It's rather urgent. I might have something, some evidence, concerning the case.' And it's slung over my shoulder.

'OK, I'll let him know. It won't be him processing your fingerprints, though, so please still take a seat.'

I sit on one of the chairs opposite the desk, waiting nervously. Then a pleasant young officer scoops me up to take me to a nearby room for the fingerprinting part of my visit. She is of British Asian appearance. I wonder how recruiting among minorities is going but decide it's probably best not to ask. This is one of those times when I should not blurt out my first thoughts.

'Ever had this done before?' she asks me.

'No, I can't say I have.' I wonder if she's trying to trip me into confessing earlier brushes with authority but then I realise she's just making conversation.

'It's very simple. I've a scanner here. Just press your right hand against the screen and try to keep still.'

'What, no ink?'

'No, we don't do it that way anymore.'

'And what happens to it?'

'The image gets sent to the Scotland Yard database so that it can be compared with the fingerprints from the crime scene and we'll know which ones are yours. Great. Now the left.'

'Did you know fingerprinting was invented by Sir William Herchel in India in 1860 to stop his locally engaged staff cheating when drawing their wages?' Maybe I shouldn't have said that?

'Um, no I did not. How do you know about him?'

'I'm a bit of a magpie. Trivia seems to stick. Watch a lot of *QI*.'

She smiles. 'I see. Well, there's not much else on worth watching, is there?'

The door opens as we finish the procedure.

'Miss Bridges, you asked to see Inspector Randall?' says Sergeant Lloyd.

'Yes, OK, right.' I stand up, then sit down again. 'Er, I need to tell him something.'

He nods to his colleague who exits with the scanner. 'So the receptionist told me. Inspector Randall is caught up, I'm afraid, briefing the homicide team.'

I almost flee on hearing that, as it sounds as if they've decided it is murder. Biting my lip, I put the laptop bag on the table. 'I'd better tell you, then. You need to know something about me first. I suffer from something called ADHD. Have you heard of it?'

His gaze goes to the buckle on the bag, realising it is significant. 'Of course, I've heard of it in children.'

'Yes, well, there's an adult form that makes the person with the condition very impulsive. That's me. If you need any more corroboration of the problem, you can talk to my doctor, er, ex-therapist. The person who was treating me until recently. Anyway, what I want to say... look, yesterday I gave in to a really stupid impulse. I knew that Jacob was hiding something from me and while I was waiting to speak to you I saw our office laptop. I took a quick peek inside and noticed that he had some things belonging to me.'

'What things?'

I move to open the bag but he holds up a hand.

'It's better if you just tell me.'

'A photo belonging to my ex-partner, a diary belonging to his wife, and a set of my house keys. Michael accused me of taking the photo but you'll see from what's on the laptop that it was Jacob. I don't know what happened to the wedding rings – they also went missing when we were broken into.'

Lloyd looks at me for a long time. 'What's going on, Miss Bridges?'

I try to tell him the best I can. 'I know it all sounds very strange, and I've not helped, have I, taking this yesterday?'

'It was very unwise, messing with the evidence. Who's to say you didn't put those things in the bag yourself?'

'I hadn't thought of that. But the entries in the laptop – can't your computer people check the dates on them?'

'But you said this was the office laptop and you were able to access the files yourself.'

'Only after I guessed the password. It's Jacob's computer really. I don't know what he did with mine when he cleared out the office.'

Lloyd doesn't like the way my story keeps shifting – nor do I, but so often the truth is less plausible than neat lies. 'How did you guess the password?'

'Inspector Randall gave it to me yesterday by accident. He mentioned Jacob's daughter, whom I'd never heard of before. It's "kaitlin", no capital.' I look at my hands squeezed together in my lap. I'm not doing a very good job of appearing innocent. 'For a secretive man, he didn't try very hard with his security.'

Lloyd reaches for the bag. 'Stay here, please. I need to take this to the inspector. Would you like another coffee?'

It's not quite handcuffs but neither is it 'you're free to go'. 'No thank you. I'd better not have any more caffeine.' I rotate the empty canteen cup that the fingerprint officer had brought me.

'Right. I won't be long.'

'It's OK. I don't have anywhere I need to be.'

He leaves.

I've done it now. I only hope that Drew is proud of me because I realise my truth-telling has just put me back in the frame for murder, as far as the police are concerned.

An hour elapses and I'm bursting to go to the loo. That's not something they cover on those cop shows on TV, is it? Everyone in them has bladders of infinite capacity. Would it be OK just to walk out and find one or will that set off an alarm? Before I can resolve that issue, Lloyd comes back in with Inspector Randall.

'Miss Bridges,' the inspector begins.

'I'm really sorry – all that coffee – is there...?'

He nods to Lloyd, who escorts me to the nearest Ladies' and stands outside the door while I go in. Washing my hands, I stare at my reflection. What am I getting myself into here?

Back in the interview room, Randall has laid out printed copies of Jacob's case notes. There are a lot of them, going back beyond where I looked in the files.

'Have you read these?' he asks.

'Not all of them. I started with the more recent ones that

mentioned me. I didn't get that far back before I realised I should hand them over. There are loads of entries. He doesn't seem to have done much else than plot against Michael.'

'Taking these at face value, what do you think they tell us?'

'That he set up the office to entrap me. I accepted the job on good faith but he made it up to drag me into his feud. He added a twist to get me in further trouble when he made a fraudulent signature on the lease to implicate me in his business.'

'Motive?'

'I can only guess that he did these things because he wanted to find out more about Michael and me, and he hated us both – anything that messed us up was good in his eyes. He clearly had a longstanding grudge against Michael.'

'More than a grudge.'

'Yes... yes, an elaborate theory that Michael has done away with four girls, perhaps more if you count Kaitlin and Ali, who I know as Emma, Michael's wife. Emma mentions a Katy in the diary who might be Kaitlin, I just don't know. She died about five years ago, shortly before I met Michael. Cancer, he said, but he doesn't talk about her much so I'm not sure of the details.'

'And when you read these accusations, what did you think?' Randall sits back. I can feel him studying my body language but I can't picture what a completely innocent person would do in this circumstance, so I sit hunched up.

'I was shocked. None of what he wrote about me is true.'

'Jacob West alludes to some incident in Eastfields – that's a school, isn't it?'

'Yes. I had some trouble there and it caused a kind of breakdown. The job with Jacob was the first I've had since then. I've mostly recovered.'

'So that part was true?'

Clenching my hand, I dig my nails into my palm. 'Yes. I meant the rest. I had no idea Michael knew any of the girls in the cases Jacob gave me.'

'So, it is possible he did know them?'

'Well, their paths could've crossed, I suppose. The dates work out. To be honest I've no idea what to make of it, which is why I brought you the computer. When I took it, I thought I'd just find the reason why I was being pursued for rent I did not owe. Instead, I found my boss thought I was living with a serial killer.' I give a strained laugh that no one else joins in with.

Lloyd, who has been standing to one side during this interrogation, takes a seat across the table. 'Did you write these case notes, Miss Bridges?'

'God, no. No, I didn't. And I'm sorry if my actions make it a question you now have to ask. Can you get someone to analyse when they were written? I didn't meet Jacob until the end of April – Michael will remember that. If there are entries made before that, then I can't have done them.'

'We will check, so if there is anything you need to tell us, it's better if you do so now.'

I hold his gaze. 'I did not tamper with the entries on Jacob's laptop, I promise.'

Randall folds his arms. 'Miss Bridges, why haven't you asked for a lawyer?'

This catches me out. 'Do I need one?'

He smiles slightly. 'Perhaps not. The fact that you haven't called for one, or considered you might require one, speaks of your own conviction of your innocence in this. But still, you've committed an offence, taking the computer from the house.'

'I saw it as taking back what was mine, mainly – you know, the picture, and the keys?' That sounded lame and we all knew it. 'Will you press charges?' I quickly calculate how much money I have access to, who I'm going to call.

Now I've got the *Ghostbusters* theme going around in my head. Dammit, I can't even control my thoughts when my freedom is on the line.

'If everything is as you claim – and we're getting the results of your fingerprint scan any moment now – then perhaps not. Not if you cooperate fully with us on the matter of Mr West's suspicious death. Tell me, is there any reason why Michael Harrison might want to kill Jacob West?'

'Only what Jacob claims – that they loved the same woman, that there's a child missing somehow, and that maybe he has some connection to the four girls Jacob asked me to investigate.'

'And from your own experience of Dr Harrison... You've lived with him for five years, I understand?'

I nod.

'Have you noticed any unexplained absences or odd behaviours?'

'Like what?'

'Such as clothes disappearing from his wardrobe or exchanging his car for a new one unexpectedly?'

'I don't think so. He's had the current car about a year – he leases them and swaps them for a new model after a while, but that's normal, isn't it? I think you could say that he prefers new things to old. He buys a lot of clothes, and chucks out the stuff he no longer wears after a few months. When he's had a clear-out, I usually bag things up for charity as they're hardly worn. But all that is standard practice for him. He's image conscious.'

'And absences?'

'He travels a lot.'

'How often?'

'Frequently. At least once a month.'

'Does he drink whisky?'

I look down at my knees, noticing I've picked up a scratch from somewhere on my shin. 'Yes, but a lot of people do. I suppose that's the one exception to not liking old stuff: he's big on his aged malts.'

'What's your opinion on West's speculations about Dr Harrison?'

'To be honest, I don't know. He has to be wrong, doesn't he? People don't just get murdered without anyone noticing.'

'You'd be surprised,' murmurs Lloyd.

Way to unsettle me, detective. 'But I don't like that there's a connection between Michael and Jacob that I knew nothing about. If Jacob did have something on him, then I suppose it's not totally inconceivable that Michael might've done something – he does have a temper. He... He can be violent when he loses it.'

'And your evidence of this?' asks Randall.

'We quarrelled a couple of nights back just before I left for the last time. He hit me. Just the once, but he did hit me. To be fair, I think he was as shocked by it as I was, but he just looked really ugly when he did it, like a man capable of anything.'

'And you didn't report it?'

'No, I just left. He's on good terms with the police. I didn't think anyone would believe me. I couldn't see the point.'

'The point is that we would have a record of that now to help substantiate your claim that Michael has violent tendencies.'

'I'm not claiming that. I'm just trying to answer your questions truthfully. I don't want to blow things out of proportion, but you did ask.'

The female officer who did my scan returns and passes a piece of paper to Randall. She gives me a smile as she leaves.

Randall reads the report and hands it to Lloyd. 'I'm pleased to say the computer matching system has good news for you, Miss Bridges. This rules you out as having touched any objects in the kitchen, including the glasses and whisky bottle. That, taken with your decision to come forward this morning, means you may go for now. Thank you for your cooperation. Please keep yourself available for further questioning and tell us if you are planning to leave London.'

I shrug. 'I'm not going anywhere. I'm flat broke.'

'Where will you be?'

'At the Feltham address I gave you. At least for the next few days.' If I haven't frozen to death in Drew's Arctic chill of disapproval.

'I'm sure we'll have to speak again but, for the moment, I have no further questions.' Randall opens the door for me. 'Sergeant, see Miss Bridges back to reception.'

Chapter 26

Michael, 13th August

The house feels empty without Jessica. She drove me crazy when she was here but at least she was a distraction. Without her, I find myself looking for Emma. I thought I had kicked that habit. She spent much of her last months on the sofa in the kitchen during our quiet weekday mornings, preferring to be near me than lying in the bed up in our room. I took to working at the table facing her rather than retreating to my study. I did this so our eyes could meet from time to time, each checking the other was still there. They were some of the best moments we had together in that final year, soothing classical music on the stereo, sunlight coming through the conservatory windows, the gentle rustle of the pages of her book. Even thin as she became, pure sculptural form with her bald head which she chose not to hide under a wig, missing lashes and eyebrows, she looked so beautiful to me, every moment of just the two of us so precious. I would've given anything to take on the illness for her and set her free. The hardest, bitterest thing I've ever had to face was the knowledge that I couldn't.

Perhaps I should sell this house? It's too full of memories. My failure. Her failure to beat off the disease – not that she ever had a choice. Failure is the wrong word. Bulldozed – cheated – by liver cancer.

I feed Colette, eat a solitary breakfast, and try to decide what to do with my day. I'd promised myself that I'd use August to get on with some research in the British Library, but I can't seem to get my act together. I wander around the kitchen, gathering up Jessica's stuff, and pile it in the corner. How has she accumulated so much crap? Books on art. Question: how many coffee-table books on Impressionism are too many? Answer: one. I've some corrections to the copy edit of my latest manuscript to complete – that seems about all my brain can cope with at the moment.

The doorbell rings. I find Lizzy on the step with a paper bag of deli croissants.

'I thought you might need cheering up,' she says.

I pull her into the hallway and close the door. 'Thanks.' I bend down and kiss her, as I know she expects it. I'd slept in our spare room last night rather than at hers. She had friends over and we agreed that it wasn't the right moment to come out about our relationship, with Jessica gone only a few hours. 'You know what I need before I do.'

'I got these on my walk with Flossie. Come on, I'll make you coffee and you can get yourself set up for the day.' She leads the way into the kitchen. 'Any news from Jessica?'

'No.' I divert her from follow-up questions by darting into my study. I don't like her mentioning Jessica. Lizzy has many virtues but she never fully chose sides in our rows, saying she understood Jessica's point of view and even liked her, despite her foibles. I pointed out that she couldn't have liked her that much, as she was sleeping with me, but Lizzy just shrugged, saying that was different. Jessica had made it OK for me to be unfaithful when she messed with that kid at school, like relationships are some game of tit for tat. I think Lizzy is waiting for me to invite her to move in now that Jessica has vacated, but I'm not ready. There's too much history between us for that to work out.

Lizzy puts two coffee cups on the table, croissants on a wooden board, butter in a white dish. She takes note of things like presentation, another way in which she outdoes Jessica. I feel hungry for the first time since Jessica stormed out.

'Thanks.'

'But you think she's all right?'

'Please leave it, Lizzy.'

'Just tell me she's got somewhere to go.'

'There's a friend over in Feltham.'

'Drew?'

'Yes.'

'Are they together now?'

'I don't know, and I really don't care.'

'I'd just feel easier about us if I know Jessica is OK.'

I want to snap that there is no 'us' but I need Lizzy's help right now. 'It's not bothered you before. Jessica will be fine. She always manages to fall on her feet.'

The phone rings. Sipping my coffee, I grab the receiver. 'Yes? Hello?'

'Dr Michael Harrison?'

'If this is a sales call, I really don't have time right now—'

'No, sir. This is Detective Sergeant Lloyd from Lewisham police station. I wonder if you might help us with an investigation into a suspicious death.'

My mind flicks through the interesting murders I've noticed recently in the news. 'The Clapham one?'

'No, sir. This one took place in Camberwell.'

'So why do you need my help?'

'The body was discovered by someone you know: Jessica Bridges.'

'Shit.' I sit down. What has Jessica got herself mixed up in now?

'You can really help us if you would clear up a few outstanding issues as to her connection to the victim and also her whereabouts over the last few weeks.'

'Are you looking at her as the killer? If so, I'd say you were barking up the wrong tree. She's fatally disaster prone but not violent. If she's involved, it would've been some ridiculous mistake. She wouldn't kill on purpose.' I worry a little over the slashed mattress but she hadn't turned the knife on a person, had she?

'That's good to hear, sir. It's just a matter of tying up some loose ends.'

Agreeing to come over this morning, I quickly down my coffee.

'What's wrong?' asks Lizzy, straightening my tie for me. I want to push her away but daren't.

'You won't believe this new development: Jessica stumbled over a dead body. Isn't that so like her?'

'Oh my word, when? Is she OK? Do you know who it is?'

'The police didn't say. I've been asked to go over to Lewisham to vouch for her. To be honest, I'd much prefer to leave her to sink or swim.'

'Michael, you can't. She couldn't kill anyone.'

'I know that – you heard me tell the police the same thing – but after what she did—'

Lizzy bags up the remaining croissant and tucks it in my messenger bag. I want to tell her to stop mothering me but the last thing I need is another argument. 'She's not been well. You need to cut her some slack.'

I close my eyes and gather the threads of my composure, reminding myself of what image I want to project to Lizzy: much wronged but still kind. 'Yes, of course.' I kiss her briefly. I don't feel even the spark of attraction for her today – that's one of my problems with our relationship. Going to bed with her is far more about comfort than the thrill. She doesn't have Jessica's willingness to experiment; our physical relationship is definitely that of equals, sometimes it feels more like a wrestling match in which I'm not always the winner. 'I'll see you later. Oh, there's a new mattress due to be delivered this afternoon. Would you mind?'

She smirks. 'Of course. I have a vested interest in it, don't I?'

I wish she wouldn't make comments like that.

Approaching Lewisham police station, my gloom lifts and I feel a flicker of excitement. I've been called in often enough to advise the police, but that is usually either at Scotland Yard or they come to me in my office at Royal Holloway. It's been a while since I've visited a homicide team at their local head-quarters. I wonder if there's some material I can use here in my next set of lectures? I'm planning a course on the effect of the police investigative process on sociopathic individuals. Confrontation is the worst way to question those with this disorder, as they've often come from abusive backgrounds and it just confirms them in their least productive behavioural patterns. I'm thinking of devising some recommendations for alternative methods of interrogation. I'd need to field test them, of course...

'Dr Harrison?' The receptionist gives me a cold look when I present her with my university ID. 'Take a seat.' She presses a buzzer at her desk and a plain-clothes officer enters, accompanied by a constable in uniform.

I get up and offer a hand. 'I'm Dr Harrison.'

'DS Lloyd,' says the officer, not coming close enough to shake hands, holding the door open for me instead. 'This way, please.'

A sense of disquiet blooms. In the past when I've pitched up at police stations I've been treated far better than this. I would be ushered in to see a senior officer, a chief inspector at least, and thanked from the outset for carving out time for my consultation. I never charge, seeing it as my giving back to the society that educated me and made my career possible. I've never been escorted by a DS and a constable into an interrogation room before. A fingerprint scanner sits on the table.

Another officer joins us after a few moments and introduces himself as Detective Inspector Randall. I rack my brains. I think I've heard good things about his work. He's not one of the highest flyers, but is known to get the job done through careful and dogged investigative techniques. Whatever his record, though, that doesn't mean they should be treating me like a criminal, corralling me in a room like this.

'What's all this about, inspector?' I ask sharply. 'I'm a busy man. I thought you wanted me to confirm Jessica's alibi for the times I was with her?'

'Yes, we do.' Randall gestures me to take a seat but I remain standing. I don't want to concede my upper hand by sitting on that cheap excuse for a chair. 'We also want to offer you the opportunity to give your fingerprints for elimination purposes.'

'Is this about the break-in at my house? I've already explained that I don't like my data being sucked into the police central database. I know you people swear it is deleted once its purpose is served, but I'm not that gung-ho about my personal details.'

'It's not to do with the break-in, not directly anyway.'

'Then what is it to do with?'

'The murder of Jacob West last Monday night.'

'What?' The news forces me to sit. Why him now?

'I take it the name is familiar to you?'

'Yes, from way back. Five years, or more, even. He pestered Emma, my wife, after she broke off her relationship with him. But what's Jacob West got to do with me?' This is a bad dream. West was the only man who ever brought me briefly into trouble with the police. It had no consequences as he didn't stay around to press charges after our confrontation and the police lost interest. Looking at Randall's cynical expression and Lloyd's pretence at blank disinterest, I quickly decide not to offer that history to the men before me. Not if they're investigating his murder. I know too much about the law not to know that miscarriages of justice happen all the time when the police get fixed on an individual. The last thing I want is them to focus on me.

'Jacob West masqueraded as Jacob Wrath. Under that name, he employed your girlfriend for three months. Do you have any idea why he might do that?'

'Wrath and West are the same person? And I thought she'd made him up. I was convinced she'd spun a fantasy.' The events of the past few days reassemble themselves in a new order. I've been way off.

'No, she didn't, but he did make up his identity and, it would appear, he got her in trouble with false claims in her name and avoided meeting anyone who might know him.'

It's a shock to find Jessica equally innocent of the rent fiasco, though I suppose that follows. And I even... 'The bastard,' I mutter. 'He picked on her because she was with me?'

'Yes.'

I'm in the unexpected position of owing Jessica an apology. 'I'd better give her a call.'

'We'd prefer it if you didn't contact her at the moment.'

'Are you seriously considering her as a suspect? If so, I'd say you are wasting your time pursuing the wrong person.'

'No, we don't think Miss Bridges killed Jacob West.'

'Thank God. Then perhaps if you'd let me give a statement,

then I can let you get on.' I want nothing more than to get out of here. West cropping up in my life again is what various branches of the military would call a situation that has gone FUBAR. I need to take stock of what it all means.

Randall ignores my signals that I want to leave. 'Would it surprise you to hear that it appears that Mr West was the person who broke into your house on Monday?'

What? 'Busy guy – breaking and entering and then dying on the same day.' The police are not amused by my attempt at gallows humour. I adjust my tone. 'Yes, it does surprise me, but now I think about it, I can see why he might've targeted me. He was always fiercely jealous that I won Emma from him. She was an amazing woman and he didn't want to admit that she'd left him for good. I'd even go as far as to say that he was obsessional about her. But so much time has elapsed, and Emma has been dead five years, I never suspected he'd wait this long to strike.'

'Miss Bridges said you thought that she was responsible for the break-in.'

'It was the only thing that made sense at the time. I wasn't very nice to her, I'm afraid. I'd really like that opportunity to contact her. I said some harsh things.'

'Just said?'

What has Jessica been telling them? My feeling of goodwill towards her diminishes. If she's made a fuss over the inadvertent blow during our quarrel, then no wonder the police are looking at me like I'm some kind of criminal. 'It wasn't a scene either of us would be proud of, on sober reflection.'

'Talking of sobriety, I understand you are partial to Scotch?'

I can spot a leading question. 'Among other drinks. What bearing does this have on anything?'

'Have you ever visited Jacob West's home in John Ruskin Street?'

'Where's that?'

'Near the Oval.'

'No, I haven't.'

'In that case, you won't mind giving us your fingerprints for elimination purposes? We have a set of prints from the crime scene that are key to our enquiries and are yet to be identified.'

'I told you that I don't like my data being taken. The less personal information out there, the better.'

'This is a murder enquiry, Dr Harrison, not a Facebook request.'

I can see that refusal to provide my fingerprints will result in a much longer stay at the station and I have things I would much prefer to do today, like write a letter of complaint to the Metropolitan Police commissioner. 'All right, I'll give my prints but I want you to make a note that I object to the invasion of my privacy.'

'You'll find, Doctor, that murder tends to trump privacy.' He beckons to the detective sergeant who takes me through the process of having my hands scanned. I tell myself it is an interesting chance to be exposed to current police practice, that I should use this in my future writing on law enforcement, but mostly I'm fuming.

'Can I get you some refreshments?' asks Randall when the scan is finished.

'I'd much rather get a decent coffee on my way to the library. I know what police station vending machines are like.' I look at my watch. 'Have you finished with me yet?'

'Not yet.' Randall waits while the sergeant exits the room with the scanner. 'Are you sure you won't have something? Water?'

'All right, water.' My tone is ungracious but what do they expect?

The inspector dispatches the constable in pursuit of a drink for me and we're alone. I'm worried now that I might've appeared too eager to leave and it has raised their suspicions.

'Look, Randall, I think I've heard good things about your work.'

He raises a brow. 'You have?'

No harm in laying it on thick. 'Yes, Chief Inspector Butcher speaks very highly of you.'

'She does?'

'Do you know who I am?'

'Yes. You're Dr Michael Harrison. You lecture at Hendon on criminal psychology. I've sat through a couple of your sessions and found them helpful.'

'In that case, if you know who I am, why are you keeping me here? I'd be happy to come back to help you with your enquiries at any time, but I really do have work I need to get to. Important work.'

'And so do I. I'm afraid I've only just started with my questions. The session will be recorded for your protection and mine, as I'm sure you understand. I'm just waiting for my colleagues to return.'

I feel like Alice through the looking-glass, everything I consider normal turned on its head. 'Is this really necessary? You can't seriously be considering that I had anything to do with West's death?'

'I have to consider all possibilities. You said yourself that many criminals with severe pathologies hide behind a mask of normality.'

Talk about your own words coming back to bite you. 'I wasn't referring to myself. I can refer you to many character witnesses who will attest to my sanity.'

'And those who know you best say you have a capacity for violence.'

The constable returns and sets a paper cup in front of me.

'Who? Jessica?' I feel a swoop of anger, finding it hard not to give in to the urge to throw the water over Randall. 'And you take the word of an unhinged woman over mine? We argued, all right? I challenge anyone to live with Jessica and not feel like driving their fist through a wall.'

'If it were only a wall, I'd not worry. And then there's Jacob West's theory about you. I have to look at all avenues of enquiry, no matter how outlandish they might seem.'

'Whatever he said, West would only want to present me in the worst possible light.'

The sergeant returns and passes Randall a note.

'I see. Right, then we can start.' Randall begins to read out the date, reference number and people present in the room. I can't believe this is happening to me. Should I call a solicitor? But as I know I've nothing to feel guilty about, wouldn't they take that as an admission I've got something to hide? I decide to let this run for a while and find out what they think they have on me.

After reminding me of my rights, Randall takes me through some easy questions to get a rhythm going. I answer with short replies, not elaborating. He asks me to repeat on record how I know Jacob West. Yes, Ali and Emma were the same person. I explain that she reverted to her first name to shake him off after having used her middle name when with Jacob. It's not exactly a lie.

Then Randall sets off in a completely different direction. 'Do the names Ramona James, Lillian Bailey, Clare Maxsted and Latifah Masood mean anything to you?'

'Who?'

He repeats them, pausing after each name. Both the sergeant and Randall are watching my reactions very closely.

'Not to my knowledge. But I meet a lot of people in my job.' The list is vaguely familiar but I can't put faces to any of the names.

'We know that you did meet Latifah Masood a year ago. We've checked with your employer and she interviewed for a place on your course.'

'She did?' I remember several bright girls who might've been Latifah in the last intake. 'I'm afraid she didn't make a distinct impression but if you say so, then yes, I did meet her.'

'Ramona James was a waitress at the reception you attended at the Tate gallery in Margate, February two years ago.'

'The Turner place? I barely remember the pictures, let alone the waitstaff.'

'Lillian Bailey left Harrogate the same evening you returned from a conference in the city a few months later – July 16th, to be exact.'

'I'll take your word for it.'

'Clare Maxsted ran away from her home in Birmingham on the same night you were staying at the university. 12th November 2015.'

'Birmingham? What was I doing there?'

'Examining a PhD,' chips in the sergeant.

'Oh yes. I wanted to fail the person but we agreed to let him pass after some rewrites. But this is all coincidental. Why have you bothered stringing all this together?'

'We didn't. Jacob West did.'

Something clicked. 'Of course! Jessica mentioned these names to me while we were on holiday! She said they were missing persons cases.'

'That's correct. We've confirmed what we could of Jacob's research, of course, but it's his work we are presenting here.'

'So, what? He was stalking me and casting round for something to pin on me? What did he think I was? Some modern-day Pied Piper of Hamlin luring girls to the city?'

'You tell us.' Randall picks up the sheet of paper in front of him. I can tell a lot depends on my next answer.

'I don't know. I'd forgotten West existed until you mentioned him to me just now. I certainly wasn't interested enough in him to keep tabs on him or his movements. He must've been obsessed with me, and as to what connection he dreamed I had with these women – girls – I've no idea.'

'So you've never visited his house in John Ruskin Street?'

'I've already told you that I haven't.'

'So how can you explain the fact that your fingerprints appear on the bottle from which he served, or was served, a glass of whisky laced with sedatives?'

'What?' Lloyd leans over my shoulder and places a photograph of a Glenfiddich single malt. It's one of their fifteen-year-old classics, a personal favourite. 'My prints are on that bottle?'

'Yes.'

My mind gallops ahead of my next words. If the police are to be believed, Jacob broke into my house. I hadn't thought to check the drinks cabinet closely, thinking Jessica the culprit – she has no taste for the stuff, so why would she touch it? Jacob, by contrast, might have removed a bottle when he took the other things. A second possibility occurs. Had Jessica set it all up with him? What if she had been involved and tipped him off about the bottles? It was obviously a good place to harvest a set of my prints.

'If my prints are on it, then it's a bottle taken from my cabinet, as I've never been to West's house. You won't find my prints on anything else.'

'Or you were careful what you touched when you went in and forgot to wipe down the bottle when you wiped the prints off other surfaces,' suggests Lloyd.

'That would make me a singularly inept killer, if I didn't think about the murder weapon.'

'The drug didn't kill him. We believe death resulted from a blow to the head from an as yet unidentified object. But still, yes, it would. Alternatively, maybe you thought it would make others look guilty, like you'd been framed?'

'That's a convoluted double bluff, if that's what I did – which I didn't. It has every danger of backfiring and ending up with me sitting here.' Panic is edging in. Everything does seem angled to make me look guilty. It is like being in some ghastly hall of mirrors where every reflection is the worst possible version of yourself. 'You can't be taking this seriously? These frail connections with the girls...'

'We're not looking into their disappearances, though we have passed the information on to our colleagues in Missing Persons,' says Randall, taking over the lead again. 'No, my concern here is the death of Mr West last Monday. The facts are that he drank a considerable dose of painkillers, hit his head, or was struck, and passed out on his way to the front door. Death followed not long after. Your prints appear on the bottle. You can see how it looks?'

'Yes. But it's another ridiculous tissue of lies and happenstance. I think I'd better refuse to say any more until I speak to my legal adviser.'

'Fair enough. Sergeant Lloyd, make sure Dr Harrison has access to a phone to make the call. We'll resume when his lawyer gets here.' Randall gets up. 'By the way, who is Kaitlin and where is she now?'

The name comes as a slug to the guts. 'I'm not answering any further questions.'

'I see. Interview ended.' Randall walks out.

Chapter 27

Contrary to what the police appear to expect, I don't have a lawyer on speed dial. I phone a colleague in the law department and ask if she can recommend anyone.

'Been a naughty boy, Michael?' Celia jokes.

'It's nothing like that,' I reply tersely. My tone must have told her that something was seriously wrong and she gives a name with no further quips.

Sally-Ann Brightwell from Farrell and Houghton, a city firm, is much more business-like than her name suggests. She marches on kitten heels into the interview room which has become far too familiar over the past few hours. Striking rather than beautiful, in a Cleopatra way, with a strong profile, I get the instant impression that I'm in good hands with her. I brush the croissant crumbs from my trousers and stand.

'Dr Harrison? I've read your books.' She shakes my hand.

'Oh, er, thank you.'

'I didn't say I liked them.' She gives me a dry smile, lets me hang for a moment, and then, 'But I did.'

I pat my chest. 'Good. I'm not really up to my normal level of banter, I'm afraid.'

She tucks one side of her sleek bobbed hair behind her ear, revealing a delicate diamond in the lobe. 'Quite understandable. Now, tell me what's going on here.'

I explain as best I can. I don't really understand it myself so I'm not sure how coherent I'm being.

'Let me put this back to you, stripped down to the essentials. Jacob West is dead thanks to a combination of an overdose and a blow to the head. The police suspect the drugs weren't taken intentionally. You have a history with the man. Your prints are on the bottle?'

I nod.

'But your case is that you hadn't seen him for years, that he was clearly stalking you and inventing all sorts of imaginary crimes for which he claims you are responsible, that he even went so far as to target your ex-girlfriend to get back at you?'

'Yes, that's about the size of it. There's one more possibility. Jessica and I didn't part on good terms. They may have colluded to frame me.'

'So are you suggesting that she killed him?'

Sally-Ann is right. That doesn't make much sense. I'd already described Jessica as not having the killer instinct – ironically the subject of my next book, so I suppose I should know what I'm talking about. 'Maybe he blackmailed her into it? She's got a serious blot on her record she'd want to hide at all costs. She might've panicked.'

'Right. We'll get to that later.' Sally-Ann makes some notes on a legal pad. 'Our priority is getting you out of here. How long have they held you?'

'Since about eleven this morning. I came in voluntarily to

help with their enquiries regarding Jessica. They gave me no warning they wished to question me.'

'Then it's high time they let you go if they aren't going to make an arrest. We have to get you away from here.'

My heart sinks. 'Why? What's happened?'

'Someone in the station has leaked that they are holding TV's favourite criminologist in connection with a murder investigation. It's not a very busy time in the press for news, unless it's the Olympics sports desk, so the crime-beat people have latched on to what they think might be a juicy story.'

'Shit.' I have always enjoyed my television and radio appearances but now they are attracting unwelcome attention. I can see what she means: I'd be gamekeeper turned poacher if I were guilty of the crime, the murdering murder expert.

'I had to barge through a crowd of story-hungry journalists on my way in.' She didn't seem too put out by the experience. It would no doubt burnish her professional image. 'We'll see if we can take you out the back.'

'This is a nightmare.'

She nods. 'Always is when the press get involved. You're telling me you've never been to West's house but that he broke into yours and removed several items?'

'Yes.'

'OK, that's something for us to work with. The police are going to have to make a very good case that you were there on Monday. You have an alibi?'

I swallow. I stayed over at Lizzy's on Sunday night when I told Jessica I was going to a hotel. I didn't fly to Berlin until the afternoon even though I pretended to Jessica that I was already there when she sent her text. I'd actually been sitting a few doors away. I could hardly tell her I had just rolled out of the neighbour's bed.

'I was with someone.'

'I thought you said you were at a conference in Berlin on Monday?'

'Yes, I was there by the evening dinner. I went a little late, catching a flight in the afternoon from Heathrow. Our neighbour rang me while I was queuing up at immigration in Germany to tell me the alarm was going off – that must've been when Jacob broke in.'

'The timeline isn't as clean as I would like. I'm not sure how close they've got to a confirmed time of death. All they are saying is Monday. They might argue you had the opportunity to take him the whisky, hit him over the head when he was incapacitated, and then left him to die.'

'My friend will vouch for the fact that we didn't get out of bed till noon.'

'I see.'

'And her call to me about the alarm should be on my phone register. It must've been a few hours later, at the end of the afternoon. I got her message when I landed.'

'So your alibi is the woman who lives a few doors down? Lizzy Huntingdon? The neighbour?'

'Yes. We're in a relationship, I suppose you'd say.'

'And did Jessica Bridges know?'

'I don't think so. I don't think she knows to this day. Lizzy didn't want to upset her.'

'And how would Jessica have reacted if she had found out?'

'I think she would've been upset but not surprised. She stepped out of line first.'

'Upset enough to collude with Jacob West to frame you?'

I shake my head. 'I don't think she has that kind of mindset. I'm sorry I suggested that. That's an unproductive line of enquiry.'

'Well, you're the expert.' She gives me another of her smiles and I feel a spark of attraction towards her. I've always been drawn to clever women. Even Jessica can hold her own in an intellectual conversation if she tries. 'This is what I'm going to do now, Michael: I'll get the police to decide if they are going to hold you any longer today.'

'They did mention restarting questions once you were here.'

'I'll shoot that down if I can. We need time to discuss your case in greater depth, particularly sorting out the confusion over the timings on Monday. If you were on a plane before the time of death, then I'd say they have to let you go.'

'My flight took off at four-fifteen. I would've been going through security about forty-five minutes before, as I had only carry-on luggage and obviously there's travel time to add to that.'

She makes a note. 'OK, I'll go and have a quick chat with them.'

I'm left waiting for another twenty minutes. My confidence that Miss Brightwell will represent my case competently has allowed my thoughts to move on to the secondary concern of what damage is being done to my reputation. I draft in my mind a statement for her to read out on my behalf – something serious and respectful of the police while projecting the subtext that they are wildly off course and complete idiots to pursue me, just because they like to put a celebrity in the hot seat. I wonder what Randall's charge-to-conviction percentages are? I don't think individual officers' records are publicly available but I might be able to pull a few strings and find out. He deserves a few dents to his image, as he's pissed on mine.

Miss Brightwell returns with Randall and Lloyd.

'I've agreed with the inspector that we will conclude the day's proceedings with a brief interrogation to establish your alibi for Monday, and then they will let you go, to resume tomorrow,' she murmurs, taking her seat beside me. 'I've stressed that you are cooperating fully with their requests to help with their enquiries.'

Randall goes through the recording protocol again and resumes his line of questioning. 'Dr Harrison, can you please give a detailed account of your movements from Sunday night until Tuesday morning?'

'Jessica and I arrived back from holiday at around eight in the evening.' I sound bored but I'm not. I'm twisted up with dread. Can I clear myself? 'We had had an argument so I needed some space from her. I was due at a conference in Berlin the next day, so I repacked my suitcase and left.'

'She can confirm this?' asks Lloyd.

'Yes, though she thinks I ordered a taxi to go to a hotel at Gatwick. I was actually flying from Heathrow and stayed overnight two doors down with a friend called Lizzy Huntingdon. Since my relationship with Jessica hit the rocks, we've been seeing each other – that's Lizzy and I.'

'You are lovers?'

'Yes.'

'What time did you leave on Monday?'

'Lizzy is a teacher so she's on holiday. We slept in on Monday and had a leisurely breakfast at about twelve. Oh, and yes, I answered a message from Jessica at about eleven, half past, it should be logged. I pretended I was in Berlin already as I did not want her to find out about Lizzy that way.' I take a sip of water. 'Right, OK, what next? I took a taxi to Heathrow.'

'Which company?'

'It was an Uber booking. The transaction should be on my phone too.'

'If you could leave the handset with us.'

I pull it out of my pocket and place it on the table, trying not to show my resentment. I don't think there's anything incriminating on there but there will certainly be some data that will embarrass me, certain messages that I'd prefer to keep private. 'I went through the usual procedures and was on the plane for take-off at 4.30. Miraculously, we took off on time.'

'So you left Miss Huntingdon around midday but weren't required at the gate until thirty minutes before departure. There seems to be some time unaccounted for in there.'

'I always leave a generous margin for flights. Ask anyone who knows my habits. It's my nature: I hate rushing for anything.'

'We only have Miss Huntingdon's word that the alarm went off late afternoon, as Miss Bridges says it was disarmed by the time she called in that evening.'

'Are you suggesting Lizzy lied?'

'I'm not suggesting anything but her relationship with you rather complicates her role in this. We will, of course, be talking to her.'

'Lizzy tried to contact me when I was in the air about the alarm. She couldn't locate Jessica and she didn't want to enter the house without permission. Others in the street must've heard it.'

'Yes, Dr Harrison, we know how to do our job. We are making door-to-door enquiries.'

Great: now my whole street will be talking about me. 'You know this is completely preposterous? Why would I want to kill Jacob West? We no longer had anything that connected us, no motive.'

'He might have gone public with his allegations against you, damaging ones even if they do not prove to be true. Fling enough mud and it sticks.'

'Of course they're not true – there's no "if" about it! And then I would've sued him for defamation, not killed him. If I murdered everyone I disagreed with, then half the psychologists in my field would be dead.'

'It was more than an intellectual disagreement.'

'That shows you don't understand the seriousness of academic debate. Careers are built and destroyed by it.'

Miss Brightwell clears her throat. 'Inspector, we are going off track here and it's getting late.'

'One more question: Dr Harrison, the nub of West's resentment against you revolves around your ex-wife—'

'Not ex-wife. I never divorced her. Emma died.'

'Sorry, I misspoke. Your wife and what appears to be her child, Kaitlin. Did she have a child?'

'Yes, before I met her.'

'Jacob's child?'

'Not according to Emma.'

'So who was the father?'

'I suggest you look for Kaitlin's birth certificate. All I know is that he wasn't on the scene when I met Emma. I respected her privacy over what had been a painful episode for her. She was trying to get away from Jacob so I wasn't going to keep on digging all that stuff up.'

'So where is Kaitlin now?'

'I don't know – and that's the truth.'

'That's not an adequate answer. Did the child die?'

'I suggest you use your investigative powers and find out what happened to her, if you believe it relevant.'

'I find it extraordinary that your wife didn't mention what happened to her daughter.'

'Inspector Randall, I believe my client has been clear with you,' says Miss Brightwell, cutting in before I can refute that. 'He is not Kaitlin's father so has no parental rights or responsibility for her. If the child went missing between Emma leaving Jacob and marrying Michael, then that's something you need to investigate, but it is not my client's business.'

That's not quite an accurate picture, as Kaitlin did live with us. I was a poor stepfather. I could fill in a few more blanks for them but it won't make a material difference in the end. Just now I'm not minded to make their job any easier.

'I assure you we will be investigating that, along with the

rest of the anomalies in this case. I sense you aren't giving us the complete story here, Dr Harrison.'

I hold his stare. Of course I'm not, you prick. Why would I when you've hung me out to dry by leaking my presence in the station?

He stands up, signalling that the meeting is finally at an end. 'That's it for now. We'll get in touch when we are ready to resume this conversation.'

'Direct your calls to me, please,' says Miss Brightwell.

'If that's what your client wants, then of course we will. Dr Harrison, I need hardly say you shouldn't attempt to leave London.'

'But I'm due in Washington next week.'

'I doubt this will have been cleared up by then. I'd be prepared to cancel.'

'But I'm giving the keynote speech! Don't you understand how important this is for my career and reputation?'

'I'm sorry, but that isn't my concern here. As I've already mentioned, murder comes first.'

'But this is outrageous!'

Miss Brightwell squeezes my elbow. 'I'll discuss this with my client and see if something can be done about the timing. However, thanks to the lamentable lapse in confidentiality in your station, I will need to escort my client out of a side entrance.'

'I hope you aren't blaming me for that?' asks Randall. 'Your client has frequently appeared on television. Anyone could've recognised him coming in here and worked out what he was doing.'

'I wasn't born yesterday, inspector. You are putting unfair pressure on my client, hoping he'll crack. The problem for you is that he is innocent and you have put yourself at risk of a claim for damages.'

I think I'm a little in love with Miss Brightwell. I almost break into a cheer.

Randall backs down. 'I have done no such thing. However, my officer will show you another exit.'

Arriving home, I discover the press are also camped out on my doorstep. I should've anticipated this. I am forced to make my way through them, head down.

'Dr Harrison, is it true you're involved in the murder of Jacob West – as a suspect?' shouts one reporter.

I can hear the cameras ticking away like a swarm of death-watch beetles. I've nothing to be ashamed of, so I lift my chin. 'No comment. If you will excuse me.' Crush them with polite-ness. I still want a television career once this is all over.

'Michael!'

'Dr Harrison!'

I let myself in and breathe a sigh of relief as the front door closes on the racket. The alarm is buzzing so I stir myself to punch in the code. It makes me think of Jacob West invading my house. The place now feels unclean. I go upstairs and get a shock when I enter my bedroom. Of course, the mattress. Had Lizzy been forced to fight her way through the press to get it delivered? What had the press made of that? They'll spin any little thing into a story.

I go to the phone and find the answer machine flashing. I

rarely use this number any more so hit playback with some trepidation.

'Michael, it's Jamie Newton from the principal's office at Royal Holloway. Can you give me a call? We're trying to put together a statement on the situation for the press.' He reels off his number.

I write it down but don't feel like embarking on that just yet.

The second message is from one of my colleagues – my head of department, Gerhart Junker. 'Hey, Michael, I'm hearing strange things about you. Had the police asking about our interviewees. Give us a call when you can so we can work out how to handle it.' His thoughts are entirely on damage limitation. To be fair, I'd be doing the same were the positions reversed.

The doorbell goes. I assume it is a ballsy member of the press, so I ignore it. I take down the rest of the messages, a variety of shocked colleagues and one from the organiser of the Washington conference, who must've been very on the ball to pick up the news on the gossip channels, as they have only just started their day in America. I can't face any of that now. I ring Lizzy.

'Michael! Oh my God, I'm so relieved. What's going on?'

'Long story.'

'I'll come over.'

'I'm afraid the press are camped outside.'

'Don't worry, I know a way.'

'It's not necessary.'

'Don't be silly. You need a hug.' And she puts the phone

down on me. I had called to tell her to keep away, not invite her in. I want to brood.

A minute later I hear a rapping at the back door. I go to open it and find Lizzy standing there looking mightily pleased with herself. She brushes off her hands.

'See, told you I had a way.'

'You climbed over the garden fences?' That meant trespassing in two other gardens.

'I did. Don't worry – no one saw me.'

I step back so she can come in. She's wearing a backpack, which she slings on the kitchen table and starts to empty.

'I made you some supper. I don't suppose you've eaten?'

'No, but I don't feel hungry.'

'You need to keep your strength up. And I've baked a cake.'

I want to shout in her face to get the hell out. The impulse is so close, I know I have to get away from her before I do something disgraceful. 'Thanks. I'll just go and have a bath. It's been a long day.'

'Good idea. Do you want me to find some scented candles? Jessica liked that kind of thing, didn't she? I can probably put my hands on some for you.'

'No candles. Just a bath.' I hurry upstairs before she can wind me up a further notch. A loss of temper with the tabloid press on my doorstep is the last thing I need right now.

Lying in the bath, I decide to ignore Randall's request and message Jessica on my tablet. No harm in rebuilding as many bridges there as possible, as I don't need someone willing to trash me to the press running around London right now.

I've heard about West. I apologise for doubting you but he

*tried hard to hide his tracks so you can see how it appeared.
You were taken in by a conman but it was my fault he targeted
you as he bore me a longstanding grudge. Do you want to meet
to talk things over?*

I press 'send' and wait for a reply until the bathwater goes
cold.

Chapter 28

Jessica, 17th August

I've discovered the petty joy of withholding communication. Before, in every relationship, including the one with Michael, I would always leap on texts and emails and fire back answers with the trigger-finger rapidity of a first-response unit called to an emergency. *Yes, let's meet for dinner. Of course I'll pick up your dry cleaning. No, I haven't forgotten we had plans for Saturday. It's fine, don't worry if you can't make it after all.* All those little pats and strokes to their egos, giving the (correct) impression that I was hanging on their every word. I've seen other women friends do it, texting after the one-night stand rather than waiting to see if the guy got in touch first, losing the chance to be the one playing hard to get, which would probably double their allure. So few of us manage dignity in our relationships.

Consider my surprise, then, when I did not immediately grab Michael's olive branch. I resisted impulse. I let it sit on the phone screen, the last in the chain of our messages. When I scrolled back through them I saw the record of a devolving relationship, his texts getting increasingly curt and annoyed with me, mine morphing from what I thought was amusing banter into abject pleas. I would've deleted the entire history but it appears the police might now need it for their enquiries. At least I had a win to end on, proof I've finally got a hold of myself and resisted the send button.

Last night on the London news I saw a segment on the Jacob West enquiry. They must be making Michael's life hell, photographing him so he looks like the serial killer everyone is whispering he is – hair blowing in the wind, eyes wild or half closed, the least flattering shot possible. He'll hate that. The police are still looking hard at Michael and the press knew this from the start, thanks to some loudmouth in reception. My money is on the sour receptionist. For lack of real evidence and Michael's uncharacteristic decision to keep out of the limelight, the media have gone after his family, friends and colleagues. His parents are fortunately out of reach in their retirement in a farmhouse in France with no wi-fi. I'm quite fond of them so I hope they are wandering their paths edged with lavender and olive trees, blissfully beyond the reach of the scandal. Michael's snobbish sister, Harriet, has appeared once, 'doorstepped' in Hampstead, I think they call it. She told them the allegations were rubbish and that her brother was the kindest man alive – this juxtaposed to one of the unflattering photographs. This endorsement is rich coming from her, as I know that they only see each other at annual family get-togethers convened by their uncle, the tedious retired judge in Hampshire. He gathers them at Christmas like a shepherd rounding up the sheep for a headcount and to see if any have dropped off a cliff over the summer on the hills. I wonder if she has actually contacted her brother to offer any sympathy? Michael's colleagues have all said anodyne comments about him being a valued colleague, the kind of lukewarm endorsement the prime minister gives someone just before they are reshuffled out of the cabinet. Even Charles wasn't as fulsome as I expected, claiming medical confidentiality as a reason for not talking about his friend. Since when has he been treating Michael? As for Michael's public appearances, these have been cancelled, including that one in Washington that he had been banging on about for months.

I can't feel sorry for him.

I won't feel sorry for him.

Now he knows what it is like to be me, floundering under a set of circumstances presented so as to make you look as ugly as possible.

The only two people who came out with anything approaching a warm defence of him were Lizzy and Mrs Jessop from next door. Lizzy told the press that Michael was a thoughtful and gentle man, a widower who wished to keep his personal life private, as was his right. There was no way he was involved in any act of violence. Mrs Jessop hobbled out on her walker and shouted at them that they should stop taking all the parking spots in the street and go and report on some real crimes for once.

I liked the bit about parking spaces, and so did the news crew, as it gave the scandal a domestic level that viewers could grasp. Murder is beyond most of us, but the frustration of not being able to park outside your own front door is right up there with potholes on urban agendas.

Drew came in from work at the tail end of the report. We have not been talking much. I know I am in the doghouse – I have spent most of my adult life there – but I thought he wouldn't hold out on me this long.

'They haven't dropped this yet?' he asked, going to the freezer to see what we could have for supper.

'Not yet.'

'It's not your fault. You did the right thing taking the laptop to the police.' He thought I was worrying about landing Michael in it – far from it. I was privately quite enjoying my ex's dilemma, and there was the issue of whether Jacob had stumbled on something with his suspicions. Michael might not be deserving of anyone's sympathy; he might be guilty of something. I still can't quite resolve what, as there seems to be a lot of smoke and little or no fire so far. The press have been ringing me to ask for my side of the story. I have to admit, their money for dishing the dirt is a terrible temptation. I've already probably blabbed too much to one of them who had a nice manner.

'I'm not blaming myself,' I said quietly. I was feeling a bit spaced out, as I've started taking Valium to help with my anxiety. Drew's GP was very understanding when I explained the circumstances. Was I slurring my words? I know that Drew wouldn't approve of my pill-popping, with his clean-living ethos.

'Good. I'll nuke this red sauce if you cook the spaghetti.'

That was about the warmest of our recent conversations.

We ate in silence with the TV taking the place of our voices and retired to separate rooms.

In the middle of this personal shit storm, I haven't forgotten that I arranged to meet my mother for lunch. The only way I can survive that is by a little medical boost so, buzzing with uppers, I am the most hyper person on the Central line. I smile manically at the Korean tourists, and at a weary Afro-Caribbean lady with worn shoes and what look like painful bunions. I offer help to a father with a fractious child in a pushchair. He is struggling to get out over a wide gap between platform and train while balancing nappy bag and too much shopping on the back. I bounce determinedly up the stairs at Tottenham Court Road only half an hour late. That's not bad for me. I've already told my mum to go ahead to the Greek restaurant she booked, so I find her sitting at a table in the window eating olives and looking quite anxious.

'Darling!' she cries on my arrival. 'You look energised, despite everything.'

I'm pretty much out of my head but we hug and then I sit down in the chair opposite her and order a glass of tonic and lemon. The new Jessica is not going to drink alcohol in the day. The new Jessica is going to be slim, beautiful and sensible. Fuck the new Jessica. 'Sorry, can I change that order, make it a G and T?'

'Of course, madam.' The server glides off to do waitery things at the bar.

'Despite what, Mum? My life's just tickety-boo. A real laugh a minute.' God, get a hold on yourself, Jessica.

'So you're not cut up about breaking up with Michael, and finding a dead body, and him being a suspect in murder?' She lays a hand over mine to stop its restless tapping.

The waiter, who is serving my drink, spills it on the cloth, overhearing this. 'I'm so sorry. Let me get you another, miss.'

'It's only a little spillage. Leave it.' I smile up at him. He looks rather startled to find me so sanguine in the face of death and backs away quickly.

'You are far better off without Michael.' Mum taps her glass to mine. 'Let's drink then: to happy endings.'

'That's not exactly appropriate, Mum, seeing about the body in the mix, but who cares?' I echo her toast.

'I remember how I felt after leaving your father. It was like the weight of the world had dropped off my shoulders.'

My father, that grumbling beast of a man in his lair. 'Is he still alive, as far as you know?' Fuck him.

'How would I know, darling? All connections cut. If there's anyone he'd get in touch with, it would be you.'

'No, I divorced him too. Unparented him, I suppose is more accurate.'

'I wondered if you'd ever get back in touch, but I think I'm pleased you didn't. He wouldn't understand you and I can't imagine him being good for you.'

'Neither can I, so I'm leaving well alone.'

'So how is the new man? Drew? I imagine he would be a generous lover. He has the look.'

'Mother, I am not talking about my sex life with you.'

'I'm your mother – you can tell me anything.'

'Not this. Besides, we're not... it's complicated.' The window behind her is dissolving into diamonds. Christ, I've overdone the pills this time. It's like being inside a kaleidoscope.

'Darling...'

I grip the cold steel of a fork to anchor myself. 'Did you talk to your mother about sex?'

She frowns. 'You have a point. I don't think my mother knew what it was. I must have been conceived by immaculate conception. I think she was too mortified to raise the subject with me. Fortunately, it was the Seventies and I don't think I was a total failure between the sheets. I learnt quite a few things from magazines.'

'Can we change the subject already?' I gulp some water. No, actually, it was the gin and tonic. The buzz blurs a little.

My mum is frowning now. 'I'm sorry, I don't meant to pry, but I've always worried about you. You never had it easy and always kept the worst away from me, I suspect.'

She is right about that. 'I made some bad choices growing up – I still make bad choices.'

'But Drew is a good choice?'

'I think so. But I've messed up already. I think he wants shot of me.'

'Why do you think that? Has he told you to leave?'

'Not yet.'

'Then don't borrow trouble. I can see how Michael might not be able to live with you, but have you not asked whether it might not be his fault rather than yours? That some people can't stand living in your light for too long?'

'My light?'

'You have a positive, sunny disposition. Old curmudgeons

like Michael think they like it, but really they prefer to mope around in the shade where their imperfections aren't exposed.'

This is unexpectedly deep from my mother. 'How do you know this?'

'It's your father and me all over again. Why do you think I married him? He thought he liked what he saw and then he went off what I had to offer. That's not my fault, is it? I didn't change; he did.'

'Actually, I think he was always a domineering bastard. If he presented another side of himself to reel you in, it was only a disguise put on over his true nature.'

'I'd prefer it if you didn't use that kind of language, even about your father. Maybe he was always domineering, but I was lonely with a young child to support, easily persuaded.'

The waiter returns with a selection of starters and pitta bread to dip.

'Jessica, I've been saving up something until I saw you in person. I want to apologise.' Mum isn't eating, which isn't like her.

'What for?'

'For not doing better by you when you were a teenager.'

'What's brought this on?'

'I'm going to see a spiritual director and one of the steps is to make things right with those you have wronged.'

'A what? Mum, you're not getting caught up in something weird, are you?' Any scam, any cult trawling for followers, and my impressionable mum is very likely to fall for it. Miriam says Mum gets drifts of charity requests, as she feels she has to give to everyone who writes to her with a sob story. 'You haven't given them any money, have you?'

'I'll have you know that it's not weird! Her name is Dorothy and she comes highly recommended by my local vicar.'

'Oh.'

'It's all very normal these days. The church seems to take faith more seriously than it did when I was a girl, when it revolved around jumble sales and gossip.'

'Well, I suppose that makes sense, as people don't go for social reasons so much. If they just want to hang out with other people, they go running or cycling now on Sunday mornings – the new fanatics. Or have an allotment.'

Mum nods. She understands my thought processes so isn't disturbed by my tangents. 'Anyway, my spiritual director is a trained relationship counsellor and she's helped me sort through some of my issues.'

'Sounds like I could do with her.'

Mum takes me seriously. 'Oh, do you want me to ask if she's got a space? But she lives so far away. I could ask if she knows anyone closer.'

'Mum, I was being flippant. But I'm pleased she's helping you.' And I'm far beyond the help of anyone recommended by a local vicar.

'I have known for a long while that you ran away because I failed to stand between you and your father.'

'You had a breakdown.'

'I know that too, but I still feel responsible. Was it so very bad, those months on your own?'

I could lie, I suppose, but Mum is trying to be honest with me. Blame it on the drink, or the drugs, but I find it all tumbles out. 'Yes, it was bad. It was mostly my fault, though. I could've gone to Miriam, couldn't I? Instead I ended up sleeping rough – not far from here. I spent half of the time out of my head on whatever I could get my hands on – alcohol mainly.'

'Oh, darling...'

'Don't say anything, Mum. You might as well hear it all, as I hope this is the last time we have to talk about it. I had sex quite a few times while drunk. I can see now that it was a kind of rape as I didn't give consent, but somehow on the streets it's easy to think you don't have rights, that you have to do what someone tells you.' The waiter returns to clear plates, fortunately halting my confession. Mum doesn't need to hear that they sometimes paid me, those men. See, I was a kind of sex worker even though I had no idea what it was all about, just fell from one crisis to the next. I don't even remember much about the sex, except that I didn't like it. It left me feeling second-best – used – and that's something I've struggled with all my life. I've never told any of my partners about this.

Mum is looking ashen. 'Oh, I didn't know, though I suppose I feared the worst.'

I'm beginning to feel tired as well as drunk. I'm coming down from the high I've been cruising. Part of me wants to lay my head on the table and sleep right there among the crumbs. 'But you understand how it happens, don't you, Mum? Your own marriage was a bit like that – abusive. I thought that was normal. I thought I had to do what I was told.'

She starts to sob. Alarmed, I reach out and cradle her hand in mine. 'Ssh, I didn't tell you to upset you. I'm fine now.' Mostly. 'When you think back to that time, you have to remember you got out of that bad place and made a home for me to come back to. I've got stuff I need to sort out but you know something? If I can get my act together, I could be with someone who sees the good in me. That's if he'll forgive me.'

She takes out a little pack of tissues and wipes her face. 'He will. He won't be able to resist you.'

'Maybe.' I go back to eating, making some silly comments about Greek food to give her time to recover. In the back of my mind, though, I'm working through what I just admitted about Drew. I've had relationships before and messed them up. Now I've reached a crossroad: I've got to do something to win him back.

'You look like you've made up your mind about something,' says Mum, taking some of the bread.

'Yes, I have. I'm going to make a new start. Drew's been telling me that Michael isn't guilty and though I think I agree with him, in my heart of hearts I've left Michael in the lurch. I've even thought about talking to the press for the money.'

Mum doesn't say anything. Her disapproval is conveyed by her expression, like I'd just handed her a lemon to suck.

'But I know if I did, Drew would think badly of me – I would think badly of me, and maybe that's more important?'

She nods. 'So horrid, all those people telling the press things that should be private. It's good you're no longer with that man but you don't need to crow about it in public.'

'And I might even be able to help Michael. There are things I know about the allegations that no one else does; there are ways in which I can help.'

'Does he deserve that?'

'Probably not.' I smile and she smiles back at me.

'I'm proud of you, darling.'

'Well, that's a start, isn't it?'

Chapter 29

Waving my mother off to join her party at the theatre, I answer Michael's text at long last. I spend about half an hour deciding on what turns out to be just six words.

Do you still want to talk?

The answer pings back immediately. *Yes, but not here. Press outside. Can you meet me at the café at the Royal Institution?* This is one of Michael's favourite little haunts just off Piccadilly, missed out by most tourists, who are drawn instead to the flashier pleasures of the Ritz and the Royal Academy.

I decide to walk as he has to travel in from Battersea. Another resolution of the new Jessica is to get fit so that I'm not so embarrassed by my body and the extra pounds sitting on my hips. The problem about living with a man as lean and toned as Drew is that I feel like a hippo by contrast – a small one admittedly, but I'm built more for comfort than speed.

I can't be thinking of Drew while meeting Michael. That's just awkward. Is there some etiquette for this situation? Should I tell Drew what I'm doing?

I stop by Nelson's lions, speculating how the tourists

managed to get up on their huge black backs without breaking a neck.

Focus, Jessica. Drew. I picture him at work. Would he want to be bothered by a message in the middle of some solemn service? Why not? Solemn is an everyday occurrence for him. He's likely to be standing outside. I owe it to Drew to tell him what's going on in my muddled head or he might take it the wrong way.

I tap out a quick message. *Decided to clear the air with Michael and possibly help him establish his innocence re girls. Meeting him in a café. See you back at home.* I send it with a slightly wobbly feeling in my stomach.

His answer comes back. *OK.*

Men! What does that mean? I look down and see that he's still typing. *You're doing the right thing.*

Is that a little crack in his Arctic displeasure? I can only hope so.

Michael has arrived before me. He's chosen a table in one of the side rooms where he's least likely to be spotted. The Institute has the air of an eighteenth-century gentleman's club, neo-classical decor and a sense of exclusivity. It's actually open to the public and involved in science education, but that's all down in the basement with fun push-button displays and Faraday's laboratory with its early electrical experiments. Up here you could pretend you might bump into Beau Brummell or Sheridan while gambling the country estate on the turn of a card. Michael gets up as I arrive. It's funny – the last time he was red-faced with anger, now he is all politeness. It reminds me how many different sides we all have – or are they a series of masks? If we kept on taking them off until we reached the real us, would there be anything left?

'What can I get you? Latte? Hot chocolate?' he asks.

'No, green tea please.'

'*Green* tea?'

I might as well have said the blood of virgins, for all his amazement. 'Yes.'

He looks like he is going to say something, resists and heads off to place my order. He comes back with a little silver teapot and glass rattling on the tray.

'I assume you don't want milk?'

'That's right.'

We busy ourselves with our respective drinks.

'So?' I say.

'So.' He pushes his black coffee aside. 'Thanks for coming to meet me.'

I almost apologise for taking so long to respond to his message but force myself to say nothing. Instead I smile quizzically.

'I... I was told by the police not to contact you.'

'Uh-oh, are they going to jump out from behind the potted palm and arrest us both?'

'Possibly – probably.' He smiles and I suddenly remember what it was I saw in him at the beginning, a certain wry humour that clicked with my more ridiculous flights of fancy. 'I decided that it was more important that I told you in person that I'm sorry my past got you caught up with Jacob West.'

'Not your fault. He was obsessed.'

'He managed to dig up just enough links between me and

those girls he had you investigating to make the police suspicious. It's been hell, trying to disprove timelines and possibilities from months, years ago. I can't remember any of them. You believe me, don't you?'

I nod. I think I do, but what if I'm just falling for another man's fantasy? In this one he is innocent. No point saying that out loud though. 'I was there at the Margate event myself. I've no idea who was handing round the drinks.'

'That's what I mean. They've dug up CCTV footage showing me on the same platform as the girl from Harrogate, Lillian something.'

'Lillian Bailey.'

'Apparently we got into the same carriage, but I don't go round picking up stray young women on intercity trains. I get my head down and do some work, if I've got a seat.'

He does talk to them at spas though, according to Emma. 'Look, Michael, I wouldn't be surprised if you did strike up conversations with good-looking women – that's not a crime. But I don't believe there's anything in Jacob's allegations against you and I think I can help. If we clear away that fog, then the police will be able to look more fairly at the evidence linking you to the crime scene.'

Michael tops up my tea for me. 'Thanks. It's the prints on the whisky bottle that are the problem, but you know that he could've got that from our drinks cabinet and planted it.'

I nod again. I hadn't known about this but it makes sense now why they were so focused on Michael. 'I thought it had to be something like that when the police were interested in what I had touched in the house.' I'm relieved Michael doesn't appear to know that I was the one who cracked the laptop password and got him into all this. I doubt he'd be sitting so politely opposite me if that were the case.

Michael toys with a sugar packet. 'Someone like Jacob was bound to have other enemies. He was a campaigner when I heard about him six, seven years ago. He tried to live an impossibly pure carbon-neutral life, chained himself to power stations, raided animal laboratories to let minks out into the wild and so on. But so far the police seem fixated on me as their number one suspect. What about his equally lunatic mates? What if one of them decided to kill him over who had the last mung bean? Or the dark forces of globalisation – that's what West would've expected, though I'm not convinced they'd be the least threatened by a small player like him. Whoever it was – if it was anyone – all I know is that it wasn't me.'

I make soothing uh-huh sounds.

'I'm going crazy stuck at home. You get to learn who your friends really are when something like this happens. I have to say most of them have behaved like rats leaving a sinking ship.'

'But I saw Lizzy speak out about you to the press. And Mrs Jessop. That was nice of them.'

Michael looks grim for a moment. 'Yes, Lizzy has been a good friend over all this. I've been coming in and out over the back gardens and through her house when I don't want to face the press.'

I resist the impulse to laugh. It shouldn't be funny to think of Michael reduced to such moves, but it is.

'The past few days have made me appreciate you, Jessica,' he says, striking an unexpectedly intimate note. 'I'm sorry about how I treated you the last few months. I think West was messing with our relationship too, and wanted me to distrust you.'

It was more than that, but if he wanted to explain away our couple's meltdown then I'd let him. 'Yes, he didn't want you to find happiness, did he, not after Emma?'

'I'm glad you agree.'

His smugness annoys me. It no longer works as it once had for me. 'I always did agree too quickly with you.'

Michael frowns and checks his watch. 'What do you mean?'

'Come on, Michael, when we met you were my tutor, I your adoring grad student. We had sex rather than tutorials, which you told me suited us both.' We'd been a cliché, now I think about it. I'd been playing out some kind of *Fifty Shades* fantasy of the powerful man and the submissive acolyte, not part of my sexual psyche that I like to look at in the light of day. The first time I'd seen Michael in his study to discuss my dissertation, I felt like I'd been punched in the midriff, so strong was the pull between us. He lounged on the sofa, arms on the back, legs spread, a glorious lion of a man, oozing power and sexual appeal. I took one sniff and I was preening, hormones going haywire, crossing and uncrossing my legs, pleased I'd worn nude tights and a short skirt. Any observer would have read our mating routine. It's a scene set to a David Attenborough voiceover in my memory. But I can recall the rush even now, feel a little sorry for myself: it was primal – mad. Soon Michael took off his jacket, turned the key in the lock and we were putting the sofa to other uses. After a few years, though, the glow faded. The problem about relationships where you make yourself so vulnerable is that your partner has to be strong in the right way. Michael, it transpires, is as fucked up as Christian Grey.

'We both enjoyed it,' he says stiffly.

Why am I the only one ever to be in the wrong in our partnership? 'You know it was unprofessional, right? You could've lost your job if I'd told anyone.'

'But you didn't and I made it OK when I asked you to move in with me.'

'Only just before too many brows were raised about our afternoon love-fests. There're no secrets in a university department and you always say academics are the worst gossips.'

'But we became an official couple.' He makes it sound as if that wipes clean any previous stain on his honour.

What was the point of arguing about this? 'We did. I even got my Masters, which was a small miracle considering I did all the research on my own with next to no guidance.'

'I helped you.'

'No, actually, Michael, you didn't, but let's not go there now. We've got far more serious things to sort out than that. Can you explain some of it to me? Why did Jacob know her as Ali and where is Kaitlin? I read a few pages of her diary. Is Kaitlin the same as Katy?'

The effect of my questions is immediate. Michael closes up, like a sea anemone prodded by a stick. 'Sorry, there are some things that I promised Emma I would never talk about. I can tell you what I told the police: that Ali was her middle name. She reverted to Emma when she left him. She was trying to shake him off.'

Such loyalty to a dead woman. It reminds me that the main problem in our relationship had been the ghost of her perfection drawing attention to my inadequacies.

'I guess that's an admirable attitude, Michael, but if telling the truth would clear you with the police, don't you think she would prefer you to do so?'

He shrugs. 'But these things really have nothing to do with West's death. And Kaitlin isn't a part of this at all and shouldn't be dragged into it. I didn't kill him, though one idea is that he tried to make it look that way. I'm thinking he was suicidal – or at least self-destructive in his behaviour – and this was his last unanswerable attempt to ruin my life. I have to say he's made a good job of it.'

'Do you know any more about how he died?'

'He took the overdose and hit his head while staggering about the place – or someone staged it that way. Though I prefer to believe it's the first – that he was suicidal. If he read Emma's diary, he would've realised she never loved him like he imagined. That could've made him flip.'

That sounds possible. My phone pings.

Finished with the ex yet?

I am pleased that Drew is a little jealous, enough to send me a text when he knows I must be sitting opposite the last guy. *Heading home soon.*

Michael tries to look like he wasn't just attempting to read my screen upside down. 'Everything OK?'

'Yes. I'd better travel back before the worst of the rush hour.'

'Thanks for coming. I appreciate it.'

'Oh, I almost forgot to say: I can help.'

'You can? How?'

'By finding the missing girls. I know you thought my job wasn't real but I truly did research them and their patterns. I think I can find at least one of them. If I do that, and she's alive and well, then Jacob's accusations can be discounted.'

He swallows, his expression showing that he is genuinely moved by me for once. 'I'd be really grateful if you could.'

'But it would help if you were entirely honest with me.'

He holds my gaze for a moment. 'Can any of us survive complete honesty, Jessica?'

Chapter 30

Jessica, 18th August

'Am I sure I want to do this?' I'm reduced to talking to myself as, with no handy sidekick, I have to take both parts: intrepid detective and sceptical follower, Sherlock and Watson. I am standing outside a launderette across the road from the Nine Elms supermarket in Vauxhall, at the address I dug up for Lillian Bailey. It's a depressing place as half the shops in this little terrace are boarded up and the rest look like they are holding on by the barest fingernail to the ledge of breaking even. With the river not far away, a main road into London, the railway into Waterloo on a viaduct, and low-flying aircraft lining up to land at Heathrow, this area could be an illustration for a child's book on planes, boats and trains. Lillian had a friend from Harrogate who lives here – or did a couple of years ago – but the odds are that they've probably moved on and I will be knocking on the door of a complete stranger.

'Now I'm here, it's worth a try.' I press the bell for the first-floor flat.

The door release buzzes. Almost missing the opportunity, I push it open. 'Trusting sort.'

I head up the stairs. The stairway is cluttered with various items of child-related equipment – a pram, a couple of dinky three-wheeled scooters, and a collapsible pushchair. I knock on the door at the top. A young woman throws it open, little blond child on her hip, another one hanging on her leg.

'Oh. Who are you?'

I take a step back, deciding I'll look less threatening if I don't crowd her. I trip over a scooter and almost take a head-first plunge down the steps, but save myself just in time.

Heart racing, I clutch my chest. 'Shit. Sorry. Didn't mean to swear in front of the kids.'

The woman waves that off. 'No problem. I'm sorry we almost killed you with the kids' booby traps.'

'Look, you're obviously busy...' I begin.

She laughs. 'Six o'clock – full-on child time – tea, bath, wrestle them into bed. I thought you were... never mind that: what do you want?' The baby tugs at her hair and manages to grab her glasses. 'Stop that, pet.'

I'm already awed by her. She's quite a few years younger than me but obviously far more competent. 'Are you Ellen Trott?'

'Yes.'

'Great. I'm looking for Lillian Bailey. She might've stayed here a year ago when she arrived in London?'

Her expression gives away that it isn't exactly good news she has to share. 'Lillian? You're the second person to come asking for her – there was a guy a few weeks ago. Like I told him, she was only here for a short while.'

That had to be Jacob. 'She's not kept in touch?'

'No, we weren't really close. We just had the same foster parent for a time, though I was a couple of years older so didn't run with her crowd.' She sizes me up. 'What are you wanting with her? She's not in trouble, is she?'

'It's nothing like that. I work for a small agency tracing missing persons. Her friends back in Harrogate are worried for her. They just want to be reassured she's OK.'

'Glad she kept some friends, at least. Lillian was always blind to a good thing and took the hard route when there was an easier one.'

'Really?'

The young mum is interested now and is in a mood to confide. 'Completely. Take our foster parent, Jane – she was one of those rare people in the system, a great woman, mother to the world. But Lillian didn't like her. She thought she was too bossy; funny that, because I made Jane my role model. I suppose it takes all sorts, and Lillian had never had anyone give her boundaries before. Oh, the arguments that caused!' She turns around. 'Tyson, do not hit your sister! No point denying it – I can hear you.' She grimaces. 'Boundaries are golden. And it's true what Jane said: that when you have kids you grow eyes in the back of your head. Look, I need to get back to do crowd control.'

'I won't keep you. Do you know where Lillian lives now?'

'Sorry, as I said, we've lost touch. She found the children too much. Didn't stay long. Surfed the sofa for a couple of days then announced that she had a better offer from a posh guy with money.' A wail breaks out from behind her.

'Is there anything you can tell me about her? Any clue as to where she ended up?'

Ellen is already turning away. 'Like I told the last guy: try that nightclub, Vaults, I think the name is. She was working there at one point. Should warn you though, it's one of those sex clubs – lap dancing and so on.'

'Great.' I grimace at the thought of trawling for information in a place like that.

'Don't go in on your own. You might not come out.' The door closes.

Lillian ran off with a posh guy with money? Michael? I shouldn't jump to conclusions. I suppose he could've picked her up on the train and then offered to set her up in some kind of love nest, but it doesn't really sound like him. From her photo, Lillian is pretty but no match for the sainted Emma, and he still had me at the time she went missing. He didn't need to pay someone for sex – though I could see him digging a lap dance. It was more likely to be some totally different guy who flashed his cash at the nightclub.

Back on the street, I look up the club. It is in a backstreet in Soho, ironically not that far from my old office. Unless I want to beg a very strange favour from Lizzy, I have no choice but to go alone as my menfolk have all disowned me. I ring her but get passed to answerphone. This isn't something about which I can leave a message to explain. Looks like it'll just be me then. It is too early yet to visit a lapdancing club so I decide to find somewhere cheap to grab a coffee and wait. I don't have the money to stretch that to a meal.

Dreaming over a bitter cappuccino at a McDonalds on

Oxford Street, I try to puzzle my way through my cloudy future. I have got to stop sponging off other people, come up with a way of earning my living. Fortunately, I haven't heard a squeak from Khan's men so I'm hoping the police have set him straight about Jacob's fraud. It was spelt out in his computer files. That's a good break for me but it doesn't stop my credit score being rock bottom. I'm just not a good bet for anyone to invest in or give a job to.

As the Mickey D crowd changes from pre-theatre to post-theatre, then clubland goers, I stand up and smooth down my skirt, telling myself to be professional and confident. Go in, ask a member of staff for information, then get out without embarrassing myself: that's the goal.

Vaults turns out, rather logically you might say, to be in the cellar of a building on Meard Street. At street level, the house, which has been converted into offices, looks like a set for a Dickens film – the kind of place Scrooge could uncheerfully inhabit with Marley for a doorknocker. From a quick look at the advertisements outside I'd say Vaults skirts the line between night- and sex-club, promising floorshows and burlesque entertainment. I wish in vain that I could be six-foot, well-built and male, going out after hours with some mates. In those circumstances, then this could be fun. As it is, I'm left with just me and not very much cash to buy a drink. The bouncers give me a quick scan and wave me past the barrier and down the steep stairs. Disorientatingly, I find myself in an ultra-modern bar and dance floor, black and silver the predominant colours, not a scrap of Victoriana in sight.

I want to feel more competent than I do. I've seen scenes like this in films. The private eye goes up to the bar, strikes up a conversation with the server and slides the right tip across to get the necessary information, all without breaking a sweat. I'm already nervous and put off by the fact that the bar reaches breast-height and there are scantily dressed women gyrating around strategically placed poles. As I watch, one hen party throws caution to the winds and gathers around a set of three poles. Ellen hadn't been quite right about lap dancing; it's become one of those clubs where you can give it a go yourself – a kind of an exotic-dancer karaoke. With much giggling the girls start to bump and grind – not exactly the sexiest thing I've ever seen, done mainly to impress each other. The professionals are giving them a hard look but aren't threatened. A party like that isn't after their customers.

'Can I give you a hand up?' A heavy-breathing businessman in a dark suit notices I'm having difficulty getting on to one of the teetering stools.

'Thanks.' I'm not meeting his eye. He won't be getting any encouragement from me.

'Can I get you a drink?'

Damn, he is trying to pick me up, despite my Greta Garbo body language. 'Thanks, but I'm waiting for someone.'

'Shame. Well, if you change your mind.' His eyes are on my cleavage rather than my face. I remember only now that I left home in a tight black skirt-suit and heels, going for professional when I visited Ellen. Here it looks like a costume. The secretary will see to you now, sir.

239

I look a little desperately for the barmaid. The music is going to make it almost impossible to have a subtle conversation.

'Look, let me get you a drink while you're waiting.' The guy won't give up. He summons the barmaid on the first attempt.

'No, really.'

'What will you have? Let me guess: champagne?'

'Champagne?' I'm so surprised, I don't intervene in time to stop the order being placed.

'Shall I add it to your tab, Mr Tudor?' asks the barmaid.

'Yes, thanks, Maeve. You'll have some champagne with me, won't you? Isn't that what Miss Golightly drinks?'

Shit, it's Khan's lawyer, the man I ran from all those days ago. The wrong side of fifty, grey hair perilously close to a comb-over, with a bit of mean in his expression. I find him a little scary and quite a lot seedy. 'I don't know what you're talking about.'

'Miss Bridges, please don't insult my intelligence. You are very memorable. I haven't had such an exciting morning since... can't say when. Losing you in Ann Summers – that was a nice touch.'

'But you must know by now about the fraud...'

'That's still to be tested in court. As far as my client is concerned, you still owe him five thousand pounds.'

'What? That's absurd. I didn't sign the lease.'

'And your defence is that a dead man did so fraudulently. What a pity he can't back your story.'

That doesn't sound good. 'Look, the police have Mr Wrath's notes about this. He admitted it. I don't want any trouble.'

'Then why come here, right into one of Mr Khan's properties? I thought you had to be looking for me – or him – to
make a deal.'

'No, no, that's not why I'm here.'

The barmaid delivers a bottle and two glasses. Mr Tudor
serves us both and mockingly toasts me. 'Bottoms up.'

I gulp half the glass. 'I'm really sorry about Jacob Wrath
but it's not my fault he ended up dead before paying for the
office.'

'We can talk about that later.' Smiling with shark-like intent,
he loosens his tie and undoes his top button. 'Maybe we can
help each other. Why are you here?'

'It's for the missing persons thing I do. I'm looking for
someone, Mr Tudor – I've had a tip that she might work here.'

'Call me Max. What's her name?'

'Um, Lillian Bailey?'

He raps on the bar, bringing the server straight back. 'Is
there a girl called Lillian Bailey on the staff?'

I feel the need to explain my interest as the barmaid looks
cagey. 'I'm asking not because she's in trouble or anything,
but her friends back where she came from just want to know
she's OK. That's all – she doesn't have to get in touch with
them.'

The maid wipes the bar. 'I don't know anyone with that
name.'

'She might not be using it. She's got a Yorkshire accent and
looked like this a few years ago.' I show her a photo on my
cracked phone screen.

She taps the screen with a lethal fingernail. 'I've seen that

241

before. A guy came in here a couple of weeks ago and flashed it around.'

I bet that was Jacob. 'What did you tell him?'

'The same as I'll tell you. That's her, over there.' She points to a blonde hanging out with some other women in a corner. Lillian Bailey used to be a sweet-faced brunette. 'That's Lily, one of our dancers.'

'Thanks.'

'So what are you going to do now?' asks Mr Tudor – Max – holding out a hand as I make to get off the stool.

'Just have a chat with her.'

'Take the champagne and a clean glass. My compliments.'

'Um, OK. Good idea.'

'I'll keep your seat warm for you.' He is still trying to pick me up.

I cross the floor, conscious of his eyes on me. 'Lillian, can you spare me a moment?'

Her eyes flick to the door in shock at hearing her name.

'I just want to talk.'

'How did you find me?'

'Want some?' I pour her a glass and set it down on the high table between us. 'It's with Mr Tudor's compliments.'

'You know Max?'

'We've met once or twice.' That seems to settle her.

'OK, I'll have a drink with you. What's this about?' She takes the flute and sips it appreciatively. 'He's sent the good stuff.'

I'm mentally adding up her age. She's only twenty and this place is supposed to be for over-twenty-ones only. It's been a rough road for the trusting teen who left Harrogate wanting something better, and I can probably guess most of the bumps along the way.

'Yeah, he's a generous man, obviously. My name is Jessica Bridges. I have a small business tracing missing persons.' As I'm making most of this up as I go along, I thought I'd just promote myself to boss. 'I find people but only on the strict understanding that if they don't want to be found, I won't tell anyone where they are. All I do is pass on reassurances that they are safe and well.'

'Who cares a fuck where I am?' She raises the glass to bee-stung lips. There's just a hint of the bruised teenager under the hard shell she has acquired.

'Your friends from Harrogate. Gina Tilbury mentioned you to me – I contacted her via Facebook. And I saw Ellen Trott earlier today.'

'God, Ellen, knee-deep in nappies still?'

'Yes. It looks like hard work being a mum.'

'But I bet she's good at it?'

'Yeah, she's got it covered.'

'I should go round and see her.' I don't get the feeling she will. She is saying that to seem normal to me.

'I'm sure she'd appreciate that. So, you're OK?'

'As you can see. Fine.'

'You've a job here?'

She shrugs, a roll of her bony shoulders in her sparkly halter top. 'It's not a bad place. Management look after you.' She glances towards Max again. He gives her a nod.

'And somewhere to stay?'

'Yeah, look, you're not my mother or anything, so I don't have to tell you this stuff.'

'No, you don't. But I know people in Harrogate who would love a text, or even a postcard if you don't want them getting back in touch, just something to say you're OK. They've let themselves think the worst.'

This piques her interest. 'Like what?'

'Like you're lying dead in a ditch somewhere.'

'Shit, they don't, do they?' She gives a horrified laugh and polishes off the rest of her glass.

'You've gone radio silent for over a year. They've started a campaign on Facebook to find you. Will you do that for them?'

She refills both of our flutes then stares into the bubbles of her drink. 'OK. I'll let them know.'

'Just one more question. Have you ever met this man?' I show her a picture of Michael.

She shrugs. 'I meet hundreds of guys each week.'

'But you'd remember this one. He was on the same train as you when you left Harrogate.'

'Was he? I didn't talk to anyone. Why? What's he done?'

'Very possibly, nothing.' I tuck the phone away, feeling I've got my drink's worth of information from her. 'And if you want out of this,' I gesture to the club, 'there are places that can help.'

Her expression hardens again. 'Fuck off, I'm fine. Nothing wrong with dancing for a living.'

That was a misstep. 'Sorry, I just meant... Look, let's finish this bottle.' We've both now put a few away and I'm feeling a great deal more relaxed. She's right. It's not so bad here, sort of sexy and fun. 'I put my foot in it all the time, saying the wrong thing.'

She grins, looking briefly her true age. 'I'm getting that about you. But I'm good at it – the dancing.'

'I bet you are.'

'It's not easy.' She gestures to the hen party. 'Most people end up looking like a dog humping a leg. You have to remember to tease, not tell.'

Could be my new motto. 'Sounds like you've had training.'

'From the girls here. They've been great.' Her glance meets Max again across the room and takes on a mischievous glitter. 'I'll make a deal with you: I'll send that postcard if you give it a go.'

'What? Jeez, I'm not drunk enough for that.'

She pours what's left of her drink into mine. 'Go on, drink up. Don't be embarrassed. Everyone's doing it.'

Even in my befuddled state, I get what she's doing: she's getting back at me for my suggestion that she might need saving. She thinks I consider myself superior and wants us on level pegging. It's not that I'm reluctant; I have few inhibitions; I'm just clueless how to go about it.

She sees I'm thinking about it. 'I won't contact them if you don't.'

No one will ever say I back down from a challenge like that. Palming a couple of pills, I swallow them and the contents of the glass in one. 'OK, you're on. Give me your promise first.'

She laughs. 'You're really going to do it? I didn't think you would.'

'Yeah, and I'll probably look like a labrador with an optimistic urge, but what the hell? Who cares? I'm ridiculous enough as it is and I get a result – a case closed.'

'I promise. Now you do your side.'

'How long do I have to dance for it to count?'

'One song – that's all. I'll look after your stuff. Take off the jacket.'

'Prepare, Miss Bailey, to be amazed.'

To Lily's hoots and whistle, I approach the pole. Whatever I do, I won't look as bad as the bridal party. Tease, don't tell. And, damn, I don't want to admit this, but it appeals to Uninhibited Me, the one who had sweaty sex with Michael within five minutes of meeting him. I roll my shoulders, unbutton my blouse a little, and begin to dance. I've pretended enough at home with the broom, but doing it for real in front of others gives me a real charge. Some of the punters drift over to see what the crazy lady is up to. I give them a shimmy and a flick of the high heels. I can see Lily applauding and laughing. Max has joined her and is now pouring more champagne. He offers me some and I reach down and take a gulp then, really going for it, pour some down my cleavage, much to the approval of the people gathered to watch my amateur act. I'm getting hot, and very drunk. I make love to that pole, channelling all my sexual frustration into it – it becomes Michael making me feel unlovable, Drew thinking I abused a boy. Believe what you want, guys. I don't care if you consider me a slut because this is fun. I can run rings round you.

The song ends and I get a raucous round of applause. I stagger a little coming off the stage.

'So you're not so stuck up as I thought,' says Lily. She hands me back my handbag and takes over on the pole. 'I'll send the postcard.'

Seeing me weaving, Max puts an arm around my shoulders and steers me over to a booth. 'That was most entertaining. I'm pleased to see you don't just run through Ann Summers but also shop there.' He flicks the next button to reveal a little more of my black lace bra. 'So, Jessica, shall we have that talk about how I might help you out of your predicament?'

There are at least three of him. 'I'm not sure I'm following you – any of you.' I focus on the one in the middle.

'Oh, I think you are. Let's take this somewhere quieter.'

So I have sex with him. That's not a surprise, seeing how the night is going. I don't really want to do it – he isn't my type, too smarmy and frankly too old, with a little belly once he has his clothes off – but it seems the best of my bad options. He explains that he occasionally helps out special clients if they are nice to him. Being nice to him means going upstairs to his office which is in the same building. We take the champagne and play naughty secretary and horny boss. I suppose that part is OK and I get off a couple of times as he bends me over his desk and makes another joke about bottoms up. I'm still oiled by the champagne at this point, so I find the kink a thrill. It is the more conventional round two on the sofa with us both naked that makes me feel like a skank. I suppose the drink and buzz are wearing off and I am left with the realisation that once again I've ended up having sex with someone I shouldn't, particularly when I am supposed to be making myself worthy of Drew. This is going in the complete opposite direction to the one I want.

At about 3 a.m., having listened to Max's light snores for a few depressing minutes, I sit up, intending to slip away before he wakes up.

'Leaving already, Miss Golightly?' Max stirs and runs his fingers over my thigh. I try not to think about how old he is, what he must think of me, how basically I've just prostituted myself again. I'm back to being sixteen. Can't I break this circle?

'It's almost dawn. I'd better head home.'

He kneels behind me and cups my breasts. 'I'll pay for a taxi. It's been worth it.' He nuzzles my neck.

I want to push him off but I can't afford to do that. Not now. 'It's been... fun.'

He smiles, reminding me how I saw the meanness lurking when we met at the bar. 'And if ever you want a job here – or even to give me another private dance – I'll fix it for you so it's worth your while.'

'Oh, er, great.' I'm feeling sick of myself and him. Please leave me alone.

His hands head south. 'So one more round for luck and then I'll get you that taxi.'

So I find myself under him again while he heaves and strains. At first, I'm not into it and he senses this but then he starts calling me dirty names and, humiliatingly, I get off at the same time as him. What is wrong with me? I'm fucked up, as well as fucked by having sex with him.

This time when I get up he lets me dress, though I feel like I'm doing a reverse strip as I pull up my tights in front of him. He gives me a self-satisfied smile. I wonder how many other women he's had on this sofa. Probably too many to count.

'Max, what about the lease?' I ask him.

'As long as you keep being nice to me, I'll make sure chasing you for the debt remains off my to-do list.'

How can I have been so naive? 'But you said you'd help me with my situation. This wasn't enough to make it disappear?'

He comes to stand behind me, admiring our reflection in the window. There are no curtains. If anyone was in the office opposite, they've had quite a show. 'You made me chase you. Consider it payment for that little escapade.' He runs his hands over my hips and pinches hard.

And isn't that the last lemon twist in this cocktail of humiliation?

Sitting in the taxi on my way back to Feltham, I reflect bleakly that now I share more with Holly Golightly than just a name. I've become a not-so-high-class call girl staving off disaster by sleeping with men. Another skeleton for my cupboard, or will I confess to Drew?

Chapter 31

After my return from the club, I sneak straight into the shower. I can't bear that man's smell on me a moment longer.

'Jessica, where've you been?' Drew is waiting for me when I emerge. Thank God I'm clean and sober.

'But I sent a text to say I'd be late. I was following up a lead.' My heart is fluttering like a wild bird trapped inside. I hope my voice is steadier.

'It's four-thirty in the morning. I messaged you but you didn't answer.'

Because I was otherwise occupied. 'You know what club-land is like. I found Lillian.'

He trails me to my bedroom door. 'You did?'

'Why the tone of surprise?'

'Sorry. Backtrack. That's great. Well done you. She's OK? Not got into trouble?'

I have a nauseating memory of me working that pole with her laughing. She had set me up for the boss, hadn't she? Did I really do that? 'She's got a job there. Dancer.'

'Good news all round then.' He reaches out and touches

my arm, a gentle stroke. It breaks me. 'You'd better get some rest. I've got to be up early.'

'I hope you didn't wait up?'

He shrugs. 'I worry. You're cold.' My goosebumps are caused by something quite different than he imagines. 'Do you want to… You could cuddle up with me if you like? I'll warm you up.'

He is making peace just at the moment when I feel least worthy of him. I can't take my sluttish body into his bed, not now.

'Thanks, but I'd better get some proper sleep.'

The moment passes. 'OK. I'll see you later tomorrow then.' He pads back to his room.

'Another time, Drew?'

He pauses at the door. 'Sure. When you're ready.'

I go into my room and crawl under the duvet. Believe me, I hate myself more than anyone else can. I'm stuck on the Wheel of Stupid: no sooner do I begin to climb free than something sends me crashing back down. I repeat the same mistakes. I should've made a deal, not just assumed Max meant to play fair. I shouldn't just fall in with a guy's plans when they push for sex. I should respect myself more. And then there's gentle, sweet Drew, hinting, asking so carefully. He's what I should want for myself, not Mr Smarmy Bastard with his office games.

I turn my face into the pillow and scream. That doesn't work, so I thump my head. The pressure isn't relieved and I'm worried Drew will hear. Fuck, I'm going to do it, aren't I, though I promised myself I wouldn't go back there? Throwing the cover aside, I go to the desk drawer and take out a box cutter I've stashed. Slipping off the plastic lid, I draw the blade across my inner arm, just a shallow scratch. Blood beads on the line. The pain cuts through the fog, giving me the release I need. I watch the trickle run down to my wrist, separate now from the anguish that brought me to this point. It's OK. I can handle this. Comfortably numb. Waiting until the last moment, I catch the drip with a tissue. I know it's an insane thing to do but it works. I feel more in control now and even ready to sleep. Slapping a plaster over the cut, I crawl back into bed and close my eyes.

The flat is silent when I get up at midday. Drew has left a note to say he is at Heathrow and doesn't expect to be home before five. I throw all the clothes I was wearing last night into the washing machine. Sitting on top of the soap powder, my phone vibrates so I check the incoming messages. There's a *hope you've had a good sleep* from Drew and a photo attachment from a number I don't recognise. With a feeling of dread, I swipe that one open and see a picture of me pouring champagne down my cleavage. 'Postcard sent' reads the message.

I curse softly, thumping my forehead against the screen. I had been hoping that I could just forget last night but nothing we do now is ever really gone. It's the modern equivalent of Ghost Marley's chains and cash boxes: we drag our embarrassments and rash moments around with us on social media.

There's a follow-up. *Max says to unblock his number and to let me know when you've done so.*

Already he's trying to control me. I've been thinking about

the rent dispute. Even if the police do back me and give me Jacob's notes as evidence, I'd still have to pay the legal costs. I can't afford to take this to court, and Max knows this. He's got me over a barrel – something he knew when he symbolically had me over his desk. It's blackmail but like many a victim before me, I opt for the easier option: giving in for the moment until I can find the exit. I go to my list of blocked callers and put Tudor Associates back on the approved list. *Done it.*

Mind cleared of that little dilemma, I try to get the rest of my life back on track. As well as being a monumental idiot last night, I did get a result. I have proof Lillian is alive and well. I try ringing Michael first but just get the answerphone.

'Hey, Michael, Jessica here. Good news: I found Lillian and she's fine. That seriously suggests that Jacob was off his trolley, doesn't it? Right, OK, I'll let the police know and work on the other cases to see if I can solve them as quickly. There has to be some reason why Jacob picked on these girls. Bye.'

I next ring the number I have for Inspector Randall.

'CID.'

'Inspector Randall, Jessica Bridges here.'

'What can I do for you, Miss Bridges?' He sounds slightly irritated to hear from me but too polite to brush me off.

'I won't keep you long. Just want to tell you that the address I had for Lillian Bailey turned out to be a good lead and I located her last night.'

'You did?' Irritation morphs into what I hope is respect for my investigative powers.

'She's fine. She's working in a club in Soho. There's no

mystery as to what happened to her; she's just a girl finding surviving in London tougher than she thought. I don't think she's using her own name and she's keeping off social media for the moment, which is why her old friends thought she was missing.'

'Which club?'

'Do you need to know? I said I'd not tell people where she was, as she didn't want to be found.' And she has photographs.

'It's part of a murder enquiry, Miss Bridges. I'm not intending to harass her. I just want to verify your information. We only have your word for it at the moment.'

'I see. Right.' And I do see. I could be colluding with Michael, I suppose. Jacob had suggested in his files that I was Michael's enabler, covering up his crimes. 'It's a club called Vaults. She's going by the name of Lily and works as a dancer.'

'Does she?'

'Yes, and she told me she had never, to her knowledge, seen or talked to Michael.'

'You've already shown her a photograph?' I hear a frustrated sigh. 'Miss Bridges, you can't go round doing my job for me. Now I can't ask her that question, as she has been tipped off as to what this is about. She'll know what possible charges we are looking into if she's watched any screen or picked up a newspaper.'

Michael has been well and truly crucified in all parts of the media, a web of innuendo where readers are invited to spin their own dark conclusions. 'But surely she's not involved? It's all a fantasy on Jacob's part.'

'We found Clare Maxsted yesterday.'

'Oh, well, that's good. How is she?'

'She's dead, Miss Bridges. So, please, keep out of this investigation. You are a witness, not a detective.' He ends the call.

Drew returns home and drops the *Evening Standard* on my lap. 'Pleased with yourself?'

My cheerful 'hi, honey, you're home' dies on my lips. I pick it up and read the article under Michael's picture.

Sex Pest preyed on female students, runs the headline. The story that follows is a salacious retelling of some of the indiscreet things I blurted out to one of the reporters who caught me at a weak moment. I'd admitted to her that my relationship with Michael had started out as a tutorial and she's run with that angle, talking to staff at the college who, of course, all knew about it at the time. The slant she puts on it, though, is that Michael habitually took advantage of younger women. She then leaves the reader to join the dots to the theory that abuse of power can ramp up to murderous rage.

'I thought you weren't going to talk to the press?' Drew is rattling around the kitchen, thumping a mug down on the side, overfilling the kettle.

'I didn't go to them. One of them rang me and I guess I must've said too much. I didn't take any money for this story.'

'You know what it is? It's fucking embarrassing, Jessica. My parents, my colleagues, are reading this stuff about you.'

I clench my fists and dig my knuckles into my eye sockets. 'I told you, Drew – this is me. I blurt things out. I can't apologise for something I can't control. It's not as if you didn't already know about... about how Michael and I started out.'

'And now the fucking world and his wife knows.'

'Why is that a story? What we did wasn't illegal. Two single adults having sex: what's the big deal?' I'm catapulted back to last night. Am I going to be making the same excuses when that gets out? Telling Drew up front doesn't seem to help with the fallout.

He stands, hands braced on the counter, head hanging. 'I suppose I shouldn't react like this. It's not about how ashamed I feel, how I can't meet the eyes of the guys downstairs, knowing what they know about you.' He takes a deep breath. 'OK, so are you all right with it – the story, I mean?'

I shrug. 'No, I'm not all right with it – but not for the reasons you imagine. I've done much worse in my life than repurpose a psychology tutorial. What worries me is that Michael will think I betrayed him, and it wasn't like that.'

'You're right. That's what matters here: how the story can be used to harm him and you.' Drew holds out his arms. 'Sorry. I'm acting like a prick.'

I walk into the hug. 'No, it's me who messed up. Again.'

'I'll cook us some supper, then we talk, OK? There're things that need to be said.'

My phone buzzes and I move away. 'Hmm. Sounds... er...' The message makes my heart crumble.

Time to be nice again. Dinner at 8. A taxi will fetch you at 7.30.

'... lovely but I'm afraid I've got to go out tonight. Can we put a raincheck on the conversation?'

Drew puts down the bag of couscous. 'I'll come with you if you like.'

'It's Lillian. I promised I'd meet her tonight – help her. I don't think she'd want anyone else there.'

He accepts this when he really should be more suspicious. 'It's great, what you're doing for this girl. Eat with me first. I've missed you.'

So I eat two dinners, one of them couscous and homemade ratatouille which I just pick at, and another in a French restaurant where the portions are artistic, so barely eating anything is not a problem. Max still makes me work off the calories with fun and games back at his office. Once we're lying on the carpet in a tangled heap, he notices the cut on my arm. I can tell from his expression he understands.

'Now, now, none of this.' He kisses it. 'We're just having some healthy adult entertainment here. No need to punish yourself.'

Then why does it feel to me like exploitation? 'And if I want to stop?'

'You are completely free to walk out at any time. I'll just go back to work, sorting out Mr Khan's affairs, chasing up outstanding matters.'

'I see.'

'I know you do. Roll over.' He licks his way down my spine, hovering at the base, mouth warm on the notch there. 'If I find you've hurt yourself again, well then, I'll have to punish you. I want you to enjoy yourself as much as I do. You need this and I'm giving you permission to be that woman.'

In some twisted sense, I know he is right about me. I hate and get excited about the illicit flavour of encounters at the same time.

Just before I leave Max hands me a boutique bag.

'Wear this next time,' he says, kissing me as the taxi hoots on the street. I open it once I'm sitting inside. It's slutwear – upmarket satin and lace, the kind of thing a man gives his mistress. Is that what I've become? Depressed beyond saying at that realisation, I pop some pills, swallowing them dry. The lights of London blink and blur. I feel dizzy and my heart is running the Grand National. Wrong pills to take. I should've taken sleeping tablets. These have only magnified my anxiety. I get back to Drew's and hurry upstairs.

'Is that you, Jess?'

'Yes.' My throat is dry. 'Just grabbing a shower.'

'How was Lillian?'

My eyes go teary. 'Sh... She was fine.'

'Good. I'll... er... see you in the morning.' His bedroom door closes.

I walk round and round in my room. My skin itches. I can't sleep in this state, can't even trust myself in the shower. A noise outside takes me to the window overlooking the yard. I hear a clatter as something falls to the ground. A dog barks. Probably an urban fox. I nudge back the curtain. The security lights have flicked on by the cold-storage area. There are deep shadows around the hearse which could hide a whole family of foxes. I hold still. The light shuts off as there has been no further movement. I then notice another shaft of light coming in from the streetlamp. The entrance to the yard is open.

I go into Drew's room and shake him awake. 'Drew, the gate's not shut.'

'Wha—?'

'The gate to the yard – it's come open.'

'Blast it. But it's bolted from the inside.'

'Not now it isn't.'

Grumbling, Drew tips himself out of bed and pushes his toes into a pair of flip-flops. 'No point us both freezing. Go back to bed.'

I nod but I am actually feeling quite anxious now. What if there is someone there – not a fox but a person? I hurry to the window to keep watch. I can hear Drew cursing as he makes his way downstairs, damning the last man to leave work that day. The wind blows the gate open a little wider.

My heart trips over itself. I think – I'm almost sure – I see a figure in a black robe with a hint of a white face standing across the road staring up at my window. The light's not good and my eyesight isn't brilliant without contacts but already my body has moved into a shaky flight response. It's probably just my imagination seeing things that aren't there, but the face resolves itself into the very unfunny features of an elongated screaming ghost, Halloween come early to the funeral parlour.

I run in bare feet after Drew. 'Drew! Don't go out there!' But he's already crossing the yard and shoving the gate closed.

He turns to look back at me, just a bathrobe between him and the night. 'Jess? I told you to stay in bed. You twit, look at your feet! You haven't even got slippers on!'

I grab his arm and drag him back inside. 'Lock the back door.'

'But I was going to check everything was OK in the yard.'

'Do it in the morning.'

'What's wrong with you? Your heart's beating like you've just run a mile.'

Where to start? 'I thought I saw something. Someone on the street.'

'Probably did. We get vandals from time to time. Idiots. Come in for a dare. How close to the coffins can they get and that shit.'

I press my head against his shoulder. He'll think I'm crazy if I start on about ghosts. 'Please, I'm scared. Stay with me.'

That's the right button to press. 'OK, OK, yes, I'll do that. Stop shaking, Jess. Take deep breaths. As you say, I can look in the morning. Let's go and cuddle to get warm again – just a cuddle. I'll rub your feet for you.'

We go back upstairs and I return to the window. The place under the streetlamp is empty. The watcher has gone – if he'd ever been there.

'Jess?' Drew is already in his bed, duvet thrown back in invitation.

'Won't be a moment.' I go into the bathroom and bolt down a Valium, then a second. No way will I sleep without a little help. Mindful of my evening's activities, I jump in the shower, punishing myself with cool water. I'm still shaking. I'd thought myself safe from my nightmares at Drew's.

'Jess? You writing *War and Peace* in there or something?'

'Coming.'

I go back into his room and slip into bed.

'I've got something to make you feel better.' Drew reaches down to rub my toes but I'm not feeling like joining in these moves that could lead to something else.

'Can we just spoon?'

With a grunt, he moves up and settles in to surround me, my back to his chest, his arm over mine.

'I'm so sorry,' I murmur, sleeping pill finally kicking in.

'What?'

'I'll tell you in the morning.'

I'm very slow to come round even though the sun is pouring through the open curtains. Drew brings me tea and helps me sit up by stuffing his pillow behind my back.

'I checked the yard. No damage. I expect Phil just forgot to make sure the gate was properly bolted when he left. I'm going to have a few choice words with him when he gets in.'

'Can people climb over?' I'm seeing Scream-face ghost slithering over the gate.

'Yeah, if they want. It's not Fort Knox. There's nothing to steal in the yard and the storeroom is secure.'

'Maybe you should padlock the gate?'

He ruffles my hair. 'Maybe we should.'

I smile blearily.

'Jess, can I ask you something?'

I sip my tea. 'Uh-oh.'

'What tablets are you taking?'

Damn. I must've forgotten to put away the blister pack last night in my hurry to get to bed. 'Ritalin for my condition and then the occasional Valium for anxiety.'

'Does the doctor know you're taking both?'

'Charles prescribed the Ritalin. I need to go back to your GP about that – thanks for reminding me.'

261

'But are you supposed to mix them?'

Well, of course not, but that seems the least of my problems. I try to appear innocently enquiring.

'Look, I'm not the expert here, but I've known guys at clubs who take both as uppers and downers, amphetamines for the buzz and Valium to quieten them down. Once they get in a pattern they need to take more to feel the effect.'

And that would be a pretty accurate description of me. 'My tablets are prescribed medicines, Drew. I'm not scoring them off some shifty bloke on a street corner.'

'I know but, I dunno, you were very jumpy last night, then went out like a light. That's not normal.'

'Drew, if when looking at me the first word that comes to mind is "normal", then I'd say you were missing the point.'

'True.' Distracted from his medical pep talk, he snuggles up next to me. 'The first word I think of is "gorgeous".'

The first word I think of is 'skank'. 'I don't deserve you.'

He leans over me and I'm worried he might make a move on me but I needn't have fretted. 'Jess, let's go and have some fun today – get away from all this.'

'And do what?'

'I've got some beans to harvest on a roundabout, and some roses to prune on scrubland in Hounslow.' He grins.

I dig deep for some of my usual enthusiasm. 'Guerrilla gardening? Count me in.'

Chapter 32

Michael, 20th August

I'm going stir-crazy. Though the numbers of the press pack have declined this morning, there are still a few of the most dedicated paying someone to keep a watch on me. I see a changing guard of young men on the wall opposite, eager, probably interns who think journalism will still exist as a paying profession in ten years' time. If I go out to buy a pint of milk, they summon their photographers and hound me like Furies to the corner shop. I want to grab their expensive Nikons, strangle them with the straps, then smash the equipment and stomp on the pieces.

The irony is that to pass the time, I'm reading Eisner's paper on reducing violent homicides. I'll have to mention to the professor, if ever I'm invited back to Cambridge, that I'm finding false accusations a real spur to homicidal urges.

Right now the person I'd most like to squeeze the life out of is Jessica. She talked to some hack, taking Fleet Street's thirty pieces of silver, and so has fed gossip-soaked fuel onto the bonfire of what used to be my career. Sex Pest. The words might as well be branded on my forehead. It's hard, if not impossible, to come back from this. Colleagues are muttering, students posting about the least flirtatious remark I made. Holding open a door has now become sexual harassment and lawyers are trawling for cases amongst my students, past and present. Christ, life is unfair.

Lizzy can sense I'm at the end of my tether. She repeatedly tells me there's no need for me to go out, that if I give her a list she'll get anything I want. I can't bring myself to admit to her that what I want most is her absence. She's hanging around like I've got some illness that needs nursing, tempting me with what she thinks are my favourite meals, trying to get me into bed. We haven't yet christened the new mattress and she's complaining that I no longer desire her. She's right, but I have to pretend it's just a temporary blip. God knows, my libido isn't crushed; I just want someone young and uncomplicated. Not the thirty-something woman next door with a spaniel, a career, and expectations.

Thankfully I've persuaded her to go home at night. I look forward to those long blanks where I can knock back the Scotch and glare into the dark. It's the most fun I have all day and I find a perverse pleasure in looking forward to these drinking sessions. I know what that sounds like, and doubtless Charles will tell me it's a slippery slope but, God, I just need the break from myself that alcohol gives me.

The back door opens and Lizzy breezes into the kitchen with the latest resupply like a plucky ship going to an Antarctic research station.

'Hello, darling. I don't think there's going to be anyone out there today. I heard on the news that there's a big fire over in Shepherd's Bush so they've moved on. Some faulty tumble-dryer scandal to cover.'

'Temporarily.' I've certainly been put on spin for weeks now.

'Poor baby.' She kisses my cheek and attempts to run her fingers through my hair but I move out of reach. Her lips thin but she doesn't say anything. Her patience is running out though, and I can hardly blame her.

'Thanks for this – breakfast, I mean. Let me do something for you for once. How about coffee? I can get out the espresso machine, froth the milk and so on.'

'Please, yes, that would be nice.' Smiling properly now, she sits down at the table and scoops Colette onto her lap. Funny how I never noticed before, but Jessica always let the cat come to her; Lizzy demands attention. 'Not sleep well?'

'Not really.' I ransack the cupboard for the pods that go in the machine.

'Nightmares?'

'No, just not sleeping.'

'I was hoping that you'd get better rest, what with the new mattress and no Jessica to disturb you.'

I'd told Lizzy as an excuse to keep her away that, after five years of being interrupted by Jessica's ridiculous dreams about some childhood bogeyman, I preferred to have some time sleeping alone. 'I'm sure I'll catch up later today. Not as if I have anything else to do.' I should've been on a plane to Washington, putting the final touches to my speech; instead I'm stuck here with everyone at the conference talking about me. 'There's a flavour here called caramel latte macchiato. How does that sound?'

'Perfect. That's Jessica's favourite.'

'Is it?' I fit it in the machine, hoping it's not more complicated than that.

'You should probably refresh the water if you've not used it in a while.'

'I knew that.' I send her what I hope is an endearing smile. 'Where does it go?' I look for a tap or hose.

'There's a tank inside.' Lizzy sits back and lets me make a hash of it but I eventually find the container. It comes out easily so I fill it up and slide it back in.

'It also helps if you plug the machine in and switch it on.'

I'm losing the will to live here. 'This is why I always make coffee in a cafetiere.' Finally, I get the damn machine working and figure out on my own how to do the milk – well, with the help of the instructions in the top drawer. I present Lizzy with her drink, feeling more respect for baristas than before I started the interminable procedure. 'How anyone can make a profit running a cafe is beyond me. I could've given a seminar in the time that took.'

'It just takes skill and patience – skill by the server and patience from the people in the queue.'

'I think there's a blog post in that. I should make a note. Or a warm-up exercise for the First Years. Psychology of the coffee shop.'

Lizzy sips her coffee – sorry, caramel latte macchiato. Is there actually any coffee in that? 'Oh, I meant to say. I found a message from Jessica on the answerphone yesterday when you were dodging the reporters to buy the milk.' She gives me a commiserating smile.

'What did she say? "Suffer, Michael, suffer"?'

She shakes her head at me. I've disappointed her. 'Of course not. Jessica's not like that. You can hear it for yourself. It's in saved messages. Something about having found Lillian Bailey safe and well and that Jacob must've been mad.'

A small glimmer of light enters the dungeon. 'She found one of those girls? I take back everything I said about her. That's really, really good news.' I rub my hands together, some of my old energy returning. 'I wondered if she'd keep on digging. I've not known her stick at things for long.' But it then strikes me that Lizzy has known this a whole day and not thought to mention it. Doesn't she get how crucial this is to me? 'Why the hell didn't you tell me this?'

'I just have.'

'I meant yesterday.'

She gets up, dumping Colette on the floor. 'Because I forgot, Michael. I do have a life of my own as well as what you persist in portraying as a walk-on part in yours. I'm trying to be patient here but I'm not going to be talked to like that. I'm not like Jessica.'

'Sorry, sorry. And you're absolutely not a walk-on part. How can you be? You're my lover, my friend – you're important to me.'

She lets the silence between us stretch. I'm not forgiven yet.

'I apologise for snapping. I'm just on edge.'

'Oh baby, I know that.' She moves in and gets her arms around my waist, head on my chest. I feel like I'm being slowly suffocated – a tree smothered in ivy. 'I'm on edge too. I hate it when you go out and get chased by those vultures. You just need to let me take care of you and not worry. No way did you kill anyone, so you have to let the police clear you and then we can move on.'

I'm fantasising about moving on to somewhere as far from here as possible. Like Melbourne or Wellington. 'Thanks.'

'I'm just worried that Jessica will keep on digging and find out things about Emma that will upset you more.'

Lizzy was always a good friend to my wife, just as she has been to me and Jessica over the past few years. She has a gift for loyalty – it's one of the things I admire most about her. 'Emma can't be hurt now. I promised I'd not say anything—'

'It was her last request. She wanted to protect her daughter.'

'You don't need to remind me, Lizzy. I'm a man of my word. When have you ever known me...' I don't finish the sentence because we both are aware of one big occasion when I didn't keep my word. 'But if Jessica does find out a few things, what does it matter now? That's all in the past. My wife is gone. Kaitlin can't be hurt by it.'

Lizzy rubs my ribs. 'I suppose. I just know what it means to you – and meant to Emma. I'd hate to see her reputation being trashed – you know how the press get? It would make what they are doing to your standing in the psychology world look like child's play.'

'OK, Emma made some mistakes, cut a few corners, but she's dead, West too, so it's not anyone's business, is it? Why would they be interested?' I'm saying this but I don't really believe it. The story is too sensational and I'd get hit with some of the backwash. I don't want it out there either. I'll be accused of being part of the cover-up.

'It might work out like that but it's too big a risk. No one will come out of it smelling of roses. Hey, I know: why don't we invite Jessica over?' Lizzy looks up at me, brown eyes hopeful. Oddly, it makes me think of Flossie, her spaniel. 'She can tell you about that Lillian person herself and you can suggest she lays off digging any deeper on the Emma side of things. It's great that she has already undermined Jacob's case so there's no need really, is there, for her to carry on pushing? I'll call her. I'm happy to cook dinner for us all to hash it out.'

What planet is Lizzy on that she believes it a good idea to put her, me and Jessica in the same room and provide dinner? 'Maybe just a quiet drink so Jessica doesn't have to stay long if she doesn't want to? You know, small steps? And let's not tell her about us, OK?'

Lizzy pouts. 'You've got to tell her sometime. I've waited long enough. I don't like lying to my friend.'

I rub her upper arms, meant as a soothing gesture with a cajoling subtext of 'get real'. 'But not in the middle of a murder investigation, OK? I don't want her to be pissed off with me – us.'

'She might be relieved of any lingering guilt. She's with Drew now, isn't she?'

'She always said they were just friends. He's not her type.' And Jessica likes her men with a bit of strength, not wimps like that Goth reject.

'Hmm.' Lizzy moves off but she has that look, the kind

of 'secrets between the sisterhood' expression that I've seen whenever Emma or Jessica were plotting with any of their girlfriends.

'What do you know?'

'Why don't you ask her yourself when she comes round?'

'I'd prefer to keep personal stuff out of it.'

'Men!' Lizzy folds her arms. 'You can't do that, not without it blowing up in your face later when she does find out. Come on, Michael, what are you afraid of? This is sweet harmless Jessica, not some revenge-minded bitch who's going to cut up your suits because you've dared to move on from her to a new woman.'

I'm not liking this experience of being hounded down a path I don't want to take. 'No, you're right. I made that mistake already when I thought she'd attacked my things in the bedroom. Maybe I should say something, but let me do it subtly, and let's not say it started before I officially finished with her. Don't push me on this.'

'If she asks me a direct question, I'm not going to lie. I'm her friend too.'

I'm getting a headache. 'I'm not asking you to lie. OK, let's invite her round and I'll clear the air with her, find out what she knows about this girl.'

'Give her a call.' Lizzy hands me the phone. I wish she would just stop nagging. I have an image of myself bashing her over the head with the handset. Christ, I really am losing it. I didn't know I had these violent urges in me. I'm afraid that one day I'm going to snap.

I put the phone down with shaky fingers. 'It's OK, I'll message her later.'

The doorbell rings, saving me from having to take immediate action. I want to think about this some more. Handling Jessica is like dealing with an unexploded bomb – you can't just rush in and cut wires at random.

'Shall I get it? I'm getting good at telling reporters to go away,' volunteers Lizzy.

'Please.' I retreat to the basement so I can't be seen from the front door. Sitting on the bottom step, I'm not sure what I'm doing down here. I don't want to raid the wine and can't bear to look at any of Emma's things right now. Some of them still have her scent. I'm worried that one day even that will have vanished and she'll really be gone.

'Michael, it's the police,' Lizzy calls apologetically.

I grab the nearest bottle to explain my emergence from the basement and return to the kitchen. DI Randall and DS Lloyd are waiting for me.

'Coffee?' asks Lizzy. 'Michael does a good line in caramel macchiatos.'

I want to growl that it's my kitchen and I'm not offering PC Plod anything but cold disdain, but I restrain myself.

'No thank you. Miss Huntingdon, would you mind? We need to talk to Dr Harrison alone.' Randall's attempt at dismissal is more successful than mine.

Lizzy kisses my cheek and takes the bottle from my hand as if I'd just been fetching it for her. 'I'll see you later. I've got lesson plans I need to prepare.'

'Yes, later.'

She goes out the front door rather than over the fence. I have to agree that trespassing in front of the police is probably not a good idea.

'So, to what do I owe the pleasure of a call at home?' I know I sound prissy, but something about these two officers makes me start acting like a jerk.

'Just some follow-up questions, sir. All routine.'

I take a seat and invite them to do the same. Randall sits but Lloyd stays standing, keeping me under observation from out of my eyeline. I know the routine, guys, I wrote the book on it.

I try to wrong foot them. 'I understand that Lillian Bailey has been found alive and well?'

Randall scowls. 'I see Miss Bridges has been busy. I told her not to interfere.'

'I'm pleased she did. One less stupid allegation that needs investigating.'

'As I explained before, our chief concern is the events leading up to Jacob West's death, not the circumstantial evidence he thought he had compiled on you. Our medical examiner has concluded that it is highly unlikely that West hit his own head. There was no object in the house that showed any sign of causing the impact and he collapsed before he left the property so couldn't have removed it himself. We are looking at murder.'

'Fuck.' I say it quietly but what else is there to say? 'Look, at the risk of repeating myself, I have no motive for killing him, surely you can see that? He was well in my past, the woman we argued over has been gone five years – I can point you to her grave if you like. As for West, his death is a massive inconvenience to me. I didn't much like the man but I had no reason to want him dead.'

'But you did get into a fight with him on the South Bank in 2010.'

So they had found a record of the incident after all. So much for hoping it was buried in the past. 'Correct. He was harassing Emma – screaming at her in fact. I protected her.'

'Can you describe the incident please?' Randall has turned to a fresh page in his notebook.

I want to say 'do I have to?' like some kid told to do a chore. 'It was all highly embarrassing. Emma had left him a few months before, as I think I mentioned already. She tried to hide from him as he was obsessional about her. I think she worried for her safety – with good reason, as his later actions prove.'

'What later actions?'

'His ridiculous fabrications about me, for starters. Unfortunately, some months after she left him, we had a chance encounter outside the National Theatre where Emma and I had been to a matinee. By great bad luck, West was part of a demonstration on oil-company sponsorship of the arts on the pavement out front. That was his kind of thing so I suppose we should've known better. I wish we'd walked out the other way.'

'Jacob West was a well-known environmental activist?'

'Yes, apparently so. I'm all for free speech and Green campaigners, but not for the lunatic fringe who send parcel bombs to scientists, or dig up the graves of their relatives. Those people have totally lost the plot.'

'So you thought West capable of a bombing campaign?'

'Don't put words in my mouth. There are enough misunderstandings going on about this case without adding to them. I am just saying that I got the impression that West was verging on that end of the scale, if not actually involved in extremist behaviour. But I'm not the expert here as I don't move in those circles or make a study of them. I'd never heard of him before but Emma told me a few things about the kind of life she had led with him, and it sounded pretty far out – living off the land and so on.'

'Shall we return to the incident in early 2010?'

'Fine. We came out of the theatre and Jacob spotted Emma. He began shouting about Kaitlin.'

'His daughter.'

'Not according to Emma. West was delusional. She was really afraid of him, I have to emphasise that or you won't understand. She said he was obsessed with her; he was claiming that Kaitlin was his child and that she – that's Emma – would have to go back to him if he took the child.'

'Go back where?'

'To live with him in some hovel in the forest where they plotted revolution and lived off scavenging – and not in the fashionable River Cottage sense.'

'Where did he think Kaitlin was – in fact, where was she at this time?'

'With a childminder, I suppose.'

'Last time we talked, you gave us the impression you had nothing to do with Kaitlin.'

'If you rerun the recording you'll see that I said no such

thing. I just said that I wasn't her parent and have no responsibility for her. Haven't you followed that up yet? Really, you don't expect me to do your job for you, do you?'

'Dr Harrison, withholding information is not going to help clear you.'

'Then ask the right questions, Inspector.' It feels good to tick him off. 'Returning to the incident, we both got quite scared when West chased us to the underpass. He tried to grab Emma – she'd already warned me he had a temper. We scuffled. It ended with me decking him – I boxed at Cambridge so I know how to throw a punch. That was when the police came. They tried to take me in but Jacob refused to discuss what had happened – snarling something about not putting himself in the hands of the fascist pigs which, as you can imagine, pleased the officers no end. He walked off, telling Emma that this wasn't over. He said that now he knew she was in London she wasn't going to get away from him again. He sounded completely unhinged and, if I'd had any doubts about the lengths she had gone to in order to break off all contact with him, I would've now seen that she was completely justified to hide.'

'And that was the end of the matter?'

'Yes. After a brief conversation and advice to avoid further confrontations, the police patrol let Emma and me continue on our way. No charges were ever filed so I'm surprised there's a record.'

'The policemen on patrol that day remembered you. You were already quite famous for your Hendon lectures, Dr Harrison. One of the officers drew the incident to my attention when he heard that you were helping us with our enquiries.'

'One of the drawbacks of fame, I suppose.'

'Would you say that you are a planner, Dr Harrison?' Lloyd is standing by the fridge where I have a calendar pinned up to remind me of household tasks like bins and maintenance calls. It was the only way to keep the place in order with Jessica's chaotic lifestyle continually breaking in like a pirate radio signal messing up the airwaves.

'Yes, I'm organised. I like to feel that things are under control. That's not a crime.' I pause, forcing myself to think professionally. They are not making idle conversation. They've probably read Hollin's introduction to criminal psychology and think they know what they're doing. 'But you are looking for someone who plans. The crime scene was staged in a certain way, almost tidy. It must have been a single blow if you even considered he might've fallen and hit his own head?'

'I'm afraid I can't reveal the details of our investigation.'

'You don't need to: I have a brain.'

'We are well aware of that.'

'And if I did do it, I was extremely foolish leaving the fingerprints behind to be found. As a planner, I would've done a better job of tidying up.'

They say nothing. I realise I shouldn't be talking to them without the redoubtable Miss Brightwell. But it is Saturday morning and calling her in would cost a fortune. I'm not going to let anything slip to them. I can handle a couple of mid-grade police officers. I deflect. 'Are you really sure you don't want coffee?'

'Positive.' Randall passes me a photograph. It's an ugly shot of a very dead body. A girl. 'Do you recognise this person?'

I wipe my wrist over my mouth, surprised to find I'm squeamish. 'Jesus. No.'

'That's Clare Maxsted. We dug the details of her death out of the files. There was some confusion because she had been using a false name but the dental records from her time with the foster services provided a match.'

I say nothing.

'Don't you want to know what happened to her?'

'Not really, but go on.'

'She jumped in front of a train in April.'

'Poor girl.'

'At least, that's what the coroner ruled. The platform was crowded at the time and there were some witnesses who claimed that she might have been pushed but nothing was proved.'

'As I said, poor girl.'

'What were you doing on the evening of 22nd April?'

I'm going to have to do the dance, it would seem. Yet more time-wasting suspicions. I get my laptop out of my bag and summon up my calendar. 'What time?'

'6.30.'

Damn – no tidy alibi. 'I finished a lecture at four and would probably have been either in my office or on my way home. Where did this incident happen?'

'Clapham Junction.'

On my doorstep. 'Then I might very well have been delayed along with thousands of other commuters, as I assume services were suspended afterwards?'

'You don't remember?'

'Inspector, you should be more suspicious of me if I claim to have crystal-clear recall. How many times has your journey to or from work been disrupted by jumpers? It's a sad fact that some desperate people see it as a solution to their problems, and they are far too distressed to consider that they are creating a tidal wave of knock-on effects, not least for the poor sod driving the train. I'm sorry I can't provide you with chapter and verse on my movements that day and I can't remember them at this distance. If I had been involved in the incident, I assure you I would've prepared a better alibi than this.'

'But you don't have an alibi.'

'Quite. That was rather my point.'

When they go, I pour myself a Scotch. I don't care that it's only eleven. What does it matter if I'm paralytic by lunchtime? I bolt the back door to stop Lizzy returning, bolt the front door just in case, and retreat to my bedroom cradling the bottle. The police haven't returned the picture of Emma yet so I've got out one from our wedding album and propped it up on the dressing table mirror. She looks so lovely – so happy. I lie in bed with the bottle resting at my side, glass balanced on my chest.

'Cheers, darling.' I toast her as I get serious about finishing the bottle.

Chapter 33

Emma, 13th February 2010

What were the odds – running into him at the South Bank today? In a city of millions, we had to come face to face. I saw him a fraction too late, waving his banner, his eyes wild while he spewed profanities at global business. This was exactly the man I fled – the out-of-control, fixated one. I pulled Michael's arm to go back inside the National but he'd seen me.

'Ali! Ali!'

'It's him – the guy I used to live with,' I muttered to Michael. 'Jacob West. I really don't want to speak to him.'

Michael clicked into protection mode – I was impressed and immensely grateful for his six-foot-one frame and visits to the weights room at the college gym. 'Then you don't have to.' We start walking fast, then running towards the bridge over the river, past the wall of graffiti and the boys doing stunts on the skateboard park. I'm not so fit as I once was, finding I get very tired since having Kaitlin. My PT instructor would be very disappointed to see me clutching a stitch in my side.

In my defence I was wearing heels and a tight skirt – you try running in them.

He, however, was as lean and mean as ever. He caught up.

'Ali, what the fuck are you doing here – and with this... this suit?' He glared at Michael. Being a 'suit' is one of his worst insults. 'Why are you fucking dressed like that? And where's Kaitlin?'

That really should've been his first question. 'Leave me alone. We're over. I'm not coming back.'

'She's my daughter – you can't just cut me out of your life!'

'She's not yours. There's no father listed on her birth certificate – oh, but you don't believe in registering your presence for the fascist state, do you?'

He reached out to grab me by the front of my coat. 'You can't keep me away from her.'

Michael stepped between us. 'Yes, she can, West, so step back. We'll get a restraining order if necessary.'

'Fuck off. That's my woman you're holding.'

'Wrong. This is my wife – and I will protect her with all the force of the law.'

'Fuck the law!' Jacob swung at Michael and they entered into a scrappy brawl. I had never seen my husband fight before; he didn't fight dirty like Jacob, which hampered him, but he must've had a punch like a sledgehammer because he had Jacob flat on his back after only a minute.

Unfortunately, a police patrol happened upon us just as Michael was standing over Jacob. I had a moment's panic that the whole business was going to unravel and I couldn't keep Kaitlin safe and out of this crap – which is absolutely my priority. Fortunately, it went no further, though, because Jacob mouthed off as usual about the police state, the same one that educated him, gave him benefits and looked after his health for free. Yeah, we're really oppressed in England.

Sorry, what little respect I had for Jacob's convictions evaporated after a couple of years living with them. He is a hypocrite and doesn't see it.

Jacob ran off after spewing a few more insults at how I had 'sold out' and 'kidnapped' his daughter.

'That was ugly,' commented Michael, wiping away a trickle of blood from his lip.

'That's classic Jacob. Now you can see why I've always been careful about keeping my identity and Katy's offline as far as possible.'

'Completely.' Michael checked we weren't being followed and we resumed our walk to the Underground. 'He shouldn't be able to trace us. You've got a new surname now and gone back to using your first name. Unless he recognises me somehow, there's no connection to make.'

I squeezed his arm, resting my head briefly against his bicep. 'Thanks. Hazard of the job, I suppose you could say.'

'But, Emma, I have to ask, is he Kaitlin's father?' Michael glanced over his shoulder. We were both anxious.

'He thinks he is – I had her while I was living with him – but he's never been a father to her.'

'That's not quite a "no", is it?'

'He's not her father, Michael. I swear.' And that's the truth in my mind. I'm her mother and that's all she needs.

Chapter 34

Jessica, 26th August

This has been a week from hell. Drew has been trying to manoeuvre me into having 'a conversation' but I'm avoiding it. He's going to ask me to leave, I can just tell. He is killing me with his kindness, so considerate, but that's what has clued me in to his intentions. That's the way he would deliver bad news, with a hug and an 'I'm so sorry – it's not you, it's me' line when we both know it is completely me. And if he saw the whole picture, the 'being nice' to Max part of my life, my suitcase would be outside the door like that pathetic character in *Evita*. I should put it there myself but where would I go next?

The cutting is getting worse. I'm doing it in places I don't think anyone will see. Add to that the fact that I'm a chemical stew. Can't sleep. Seeing the Scream – or fearing to see it – every time the lights go out.

I don't want to talk about me right now.

The irony is that Lizzy has asked me over to supper at Michael's to cheer him up – as if I could be anyone's cure.

Maybe seeing me so wretched will bring sunshine into his life, I don't know. I didn't want to agree, as that house has nothing but bad memories for me and I'm not in a good place to go back there; but there is something about Lizzy that is hard to resist. She has been so kind to me, standing by me when others didn't, introducing me to Drew, so when she laid it on thick about how Michael fears his career is in ruins, I found myself saying 'yes'. I wanted to say that he should've thought about being nicer to people on the way up, but what is the point of 'I told you so'?

Drew knows I'm going but doesn't approve. He must be wondering by now about all my mysterious evenings out but that's another thing I'm not letting us talk about. Fortunately he's got his own plans for tonight: tickets for a Kraftwerk gig with a mate from his schooldays. He said weeks ago how he queued up for hours at the box office to get hold of good seats. I tell him to go ahead and enjoy it. A couple of hours with Michael won't kill me.

After Drew leaves on the moped bound for Hammersmith, I dress carefully, trying for the 'I'm flourishing away from you, you bully' look, which translates as a red dress for confidence and black high-heeled shoes. I scrutinise my face in the mirror. I'm looking pale and unhappy. That won't do. I apply blusher and a bold red lipstick. Shit, now I look like a clown. I tone it down a little but I still seem a little manic even to my own eyes. Psyched up, I arrive at the house only to find no one home. Brilliant. A little of my attitude escapes like air from a balloon, leaving me sagging. I go along to Lizzy's, thinking maybe I misunderstood her message and she is holding the supper party at her house. I'll look a complete chump if I've got the wrong day. She comes to the door, up to the elbows in flour.

'Oh, Jessica, sorry, I'm running way behind. Flossie got a stick lodged in her throat so I had to make an unscheduled visit to the vet. Then Michael got summoned to see the Principal at Royal Holloway at the last moment but he shouldn't be long.'

'Is it serious?'

She smiles grimly. 'Flossie or Michael?'

'Both.'

'Dog's fine but as for Michael, I don't know. Maybe. He's certainly going to need us. Look, I've got the keys. Would you be an angel and feed the cat for me and lay the table? My kitchen is a mess – I've totally gone overboard with what was supposed to be a simple meal.'

'You shouldn't have bothered.'

'You know me – I get caught up once I open a recipe book. I thought it was better to keep the chaos here and then we can eat like civilised beings at Michael's when he gets home. You know how he hates mess.'

'Sounds a plan. Is there anything I can do though? Chop stuff? Feed cough drops to Flossie?'

'Ridiculous dog.' I can hear the spaniel whining in the back of the house, scrabbling at the door to get out to greet me. 'Oh, I know what you can do. I've cheated on the bread.' She passes me a packet of part-cooked rolls she has ready by the front door for transportation. 'Can you put these in the oven at eight?'

'Contrary to Michael's opinion, I'm not entirely clueless. I think I can just about manage that.'

'Jess, I know you're not clueless. Thanks.'

I take the keys and let myself into what was once my home. Weird – it smells different somehow, some kind of heavy cleaning spray lingers in the air. The alarm buzzes, bringing with it all those unpleasant memories of the accusations Michael levelled at me. I punch in the code and open the door to go through to the kitchen. Colette scampers in – at least she is pleased to see me. I lift her to my lap and bury my face in her fur.

'Colly, I've made such a mess of everything.'

She kneads my thighs in pinprick punishment.

'Yeah, you're right. I should feed you.' She transfers her attention to the kibble I pour her and then I set the bread out on a baking tray. Lizzy has picked a pretty pinwheel of different buns, some seeded, some with a glaze. They look too good to eat. Jeez, what is wrong with me? I'm weeping because we're going to spoil the pattern. Biting a knuckle to bring me back to some semblance of calm, I check my watch. It's close to eight. I decide to delay putting them in as the instructions say they only take six minutes.

Don't stop. That's when the thoughts come. So, what next?

I lay the table as asked. Lizzy has already put out the things we'll need, even down to the tablecloth, wine-red napkins, and candles, so it is just a question of piling Michael's papers up on the sideboard. I flick through them, of course, and note that his new book is nearly finished. Ironically the title is *The Pathology of a Killer*. His publisher must be anticipating bigger-than-average sales thanks to his notoriety.

Killer, killer, who is the killer? I realise I'm chanting it like some playground rhyme. Focus. Knives and forks. I then set three places, light the candles, dim the overhead lights and sit down to see what it all looks like at table level. I don't like this, being alone here. Where is everyone? Still hearing no one at the door, I open the bottle of red to let it breathe. I persuade myself that it also needs tasting so I help myself to a healthy glug in one of the big-bowled glasses Michael prefers. They were a wedding present, he once said.

Sitting with the wine in my hand, mesmerised by the ruby glow, it dawns on me that this is the first time I've sat here and done nothing for weeks. It's an odd position to be in sole occupation of the house from which I was thrown out so unceremoniously. The oven hums away to itself on its ascent to the required temperature. The refrigerator joins in with a smoother purr. Even Colette butts in as she circles on my knee and sits down to rumble her happiness on my lap. I'm horribly reminded of Jacob, sitting with his final whisky. Was he alone or did he have company for that last drink? I'm still thinking he was his own killer. It was some weird way of committing suicide – lace the fatal drink as a 'sod you' to Michael, miscalculate the dose so he had time for doubts, stumble to front door, hit head somehow and end up killing self in an unintended manner.

A little Byzantine maybe, but it is plausible. His behaviour trying to frame Michael shows an obsessive, possibly depressive man flailing about for some kind of payback. The real cause of his grief was dead though, so he was always going to miss his true target.

'Tell me about Emma and Katy,' I murmur, scratching Colette under her chin. 'What really happened to them?' Jacob said in his files that he had found no record of Emma's treatment, but then he was looking for her under the name Ali, or variations on that. But what about Katy? Was she Jacob's child? I listen hard, almost persuading myself I can hear the cries of that lost girl in the walls of the house, or shut in the basement. Michael had dismissed that question but he doesn't appear to have pressed Emma for an explanation as to who the father was, and Emma is very cagey in the diary entries I've read. I think Jacob was the parent. It would certainly explain his desperation to find the answers if he was fighting to reclaim his daughter. Where did she go after Emma's death? Off with that Biff person? From the evidence in the diary, Emma and she were thick as thieves. Biff was a she, wasn't she? I can't remember now if Emma ever said. I was reading backwards in the diary and only got two-thirds of the way through. Maybe if I got home early enough tonight I'd have another go at finishing it off. I hadn't taken very good photos of the pages so it has been slow going. I thought I'd have more time but my other life, keeping Max happy, is taking up my evenings. From what I've got through, Emma spends a lot of time complaining about living in the woods, so it's frankly got less interesting than the later entries about her marriage and experience of cancer treatment that I read first. I liked that Emma. I'm not so sure what to think about the earlier one I'm meeting now.

I no longer think we'd get on.

It's no good. My mind circles back to the thought I've been

avoiding all evening. What am I going to do? I had a chance
a few days back, a life raft with Drew, but instead I'm hanging
off the side, doing a Jack from *Titanic*. Drew can't pull me in
because my messed-up sex life is dragging me down. I do the
wrong thing, the thing I don't want to do each and every time.
I should tell Max 'so sue me' but I can't because he's got his
hooks in. He knows it's not just about the money for me.
Some shameful part of me wants to be fucked over by him
– and I hate that. I can see that if I don't change, don't kick
free, I'm going to die. Not literally – I'll keep breathing – but
inside.

It is getting dark. The kitchen clock hands are halfway to
the splits, pointing to eight-twenty. I used to be able to do
the splits when I was a kid – fat chance of that now. Shut up,
brain. Think happy thoughts for once. Should I go back and
knock on Lizzy's door again, see what the hold-up is? Maybe
I could even talk to her about all this, unburden myself? She
was a good listener after Eastfields. I should've thought of
her earlier. I don't move even though I don't like sitting here
on my own in the conservatory. I'd asked Michael to get blinds
but he hadn't wanted to change anything, saying roof ones
were enough, that we weren't overlooked. How does he know
that? With all the lights on, I'd be visible to someone outside
like a fish in an aquarium. Anyone can see that I'm alone,
creep up on me and...

Oh God, I've conjured him up again – the screaming ghost.
I knuckle my eyes, trying to drive him away.

'I will not think about him. I will not think about him.'

My heart is racing, pulse pounding in my ears. Not going

there. I take a Valium, trying to muffle the noise inside, slow everything down. How long will it take to kick in? Too effing long. I don't want Michael, or Lizzy for that matter, to see me like this. I must stop sabotaging myself by summoning up these demons as soon as I sit still for a few moments. Leave the past in the past.

Colette doesn't like the way I'm holding on to her and jumps in disgust from my knee. She disappears into the laundry room.

I brush the fur from my lap. Calm down, Jessica. Calm. Down.

I close my eyes and try the breathing Drew has been telling me to practise. In, two, three. Out, two, three. It does help. My heart goes from canter to gallop. Slowly I lift my chin and open my eyes.

A dead white face is pushed up against the glass, mouth a black O of horror, staring right at me. I have time to register the glint of the eyes in the cut-outs before my screaming begins. The ghost steps back into the darkness. It vanishes as quickly as it came.

Oh my God, oh my God. I crumple onto my knees and crawl under the table, pulling the tablecloth with me with a crash of crockery and glass. I want to run but I'm too scared to go outside. I want Drew. I grope in my pocket and try his number but he doesn't pick up. Why doesn't he pick up? Oh God, God. The screaming won't stop.

Chapter 35

Michael

I meet Lizzy on the step. She's trying to juggle a casserole dish and knock at the same time.

'Oh, good timing, Michael. I can't get a reply from Jessica and she's got my key.'

Grimly, I get out my own set. The last thing I feel like tonight is a merry dinner party with my ex who shopped me to the press and my current girlfriend with her chipper attitude, but Lizzy is difficult to divert once she decides on something. Personally, all I want to do is drown my sorrows. I'm going to throw them both out, after telling Jessica what the fuck she's done. The Principal told me my contract will be terminated for inappropriate behaviour with a student. Congratulations, Jessica, you got your revenge and I am completely destroyed. I won't even be able to get a job in an FE college now.

Aware that I'm a little too angry, I open the door to let Lizzy through to the kitchen. Giving myself a moment to regain control, I pause to take off my shoes.

'Jessica?' Lizzy calls. 'Michael, come quickly!'

I find the conservatory half of the kitchen in a shambles. The best white tablecloth, my grandmother's Irish linen, has been dragged onto the floor and under the table. Plates, glasses and cutlery are smashed but the worst damage is done by the lake of red wine.

'Damn it, Lizzy! These tiles are limestone – porous – I'll never get that stain out.'

'Shut up about the tiles, Michael. It's Jessica. She's under there.' Lizzy is kneeling now and reaching towards what I now see is a white bundle of person. 'Jessica, it's us – Michael and me. Are you OK?'

Jessica's reply is a whimper.

Lizzy turns to look up at me. 'Have you ever seen her like this before?'

'Only once, the day I checked her into the clinic at Willowbank.' I fear Jessica has finally cracked but it's bloody awkward that she's chosen to do so on my turf. I'm bound to get the blame somehow. 'Shall I call an ambulance?'

'Let's find out if she's hurt first.' Lizzy pats Jessica's ankle. 'Are you injured, honey?' I hear the voice that she must use for tumbles in the playground. 'Can you come out of there so we can check?' She gently pulls the tablecloth away from Jessica's face. 'I only left you here on your own for half an hour. What happened?'

Jessica looks so pale and exhausted. The clock is reset to February, when I picked her up from the headteacher's office at Eastfields. 'I saw something in the garden,' she whispers. She's shaking violently.

Lizzy glances at me so I do what is expected and look

outside the back door. It reminds me of how my father used to check the wardrobe and under my bed when I was five and haunted by the idea of monsters.

'Nope, nothing there.' I almost say that she must have been imagining it but bite back the words. I can see that it was real to her, just as a boy's night-time fears were to me.

'What did you see, Jessica?' asks Lizzy softly.

'The Scream. Ghost face against the window.'

Lizzy looks to me for explanation.

'That's one of Jessica's nightmares. She must've dropped off to sleep and confused a dream with reality,' I suggest.

'No, he was there – really there.'

'Where?'

'Middle window.'

I take a closer look at the pane. There does seem to be some kind of smudge on the glass, I'll give her that, but what caused it is impossible to say. Could've been me getting my balance to put on wellingtons, or when Lizzy knocked on the window yesterday to be let in. Had her imagination taken the smudge and transformed it into her bogeyman? 'He's definitely gone if he was there,' I say, remembering that the one thing I wanted from my father was certainty to drive off the monsters. 'You're safe.'

'Oh God, why is this happening to me?' Jessica puts her head on Lizzy's shoulder and sobs.

I have to get her out of here. I'm the last person in a fit state to help her. 'I'll phone Charles.' It's a sign of how broken she is that Jessica doesn't protest. I make the call from my study, explaining the situation.

'It's probably been too much for her – finding the body, our argument, the accusations,' I say.

Charles is, as ever, a pillar of strength for me, reacting without fuss. 'I'll come and collect her. We'll keep her in Willowbank for a day or two on complete rest, see how she is in the morning. Will she come willingly or will I need to persuade her?'

I suspect right now Jessica is as malleable as Plasticine. An ugly part of me is glad she is suffering as much as I am at the moment. 'I think she just wants to feel safe.'

'We can do that but I can only legally remove her from the premises if she agrees. She dismissed me as her clinician, remember?'

'Thanks, Charles.'

'No need to thank me, Michael. We've been friends long enough now for you to know that. You'd do the same for me if the position was reversed.'

I return to the kitchen. Jessica is bundled up in a blanket on the sofa. I have a disconcerting flashback to how Emma looked, sitting in that exact spot. Even at the end she was never as fragile as Jessica.

'Jessica, Charles is coming.'

Her eyes go to mine. She looks helpless – shattered. I shouldn't be irritated but I am.

'I know you don't trust him completely but he really does have your best interests at heart. If you can't take my word for it, just think that his professional reputation is at stake. He'll treat you as he would any patient. He thinks you need to rest. At Willowbank.'

293

She rubs her face with a hand. 'I can't go back to Drew's alone – he's there too.'

'Who are you talking about?'

'The Scream face.'

'Right, OK.' I exchange a glance with Lizzy. 'It sounds like Willowbank is a good option then.'

'I don't want to be locked in – not again.'

'You won't be – I promise. Just bedrest.'

'One night only – just tonight.'

'That's right: just a night.' Tomorrow it would be Charles' job to persuade her for a longer stay if she needs it. To be honest, I need her to bounce back quickly as she is doing a far better job of clearing up the confusion around those girls than the police. 'And don't worry about the bill. I'll cover it.'

She closes her eyes and rests her forehead on her knees. 'Thanks. Tell Drew for me?'

Lizzy eases Jessica's phone out of her hand. 'Is he on this?'

'Yes.'

'I'll send him a text, giving him my number. It might be easier for him to call me than Michael.'

'He hates Michael's guts. Thinks he's a prick.'

I'm a little relieved by the insults. Sounds like Jessica is getting her feet back under her. 'The sentiment is reciprocated,' I say.

'That's what I told him.'

Jessica doesn't speak much after that. She barely registers Charles' arrival and follows him, docile as a lamb, out to his car. I listen in on what little conversation she does hold with him. I can't escort them all the way to the vehicle in case the press are watching but I remain just inside so I can see that they get away without intrusive questioning. 'Sex Pest's girl-friend in emotional collapse' is not a story I want on the next twenty-four-hour news cycle.

'Is he really there – the screaming ghost?' she asks. 'He feels so real – I can't tell the difference.'

'I don't know what you saw, Jessica, but I do know that ghosts aren't real. I'm wondering if we need to adjust your medication.' Charles opens the door for her. 'You might be reacting badly to the Ritalin. It can have side effects in some patients, including hallucinations.'

'So I'm not going mad? It's the pills?'

'That's my hunch. Your mind is dwelling on those stories in the news about murder – of course all the horrors in your past will surface – it's a natural reaction. But let's get you to Willowbank and do a complete assessment.'

They get in the back and the car pulls away. I wonder how much all this will end up costing me. Bloody ironic that I'm footing the bill for the woman who just lost me my income. But at least she's gone.

I return to the kitchen and find that Lizzy has made a start on cleaning up the mess. She's staring at the wine stain, hands on hips. Despite her attempts to mop it up, there's a distinct pink tinge to the slabs.

'Any ideas what we can do about this?' she asks.

'Leave it. I'll ask a flooring expert when I can be bothered.'

'There's supper if you can manage it.'

We both look at the casserole, neither of us making a move.

'I've never seen her like that,' Lizzy admits. 'It shocked me.'

'Jessica does a fairly good job of hiding how fragile she is most of the time. People never believe me when I try and tell them.' Kicking myself mentally into action, I open a cupboard and take out two plates. 'Let's eat. No point letting it go to waste.'

'OK. You serve. I've just had a text back from Jessica's Drew. He wants to know where she is.'

'It's best Jessica has a quiet night. Tell him she's receiving care and you'll send him the address when you get it in the morning.'

'But she's at Willowbank, isn't she?'

'Yes – and do you know the address?'

'No, but you do.'

'And I'll tell you in the morning. That way, you don't even have to lie.'

Lizzy doesn't look too happy but sends the text. 'I'll have to put it on do not disturb or he's going to be ringing me next.'

'Do so – and then we'll eat.'

'You haven't told me what the principal said to you.'

'How much bad news can you stomach in one evening?'

'I see. Let's get out another bottle of wine and soften the blow.'

Feeling more grateful to her than I have in a long while, I put the plates on the table as she uncorks a second red.

'To Jessica's recovery and your vindication,' she suggests, holding her glass to mine.

'I'll drink to that.'

Chapter 36

Jessica, as for the date …

I'm drifting. I can't remember if I ever left this place. I was here in February – I remember that. Two skylights, sometimes with frost patterns.

They are dark now. I don't dare open the curtains at the window in case he is there. Can he climb on the roof? He can probably come through walls, can't he?

I turn over and bury my head under the pillow.

You dozed, and watched the night revealing
The thousand sordid images
Of which your soul was constituted.

Shut up! Shut up! Stupid T. S. effing poet – get out of my head!

These fragments I have shored against my ruins.

Things are beginning to make sense. I'm at Willowbank again. I love/hate Charles. He is like my bungee rope. I think I'm leaping off the bridge, free at last, but at the bottom of the fall, he snaps in and pulls me back. I don't smash on the rocks, I'm left alive and swinging in the wind.

I want Drew.

But do I want Drew to see me like this?

I'm coming back a little, like a shape emerging from fog. I'm not going to sleep anymore because what happens when I close my eyes isn't sleep – it's torture.

Charles said in the car that it was best I didn't take any more pills until my system has 'levelled out'. The care assistant brought me warm milk and a relaxation download for the sound system. I got fed up listening to whales moaning so switched that off after a few moments – sounded too much like sex noises. Probably are. They sell it as suitable stuff to make you wind down but if you ran it through the animal equivalent of Google translate you'd probably get lots of 'c'mere baby, I am so hot for you', 'come rub your white belly against my enormous dick'.

Fact – blue whales have the biggest penises in the world, stretching up to ten feet when aroused. Thanks, *QI*, for filling my brain with yet more show-stopping images.

God, I'm a terrible mush of random thoughts.

I have to move from this bed. I'm just not safe here.

Dragging the duvet with me, I get up and go into the bath-room where there are no windows. I shut and lock the door, make a nest of towels in the dry bath and turn off the over-head light so only the one over the mirror is lit. That shuts up the fan after a time so I don't have to listen to its dementing rattle.

You know only a heap of broken images.

Eliot had that right. *My nerves are bad tonight.* I cocoon myself in the duvet and curl up in the bath. I'm still clutching my phone but haven't checked it for some time. I see now that it has been switched off. When did that happen? I switch it back on. The percentage symbol is near red and I have no charger. This brand is the teenage boy of battery-lasting power – gets all excited then goes off prematurely.

I see Drew has been texting me non-stop since about ten – that must've been when he got out of his concert. I decide it's best to call him directly.

'Jess, where are you?'

'In the bath.' It's so lovely to hear his voice. *Stay with me.* The pieces of me start to glue back together.

'What? Tell me where you are!'

'How was the gig?'

'Jessica!'

'OK, OK, look, I had a bit of a meltdown at Michael's—'

'What did that bastard do to you?'

'No, he wasn't even there. It's not his fault. I think I'm having a bad reaction to my pills and saw something – you know, like a hallucination? – or that's what Charles thinks.'

'You believe Michael's best mate, the mad doctor?'

'*Mad* doctor – good one.'

'I'm not making a tasteless joke about your state of mind, Jess, but warning you about him. You always said that you can't trust him.'

'I just want to survive the night. He's taking me off the medication. Wants me to let my body chemistry settle so he can see what's really going on with my condition.'

'I'm not arguing this with you in the middle of the night. Jessica, where are you?'

'Willowbank.' I reel off the address.

'I'll come and see you tomorrow – and I'll have a talk to this Dr Charles of yours. I don't like the sound of him.'

'That'd be nice – to have someone on my side. I miss you.' God, I don't deserve you.

'I miss you too. Why are you in the bath at three in the morning?'

'There are no windows in here.'

'I guess that makes sense – in a Jessica way.'

'I knew you'd get it. You're the only one who does.'

'It would be better if I were there to keep the bad guys at bay.'

'I'll be fine until tomorrow – honestly. I'm feeling a lot better just having talked to you.'

'OK, that's good. I'll be there at nine. Try to get some sleep.'

I hug the phone to my chest. I'm not going to be able to trust what happens when I close my eyes so I decide to dip into the cache of deleted photos. I still have Emma's diary in there on the thirty-day rule. It's going to be hell to read but I'd much prefer to keep company with a familiar ghost – she's less scary than what my imagination can conjure when I don't keep it busy.

Chapter 37

Emma, 25th December 2007

My Christmas gift to myself is to tell the truth in this diary. My life has so little room for honesty but if I can't think this out somewhere I'm going to explode. I'll make sure he never finds it – put it at the bottom of the Tampax multipack I smuggled in – that's as good as a 'no fly' zone to a man like him.

As well as the carbon-guzzling 'luxury' of tampons, he doesn't believe in celebrating Christmas. He has hauled in what he calls a Yule log from the forest and thinks he's recreating some midwinter pagan festival in our garden as he sets it on fire. I can see him now from the upstairs window, standing with Biff, Gerry and Sparrow, all watching the sparks fly. Biff turns around and gives me a look. Thank God for her. She is my sanity. I'll have to go down eventually and pretend to enjoy it but I need a few moments after having just thrown up my dinner.

OK, diary, here's the thing: I think I'm pregnant. Shocked as I am? You bet. It was probably that bout of food poisoning in November when we had that undercooked rabbit he had snared. I'd forgotten that profuse vomiting can stop the pill working and he doesn't believe in suiting up for sex, the selfish git. Says he doesn't want to add to the landfill, and I as his equally committed girlfriend go along with that, but did he stop to think how much an extra human life adds to the waste mountain? That's these environmental purists for you. It's all about them and their perfect lifestyle. They're like a modern form of Jesuit getting a kick out of standing apart from the rest of us sinners. Holier than thou.

What am I going to do about this though? My Catholic upbringing is making a horribly timed appearance. I haven't even been to mass since I was twenty and still it has a grip on me. My instinct is that this life is innocent even if her parents are fuck-ups. And forgive me, bun-in-the-oven, self-ishly, it would cement my place with this crew – a very astute strategic move. He's been looking at me with suspicion recently. I know I've made too many dashes up to London to keep the bosses happy and had too many whispered conversations with Biff. Neither of us have adapted well lately. We're not sure we're on to anything here and the sacrifice of sleeping with these guys suddenly seems – just tawdry. Biff and I agreed we'd have to bend the rules but somehow we've bent ourselves out of shape.

My mother would certainly see it as whoring. I can hear her voice now, her Irish coming out with her emotion. 'What do you think you're doing, Emma, a nice girl like you?'

Ma, I was never a nice girl. She was afraid that I would turn out more like my dad, the charming actor who drank himself into an early grave when work dried up. As a kid, I always wanted to be a kick-ass superhero, but that didn't go down well in the world of dollies and cake bakes that Ma inhabited. If breast cancer hadn't got her, she would be in her element now, knitting baby clothes and dishing out advice.

And Ma, I'd have finally listened.

I'm getting maudlin. I'm in a fix. I have to carry on until there's a sign for the exit because the fallout if I left now would be career-ending. Living the life I do is like being a Christmas present – a shiny wrapper around the box with a secret inside. And boy, do I have one hell of a secret. Sometimes I can trick myself into thinking I'm all foil and box, and forget what's hidden, but then something rattles me and I remember. This isn't my life. My life is missing.

Chapter 38

Michael, 27th August

Lizzy is humming as she makes breakfast. I know why –
and she knows that I know why: she's celebrating that
we finally christened the mattress and is going to be as in-your-
face about it as she can manage. I can't burst her bubble just
yet. She's mistaking what we did last night for the beginning
of a new phase rather than the end of something.

'Have you fed Colette yet?' I ask, carrying the wine glasses
down from the bedroom.

'Haven't seen her.' She switches on the radio, choosing
something with pop music rather than my preferred Radio 4.
I don't know how she can stand all that chirping away between
records. It feels like a worm burrowing into my brain to listen
to five minutes of it.

I take the kibble and the food bowl and go outside for
some peace. I rattle the box and Colette appears with her
usual Ninja-warrior skill from the roof of the neighbour's
shed. Silhouetted against the skyline for a second, she looks
magnificent. I put the bowl down and stroke her along her

flexible spine. Emma was very astute giving me this last present.

'It'll be just you and me, sweetheart, very soon,' I murmur. It'll be a bore to get a new cat-sitter but maybe I should move right away to somewhere in Surrey? A village full of the kind of kids who do odd jobs for neighbours without it being weird or something you'd report to Child Protection. Somewhere with a Cub and Brownie pack. Do they still exist? I went to Cub Scouts as a boy in Wanstead. I liked the badges. They gave you a sense of gathering skills, steps along the path to adulthood. To this day I can make a pretty good fire and light it without matches. I impressed the hell out of my colleagues on our department away day last year – a weekend in the wild with one of those ridiculous training companies. Sometimes your talents take decades for their moment finally to arrive and mine did in the rain at six-thirty in the evening, Brecon Beacons, just when everyone had begun to despair of getting a hot meal.

I'm letting my thoughts wander. That's more Jessica's habit than mine. I lean against the fence, looking back into my own house. The kitchen feels occupied – Lizzy the conqueror as she commands the cooker. Last woman standing. I never really understood her connection with Emma. For the duration of our marriage, I felt she was jealous, not of Emma, but of me, being so close to her best friend. Emma had started to rely on me rather than her. That's part of my difficulty with our relationship now – it's like we're betraying Emma, which is illogical and doubtless a product of my own grief. But I should be grateful that Lizzy has always been there to catch us when we fell.

Don't Trust Me

She was dead set against what happened to Kaitlin and pleaded with me to take a different route, but for once I stood firm. I knew what Emma would've wanted, no matter what Lizzy claimed. God knows how I did it, because I was as fragile as a blown bird's eggshell – I collected those too as a boy. I don't think children do that kind of thing any more – probably laws against it now.

These leaping thoughts – I laugh suddenly. Just listen to me: I'm turning into Jessica. It's as though the house demands one chaotic thinker and I'm up for this round.

My eyes refocus on the windowpane. The smudge I saw last night – it's on the outside, quite distinct in the morning light. It's a whole handprint, as if someone leant against it, fingers splayed. Small – a woman's hand. I lean over and touch it with my fingertips. They come away white. I rub the pads together and feel the silky powder of flour. I lift my gaze and find Lizzy staring at me.

Chapter 39

Jessica

I wake up with a crick in my neck. Note to self: sleeping in the bath is not recommended. I take a few moments to surface before I realise what disturbed me. Someone is banging on the door.

'One moment!' I clamber out and drop my phone in the process. 'Bugger.' That's probably done for the already spider-webbed screen – and just when I thought I was getting a handle on Emma. I release the door catch. It's the sort that can be undone from the outside in case I'm in here slitting my wrists, but I gather they're not that worried about me yet because no one has broken in.

I find Drew on the other side.

'Drew!' I burrow into him as he gives me a tight hug. He's looking a bit rough, beard untrimmed. I'm always teasing him: why have a beard if you still have to use a razor to shape it each day? But it shows that he's been as good as his word, coming straight here as soon as he could.

'They wouldn't let me in at first,' he explains.

'What?'

'It's 9.30. I'm sorry I'm late.'

I frame his face in my hands. 'I was out like a light. I didn't finish reading until about four when my phone went "phut!" I hadn't noticed the time.'

'Phut? That's a technical term, is it?' He cups my chin tenderly. 'You look like hell.'

'Oh God, really?' I go back into the bathroom. I didn't take my makeup off last night and my face is indeed grim, mascara halfway down my cheeks. I'm wearing a borrowed white knee-length nightshirt that makes me resemble a mental patient escaped from a Victorian asylum. 'Don't look for a moment.'

He smiles and carries on watching as I wash my face. 'I know what you really look like, Jess. You don't have to hide.'

Oh, but I do. 'It's not hiding; it's called salvaging my pride.'

He holds out a bag. 'Will these help? I've packed some of your clothes.'

'You are an angel.' I grab the bag and shut the door.

'Spoilsport.'

'You'll survive the deprivation.'

I come out feeling several degrees more human.

'There you are.' Drew kisses me and I know he means more than just acknowledging my return. He is saying I look like I'm back to my old self. 'Feeling OK now? You sound OK. I was expecting you to be in more of a state.'

'Yes, much better.' I shudder at the memories. 'God, it was so embarrassing. I had a complete collapse in front of Lizzy and Michael.'

'You said you saw something?'

'Let's not talk about it. I haven't seen anything odd since – unless you count your face.'

'Hey, you.' He tweaks my nose.

'Charles thinks it was the pills playing tricks.' It's a relief to find something to blame. Can I find them responsible for my shitty choices too?

Drew sits on my bed, head resting against the padded headboard. I snuggle beside him. 'Well, if he gets you off those, then maybe last night wasn't such a bad thing?'

'Maybe.' I play with the cords on his hoodie. I don't want to admit that I'm itching for my usual morning dose of Ritalin. Some people can't move without a shot of caffeine; I can't get my brain in gear without my tablet. But I'm going to have to learn how to live without. I can't go around seeing things that aren't there.

'So you fell asleep in your bath nest?'

'I'd be lying if I said it was comfortable but it was what I needed at the time. Oh, and I read something really interesting before my phone gave out.'

'Yeah?'

'I've been reading Emma's diary – I took photos of it. The real one is with the police.'

'Jess, you have to be the nosiest person ever.'

'And your point is? Do you want to know what I found out or not?'

'Go on then. You're going to tell me anyway.' He closes his eyes, pretending he is listening only on sufferance.

'I think Jacob was Kaitlin's real dad. Emma told Michael that Jacob wasn't the father, but there's one entry where she seems to admit that he is, though she never mentions his name directly. Who else could it be though – she's hardly having a fling with two blokes at once, is she?' I'm the only slut doing that. 'It's weird – it's like she already hated Jacob long before they split up.' I'm getting into the story now. 'They're living in this cottage in the woods, right? And she pretends she's all save-the-whale for him but she really isn't. She gets very sneery then very angry about his lifestyle. It doesn't make sense. I can understand pretending to be something a man wants if you're already head-over-heels in love, but not when you despise him. So, do you know what I think?' I get up on my knees.

'What, Jess?' Drew is smiling at my eager expression.

'I think she was like a spy or something, living a double life.'

'A spy?' Drew quirks a brow. 'The name's... What was her surname?'

'She took Michael's.'

'The name's Harrison, Emma Harrison. Nope, it doesn't work.'

'I'm being serious.'

'People don't go having children as part of spy cover. That is very uncool. James Bond with a nappy bag: see? Not happening.'

'But what if someone did? What then? Wouldn't that mean you'd never want to see the father again once your mission was over, because you weren't who you said you were when you were with him?'

'Jess, I know you think you know her because you're reading

her diary, but people just don't do that kind of thing. It's illegal.'

'No, look, I'm not bullshitting you. I already knew that she was a police officer – that's how she met Michael – at one of his Hendon gigs.'

'She was in the police? I didn't know that.'

Things are falling into place in my head, like I've just fed in the right ten pence to start the coin waterfall tumbling into the slot. Jackpot. 'That's the answer! It's been staring me in the face all the time. The photo in the frame that Jacob took – that was Emma at her graduation, or passing-out parade, or whatever they call it when they qualify for the Metropolitan Police. She's in uniform.'

'Jessica, no one would sanction an undercover policewoman having a child with a target.'

'I'm not saying anyone did. There've been cases when officers go against the regulations, dating people to get under the surface of an organisation. If it's a woman doing the romancing, well, stuff happens – you get knocked up because you have food poisoning, not because you do it deliberately.'

'Why go through with it?'

'Because she was Catholic – she was in a moral fix but thought it better to go through with the pregnancy.' I take a breath, reviewing what I think I've discovered. 'It's all so bizarre, isn't it – the lengths the undercover police went to then? Do you remember how, back in the Noughties, they were in a panic about animal extremists and sent people in to monitor groups?'

Drew nods. 'Yes, I remember. It's all a bit close to home. I went on some marches myself but steered clear of the loony brigade.'

'Of course you did, you guerrilla gardener, you.' I pat his cheek. 'They seem oddly innocent, compared to today's terrorists.'

'Not if you were a scientist and had a bomb sent to you through the post.'

'True. So, back to my boss. What if Jacob hadn't suspected Emma was the Fuzz and the first time he realises it is when he sees that photo? Just imagine: it would be like everything he thought about her – their relationship, the child – was all make-believe. What would he want to do then? He's going to be so angry. She's left him off the birth certificate so he'd find it next to impossible to trace Kaitlin – Michael would prefer to punch him than tell him anything – and maybe it was always Emma that Jacob wanted rather than the kid? But the real bummer is that he can't hurt Emma because she's dead, so he kills himself as a kind of desperate revenge, hoping to take Michael down with him if he can stage it right.'

'I don't know, Jessica, it all sounds... way out there.'

'Read the diary. You'll see what I mean. Michael needs to tell the police who Emma really was. It'll go a long way to clearing him. And, he's got to come clean as to what happened to Kaitlin. Where the heck is she, by the way? God, poor Jacob.'

Drew pulls me back to rest beside him before I shoot off across the room like a ball in a pinball machine. 'But the detectives have the diary, you said. They're not going to be so slow at reading it. Maybe they already know?'

I'm pretty buzzed by my new theory. It explains so much about the odd dynamic between Jacob and Emma. But how can I confirm it? I suppose I can ask Michael right out but he's always been very secretive about his wife and I'm guessing that won't go well. What I really want to do is get hold of the diary and read it right from the beginning, not try to squint my way through the poor photos I took.

'Jessica, your pulse is a little elevated,' says Charles as he takes a set of morning vitals. 'I suggest you stay on bedrest for twenty-four hours and we'll reassess tomorrow.'

'I'll make sure she rests at home.' Drew has stood his ground and refused Charles' polite attempts to have him evicted from the room.

'Mr Payne, I don't think you understand how serious Jessica's condition was last night.'

'Don't tell me what I understand, Doctor.' Drew is so sexy when he's stern. I've not seen him like this before. 'Is there anything you are going to do for her that I can't?'

'Care for a patient like Jessica,' says Charles pompously, 'takes more than a single person. Her body has become used to the tablets. Coming off them, she'll have mood swings, restlessness, cravings, she might even try to find a new source for her tablets.'

'*She* is actually right here,' I mutter.

'My parents are willing to help,' counters Drew. 'I live over the family workplace so they are on hand all day.'

'I suppose you mean your firm of funeral directors?' Charles looks amused.

'What's so funny about that?'

'Nothing funny at all. It's just that someone... it doesn't matter.'

'He and Michael don't get along,' I slip in, understanding where Charles is coming from on this. 'He's got some funny ideas about Drew.'

Charles continues to address Drew. He would be much less of an old fart if he actually joined the twenty-first-century gender-equality movement. 'I'll need to see Jessica to continue her cognitive behavioural therapy.'

'Not at the weekend though,' points out Drew.

'True.' Charles walks to the window. He shoves a hand through his hair, an artfully swept-back pepper-and-salt cut to make him look as much like George Clooney as he can. Dream on, Charles. 'Michael won't be happy when he was all ready to get out the cheque book for her, but I think Jessica might actually do better with you. I noticed she doesn't sleep well here.' So my bath nest has not gone unremarked by the staff. 'OK, Jessica, if you're happy with that, I'm content for you to go home with Mr Payne here. But you have to keep off the tablets – no sneaking them behind his back to give yourself a little lift. Like with an alcohol addiction, you have to stop completely. No falling off the wagon.'

'Are you saying I'm addicted to the amphetamines, Charles?'

'Of course. Didn't you realise?'

'But you gave them to me.'

'And you took them as instructed?'

Got me there. 'Not exactly.'

'And you wouldn't be the first to abuse prescription medication. Try life without them for a while, Jessica. Let's see who you can become with non-medical interventions.'

On the moped heading back to London, Drew calls back to me, 'You know, Charles doesn't suck as much as I expected.'

'Why? Did you think he was plotting my downfall with Michael?'

He shrugs. 'He might've been.'

'I never thought he was out to get me, just that he didn't listen to me.'

'He seemed very reasonable today. He listened to me.'

'Yeah, but you have something that I don't have.'

'What's that?'

'A Y-chromosome.'

Chapter 40

Michael

I'm not sure how to broach the subject with Lizzy. I think
I know what she did but why on earth would she? She's
always been a model of kindness. I've known her for years
and never seen any hint of cruelty in her. She helped me nurse
Emma, looked after Kaitlin when Emma couldn't, showed
real gentleness towards Jessica when she went through her
breakdown. I had her tagged as one of life's carers. Did Lizzy
fear I was going to invite Jessica back to live with me? Is she
trying to keep the field clear for herself? Does she love me so
much that she briefly lost a grip on her reason?

Still wondering if I'm going to say anything, I go back into
the kitchen. Letting sleeping dogs lie has some wisdom. I'm
sure I'd get a better handle on it all if I just could get some
distance from the house.

'I think I'll go out for a while today,' I begin.

'Is that wise?' she asks, putting a plate of scrambled egg
and bacon in front of me and a large mug of coffee.

My stomach is churning but I can manage the drink. 'It

has to be. I can't leave clearing my name all up to Jessica, not now she's had a relapse. I've got to make some effort myself.' I take a gulp and wince – it's searingly hot.

Lizzy gives me a saccharine smile. Yes, she is definitely pissed off with me. 'Taking your cues from Jessica now?'

'She's got the right idea and is making headway with these girls, so yes.'

'And what are you going to do about it?'

Something in her tone puts my back up. As Charles always says about women: give an inch and they'll take a mile. 'Sorry, but since when have I had to report my every move to you, Lizzy?'

She butters her toast as if it has personally offended her. 'I think that you are about to make a big mistake, stirring all of that up again.'

'I don't think I'm the one making the mistakes.' OK, so we aren't going to avoid the subject after all. 'You climbed into the garden last night and deliberately scared Jessica, didn't you? She wasn't hallucinating.'

Lizzy ignores me, pretending to take her time choosing between marmalade and honey.

'You knew about her nightmares – I'd told you myself – and you exploited that confidence. Why? Why would you do that? I'm hardly going to like you more for using such cruel tactics on a rival.'

She gives a scornful laugh, her facial expression becoming quite ugly. 'You think this is about you? Can you be any more self-centred, Michael?'

'So if it's not about me, what is it about?'

'Emma, of course! I can't believe how stupid you've been recently – you actively encouraged Jessica to go on digging into Jacob and his fixation on you. How long will it be before she starts to circle near the truth?'

'She has no idea about Emma's job.'

'She knows Emma was in the police. She knows Emma lived with an eco-terrorist under a different name and had a child. Jessica, despite everything you like to pretend, is no fool. She'll put it together.'

'And maybe it's time. Maybe I should just explain…'

'You can't do that. You promised Emma.'

'But Emma had no idea where that would lead.'

'I disagree. She asked you to promise because she knew there may come a day when it would cost you to keep silent. She cared what happened even after she was gone. That's why it was pretty much her last request. We've got to keep Jessica away from it all – for Emma's sake, for Jessica's own sake.'

'I can't believe this. I wanted you to say that I was wrong but I'm not, am I? You, a grown woman, climbed over the fence in a Munch's scream mask and scared the bejeezus out of her on purpose like… like some teenager in a cruel prank at Halloween.' My throat goes dry just at the thought of it, how terrified Jessica must have been. I swallow some more coffee. It leaves a bitter taste in my mouth, but then everything does at the moment.

'It's better that Jessica spends a few days on bedrest than gets caught up in things that should stay in the past.' Lizzy sounds so reasonable. It's hard to remember what we're actually talking about.

'But don't you see how crazy, not to say mean, it is to scare a woman, and one who considers you a friend? Are you hoping to precipitate a breakdown, just to protect a stupid secret? Because if that's your goal, then you are going the right way about it. Jessica left here in pieces!'

'It's not stupid, Michael.'

'No, I suppose it isn't, not to you.' I push the plate away. 'Oh, I get it now. It's not Emma you're protecting but yourself. You're scared I'll ask Jessica back.'

'Rubbish. I'm defending Emma's memory – I loved her, I sometimes think I loved her more than you.'

'Don't you dare say that! Don't you dare!'

'I knew her long before you even met her. We were like sisters. What were you but a final fling?'

'I was her husband, for God's sake!'

'I bet you'd have been divorced by now if she had lived. She would've seen through you, your selfishness. We swore to stand by each other, through thick and thin, and I stick to my promises.'

'This has gone far enough!'

'I'm doing it for her.'

'You're doing it for yourself.'

'If you really loved her – selflessly, properly – you'd under-stand. She made mistakes, yes, but we all do. I forgave her when she went and had that baby on the job with that dangerous fool, Jacob. I helped her. As her husband, you should be standing right by me, defending her too, not sending someone to dig up the dirt to save your own skin.'

'Hang on, are you saying... you're saying... Look, I knew

that Kaitlin was conceived while she was undercover, but Emma swore—'

'Emma said what she had to. What we agreed. She only wanted what was best for Kaitlin.'

There's a hole in my chest – a sinkhole into which my belief in Emma has just driven. I think I suspected it was there, saw the cracks developing in the tarmac, but I drove in anyway and I'm at the bottom, wheels spinning. Frankly, I've been a willing dupe and I don't love Emma any the less for it. But because I loved her, I had rationalised that Emma had had another 'real world' relationship parallel to the one with her target because she had sworn to me that Jacob wasn't the father. I knew it was a lie, didn't I, even as she looked straight at me and promised? I went along because I tacitly agreed with her that Jacob was a danger to a child and the truth was inconvenient.

'I'm tired of all this.' I rest my head on my hands. Before Emma died, she asked me to destroy her diaries without reading them, probably so I wouldn't be faced with incontrovertible proof, but I couldn't bring myself to do that. I boxed them up with her other things. I meant to destroy them; I even brought one up to the bedroom to see if I could bring myself to tear it up. I couldn't. That was in part why I was so furious when I thought Jessica had taken the one from the bedside. I hadn't done what Emma asked, and now my weakness meant they were out there for others to read and judge her. 'You're wasting your time, Lizzy. It's too late now for your falsehoods. The police have one of the diaries – the key one.'

'That won't matter. I doubt they'll bother to read a diary

that ends five years back – not when they're investigating an incident that happened just a few weeks ago. Anyway, if they do, we can tell them they were a story she was writing – a case study for her training course with new recruits. There's no proof. No Jacob to make a fuss.'

She's reaching. I can't believe they'd spend even a second on those tissue-thin excuses. 'The police won't believe me if I say they were a story and it would be a stupid lie. We've tied ourselves in knots for Emma and look how that turned out? Jesus Christ, Lizzy, I've defended her memory for five years. I've lived with her loss, grieved for her, suffered all during that time, but we've come to the end of that road. I'm not getting involved in this insane cover-up. Both of you shafted West, didn't you? Took his child from him?'

'He was a terrible father.'

'That wasn't for you to judge. Who did you think you were? He had rights but you rode roughshod over them. I'm going to have to tell the police.'

'You can't—'

'I bloody well can – and at the very least I've got to tell Jessica about the mask so she knows she's not going mad. We've already lost Kaitlin. We can't make Jessica into yet more collateral damage in this ridiculous attempt to sweep lies under the carpet. She deserves better from both of us.'

Lizzy slams down her mug. 'Damage? If Jessica's damaged that's on you. You should never have encouraged her to clear your name. When she suggested it, you should've firmly told her to keep out of your business.'

'Oh, so it's my fault, is it?' My head is swimming. This

woman gives me a headache – this whole situation makes me sick.

'Yes. And Jacob went way too far bringing her into his investigation – I would've stopped that if I could.'

'And the memory of a dead woman means more than my career and Jessica's sanity?' I am desperate just to be alone but I can't be until I can force her to leave my house and shoot the bolts. I've got to get her out.

'Neither would be at risk if you'd just do as I tell you. Consider this a final warning. If you go to the police with any of this, or speak to Jessica, then I'll do my own tale-telling.'

'And what have you possibly got to say? You're up to your eyeballs in this shit.' I get up and go to the sink to get some water. God, I feel so woozy.

'That I know you went from my house to Jacob's that Monday. That you told me you were going to silence him. That you were going to set it up to look like suicide.'

'But that's not true!'

'Who are the police going to believe, the nice schoolteacher who lives next door, or the prime suspect whose fingerprints were found on the scene?'

'You're mad.'

'No, just loyal. You're the crazy one if you think you can get away with betraying Emma.'

'Get out of my house.' I feel as though I've never seen her properly before. It's like a stranger has taken over her body and is mouthing these terrible lies.

She comes towards me with the coffee pot. 'It's too late, Michael. You're not getting rid of me now.'

Chapter 41

Jessica, 30th August

Drew and I have been tiptoeing around each other since we returned from the clinic. He has done everything to provide a safe place for me to recover and I'm beginning to remember what normal felt like. Charles was right: the continual head-rush given by the pills had been playing silly buggers with my perception. Though I itch for a dose, so far I've managed to keep the lid on the bottle. I've been rewarded by not seeing the ghost again or feeling the slightest bit spooked even when alone in bed. All I need to do now is sort out the rest of the crap that's getting in my way.

When I get up, I am pleasantly surprised to see Drew waiting to share breakfast with me. I wish I had remembered to put on something more attractive than the shapeless T-shirt advertising a language school – my only relic from an abortive attempt to learn Chinese – and baggy grey pyjama trousers.

'Oh, hello. Got the morning off?' I ask with faux cheer.

'I told Dad I wouldn't be down until eleven. He knows I'm looking after you. Jessica, we need to have that talk you keep avoiding.' Drew is looking particularly edgy this morning in his black vest and black jeans, arm tattoos on display. The joker is grinning at me – or is it snarling?

'Uh-oh.' I have heard this opening before. 'Perhaps I should get dressed?'

'You're fine as you are. Tea? Coffee?' He fills the kettle.

'Double brandy?'

'If you like.'

'Tea's fine.'

He sets the kettle down and roots around among the teabags. 'Indian or green?'

'Whatever you're having.'

God, we've become so formal!

He puts two cups down on the table, and a little see-through pot with tea brewing in poisonous green curls like some witch's potion. 'Right, let's talk.'

'It's OK, Drew. I know what you're going to say and I'll—'

'I don't think you do know what I'm going to say.'

'You're going to say that I'd better start looking for somewhere else to stay. That's what any reasonable person would say.'

'Let me get a word in edgeways, please.'

'Sorry, when I get nervous, I babble.'

He reaches out and takes my hand. 'Just listen then. I'm not throwing you out. I promised I'd look after you but it's more than that. I'm sorry I've been so quiet the last week since you told me about Eastfields. And then you had your...'

'Breakdown.'

'Yeah, your thing last Saturday. I had to work through some

issues of my own after what you said about that boy. I had a bad experience when I was a teenager, with someone I should've been able to trust, so any hint of sex between child and adult, and I tend to think the worst.'

'Oh Drew, I'm so sorry.'

'It's OK now. I got help. The person was dealt with.'

'By whom?'

'My dad. It was his cousin.'

'What did your dad do?'

'You know we're a family firm of funeral directors, Jess?'

'You killed him!'

Drew actually laughs at my wild guess, lightening a serious moment. 'No. We're not Feltham's answer to the Godfather, though I love your imagination. Dad put the fear of God into him though, rearranged a few features, and sacked him. Then Grandad got hold of him, did the same, and told him to fuck off and seek his fortune in another country – Australia, Canada, if either would have him.'

'He used to work here?'

'Yeah.'

'I'm sorry.'

'Don't be. It wasn't your fault. I was messed up for a bit, felt guilty as if I caused it somehow, but I got a good therapist, and that really helped. It took me a while to feel clean of it all but now I can say "water under the bridge" and mean it. I just needed to explain that when you told me that you and the boy had been at it in a cupboard...'

'He was eighteen, a young man,' I mutter.

'... it touched an exposed nerve. But I made myself think

about it some more. The person who did it to me definitely made all the plays, getting me on my own, making me think I had to do the things he wanted, threatening to tell my mother, which of course he would never have done, but I had no perspective at thirteen. It went on for about six months. I just thought it was all my fault. But you – I know you. You wouldn't pursue someone, you're not predatory.'

'Hardly.'

'You're sexually more on the submissive side of the fence.'

'Geez, I sound pathetic – and there's a fence for this?' I'm imagining one very strange field with us all lined up according to our sexual behaviour, a kind of sheep-and-goats scenario, Michael and Max on one side, me on the other. On which side is Drew right now?

He shrugs. 'It's just the way some people tick. So I had to ask myself whether the boy was the one who moved on you. Maybe he sensed that you were vulnerable, the kind of person who responds to an alpha personality. The assumption is that teachers are in control, but we all remember from our school-days that that really isn't the truth.'

I grimace. 'Look, I know I'm the dictionary illustration for Beta, one of life's followers.'

'You're not that much of a doormat – you just think you are. I think you can be bloody stubborn sometimes. Anyway, as you say, he was eighteen too, much older than I was. I decided I should stop replaying my own history and instead look at it through what I know of yours. You have a terrible taste in men, Jess.'

'What?'

'Michael: dominant, sneering, bullying, doesn't know a good thing when he sees it because he lives in the past. This kid? I'm guessing: full of himself, proud of having pulled a pretty female teacher, persistent?'

I nod.

'You've been badly led by your instincts and you were professionally way out of line. You even make too many excuses for yourself, you know that?'

I'm not sure whether to nod or put my head in the gas oven.

'But we can't be defined by a single mistake – we should learn from them.'

'What if it's more than one mistake?'

'Then you have to break the cycle. I think you should try to like someone who would be much better for you, who would keep you out of trouble, who is around the same age. In fact, I think you should try to like me.'

'I do like you!'

'No, I mean, like this.' He pulls me up from my seat and kisses me.

'I haven't brushed my teeth yet!' I wail. 'God, I must be as attractive as the sawdust at the bottom of a hamster cage.'

'Ssh!' He offers me a cup of the green tea. 'Have some of that and we'll try again. You're messing up the big moment here. I'm trying to take the lead, like you need me to. I've realised you'll never come to me.'

I take a sip, swash it around my mouth, and put the cup down. 'Thank you for understanding.'

'It's my job to make you feel good about yourself, and I'm patient. Now, if you're ready, we're taking this tea to bed.'

He is getting into being this alpha guy even though it's not his usual play. 'At nine in the morning?'

He nods, his eyes twinkling.

I panic a little. I'm the idiot letting herself be blackmailed into sleeping with a guy I don't even like. Here's a man I do like and I feel terrified.

'Stop thinking whatever it is that you're thinking. You are perfect to me.' Drew draws me after him to his room. He has a totally decadent king-size bed with maroon covers, black scatter cushions and Japanese prints of galloping horses on the wall. It's unexpectedly flamboyant.

I giggle a little desperately. 'Flamboyant in Feltham?'

'That's better. I hate seeing you look so miserable. I did that to you the last couple of days.'

No, Max and I did that.

Drew takes the tea and puts it on the bedside table. 'You OK with this?' It's weirdly domestic and sexy at the same time.

'Yes, but don't expect too much, OK? I've got quite a few miles on the clock.'

'You're beautiful, so shut up.' He lifts my T-shirt over my head. 'Stop over-thinking.'

I'm not sure of the time but there's nowhere else I'd rather be. We lie together, my head on his chest, sun spilling over us like a gentle continuation of the superb feelings Drew had stirred in me. He is playing with a lock of my hair, dusting my shoulders with it. I don't feel used like I do with Max; I feel completed.

'Do you know that you have three freckles on your shoulder blade? They make a little equilateral triangle.'

'No, I did not know that. Gosh, I may not be sexy but I am geometrical.'

'You're sexy too, you muppet, or do I have to prove it to you again?'

'Maybe I do need to be reminded.' I run my fingers over his chest. He has a little smattering of hair which concentrates at the centre and arrows south. Just above his hip bone there's a tattoo of a phoenix I've not seen before. 'How many of these have you got?'

'I'll leave you to find out.'

'Ooo, homework from the teacher. My favourite kind.' I take a playful nip at it.

'Steady, or you'll be in trouble again.' He rolls over so I'm now on the pillow, his face hovering over mine.

'Yes, please.'

His alarm goes. 'Damn and blast.' Drew turns it off, looks once at me, considering, then sighs. 'I've got to get going.'

I stretch and yawn, feeling decadent. 'Really?'

'It's quarter to eleven. Cortege leaves in fifteen minutes.' Drew is shimmying into his trunks and I catch a glimpse of new tattoo number two, a panther.

'You've got a panther in your pants?' I start to laugh.

'You know, you are the first girl to get the joke.' He grins at me.

'I don't want to hear about other girls.' I grab my discarded clothing.

'And I don't want to hear about the other men. Fresh start for us both.'

'Yes.' I hope so. 'Good idea.'

As he leaves, I summon up the contacts on my phone. Do I have the courage just to delete Max Tudor and take what follows? Maybe, like Drew's experience, the threat is more in my head than real and Max wouldn't want to tell anyone what we've been doing? There must be professional guidelines he's breaking? I stroke the screen. Do I dare?

Fuck this.

No more being nice. Don't contact me again. I press send.

Energised by doing what is right for once, I go back to clearing Michael's name with more enthusiasm. I start pulling on the threads and the tangle around him begins to unravel in a very satisfactory fashion. I find Latifah. A colleague of Michael from Royal Holloway – one of the few who returned my calls – who does me a favour and rings round London colleges. She discovers that Latifah is on the enrolment for this year's Psychology intake at University College London. It's probably against all sorts of regulations but she knows how serious things are for Michael – she was the one who found him his lawyer – so she gets me a mobile number on the strict understanding that I won't say where it came from.

'Hello?'

'Is that Latifah?'

'Who is this?' I can hear street sounds at the other end. It sounds very busy, wherever she is.

'My name is Jessica Bridges I look for missing persons – please don't hang up.'

'How did you find me?'

I'm going to lose her if I'm not quick to defuse her alarm. 'Listen a moment: I'm not going to tell your family where you are, I promise. I'm looking for you for a completely different reason. Your name has got mixed up in some ugly allegations made against my ex-partner, Dr Michael Harrison.'

'Oh.' She must've seen some of the press stories as she doesn't ask what the allegations are. I suppose if you are about to embark on a psychology degree you would pay attention if one of the leading figures in the field is splashed all over the front pages. 'But what's that got to do with me?'

'When you went missing, someone decided that Michael arranged it.'

'But I only met Dr Harrison once – at my interview. I've not seen him since and I decided in the end not go to his college.'

The question has to be asked. I remember my own time in Michael's study, the sweaty coupling on the sofa. 'Was it anything to do with him – the way he treated you?'

'What? No! It was just that when I decided to get away, I thought my parents would know too much about where I was if I went to Royal Holloway. So Dr Harrison has absolutely nothing to do with me.'

'I'm glad. But it would help him a lot if you could confirm to the
police—'

'The police? No, I can't talk to them.'

'You're over eighteen, Latifah. The police have no reason to take it any further once they know you are safe.'

'How do I know that? I don't know you.' This is one cautious woman I'm talking to – I approve.

'The only interest the police have is in hearing that you're fine. You are fine, aren't you? I mean, do you need money or help ór anything?' I think of Lillian and hope Latifah hasn't gone down the same rocky road. And listen to me, the penniless loser, more or less offering to bail her out!

'No, I'm fine.'

'How have you managed? Sorry, you don't need to answer that. It's just that I ran away once and didn't come through the experience very well.'

'I suppose there's no harm in telling you, is there? I've been working for a charity fundraiser this year. Saving for Uni.'

'So you're what, chugging?' The street sounds make sense now.

'Yes.'

'Brave of you. I can imagine few things worse than going up to complete strangers, who would wish you in Hades for interrupting their day, and having to ask them for money.'

Her tone is unbending a little as I make the connection with her. 'It's OK. Teaches you a lot about the weirdness of people when they're asked to give.'

'I bet. Plenty of material for your essays next year.' I'm liking this girl. 'Please, I don't want to upset the new life you've made for yourself, but Dr Harrison could really do with some help. He's been falsely accused and the question mark over your whereabouts is part of that.'

I can hear her tell someone that she won't be much longer. She comes back to me. 'But you don't understand, Miss Bridges, I'm with someone now. If my family find out, we could be in real danger. You don't know what they're like. My uncles ...'

I can guess because I've researched them.

Drew comes into the kitchen, removing his black tie, and, seeing I'm busy, starts on a late lunch. I wave.

'They wouldn't like his family background,' continues Latifah. 'They won't think he's good enough for them. They can't know.'

I really don't want to make trouble for her. There has to be a way to keep her safe and get Michael off the hook. 'How about I give the police investigating the accusations about Dr Harrison your number, and you confirm that you're OK over the phone? You don't have to see them – or go to them – nothing like that.'

'You're not giving up, are you?'

'Dr Harrison's liberty might depend on you. Besides, if the police really start looking for you, they're going to find you and then it'll be much more difficult to control how that all unwinds.'

She goes quiet for a few moments. 'All right. No, actually, you give *me* the number and I'll call them. And I'll be changing this one, so please don't try to ring me again.'

'OK, Latifah, you're in charge. I'm sorry if I've made you feel that you're not.'

'It's fine, I get it. You're only trying to help your friend. I know I can't hide for ever but I've spent a year trying to disappear. I don't want to come back right now. I'm not ready.'

I remember some of the appeals I had read in the local press in her hometown of Bradford. She has sisters, a mother and father. 'I think I should mention that your family is worried something bad has happened to you.'

'It would if they got hold of me and Jamal.'

'I understand that. But if you need a go-between, I can pass them a message on your behalf, put the worst of their concerns to bed. You've got my number now.'

'I'll think about it.' She ends the call.

It's not quite the hundred per cent outcome I hoped for – a daughter reconciled with her family, the allegation hanging over Michael refuted immediately – but it's good enough. If she doesn't contact Randall, I'll at least be able to point him in the direction of UCL if it becomes absolutely necessary. However, on balance, my money is on Latifah coming through for Michael and contacting the inspector.

When I put my phone down, carefully because the screen is only just attached by the equivalent of an electronic thread, Drew actually applauds.

'You sounded good, Jess. Firm, persuasive, but not pushy.'

'Thanks.' And I do feel good about myself for once. I think I handled her OK. 'What I can't understand, though, is where Jacob got all this... this guff from? That's clearly not a raped and murdered girl left in a shallow grave. Why had he ever thought she was?'

'Yeah, really bizarre, isn't it? You're going to find Ramona though, aren't you, even though you're no longer worried for her?'

'I have to close the case. And I've got an idea on that too.'

Drew comes up behind me and shuts the lid of the computer. 'Enough for today. Right now, we are going to take the afternoon off and make sure you are fully recovered.'

'Are you giving me a choice here?'

He kisses my neck. 'Yeah. In the bedroom or on the sofa?'

After that pleasantly enforced break, I only get back to my investigation the next morning. My idea is to trawl through the images of life models in the exhibitions of graduating students from the major art colleges. Ramona is distinctive looking, in an African-princess way: swan neck and the last picture had her with close-cropped hair. She would be a joy to sketch and I have a hunch that Ramona will be hanging around in the world she loves.

After three hours of internet searches I'm beginning to think I'm getting over-confident with my investigative instincts. I can't see her. There are fat saggy guys, old wizened ladies, buff men and middle-aged women with pouch bellies, but no Ramona.

Drew comes back at lunchtime, relieving his mother who has been doing paperwork to keep me company. Fortunately, I've been too busy to feel my usual itch for a tablet so I've not embarrassed myself by giving her any trouble.

'How's it going?'

'There are some right frights on there,' comments Mrs Payne, gathering up her files.

So she wouldn't wonder why I am trawling the internet for sketches of nude people, I explain what I am up to and show her the picture I have of Ramona.

'Isn't she a lovely-looking girl?' she says. 'People are going to remember her.'

Off babysitting duty, Mrs Payne heads down to the reception.

Drew massages my shoulders. 'Mum's right – your best lead is that she's distinctive. Hoping that she might've been in one of the featured graduate shows is a long shot. And shucking your clothes is not everyone's cup of tea.'

'It is mine.'

'I've noticed and thank my lucky stars every day.' He grins. 'She might be too shy.'

'You're right, of course. I was reading into her what I would do in the same circumstances.'

Drew walks over to the kitchen counter and fills the kettle. 'What else do you know about her? She was working for a caterer at the Tate reception you went to, right?'

'Yes.'

'Then why wouldn't she think to do the same thing in London? There are two Tates here that host loads of events and have their own cafes and restaurants. She might even have found out which companies run them before she left, organised herself a parachute.'

'How do we find that out?'

'I have a cunning plan: go and ask.'

The Tate Modern, an old power station on Bankside which has been successfully converted into an art gallery, is a difficult place to search. It teems with tourists, and has lots of confusing escalators, lifts and stairs that don't seem to interlink logically. Maybe it is all one big art installation project set to run for years called 'Just how confusing can you make a gallery visit?' As Drew has to work, his mother has come with me. It's faintly ridiculous that I need a minder but that was the only basis on which Drew said he wouldn't ditch his afternoon funeral.

Mrs Payne proves very useful, however, as she has the knack of striking up conversations without rousing people's suspicions. She has a motherly vibe. On my suggestion, she starts first with a young security guard, extracting quickly from him that he is originally from Nigeria and has a wife and three children.

'Do you know if Ramona is in today?' she asks when his defences are fully lowered.

'Ramona, ma'am?'

'Yes, she's a friend of my daughter-in-law here.' Mrs Payne waves to me. I try not to blink at my sudden promotion from girlfriend to wife. 'Pretty girl. Jessica, where's that photo you showed me?'

I hand over the picture. 'It was taken a while ago. Sorry I've nothing more recent. I think she said she works in the cafeteria.' Look at the pair of us, making up this stuff, like we've always worked together.

'We were hoping to be lucky and find she was in today. We don't often get up to town. I was sure you'd know.' Mrs Payne makes us sound the most clueless of country bumpkins who think everyone in London knows each other.

The man smiles. 'No, ma'am, I'm sorry, I don't know all the canteen staff by sight. It's a big place, this. I suggest you try the manager. She will know the shift pattern.'

'Thank you.'

'Just say Femi sent you.'

'Thank you, Femi.'

Keeping my lips sealed until we are out of sight, I can't help laughing when it's safe to do so. 'You are brilliant, Mrs Payne.'

'Call me Glenda.'

I nudge her. 'Of course. After all, I'm your daughter-in-law.'

'Give it time,' she mutters.

'Oh my word, a mother with a mission. Should I tell Drew what you plan for him?'

'He knows. I'm serious about wanting grandchildren.'

'Stop, stop, this is weirding me out.'

She chuckles. 'Oh yes, you'll do.'

We reach the canteen level and again Mrs Payne takes the lead, asking to see the manager.

'Is there a problem, madam?' asks the counter staff, going all formal as soon as she makes the request.

'Not at all,' she says airily and smiles him into compliance.

I wander off to overlook the Turbine Hall with its puzzling display of flying fish. That is stranger than anything my hallucinations can conjure up. Perhaps I should go into modern art and turn my visions into things like this? I'd find myself on the normal end of the artistic spectrum.

I turn around and see Mrs Payne is engaged in conversation with a slight woman in a black uniform who appears resistant to her charms. I suppose it is too much to expect she'll dish out information on a staff member but I was hoping at least for a confirmation or denial that Ramona works on her team.

But then I realise I don't need it. On the far side of the large canteen I catch a glimpse of a girl clearing tables. Before I lose her, I make my way through the school parties and pushchairs. This is more difficult than it sounds as it is a big place and stuffed to the gunnels with people. It could be a new Olympic sport: steeplechase with tourists.

'Ramona?'

The girl freezes. Her badge says 'Monica'. Close enough.

'Please, don't run away. I'm not here to cause any trouble for you.' I glance to check that Mrs Payne has kept the manager talking. I don't want to be kicked out before getting my questions asked. 'I look for missing persons, but I promise the people, when I find them, that I will only reveal where they are with their permission, and if they think it's safe to do so.'

'I'm sorry. You've got the wrong person,' she says, picking up a tray laden with empties.

'We met once – at the other Tate in Margate.'

'I don't remember you.' But she doesn't deny that she's from there.

'You were serving at a reception my ex and I attended. To be honest, I don't remember you either, but that coincidence has caused my former partner a huge amount of trouble.'

She puts the tray down and gazes out of the window. Her profile is the kind that would send a photographer into ecstasy. She's wasted on clearing tables. The view is also fabulous: the river, the bridges, the white dome of St Paul's – iconic London.

'I can see why you'd swap Margate for this,' I say, keeping it light.

'What kind of trouble?' So she has been listening.

'The stupid but major kind. Someone said my ex abducted you, or lured you to London.'

'That's not true. I came on the bus. On my own.'

'I don't doubt you. It would just be really helpful if I could tell the police that.'

'Why?'

'Michael is being investigated in connection with even more serious allegations – another set of false ones. I think someone has tried to frame him and managed to concoct just enough to make him a plausible suspect. And until what happened to you is cleared up the police won't give up the idea that he's a bad man.'

'OK, you can tell them I'm safe.'

'They might want to speak to you.'

She sees the manager approaching. 'I thought you said you didn't want to cause trouble?'

'Monica, is this woman bothering you?' asks the manager, giving me a cold look.

'No, miss. She's an old friend from home.'

Thanks, Ramona. 'Sorry to interrupt her at work,' I add. 'I'm only in town for today and I didn't want to miss my chance.'

The manager relaxes a little. 'So your mother was telling the truth?'

Mrs Payne has edged one step closer in kinship, it would appear. Next she'll claim to be my twin. 'Yes.'

'Well, it's almost end of shift. Monica, if you want a few moments with your friend, feel free to go off duty now.'

'Thanks, Miss Dunwoody.'

The manager pauses. 'By the way, what is your first name? That lady over there seems to think it's Ramona.'

My turn to give Ramona a break. 'Sorry about that. My mum always gets names muddled. She's got it lodged in her head that Monica here is called Ramona.'

The lady smiles in sympathy. 'Oh, I see. I know the feeling. I'm always getting my kids' names mixed up. I'll leave you to it.' The manager takes the tray from Ramona and heads back to the kitchen.

'Thanks,' mutters Ramona.

'Don't mention it. Do you have a moment to sit down?'

She nods and pulls out a chair. 'Do you want me to get you something? I get a staff discount.'

'No, really, I just want a quick chat.' I press my hands together, wondering how best to start on the subject. 'When I took on your case, I felt for you because it echoes elements of my own experience.'

She says nothing and keeps her gaze fixed on the view outside. A seagull lands on a window ledge and savages a crust. It looks too big to be in a city. It's easy to forget what things are really like until you see them up close.

Jessica, keep your head in the game, not flip-flopping in your usual random pattern.

'I ran away too, but when I was younger than you. I managed very badly. Still am a disaster area, if the truth be told. But you've done a good job looking after yourself. Someone needs to tell you that.'

'Thanks.'

'I ran away because my father was abusive, not sexually but physically and mentally.'

Her eyes meet mine.

'While I was away, my mum finally summoned up the courage and left him. She got a divorce. I've not seen him since.'

'Good.'

'Yeah. The thing is, I spoke to your mother a couple of weeks ago. I don't think you know, but she's given Barry the boot. She didn't realise until you left what had been going on.'

'She should've done.'

'She knows that. It's hard to look at something so terrible. You give yourself all sorts of reasons why it can't be true. The main thing now is that she's done what she should've done a while back and she's desperate to find you.'

'You won't tell her?'

'I made you a promise and I'll keep it. You know, I really have been sitting where you are. It took a while but I'm reconciled with my mother. Funnily enough, we only really talked about what happened to me just recently. These things take time, and forgiving others, forgiving yourself is sometimes best done in baby steps. Your mum's taken the first; I know it would mean everything to her if she just knew that you were OK. Could you make that small concession?'

'I suppose.'

'And maybe there's no one to say this to you, but I've been looking into a number of missing persons cases to help Michael. Two of the girls had no one. The other – well, her family is still a problem. I look at your case and I think there's a mother who's made really bad choices, recognised it, dealt with the root, and will now do anything to make it better. She's on your side. That's not to be dismissed as worthless. Think about it.'

'She's left him?'

'I think she threw him out.'

A small smile plays on Ramona's lips. 'Good for her.'

'You can get the law involved if you want, make it legal that he can't come near either of you. He can be prosecuted for what he did, if that's what you want.'

'I don't know. It's all too...'

Too difficult. Too painful. Too ugly. Yes, I know all of those feelings.

'OK, I've said enough. Everyone's experience is different and I respect that. But I really hope you do get in touch with your mum. She's a nice woman.'

'Yeah, yeah she is.' Ramona reaches out and touches the back of my hand. 'Thank you. I suppose I knew I'd get back in contact but I was just scared in case he answered her phone or read her messages.'

'I totally get that.'

'I'm pleased you got away from your situation.'

'Not without scars, but yes, I escaped.' I write down Inspector Randall's number on the back of a stray receipt. 'When you're ready, can you phone this man? He is the one investigating the charges against Michael – that's Dr Michael Harrison.'

'Oh, I saw the story about him in the *Metro*. I'll go ring the police now. No point leaving it once I've decided.'

344

'You know, Ramona, you are one great person. You are going to be fine.'

With a smile worthy of a *Vogue* cover girl, Ramona heads out back to change out of her uniform for the end of shift.

Mrs Payne takes Ramona's place. 'I told you she was a pretty girl.'

'She is beautiful on the inside too,' I comment, feeling quite tearful as I watch her go. I'm proud of her and I've only just met her.

Mrs Payne hands me a tissue. 'So are you, dear. So are you.'

I'm not, because I've not yet dealt with the threatening text I received from Max after my message ending it. I'm afraid I'm not going to be strong enough to resist going back there and doing what he asks.

Chapter 42

Drew and I sit on the lounge sofa with the TV switched on, two pairs of feet up on the coffee table, his in black socks, mine in ones with cats on them, and holes in the big toes. It is gloriously normal and for a brief moment I can pretend I'm not someone else's mistress. I realise now that I hardly ever had a relaxing evening with Michael, certainly never one watching any old thing on the telly and eating microwave popcorn. I spent a lot of time on my own, especially after I stopped going out after my first breakdown. If Michael did stay in with me, he was writing his books while I fussed around doing house-hold chores or one of my hobby crafts. I found it awkward to sit down when he was so clearly working. Thinking back, even before my crisis, when we were still out there as a couple, a typical evening together would mean meeting up with his friends to see something cultural. Michael had a mental list of all the things he needed to do each month to keep up with the trends. Maybe one of his fears was to be stuck at a drinks reception and have to admit to not having gone to the must-see exhibition, play or private view. It was an exhausting race always to be with or ahead of the cultural curve.

'You know what, Drew? Thanks to you, I have discovered my inner couch potato.'

'Glad to be of help.' He switches channel away from a soap neither of us like to a cooking programme which seems to involve the straggly-haired chef and his dog doing some kind of foraging in the forest. The chef looks like one of the weasels from *Wind in the Willows*, wilder than his handsome chocolate Labrador. I think of Emma and her food poisoning. Fate is a bitch sometimes.

'I'm surprised such a dietary purist as you has popcorn in the cupboard.'

'I thought you deserved a treat after your triumphant day.'

'I know. I'm pretty darned good at what I do.'

He takes a handful of kernels from the bowl on my lap as the chef cuts some green broad-bladed leaves with a bowie knife. 'Do you think you can make it into a business? When you've cleared up your cases, will you go looking for more?'

'Did I tell you that I had a text a few hours after meeting Ramona?'

'No. Who from?'

Don't say Max. Don't say Max. 'Her mother, ecstatic that her daughter has contacted her.'

'Hey, champ, well done!'

'She said she wanted to pay me for helping her and asked how much I wanted. I've not replied yet because you know how mixed up my motives were. I'm not sure it's right to charge her anything.'

'Jess, if you want to go into business you need to bill people for your services. It's not as if we like to charge people for getting dead.'

'I know, but I would've looked for Ramona anyway.'

'Fine, I understand. I've an idea. There are all kinds of payback. You can ask her to give you a testimonial and be a reference if someone wants to check you out.'

I reach up and give him a buttery kiss. 'I knew I kept you around for a reason, other than the sex and the popcorn, of course.'

'You forget the nifty foot rubs and neck massages.'

'I had that filed under sex.'

'That's a distracting thought. Where were we?' He sucks on one of my fingers. 'Oh yeah, Jessica's future.'

It was time I joined the real world. 'I think the idea of looking for missing persons was something of a fantasy, one that Jacob concocted for me, not a viable business. I'm going to need something more, I dunno, everyday, with a steady income.'

'You could work for us part-time on reception.'

'But aren't I the shameful skank who had sex with her tutor? I thought you were embarrassed by me.'

'I told you, I'm over that. Besides, you're having sex with me now, that earns you loads of plus points. If any of the staff make any comments, you tell me.'

'No one will mind?'

'Who's to mind? Mum and Dad really like you. They'll back you.'

I groan, remembering.

'Problem?'

'Your mum. She's got plans.'

He laughs and nuzzles my hair. 'She's had plans for me since I was born. I'm used to it. I'll be your human shield if you need one.'

'Just don't ask her to buy your condoms. She'll secretly be sticking pins in them.'

He looks fairly green at the prospect. 'I have never and will never ask her to do that.'

'I know – it's a gross thought. I have them. Frequently.'

My phone rings. The screen has reached the point where I can hardly see the name listed.

'Hello?' I'm fearful it will be Max asking why I'm a no show this evening but am relieved when I hear Lizzy's voice.

'Jessica? Jessica? Is that you?' She's sobbing.

'Lizzy? What's wrong? Are you OK?'

Drew mutes the programme just as the chef slices off some yellow fungus like dead fingers from a stump.

'No, I'm not, not OK. Can you come over?'

'What's happened? Is it Michael?'

'Yes. No. Oh God, I don't know what to do!'

'OK, hold tight. I'll ask Drew to bring me over. I can be with you in about,' I look to him, 'twenty minutes?'

Drew nods and gets up.

'Thanks. I really need a friend right now.'

'You've been there often enough for me. Want to give me a hint of what's happened?'

'Horrible, horrible argument with Michael. I'm feeling very shaky.'

'Is he there?'

'No. I'll explain when you come. Please, just get here as quickly as possible.'

I ring off. 'Sorry.'

'No, no, she's our friend.'

When we get to the street I've been trying so unsuccessfully to relegate to the past, I find myself looking for lights on in Michael's windows. The house is dark. Drew parks the moped and I knock on Lizzy's door. She opens it a crack, then all the way.

'Come in quickly please. I don't want anyone to see.'

She practically pulls me inside, Drew only managing to slip in because he's stepping on my heels. Once we get into her hallway I see why she's so anxious not to show her face. A bruise marks her jaw and she's got the start of a black eye that she's nursing with an ice pack.

'My God, Lizzy, what happened to you?'

She bites her lip.

'Was it... Was it Michael?'

I can hear Drew muttering something about going round and sorting him out.

Lizzy nods. 'We... We argued. I didn't expect him to get physical. Oh Jessica, there're things you don't know. Do you mind if we sit down?'

We follow her through to her kitchen. It's the mirror image of Michael's, conservatory on the left rather than the right. Flossie runs up and jumps to greet us, barking hysterically. The sounds goes right through my brain.

Lizzy tries to restrain her. 'Sorry, she's not had a walk. I couldn't go out like this. Tea? Coffee?'

Drew crouches and attempts to calm the spaniel. His gets a face-wash for his trouble. 'Would you like me to take her out so you two can talk?'

'Oh would you, Drew?' Lizzy fetches a lead which produces yet more bouncing. 'There's a park – oh, but it'll be closed now.'

'Don't worry. Flossie will show me where she wants to go.' He pockets some little black bags and heads out with the spaniel towing him along the street.

'You've picked a good one there,' says Lizzy, looking a little grim.

'And I have you to thank for introducing us. He and his family are so kind to me.'

'Jessica, I should've thought! How are you after Friday? I shouldn't have rung you. You need to rest.'

'I'm OK. I only stayed in overnight. There was only the one, you know, hallucination when I was in the kitchen. When I settled and got over the fear, I felt more or less normal. Normal for me, that is.'

She nods and pours water into a teapot. 'I'm making decaffeinated – is that OK?'

'Fine. Now sit down and tell me what's happened.'

She puts two mugs on the table, a little jug of milk, and the teapot under a cosy in the shape of a thatched cottage. There are kids' drawings on the fridge – thank-you cards from her last class of leavers. It's odd, now I think about it: I don't come over here very much. She tends to come to us. There's a dream catcher hanging at the window and a large picture of a moon over a dark sea, rather gloomy for a kitchen.

'OK, there's something I need to confess first,' begins Lizzy. 'Michael and I have been... have been lovers for a while now.'

'Wow.' I put my hands to my face. I hadn't been expecting that. 'How long?'

'Since Eastfields. I've wanted to tell you but Michael said that he didn't want to do so. He couldn't afford to have you even angrier with him than you already were while he was being investigated.'

'He was sleeping with you? Behind my back?' I say it more to make it a fact than to get an answer. Weirdly, it is a relief. I'm not the only slut; Michael is one too.

'I think I was a kind of revenge relationship to start with, but since you left we've spent more time with each other and... well, I've been practically living with him for a few weeks now. I'm sorry. I love him.'

I take a breath. I need to work this out for myself. I can hardly complain about betrayal when I'd been the one who started it. I'd long since worked out that I no longer loved Michael. 'Right, OK. Don't apologise to me. Stuff happens.'

'It certainly does. But that's only a kind of introduction to what went wrong, so you'll understand.'

It's clearly gone hugely, horribly wrong for her to be sitting there with an ice pack. I pour the tea for us both. 'I'm listening.'

'I've spent most of my time over at Michael's since you left. I thought I was a comfort to him.'

'You probably were.' I'm trying not to be cynical but Michael is the kind of man who needs a woman to offer him a flattering reflection of himself. Lizzy, an attractive woman with her honey-blonde hair and doe-like brown eyes, fitted the bill.

'You know, it all sounds so stupid! I can't believe myself sometimes. I'm normally a better judge of character than this.' She shakes her head at herself.

'What happened, Lizzy?'

'I did some ironing – I did his shirts for him because he mentioned that he was running out.'

'So you are an ironing kind of person,' I murmur.

'What?'

'Nothing. Go on.'

'I was hanging them up in his wardrobe when I noticed a lump in his jacket pocket – the green linen one, very rumpled.'

'His conference suit.'

'Yes, it survived the bedroom slashing.'

'He was wearing it in Berlin.'

'Of course. Anyway, I thought he might've left something he needed in there, so I fished around and found this.' She puts a dark-blue box on the table and opens it. A plain gold band and a sapphire flanked by two diamonds. 'They're Emma's, aren't they – engagement and wedding rings?'

'Yes, they are.' And Michael had said they were stolen. First, he accused me, then we had all assumed Jacob had taken them. 'Have you told him you found them?'

She gives a dark laugh. 'Oh yes.' She points to the black eye. 'I asked him how he came to have them when he'd told the police that they'd been stolen during the break-in and the attack on the bedroom. He tried to deny they were the same rings. I called him on that and he got very angry – I mean, really scarily angry.'

'I can imagine.'

'I tried to push past him but he got in my way. He's a big man. I have to admit to getting scared at this point. We had, I suppose, what you'd call a fight. I hit him with the coffee pot to get away. He was bleeding, dazed, so I took my chance and ran home and locked the door.'

'You should've called the police.'

'You think? I don't want to get him into more trouble.'

'Lizzy, if he had the rings, then he's not been telling us the truth, has he?' I'm having to rethink my assumptions. 'Just because Michael's been cleared of Jacob's wild accusations doesn't mean he can't, after all, have been involved in his death.'

'How do you mean?'

'I'm not sure. I can think of several alternatives. Maybe Jacob broke in and took most of the stuff, as we know. When he came home, Michael found the damage, decided it was me, and pocketed the rings to make me look more vindictive to the police he called in.'

Lizzy frowns then winces as it hurts her bruises. 'That's possible, I suppose.'

'Or Michael staged the break-in himself. Drew suggested that as a possibility early on to me, but I'm afraid I dismissed it.'

'So how did Jacob have some of the things at his home?'

I don't want to think this way, I really don't, not when I've spent the last few days convinced Michael is the victim here. 'Maybe Michael took them to Jacob's house, got into a show-down with him, killed him and then made a botched attempt at making Jacob's death look like suicide.'

'The drugged whisky? Was that him too?'

'I... I don't know. Perhaps.'

'Are you saying you now think Michael did kill Jacob?'

'I don't know what to think, but I do know you need to tell the police. I know that the ring box has opened up various doors that I thought we'd shut.'

Lizzy puts the ice pack down. 'There's something else you need to know. Michael's gone. His car, some of his clothes, his passport.'

Now she mentions it, I can see with my own eyes that at least part of that is true. The BMW isn't on the street outside the house as it normally should be. 'You went back in the house?'

'Only when I was sure it was empty. There's some blood on the sink, as if he only had a chance to have a quick wash-up, otherwise there's no sign of him. I think he might've made a run for it, knowing that I had got away and had the rings as evidence. He must feel as though the net is closing in.'

I pick up her home phone. 'Lizzy, phone the police right now. They'll want to send out an alert.'

'Right. OK. I'll do it. Which number shall I ring? 999?'

'Try this one first.' And for the third time in two days I hand over Inspector Randall's details to a woman with something to tell him about Michael.

Chapter 43

By the time Drew is back with Flossie, the police have arrived. The press, piranhas, smelling blood in the water, swim up soon afterwards, filling the street with their noise, equipment and lights. I stay inside Lizzy's as she escorts DS Lloyd around Michael's house. They have asked to see the broken coffee pot and the gaps in Michael's wardrobe.

Inspector Randall sits with me, drinking a fresh cup of tea. 'You've been busy, Miss Bridges.'

'For all the good it's done.'

'You helped tie up some loose ends. Though I told you not to interfere, I suppose I should be grateful you've saved me the man-hours that would've been expended checking out what had happened to these girls.'

'Is that a backhanded kind of thanks?'

'If you like. Did you ever read all the way through Jacob's files?'

I shake my head. I guess that he is subtly checking my earlier statements, hoping I'll slip up now over a week has passed. 'No. I mentioned that I read the entries from where he first decided to employ me. I then had an attack of conscience and handed the laptop over to you. I didn't know how the earlier stuff would connect to Michael.'

'It's a very odd case.' Randall leans forward as if to confide in me. I have to remember I still could be a suspect here and not get too friendly. 'Jacob West appears to have a tendency to believe a number of conspiracy theories. He contributed to online chats with that profile.'

'I didn't know that about him. What kind of theories?'

He gives me a rueful smile. 'You name it. Anything to do with big business or influential figures in the establishment plotting the downfall of free society. There are some you'll recognise: 9/11, the intervention of a shady group called the New World Order, the Roswell alien incident, NASA faking the Moon landings, the assassination of JFK.'

'So you're wondering if he invented his own conspiracy about Michael and those girls?'

'Actually, no. I think it's more complex than that. You have to understand that most conspiracy theorists I've come across honestly believe their alternate reality. It's a kind of mentality – I was going to say modern mentality but I think it has been around for a long while; the internet has just allowed like minds to meet more easily.'

'The opposite of Occam's razor. If there's a wiggly twisted route, the conspiracy theorists take that rather than believe the straight road of the evidence.'

'I'm sure there's all sorts of psychological reasons why quite a large proportion of society are susceptible to the opposite of, what was it you called it, Occam's razor?'

'Yes. Sorry. I like trivia.'

'Please, no need to apologise. I'm impressed. But then again, from the start I've had you down as an intelligent player in this particular case.'

'I think that's a compliment – unless it gets me in trouble.'

'I'm coming to that. You see, we believe Jacob was fed selected information on the girls by someone who knew that he would likely spin the little he was given into some complicated theory. He refers, back around New Year a couple of times, to anonymous tips.'

'Do you know the identity of the tipster?'

'It's someone who knew where Michael was at certain times and on specific dates; someone who knew just how to throw tempting titbits to a paranoid character like West, getting him to snap them up without question even if they were poisoned bait; someone who has a good understanding of the psychological profile of such an individual.'

The silence is broken by the sound of Drew playing fetch with Flossie in the back garden. She got hysterical again when the police arrived so he has done us all a favour by removing her from the room. I wish he were sitting with me to give me moral support. 'Inspector, are you accusing me of doing this?'

'No. I'm asking if you did.'

'Why would I? I was part of Jacob's whole evildoers fantasy, wasn't I?'

'That could be a very clever smokescreen – hide the fact that you started it by taking a minor part in the drama.'

'Who's making up the conspiracy now? Let me give you a straight answer. No, I did not tell Jacob to look into the four girls or suggest he employ me to do so.'

Lloyd and Lizzy come back in.

'Sir, Miss Huntingdon is correct,' reports Sergeant Lloyd. 'Michael Harrison has left in a hurry. An officer from the crime scene team swabbed the sink and will check if it is Harrison's blood, and I've locked up. Shall I put a police guard on the place?'

'Have an officer stand out front for a couple of days to keep the press from intruding. That should be enough.' Randall gets up. 'Thanks for the tea and use of your kitchen, Miss Huntingdon. We'll be in touch.'

'What happens now?' I ask.

'We look for Dr Harrison and for the car.'

'Will you arrest him?' asks Lizzy, touching her black eye lightly.

'If you wish to press charges on assault, then yes. As to the other matter, I have plenty of questions I now need to ask him, so you can rest assured Dr Harrison will not be returning home any time soon. Thank you for handing this over to us.' He holds up the plastic evidence bag containing the ring box.

'No problem,' says Lizzy.

The inspector pauses on the way out. 'I looked you up, Miss Huntingdon. You were on the job, weren't you?'

'Long ago.'

'Why did you leave?'

'I lost my appetite for that kind of work. I decided teaching was more my thing.' She walks him to the front door. 'Good night, Inspector.'

Chapter 44

Michael is still missing. The media report the next morning that his vehicle has been found in a short-stay car park at Heathrow. Being an area of high security, the garages have CCTV but the BMW had been parked in such a way that the driver was hidden behind a pillar when he got out. He then ducked into a stairwell and mingled with the crowd. Further checks with the airlines don't find him booking in for any onward travel, so the media are speculating that Michael either used a fake passport, or driving to the airport was a bluff to make everyone think he's fled the country. The local reporter on the BBC points out that the central bus station has coaches departing for all corners of the UK at regular intervals and no one document-checks the passengers. He could have gone anywhere.

Drew switches off the breakfast TV. I lie with my head on his chest, letting him soothe me.

'This is so strange, to be close to a major news story,' I murmur.

'Yeah. So are you thinking Michael did kill Jacob after all?'

'I don't know. The ring box – where does that fit? The

inspector told me last night that Jacob was a committed conspiracy theorist. He thinks someone manipulated Jacob into creating a case around four random girls who just happened to go missing on days when Michael was in their area. Like, if it had been Manchester rather than Harrogate, he'd have picked one from there.'

'Not so random then. That would take dedicated research.'

'And a knowledge of Michael's movements. It's not as if he posts his diary online or anything.' I turn to look up at him. 'Randall suspects me.'

'He suspects everyone.'

'I knew what Michael was doing during that period and I worked with Jacob. I join the dots.'

'But unless you've got very good at falsifying data input on a laptop, then you're clear. You didn't know him before April.'

'There's only my word on that. But what if I knew about Jacob before I started working for him? That diary of Emma's had to be lying about the house somewhere and Randall can theorise that I found it earlier than I claimed. What if I saw the animosity between Jacob and Michael and decided Jacob was a perfect tool to undermine my partner as our relationship crumbled?'

'How very Machiavellian of you.' Drew kisses my equilateral triangle of freckles. 'Good attempt, Jess, at persuading me to doubt you, but I don't buy it. Can't see you having enough mental energy for a plot like that. So little for you to gain. And plus, you're too nice.'

'Aw. OK, I own up. It wasn't me. But someone did. Jacob is

unlikely to have enough insider knowledge on Michael to come up with all that stuff himself.'

'OK, here's a thought, going with my earlier idea that Michael trashed his own bedroom: what if Michael was the one feeding Jacob this false material to destroy his reliability as a witness if he did come forward to make allegations against Emma?'

'Go on.'

'So Emma did go wrong, trying to hide Jacob's child from him. Michael would've been well aware that Jacob could've sued the police and made a huge scandal. It's bad enough when cases involve male officers duping unsuspecting females and having kids with them; think of the shitstorm when it's a female officer who tricks the dad and runs off with the child.'

'It would be brutal – and, no question, Michael still loves Emma. He would hate that to happen to her reputation, even though she's dead.'

'Right. So, Michael drips these cases into Jacob's suspicious little mind and builds a picture of himself as some monster, so way out there that any rational person would dismiss it. He's the famous TV psychologist, he can claim, bound to be the focus of some nutter's fantasies. The police will just brush the allegations off like so much lint. He knows just how to work the con because he's the fricking expert on deviant minds, so it plays right into the way Jacob thinks. Am I making sense so far?'

'Yes, you are.'

'So when Jacob decides to go public – hey, this woman

stole my child from me and she went to live with a murdering bastard who killed all these girls and possibly my daughter too – Michael can just produce three living women and say "no, I didn't". He couldn't have predicted that the fourth was depressed and would take her own life, but still that's not on him. No one has put him at the station when it happened. His reputation would stand. Jacob's would nose-dive. No one would listen to Jacob after that.'

'How does that fit with the way Jacob died? I feel like we've got some of the right pieces but they don't fit easily together and it's no good forcing them.'

'Yeah, it's not quite working, is it?'

'It still must be to do with Jacob finding out somehow that, for once, he was right, that he had been the victim of a conspiracy, Emma had been undercover. What then?'

'That's where it gets a bit shaky. Maybe he threatened to blackmail Michael and they argued? Michael went over to Jacob's house on his way to Berlin to sort it out. Push came to shove – I meant that literally – and Jacob died.'

'But the drugged whisky?'

'I told you it was a shaky theory.'

Something is bugging me. I can't lie in bed any longer until I get this niggle out of my brain. 'I hope you've got plenty of ink for your printer because I want to print out Emma's diary – all of it. I've been dipping in, mainly reading it backwards in the order I took the photos, but it's time I put it all together chronologically.'

Drew groans. 'I was hoping I could persuade you to stay under the duvet with me a little longer.'

'Tempting, but from the glint in your eye, I don't think it would be just a little while.'

'I can be quick.'

I dance away from his outstretched arms. 'Later. There's something I want to check.'

I set the printer going while I get dressed. Drew shows he's a good sport by solving a couple of paper jams caused by the recycled paper I'm using. By the time I'm dressed I have a complete set of Emma's entries. I carry them to the kitchen bar.

'Got a couple of highlighters?'

Drew opens a drawer and chucks me two in rapid succession. I obviously drop them both because I'm a klutz. 'What are you planning to do with them?'

I scrabble on the floor to retrieve the pens. 'You can help if you like. I'm a great believer in highlighters. I want you to underline in yellow every mention of Jacob, and then in orange, Emma's best friend, Biff.'

'Biff?'

'Yeah, I think she'd been there all along.'

'Your mind is a fascinating place.'

'Sherlock has a mind palace; I have a mind jumble sale. Eventually, if I rummage around enough, I'll spot a bargain.'

'And right there's the slogan for your T-shirt.'

I grin. 'It was my mistake that I didn't see it earlier. I've always thought of Lizzy as Michael's friend because I never saw her with Emma. Michael doesn't have photos of Emma out on display, no group shots, no party selfies, and Biff doesn't appear in the wedding album – that was obviously because

Michael and Emma went alone to Vegas. I'll bet "Biff", or Lizzy, who I think are one and the same, stayed home looking after Kaitlin for them.'

'There must be more images, something that puts them together if they were that close.'

'I'm sure there are. Michael will have more photos but in cloud storage or on a device somewhere. I've never thought to check. Anyway, it would all be pass-coded. He never liked me to see that part of his life.' Speed reading, I find the first mention of Biff and highlight it. Drew, who is starting at the other end of the diary, grabs the pen from me and makes several marks. 'Yesterday, as he was leaving, Inspector Randall mentioned that Lizzy had been on the job.'

'I noticed. It was an odd moment.'

'She admitted it – she could hardly deny it to a serving officer if he's got the records. I've been wondering why she has never told me, in all the years I've known her, that she had a career before primary teaching?'

'Playing devil's advocate here: maybe she just didn't like to be reminded that she washed out?'

'Or maybe she was hiding it because I would know that Emma was also in the force and start to ask questions. And the name – Lizzy – Elizabeth – Biff – it's not so much of a stretch to think Emma might've called her best friend that.'

'I bet it was useful – something Emma would use naturally without giving Lizzy's real name away while they were on the job.' Drew has found more mentions of Biff than me. I can see from a glance that she had greater involvement in Emma's life towards the end than at the beginning of the diary.

'It's a shame Emma's notes don't go further back. They start when Emma is already living with Jacob. The decision to do that must be in another book somewhere, that's if she risked writing it down at all. She must have known she was going far outside procedure.'

'I'm more cynical. I can imagine the two women officers were given unofficial sanction to use a honey trap, if their bosses really thought Jacob's group was planning an attack.'

'OK, I can work with that. So imagine the pair of them sashaying into a protest march and sticking around for the pub. Those eco-guys must've thought their luck had changed when two good-looking girls flattered them into thinking living in the wild with them was their idea of fun.'

'I imagine their dicks rather than their brains were involved in the decision to let them into the inner circle.'

'You men are so predictable.'

'It's a burden we all just have to bear. Women are obviously the only rational sex. Never think emotionally.'

I snort. I move to yellow, highlighting Jacob's name. There are lots of entries in this early part of the diary that I haven't got to yet in my read-through. 'What would be really helpful is if we could find a place where Emma doesn't call Biff by her nickname. Just once, then I'll know that I'm correct that they were friends before she met Michael.'

'But you think you're on the right track, I can tell.'

'It would be good to have evidence to show Randall.'

'But can you trust the police with this? Aren't they involved? You know, you're selling this theory of yours to me, so I've got to think the worst.'

'Which theory?'

'The undercover-cop one. I thought it was a little out there when you first mentioned it.'

'It is – it's mad. That's why it's not been anyone's first explanation of what's going on in Emma's diary.'

'But people do mad things every day.'

'Like shack up with me.' I hip-bump him.

'Exactly.'

'When I first read the diary, I thought it was a young woman thinking she's saving the planet, falling out of love with the idea once she has her own kid, then trying to hide from an obsessive lover. Please rein me in if you think I'm getting carried away with my spy story.'

'I will, but so far you are carrying me along with you. But I've another question. If Biff-slash-Lizzy was so involved in Kaitlin's early days, why isn't Kaitlin with her now? Michael's not the fatherly sort. She could've put in for adoption if Emma agreed.'

'Would she agree?'

'Emma had warning that she was dying. Wouldn't her first concern be for her baby girl?'

'Yes, I think it would.'

'So what happened? Why not entrust her to her oldest friend?'

I highlight another string of mentions of Biff. 'I think only Lizzy and Michael know, and somehow I get the feeling neither of them want to say.'

Chapter 45

Michael

So cold. Ice.
The pain.

Emma's here. I can smell her.

Even Kaitlin, that little-girl scent that scared me senseless. God, Kaitlin, sorry, sorry, sorry. You, so lost after she went, so demanding. And me, so unable to be what you needed.

I'm sorry I couldn't...

How much time has passed now? It feels like forever. I don't know how long but I know I'm fucking dying. My rage is monumental, like I've got an alien trying to burst out of my stomach. I have howled myself hoarse but no one came. No one has ever fucking come to help me. I have nobody – that's a bloody depressing truth.

I swig the last of the bottle of Spanish red. I've given up trying to piss into the empties. I threw one at her last time she came, but got doused with the splash-back. I've had enough humiliation without that. At least it kept her away, fucking rabid bitch.

I can hear her coming.

'*Ten green bottles, hanging on the wall.*'

'Singing now are you, Michael?' She hovers at the top of the stairs.

'*Ten green bottles, come and take them all.*
Cause if you do, then you'll accidentally fall
And there'll be one bitch less to torment us all.'

I laugh manically.

'And to think the great Dr Harrison is reduced to spending his last hours making up playground taunts.'

'I'm a fucking dying swan, I am, singing out my heart. Recognise yourself, babe?'

The door closes, shutting out the light. I open the freezer and scrabble around until I find another carton of ice-cream. I stretch – and the pain is blinding.

I must've lost consciousness again because when I wake the ice-cream is in a puddle on the floor. I scoop up what I can and cram it in my mouth.

'You're not going to fucking beat me, bitch.'

Chapter 46

Jessica

I pull together all the diary pages and flick through them, getting a sense of the pattern.

'OK, here's how I read it. Emma goes undercover with Biff, working the same group, but they pretend not to know each other. That means the first year or so they only meet in passing when Jacob's around and save their big get-togethers for reporting to the bosses in London.'

'That goes with the idea that their managers knew what they were doing.'

'Or preferred not to ask questions as to how they got their information. Then in November 2009, when Kaitlin is about eighteen months old, Emma's priorities are shifting from her career to finding a decent place to raise her child. She expresses it as too much nappy washing by hand but I think the double life is tearing her apart. She's had a kid with a guy she doesn't like very much, after all.'

'Would screw anyone up.'

'So she bolts back to her secret life in London, leaving Jacob high and dry. Biff extricates herself shortly after and helps support Emma. Maybe that was when she quit the police, to do childminding. She probably combined it with teacher training.'

'Noble of her.'

'Agreed. I don't think there was much she wouldn't do for her BFF. OK, so Emma moves over to a training role in the police, drawing a veil over her own mistakes by not making a song and dance that she has a kid now. She might even have inferred it was Lizzy's kid if colleagues asked. Biff was no longer in the police, so what would they care? The two conspirators – that's Emma and Biff—'

'Yeah, I am keeping up, Poirot.'

'I prefer Sherlock – he's sexier.'

'Only because you're in love with Benedict Cumberbatch.'

'Who isn't?' I kiss Drew. 'Moving on. They seemed to have treated the arrangements for Kaitlin as a joint operation. Anyway, Emma meets Michael while she's on a training course and, thunderbolt moment, they fall in love. That wasn't in the plan and would have put Lizzy's nose well out of joint. Whirlwind romance, marriage, and the rest. Emma's hardly going to hide the fact she's got a daughter from Michael, so Lizzy finds she's being relegated there too.'

'To what?'

'An auntie-type figure. Not a co-mother.'

'Did the house originally belong to Michael or Emma?' asks Drew.

'I don't know. Good question.'

'I bet Emma and Lizzy bought properties conveniently

situated for playing pass-the-kid some time before. Emma's property would've become Michael's when she died.'

'Makes sense, Watson. Everything goes up in the air at that point. Lizzy has no legal right to Kaitlin. There's no father on the birth certificate. Michael's not the most involved step-parent. So what happened to Kaitlin?'

Drew brushes the hair back from my face. 'Maybe Emma had distant relatives you don't know about? They might've swooped in and claimed her.'

'That would've really pissed Lizzy off. She's given up her career to help with the kid and now it's as if she were no more important than an au pair.'

'So we've got a picture of how that went, but what about Michael? Why's he run for it now? You know him best: why would he do that?'

'I can believe he came to blows with Lizzy, but do you know something, I've realised the one thing that's been bothering me. Emma's cat. Colette.'

Drew shakes his head. 'A cat? We're talking domestic abuse, possibly murder, and you circle back to animal welfare.'

I'm pacing with excitement; it's all falling into place. 'Michael loves that animal. He would not walk away without making sure she was taken care of – or he'll sneak back to do so himself.'

Drew takes my shoulders and forces me to face him. 'Oh God, I know what you are going to say. Jess, stop. This is one of your impulses. You're coming off your meds and you're going to be up and down, reckless one moment, zonked out the next.'

I'm so revved, I'm bouncing. 'Faint heart never won fair lady. Time for some cat-napping.'

'You don't mean going to sleep, do you?'

'No, I mean revisiting the scene of the crime to see if Colette is still waiting at the back door.'

'If she's there?'

'Michael's in trouble.'

'If she's not there?'

'He's in even more trouble but at least he has company.'

'Just to think my life was normal before I met you.'

'Yeah, so normal, dealing with all those dead people in fridges at the end of the garden.'

He bats me overhead with a seat cushion. 'Fairly normal. So we're going back?'

'Yes. This time we're breaking in for real. I've been accused of it enough times so I might as well have a go.'

'And what's the excuse you're going to offer the police when we inevitably get caught?'

'That we mean well.'

'Yeah, like that's going to work.'

I spend the journey to Michael's house plotting our way inside. The thing about a house where you've lived for five years is that you know it like no one else does. I know, for example, that anal Michael keeps a special key box in his small tool shed, screwed under the workbench, and that is pass-coded. This is after I lost or forgot my keys several times and he had to come out of work to rescue me. Inside is a back-door key. I also know, because Randall was so kind as to announce it in my hearing, that the police patrol is only on the front of the house. They won't be watching the side passage. You can sneak into that through the bush in the neighbour's garden and then there's another push-button gate lock to which I have the combination. Unless the police are being particularly vigilant, no one should see us.

We park around the corner. Drew locks our helmets in his seat compartment.

'OK, what do we do now?' he asks.

'First, we stroll along on the opposite side of the road as if we're just on our way somewhere. I want to see what, if anything, is going on at Lizzy's and in Michael's house.'

'OK.' He puts an arm round me. 'Where are we pretending we are going? I like to have a visual.'

'Cinema?'

'Brain-dead comedy or raunchy love film with handcuffs and whips?'

'One where stuff blows up,' I say repressively. I don't want to be reminded of Max, not now. 'Superheroes.'

'Ugh. OK. I'm imagining that.'

'Would it have made a difference if I'd picked one of the others?'

'I'll show you later.'

Carrying on our banter, we stroll past the houses. There are lights on at Lizzy's but I can't see any movement behind the curtains. Michael's is dark apart from the alarm on the front wall glowing blue in set mode. Incident tape wraps around the gate but there is no one standing guard on the doorstep.

'Do you think they've gone home?' I ask Drew in a low voice.

'No, black car, across the road.'

Two men are sitting drinking coffee. One flicks through a copy of the *Evening Standard* while the other is talking on his phone. He might be reporting in, of course, but I imagine he's just phoning home.

'I guess it must be tedious, watching nothing happening,' I comment as we carry on past then circle back again. Our luck is in because the police have parked so they look across at the front door. They shouldn't see us heading into the neighbour's unless they turn around. We get into the shelter of the privet. It's not been cut for years as Mrs Jessop has rather lost interest in the world outside. She tends to live at the back so I'm not worried about being spotted. The foliage hides us completely. Drew doesn't say anything but does roll his eyes as I start to force my way through what I had generously called a gap when I explained my idea back at his house. It's more of a slot where it meets a fence. We get into the alley without mishap, unless you count ripping Drew's T-shirt and my leggings. I enter the combination and we're through to the back garden.

'OK,' I whisper, 'if Colette still is here then she'll come when we shake some kibble.'

'And where do we get that?'

'From inside.' I point to the container on the window ledge.

'You know we could've bought some from a shop and then not have to actually break in?'

'*Now* you suggest that. It's a bit late to actually plan this,

Drew.' We exchange a smile. God, this is fun. He really is my partner in crime now. 'Give me a sec, I'll just get the spare key.'

'Won't we set off the alarm?'

'Not if the person who left remembered to push the button so the cat's designated zone isn't active.'

'And if they didn't?'

'Then we're going to have to do a great deal of explaining.'

Chapter 47

Michael

'Why are you here again?' I try to lift my head. I can't believe the pain – like ice-bladed knives sticking in my side. I prefer that, though, to the parts I can't feel. This has been going on for so long I've lost track of time. I smell worse now because some hours ago I lost control of my bowels – no fucking choice lying here like a puppet with strings cut. I can't move my legs. I am so cold. Frankly, I'm surprised I'm still alive. Self-medicating on the wine I can reach from the rack only goes so far to dull the agony. I might be able to bear it, die quietly with some dignity, if only she would just shut up and go away. The mad bitch is clearly not getting me help. It was her who pushed me down here so she's hardly going to say 'oops, my bad, let me call an ambulance.'

'Fuck this!' I heave an empty bottle at her but it smashes several steps from where she's sitting. I'm angry that my aim hasn't improved.

'Temper, temper, Michael.'

'You're a sadistic cow, aren't you?' I'm slurring. Probably

thanks to the bottle of Chianti I downed just now. 'I can't imagine why I didn't see it.'

'Because you didn't take even a few moments away from your self-absorption to look. To be honest, I'm surprised you didn't get suspicious when I moved on you in February. I wondered if that would put you off – a girlfriend in distress and her best pal taking advantage, but no, you lapped it right up, a new little woman to hover over you and boost your ego between the sheets.' She sits at the top of the stairs like a spectator in the Colosseum come to watch the dying gladiators. She should sell bloody tickets. 'Not such a great psychologist now, are you, Dr Harrison?'

'Just shut the fuck up.'

'No, you listen. You knew Emma and I used our relationships with men to get the information we wanted. Why didn't you wake up to the fact that I was using you to get my own back? Do you think you're so irresistible to women that I would just fall for you like that?' She snaps her fingers. 'News flash, Michael: you're just another job. Why else do you think I've been putting up with you these last years?'

Something's really wrong with me. I can't see her now, vision tunnelling, just hear her hateful mocking voice. 'You're still working for the police?'

'Call it a private mission.' She gets up. 'But I think it's about to come to an end, don't you? How many more days of this do you think you can survive?'

'Until I'm found.'

'No chance of that. They think you've fled. I left your car at Heathrow. I hate to think what the parking charges are by now.'

'But why are you doing this?' That's what I'm wondering in my lucid moments, which are mercifully few. I prefer the drunken stupor. It hurts so much less. Chianti kicking in, I'm heading that way now; just need to keep as sharp as I can while she's here. I wouldn't put it past her to slit my throat if I were lying here unconscious. 'This can't still be about Emma's diary, the cover-up of what you both did. What have I done that you've decided I deserve to die by inches like this?'

'Katy.'

'What?'

'You sent Katy away.'

'Of course I did – I had to. You remember how I was after Emma's death? I was in no fit state to look after a little girl. I couldn't take up the guardianship.'

'You were never fit to look after her. You barely took any notice of her. She was supposed to come to me. Emma said.'

I'm getting angry now, which helps as it gives me some energy to fight this sapping cold and alcohol-induced dullness. I feel like Socrates dying from the feet up. I hug Emma's ski jacket to my face. 'Well, she must've changed her mind because there was no mention of that in her will. You know what? She probably realised what a psycho bitch you were. I'm pleased I didn't let Kaitlin go to you.'

'You did that because you couldn't bear the reminder of Emma living a few doors down. You were just being selfish, putting your needs first.'

'I did that because I thought it was best for Kaitlin – and I was right, if your actions now are anything to go by. My God, woman, you pushed me down the stairs and now you're gloating – that's not sane. Well, you're going to have to come and finish the job yourself, as I've got enough food and water within reach to last quite a few more days.' I must be drunk if I'm baiting her.

'Don't think I won't.' She takes a step. I see now that she has my old cricket bat in hand. Somehow the fact that she's intending to use a treasured possession from my college days to kill me seems the last insult.

'Well, fuck you. Go get your own murder weapon, bitch. You're not using that.' I heave another bottle at her, this time managing to smash it at her feet so she has to jump back. I can't afford to throw any of the full ones so I only have one left to drive her off. I'd better make it count.

'Hello?'

There's someone out there.

'Help! Down here! Help!' I shout.

The door opens all the way. It's Jessica and that Goth man she has been staying with. I don't care who it is: right now to me they are the Archangel Gabriel and all his army.

'Oh my God,' exclaims Jessica. 'What's happened?'

'He must've fallen,' says Lizzy quickly, leaning the bat against the wall but not before the man spots it.

'The bitch pushed me,' I tell him. 'Keep away from her.'

'He's raving – must've been lying here for days,' protests Lizzy, sounding oh-so-innocent. 'I was only checking on the house and thought I heard something.'

'Well, call an ambulance then! Can't you see he's hurt?' Jessica says irritably, hurrying past her and coming down to me.

'Stay away from her – don't come down here,' I try to warn her but Jessica's impulse is to comfort, not to take care of her own safety.

'Jess, I don't think we should try to move him,' says the guy, still standing at the top. I'm pleased to see he's looking hard at Lizzy and keeping his distance. 'Come back up here.'

'What's that smell? Oh Jesus.' Jessica grabs a picnic blanket from a high peg – it's been hanging there taunting me for days. She covers me. 'You're OK now, Michael. We're here. Drew, call an ambulance. Lizzy, snap out of it. We need to make him comfortable.'

There's a mew and a rattle of the cat flap. Phone in hand, Drew turns as Colette winds around his ankles. 'You called that one right, Jess. The cat is still here. I'll just go into the garden to ring for the ambulance. I can't get any reception in this corridor.'

'Watch out!' I shout.

Jessica shrieks as Lizzy swings the bat at the back of Drew's head. Reflexively, he ducks, taking the blow on his shoulder. Jessica is up and dashing up the stairs even as Lizzy lines up another shot.

'Are you mental?' Drew exclaims. 'What the hell are you doing!'

Lizzy kicks out at Jessica, at the cat, intent on taking out the man she sees as the biggest threat. She'll then turn on Jessica, leaving me till last. She swings the bat. Spooked, Colette streaks away from the violence. She must've headed for the front door because the next thing I hear is the house alarm wailing. Thank you, thank you: someone has forgotten to shut Colette in her zone and that blessed animal has tripped it. Realising her private little massacre is about to be interrupted, Lizzy makes a dash for the back but Jessica – Jessica! – jumps on her.

'You take a swipe at my guy, would you?' she bellows, pulling at Lizzy's hair to bring her to the ground. They fall over backwards and out of my sight.

'Answer the fucking door, would you?' I shout, as I can hear pounding at the entrance.

I don't know who eventually does open up, but the next thing I know is, the police are inside and an ambulance has been called. I'm not aware of what is happening upstairs because my view is blocked by the people clustering in the cellar. I find myself being assessed by a serious-looking paramedic who is calling for a backboard and head stabilisers.

He touches my ankle but there's nothing.

'I can't feel my legs. I'm fucking terrified.'

'I understand, sir. There's possibly damage to the spine. It's good that you've got arm movement.'

'My bladder – bowels ...' I think I would prefer to die here than spend the rest of my life pissing in a bag.

'It's Michael, isn't it? Can I call you Michael?'

'You can call me what the hell you want as long as you get me out of lying in my own shit.'

'Michael, you've been down here a long while. Don't jump to conclusions as to how severe your injuries are. We need to take you in to see what's going on.' A colleague appears at the top of the stairs. 'Quickly now: where's that stretcher? How are the pain levels, Michael?'

'I'm so fucking beautifully drunk, I don't know.'

He glances around at where he found me: crumpled at the bottom of the wine rack next to the box of Emma's things. I'm surrounded by empty cartons.

'I'm sodding sick of ice cream.'

'Don't blame you, but Ben and Jerry's cookie-dough ice cream might just have saved your life.'

His colleague brings down the stretcher and they line it up, ready to lift me on.

'This might hurt.'

'I don't care. Just get me out of here.'

'Do you want me to bring anything with you to the hospital?'

I hand him three of Emma's diaries, ones that fell on top of me when I upended the box to get at the clothes. I can't leave them here in this mess. 'And can you make sure someone feeds the cat? She's a bloody hero. I'm leaving everything to her in my will, you got that?'

'Yes, Michael, she's a hero. Now, brace yourself.'

Chapter 48

Emma, 10th May 2011

Today I called in the solicitor to see me in the hospice. The staff have warned me that I should put my affairs in order – God, that's such a strange phrase, like I'm having illicit flings with at least six lovers. How disappointing to find that at the end of life it just means sorting out the important things, like your daughter's future and your estate.

I told the lawyer that I wanted to change my will. I'm now trying not to feel guilty about it. I know Biff has been a good friend to me – my best friend since we were in Mrs Mandy's class in our Dorchester primary school all those years ago – but I've decided to make Michael Katy's guardian. There, I've said it – gone and done it. Biff is not going to like that, not one little bit, but I genuinely believe it will be the right thing for my daughter and that's what matters now. Us adults will have to muddle through as best we can with the crap hand life has dealt.

I have quite a few reasons for this decision. I haven't made it lightly as I know it will be upsetting to both Katy and Biff, at least to start with, that's until they get used to the new arrangement. Katy will recover quickly – she's at that age. She won't even remember me in a few years so she'll certainly get over being eased away from Biff. It might take Biff a few years to see I meant what was best for her too, but hopefully she'll be mature enough to get that eventually. She was an only child, like me. We both need more people around than fate has given us. It's time she made a start on that.

My first reason is perhaps not the most noble. There have been occasions over the last few months when Biff has acted as though I'm already gone. I think it's partly push-back for me having married and made our trio a quartet, but I can hear her talking to Katy sometimes. 'When Mummy is gone, we'll…' 'Those are Mummy's favourite flowers. We will have to remember her when we see them.' It might be that, so close to the end of my own life, I'm jealous of the living, but something feels just off about Biff's behaviour lately – this past year, in fact. Unhealthy. That's ironic coming from me, with the non-functioning liver and toxic blood. I've been telling Biff to get out, create her own life with a relationship, as we both should've done years before. It was fine to join the police together but we should've taken separate paths just so we had the chance to form our personalities apart for a while. The wisdom of hindsight. We made it too much like a three-legged race. Even when I left special ops, thinking she'd stay on, she followed me. I should've put my foot down then but she made it easier, sharing the childcare so I could still have a career, and go on to meet Michael.

Don't get me wrong: I'm grateful. She made real sacrifices,

going part-time and changing to teaching so she could have the holidays off to look after Katy. I was hesitant to question my good fortune but I might've been reading the signs wrongly – I thought she was helping me but I think in a way she was trying to be me. I think she'd reached the point where she couldn't, wouldn't disengage, and that's a bit frightening. I don't doubt that she loves me and loves Katy but no one wants to be the focus, to that extreme, of someone else's existence. We all in the end have to be free to stand alone. I can't leave Katy handling that attention.

But enough. The prospect of death might be making me more clear-sighted, more prone to cutting through the crap, as I just don't have time for it any longer. Biff is still young and has so much ahead of her. She could have her own children, her own life. None of my hints in the past have worked: she's carried on living, or trying to live, mine. It has felt oppressive.

But the main reason for my decision is that Michael will never learn to be a proper dad to Katy if Biff is hovering over him, breathing down his neck like she does mine. She'll undermine his confidence and have Katy with her too much. With Biff kept more at a distance from day-to-day matters (I can't see him letting Biff wander in at all times of night and day, as she has with me), and with him given the power of the guardian, the father that I know is inside him will have time to emerge. And he can protect Katy much better if Jacob comes sniffing around – a respected academic versus a crazy guy who lives on the fringes like Jacob? No contest. Biff and I, well, we made mistakes, so we are vulnerable if Jacob wants to challenge what we did. That's the price of our taking those risks. Michael is the safer pair of hands. If it goes to court, they'll rule in the best interests of the child, and by then that will be Michael.

Biff will think the forced break from Katy is cruel, but I'm being cruel to be kind. You've got to move on, Biff. Live a bit.

I don't think I've spelt it out too clearly, not so as to endanger Katy, but I don't want to leave any hostages to fortune. Except maybe that weak moment at Christmas 2007 – I had to vent somewhere or I would've just burst – but I should've ripped that out. God, I need to rip that one out. Can I get Michael to bring it in? Or just ask him to chuck that whole notebook? I don't want to draw his attention to it. And I don't want Katy to read them ever...

It is an hour later. The nurse came in because my heart rate peaked. She said I was overdoing it with my meetings and my scribblings, as she puts it. She is Irish, would you know. I feel like there's a touch of my mother in her which makes me forgive her badgering me to rest. I'm soon going to get plenty of that. I had to promise I'd calm down. The pause gave me a chance to think it through. There's no need to panic. I'll ask him tonight. I'll get Michael to destroy those diaries of mine – all of them, including the embarrassing teenage outpourings as well as the more incendiary stuff of my twenties. That's not the version of me I want to survive. Given the choice, I'd prefer Michael not to know exactly what happened, not for sure, so I'll ask him not to read these words. I don't mind him knowing, though, that he has been my huge consolation prize these last two years. Life has kicked me around but at least it gave me him towards the end. My love for him has changed my view on what love can be. If there's a way of being there for someone when they die, then it'll be him I'm waiting for – that's until Katy joins us, many, many years later. I don't mind him reading that. But burn the rest, my darling.

Chapter 49

Michael, 2nd September

She's managed to come back to me, like she promised. We're wandering, lovers in no hurry, passing over the Accademia bridge in Venice. She's laughing, head thrown back, hair rippling to her shoulder blades. My soul walks beside me.

That's not right. She was ill already when we were in Venice.

'Where's Katy, Michael? Why isn't she here with us?' asks Emma.

'We left her at home, remember? It's just us for a few days.' I try to lace her fingers in mine but suddenly she is at the other end of the bridge and she's holding Kaitlin's hand. Coppery glints shine in Kaitlin's bobbed hair and she's talking earnestly to her mother, a stream of her babbling chatter. She offers her mother a purple iris, Emma's favourite flower. They're walking away from me, not taking any notice of my shouts for their attention. I can't reach them because my legs won't work.

'Emma? Emma?'

I feel a hand on my shoulder. 'Sssh, Michael, it's just a dream. They're gone now.'

I open my eyes and it's Lizzy standing over me. She has the bread knife raised above my chest – the same one as was stabbed in the mattress.

I yell and throw my hands out. They crash onto the bed rail, the IV port in the back of the left hand taking a fierce rap. My eyes really open this time, shocked awake by pain, and I realise I'd dreamt it all – Venice, Emma, Lizzy.

'Are you all right, Dr Harrison?' It's the policeman guarding my room who is asking. Alarmed by my shouts, he has poked his head round the door.

'Ye... Yes. Just a nightmare.' I try to reach for the water but my hand is shaking too badly.

'Shall I call a nurse?'

'I just... I just want some water.' Humiliatingly, I can feel tears beginning to fall.

'I'll get someone for you.'

I collapse back on the pillows, remembering, as I had in the cellar, that there is no one.

Chapter 50

Jessica, 3rd September

I'm a little fearful about what I will find when I visit Michael in St Thomas' Hospital. When I last saw him he was being carried out of his house, strapped to the same kind of stretcher that they use for mountain rescues – this was made necessary by the narrow cellar stairs. Michael had been grey in the face but spewing swear words like an irate TV chef as they bore him out of the house before the cameras of the national media. It hadn't taken those vultures long to circle the carcass of our drama. Michael's foul language had the advantage, though, that none of them could print or broadcast his words without asterisks and bleeps, so they got barely a repeatable word from him. He instantly became an internet sensation in a few uncensored clips that slipped through on YouTube, telling the press to go fuck themselves sideways.

The paramedic explained to me afterwards that Michael was rip-roaring drunk as he had survived on alcohol and ice cream. I wanted to quip that that was my normal diet but held back, as it wasn't the right time for jokes. As they packed up, the ambulance guys were saying the press should be ashamed of themselves, filming a seriously injured man in a vulnerable moment. I suspect, however, that Michael won't be too upset. He got a chance to say what he really felt without his usual gloss and the press have to feel bad about the way it came out. He is now above criticism. After putting him through trial by media, they are now finding themselves castigated, by the few outlets that held back, for failing yet again to learn the lessons of responsible journalism.

I show my ID to the policeman on the door who checks my name against the list of allowed visitors. Inspector Randall only now is taking care that the press don't get in to maul Michael again. Randall is another one who is facing criticism for the way he's been handling this case.

'Anyone else been?' I ask.

'His sister, but she didn't stay long. His parents are coming later. Some uncle is expected tomorrow.'

The retired judge. Good God, that's enough to polish anyone off.

I enter. Michael turns his head to look at me.

'Jessica.' There is more warmth in his tone than I've ever heard.

'Michael, how are you?'

'Seriously fucked up. Looking on the bright side, it's an L4 break which means it could be worse. I might even be able to walk short distances one day but will probably be in a wheelchair for most of the time.'

I say nothing, just hold his hand.

'At least that's what they think. Because I was lying down

there so long there's a lot of swelling and bruising. They're going to do some more scans next week, see if there's any room for improvement on that prognosis. I've got cracked ribs too, but that seems rather minor by comparison.'

'I'm sorry.'

'Don't be sorry. Thanks for riding to the rescue.'

'It was Colette who did that.'

'Yes, I suppose she did.' He manages a smile, lips curving in a prickled chin, some grey stubble showing on his upper lip. It annoys me that no one has helped him shave. He would never normally want to be seen like this. I wonder if I should offer but it seems awkwardly intimate, considering where we've reached in our relationship. I offer instead what comfort I know I am able to give.

'I've taken Colette to my house temporarily until you get home. I'm keeping her in so she doesn't run away, but it's a large flat. Is that OK?'

'Thanks. I might be in here some time – and then there's rehabilitation. Not sure where I'll be for that.'

'As long as it takes.' I've also adopted an abandoned spaniel, but perhaps he doesn't need to know that.

We sit in silence for a little while.

'Go on then. Tell me what happened after you tackled Lizzy,' he says.

'You saw that?'

'The start of it.'

'It turned out that was a stupid idea as, hello, trained former policewoman? But that's me – dive in without much prior thought. I ended up with her straddling me, about to bash out my brains with the butt of your cricket bat. Drew hauled her off, kept her in a half-Nelson while I let in the policemen. They were parked outside keeping an eye on the place.'

'Are you telling me that the police were there all the time – while I was lying in the cellar?'

'I'm afraid so. Lizzy was the one who showed the original investigator around the house and he was working on the assumption you'd fled. You have to say she had balls. It didn't cross anyone's mind that you might still be on the premises, so he only checked the main rooms and that your passport and some clothes had gone – which of course they had, as Lizzy had already taken them. The police are getting a lot of criticism for that.'

'So the police came and then what?'

'It was a mess. Lizzie jumped right in and said we'd done it – that Drew and I had pushed you down the stairs and she'd just found us. The ambulance came and carted you off. No one was allowed to talk to you to get the truth, as you were in a bad way.'

'I was drunk as a lord.'

'That too.' I squeeze his hand. 'Randall and his team turned up and things began to calm down somewhat. We were taken into separate rooms and each asked to account for our movements. I think he was already suspicious of Lizzy. His team had got to the diary and it's pretty clear from that that Emma was colluding with someone she called Biff.'

'She always called Lizzy that – a childhood thing.'

'Randall had been going through their service records and putting it all together.'

'I've heard that he's meticulous.'

'Good thing too. Of the three of us, Lizzy had the most to hide. But it was still unclear why she turned on you in such a horrible way.'

'She told me that in one of her gloating sessions. Revenge. I didn't let her have Kaitlin.'

'Oh, OK. Yeah, that makes sense.' The missing child. In the end it keeps coming back to Emma and her daughter. 'I thought it might be to cover up the fact that she murdered Jacob.'

'She did that too? I did wonder if she was responsible, after I found myself at the bottom of the staircase. I think she drugged my coffee to slow my reactions.'

'I suppose if it worked once, why not again?'

'She had already opened the cellar door, so all she had to do was manoeuvre me in front of it while I was staggering, and push. I thought I was going to die down there.'

'You might've done, as no one was looking in the house for you. You missed the bit where she produced Emma's rings as a way of implicating you – that's why we all thought you had fled. It turns out that Lizzy, as her alter ego, undercover cop Biff, had kept up some contact with Jacob through the eco movement. She was the one who had fed him that information that started him off on the wild goose chase about you and those girls. She played him like a Stradivarius. Her intention was to destroy his credibility in case he found out that Emma had been a policewoman. If he started making wild accusations against you, then who would listen to what he said about her? Plus it was a major pain in the butt for

Joss Stirling

you, potentially career damaging, with whispers and rumours doing the rounds. You only have to pick up a paper to see that allegations of sex abuse taint the target even if they're innocent. Lizzy had an interest in making your life a misery, as you know.'

'Yeah, she's good at that.'

'I don't think she expected him to go so far, though. When he broke in and she found the damage after turning off the alarm, she knew he was out of control, and worse, was in danger of finding out far too much. She had to think quickly. I'm guessing she went round there that night when you were in Berlin and I was with Drew, taking the whisky with her. He had no idea it was yours but she was already thinking of a way of making it look like you did it. She turned up – an old pal from the eco movement – to find him railing against the fact that his ex-partner had been in the police. That picture you keep beside the bed was the tipping point – he hadn't even got to the diary yet.'

'And when he did, he would find Biff in it?'

'You're keeping up – well done. So she thinks, let's shut him up permanently. If she's successful, her two problem guys are out of the way – one dead, one in jail. She gets her revenge and rides off into the sunset. She's not a totally competent assassin, though.'

'Tell me about it.' He lifts the sheets covering his legs.

'For which I am grateful. Anyway, she misjudges the dose and ends up having to bash him over the head before he gets out onto the street to raise the alarm.'

'Did they find the weapon?'

'No. She probably chucked it. It could've been anything handy in the kitchen. She might've made a quick search for the diary but she didn't see it in Jacob's messenger bag, which was in another room between the sofa and the wall. Her priority at this point was to get away and she couldn't risk turning the place upside down. She must've frisked Jacob and found the rings in a pocket, but the rest she had to leave. She gets away undetected to slip back to being the innocent neighbour. She knows how crime units work so has been careful not to leave prints or any of her own DNA on the scene. She is aware that it is not a perfect fit-up for you, but enough to ruin you, possibly to jail you – she's having to improvise quickly here. The main aim was to shut Jacob up, and she succeeded in that. As long as it's a few days before someone finds the body, they wouldn't be able to pinpoint time of death, and that gives you opportunity to have done it.'

'How do you know this? Did she confess?'

'No, it's what Inspector Randall thinks happened. I'll come to her in a moment.'

'Has something happened to her?'

'In a manner of speaking. Just to wrap all this up, she takes the ring box, as it has sentimental value to her but she's also hedging her bets. She can plant it on whichever of us she most wants to implicate. No one, after all, is looking at her, so she doesn't have to worry about keeping it. Then ta-dah, she gets it out after she's pushed you down the stairs, and the rest you know. You have to admit, she was a pretty good schemer. I'm still finding it hard to accept the lengths to which she went. Did she have nothing better to do than mess with other people?'

'She was your hallucination, Jessica.'

'What?'

'I told her once that you had nightmares about the Scream. She climbed over the fence, knowing you were sitting on your own, and gave you that scare. She was hoping to push you into having a complete breakdown again so you wouldn't dig up any more secrets.'

'You mean I really did see a scary ghost?'

'Yes.'

'Did she come over to Feltham and do it to me there too?'

'I haven't heard about that one.'

'It was a few days earlier. I really thought I was losing my grip.' I get up and go to the window. Michael has a view of Big Ben and the river, pretty jaw-dropping for an NHS bed. 'So it wasn't the pills causing me to hallucinate – maybe I can start them again?'

'Jessica, I don't think—'

I turn round and grin at him. 'I'm not your problem any longer, Michael. You don't have to worry about me. I'll talk to Charles. He is comping me my treatment, as he thinks I saved your life. We've reached an understanding, he and I, but it's good to know I'm not seeing things.'

'I can't swear she went to Feltham. I just know about that time at my house.'

'It's OK. I'll deal with it. It already feels far less scary, now I know I was stalked by a psycho bitch rather than a figment of my imagination.'

He laughs at that, as I intended. 'I wish I could persuade

you to be my problem again, Jessica, but I know I don't have much to offer a woman anymore.'

Difficult area, that one. 'Enough with the pity party. You, Dr Harrison, are going to be zooming down the corridors soon in some cool electric wheelchair like Dr Xavier from *X Men* – James McAvoy version – and if I know you, there will be a pretty nurse sitting on your lap. Your new book, and no doubt the one you write about all this, will make you a fortune. Celebrity status will return with a new shine after being dunked in the dirt. Everyone is going to be falling over themselves to be nice to you.' I go to a large bunch of flowers in the corner. 'See, this has been signed by the principal at Royal Holloway herself, looking forward to seeing you back as soon as possible. Make them eat crow, Michael.'

'Thank you, Jessica. It might be an overly rosy version of my future, but it's better than the gloom my sister dished out. I think she's just scared I'm going to go and live with her.'

'Michael, it really is early days, but I can't see you living with her.'

'God, no, then I absolutely will have to turn into a killer.'

'You'll find your way through this.'

'So are you going to tell me what happened to Lizzy? Has she been arrested?'

'Ah, here's the thing. You need to talk to Randall because he's spitting mad about it.'

'He'll probably come in to question me as soon as the doctors give him the all clear.'

'When he does he'll tell you that he was about to make

the charges of murder, attempted murder, conspiracy to pervert the course of justice and assault, when three senior officers turned up and took Lizzy away with them for further questioning – whisked her right out of Lewisham police station to destination unknown.'

'What?'

'Inspector Randall thinks they're from the special operations unit. They prefer to police their own.'

'Not when it's murder, surely?'

'You'd think not. Randall is afraid he'll be gagged, so he's rather hoping you get well enough to blow the gaff. You can say the things he can't.'

'Go public that my wife was part of this?'

'I'm afraid it would involve that, yes. Lizzy might escape a proper trial if you don't.'

'But I promised Emma.'

'I know. But who are you protecting now? Kaitlin?'

He shakes his head.

'What did happen to her, Michael?'

He lies back on the pillow looking exhausted. I probably shouldn't have asked. 'Nothing. I mean, nothing dramatic. Emma named me in her will as Kaitlin's guardian but I couldn't look after her – I could barely look after myself. So, to my eternal shame, I broke my word to my dead wife and Kaitlin – Emma's Katy – was put into temporary foster care. Lizzy predictably wanted Kaitlin to stay with her but I put my foot down. We were both grieving and I already had an inkling that I would never be in a fit state to parent a child. Kaitlin had no living relatives that I knew of, and I was aware that

Emma felt it best that Lizzy didn't have any closer involvement in her upbringing – she told me this in confidence and even today, I've just read about it in her last diary, so my memory of our conversation is accurate.' He gestures to a notebook lying on the bedside table. 'Emma had been clear that she didn't want Lizzy to have Kaitlin – pretty astute, considering the outcome. After a few months I didn't feel any better, so I asked Social Services to place Kaitlin for adoption. I did what I hoped was best in the long run. I gave Kaitlin away so she could live without shadows.' He swallows. 'I've never wanted children and I was a hopeless stepdad. Do you really think she would've flourished with a man like me, paralysed by grief?'

'It's not my place to judge you. If you didn't want her, then you did the best thing.' I have to admit that I'm surprised that he would let any part of his beloved Emma go. He wasn't the hero Emma imagined him, but then again she wasn't the perfect woman he thought her, was she?

'I don't know if it was as simple as not wanting. I know I can be selfish but I was just incapable at that time. Emma thought I'd grow into a good father but she was wrong. I don't have that in me.'

'It's OK, Michael, you don't have to explain it to me. I just wanted to know where she was – the last missing girl.'

'She's still missing.'

'From her old life she is, but I expect you are right that she's happier in the new one she found.' I check the time. 'I'd better go. Drew is waiting downstairs in the cafe for me.'

'Thank you for coming to see me.'

'I'll come back – at the very least, to tell you how Colette is doing.'

'And tell Randall to get in here. I'll try to help him to get justice for Jacob. If it's publicity he wants, that's something I seem to have plenty of to share around.'

I lean over and kiss his cheek. 'Get some pretty nurse to shave you, Michael, before you let the cameras in. I'll see you soon.'

As I leave, I come across a woman in the corridor, standing next to the policeman. She is in an emerald-green trouser suit and is applying lipstick, one of those shades with a name like Red Fox or Flirty Fuchsia.

'Hi, have you finished with him?' she asks.

'Yeah, he's all yours.' I hold the door to let her enter.

'So, Michael, who shall we sue first?' she says, striding into the room.

'I suppose that's the lawyer?' I ask the policeman as I let the door close on their conversation.

'Ms Sally-Ann Brightwell,' he confirms. 'She told me she was after the Met and looking forward to her day in court. There goes my pension fund.'

Drew is waiting for me where I left him, drinking green tea in the cafe, my Elizabethan pirate washed up at a Formica table in Westminster. 'How is he?'

I sit down and blow out a stressed breath. Being cheerful is taxing sometimes. 'He might not walk again.'

'Bugger.'

'But otherwise he's doing OK. He kind of asked me to go back to him.'

'Did he?'

'Only in an "I know you won't but I wish you would" way.'

'And what did you reply?'

'What do you think? No, of course. Even if I weren't in love with you, I'd still find it poison to live with him. But he has an illusion that we could be a good thing together, now the misunderstandings are cleared away.'

'But you know it's an illusion, right?'

'Of course. There's been far too much of that around. Emma pretending to be Ali. Jacob pretending to be a private eye. Lizzy pretending to be a decent human being. The only person not pretending was Michael, and we all thought for a while he was a serial killer behind the mask.'

'I thought you said you never believed it.'

'I had a few bad moments. I've never claimed to be consistent. Anyway, I've had enough of other people's fantasies; I want to live a real life with you.'

'Now that sounds like something I can get behind.'

'Drew, I've been thinking, can we offer to bury Jacob?'

'Jacob?'

'Yes. He's in danger of being forgotten in all this. I know he set me up and everything, but he was set up himself.'

'And got dead.'

'And got dead. He lost his kid too. In fact, every way you look at it, his situation sucked out loud. A conspiracy theorist who finally had a conspiracy come true, but it cost him his life. And I doubt anyone else will step in to give him a funeral once the police release his body.'

'Well, I suppose I can give you a staff discount.'

'Drew!'

'Yeah, of course we'll do it. Won't cost much because as an eco-terrorist he'll want the cardboard recycled coffin, won't he?'

'Stop it, I'm serious.'

'I think I am too. Yes, we can give him a decent send-off. Are you ready to go?' Drew stands up, jingling his keys.

'Yes. I'm not a fan of these places. Too much for my imagination to picture going on behind closed surgery doors. Frankenstein and so on.'

'Muppet.' Drew's gaze lifts to focus on something behind me.

'What?' I turn.

Max Tudor is standing there, suit, briefcase, the whole works. Oh God, not now. 'Jessica, I saw the news about Harrison, so I thought I'd find you here.'

'Who's this, Jess?' asks Drew.

Max holds out a hand. 'Max Tudor. I'm a lawyer.'

'He's a snake. Don't shake his hand.' I don't want Drew touching him.

'Jessica?' Drew is trying to make sense of this.

'Come, come, Jessica, that really isn't very nice of you.' Max makes to sit beside me but I stand up, arms folded across my chest.

'I told you I'm done with being nice to you.'

He looks over my head. 'Did your little girlfriend tell you about our arrangement?'

'Don't you dare!'

He puts down his briefcase on the table. 'I have to say she

is very creative in bed – not that we ever did it in bed.' He leans towards me, voice lowered. 'I have some very invigorating footage, not to mention photographs, in my briefcase. So unless you want me to get them out right now, what do you say? Tonight? My place?'

I close my eyes briefly. I see that it's one of those moments where I get to decide what kind of person I'm going to be. I know what I should do – not take the easy way out, because that's not really easy – but I don't know if I've got the courage. I can feel Drew behind me, full of questions.

Remember who you want to be, Jessica.

I open my eyes and drop my arms to my side. 'Max, I've only one thing to say to you: go fuck yourself sideways. I'm not doing that with you anymore.'

He gives me his shark's smile and reaches for the briefcase.

'As for your photos and the rest, publish and be damned. I'm not ashamed. I expect I'm fucking beautiful in them and you're the old man who has to blackmail a woman to get sex – who comes out of this worse?'

His eyes narrow. 'But the rent...?'

'Fuck that too. Sue me and I'll explain in great detail just what you've been asking for in payment.'

Drew comes around the table. 'This guy's been making you have sex with him?'

'I broke it off when we... you know, but yeah, basically, that's the situation.'

'Well, screw that!' He slams his fist into Max's stomach and follows through with a punch to the face. Max stumbles back and crashes into the display of cupcakes as various customers scramble to safety. Drew takes my hand and leads me to stand over the crumpled lawyer.

'If you want to make an issue of it, you wanker, like she said, sue me!' Drew strides out, pulling me along at a rapid pace before security arrives.

Once we get outside, I jump him, legs around his waist. 'Drew, what was that?'

He laughs, very pleased with himself and deservedly so. 'That was me defending my girl.'

'Oh my God, you are so going to get laid when we get home.'

'Then we'd better hurry.' He kisses me and drops me back to the ground. 'You've got to stop these fuckers exploiting you.'

'Oh, I will. I promise that's the last mistake.'

We head out of the hospital to where he's left the moped, our trusty steed.

I climb on behind him. 'Ready.'

On a powder-blue moped, winking with shiny possibilities, we ride over Westminster Bridge towards Big Ben and turn west for home.

Acknowledgements

Special thanks to Debra and Matt Walker for telling me about murder investigations as part of their work for the Metropolitan Police. Any procedural irregularities are entirely my own!

Thanks too to Alan Schwarz, author of *ADHD Nation: The Disorder. The Drugs. The Inside Story.* This is the book that started me thinking 'what if...?'